THE PHOTOGRAPHER'S WIFE

THE
PHOTOGRAPHER'S
WIFE

SUZANNE JOINSON

BLOOMSBURY CIRCUS

LONDON • OXFORD • NEW YORK • NEW DELHI • SYDNEY

Bloomsbury Circus
An imprint of Bloomsbury Publishing Plc

50 Bedford Square
London
WC1B 3DP
UK

1385 Broadway
New York
NY 10018
USA

www.bloomsbury.com

BLOOMSBURY and the Diana logo are trademarks of Bloomsbury Publishing Plc

First published in Great Britain 2016

British Library Cataloguing-in-Publication Data
A catalogue record for this book is available from the British Library.

ISBN: HB: 978-1-4088-4077-1
TPB: 978-1-4088-4078-8
ePub: 978-1-4088-4079-5

2 4 6 8 10 9 7 5 3 1

Typeset by Integra Software Services Pvt. Ltd.

To find out more about our authors and books visit www.bloomsbury.com.
Here you will find extracts, author interviews, details of forthcoming
events and the option to sign up for our newsletters.

One has to be careful what one takes when one goes away forever.
Leonora Carrington, *The Hearing Trumpet*

Jerusalem, 1920

The man opposite Prue was trying to force a canary through the train window and such a hash he made of it: a yellow fluttering blur, bright black accusatory eyes, and then – *pouf* – gone. The empty birdcage on the table in front of him was a perfect dome with a wooden swing in its middle suspended for a bird to rock and pretend to fly. She longed to touch it, but didn't dare.

He hadn't remotely noticed her, despite the fact that they were the only two Europeans on the train. Most passengers appeared to be Armenian, Egyptian, Jerusalemites and others Prue couldn't easily identify. She watched him steadily, hoping he would look over at her, but he never did. His cheeks were awfully red and he was sweating despite the cold; she guessed he was English. A framed picture on the back of the train door stated RAPID AND COMFORTABLE TRAVELLING FACILITIES TO ALL PARTS OF PALESTINE *with connections to* EGYPT, SYRIA AND BEYOND, wherever BEYOND might be, but the train was not particularly comfortable and had been still for some minutes now. There was no sign of the purser.

The slam of a door could be heard further along the carriage. The air was suspended, everyone waited.

Prue was travelling alone, despite being just eleven years old. Her father had given her permission to visit a village called Yibna for the day to photograph a Mamluk tower. It had gone well, all things considered. She was intact, not murdered. Not a person had spoken to her. Bandits had not stolen her much-cherished camera, a Kodak Eastman. True, she had been unprepared for a flurry of snow that left her damp and cold, but now she was returning to Jerusalem full of hope that it would be friendlier, warmer.

She could see from the luggage tag dangling from the suitcase in the rack above that the man had travelled from Cairo, via Alexandria and Kantara. The handwriting was clear, very black, and looking at it Prue realised who he must be. She had overheard him saying to the purser earlier that he was going to Jerusalem. He must surely be the new pilot, then. Eleanora's *great friend*. There were no other Englishmen on the train, and he was due about now. She tried again at getting his eye, but he avoided hers, and the loneliness which had lifted for an instant resettled on her, like dusk.

She looked out of the window. Steam from the train's engine dispersed to reveal a stretch of stony ground, the suggestion of hills in the far off, a pure, blank sky. Prue was still not used to the lack of grass. She missed hawthorn blossom and damp tree bark and ladybirds and the hairy strength of daisy stalks so much that she was sickened by the memory of these things. Might she ask him? *Hello, sir, are you the man my father has employed to fly aircraft over Jerusalem?* Just as she was about to speak the man jumped back in his seat.

'Good heavens,' he said. A face was pressed against the train window, a bottom lip dragging along the glass, revealing gums, teeth, and then just as quickly it was gone, dropped down presumably towards the tracks, and all that remained was a streak of spit on the window. Nothing happened for a moment. The man, who might or might not be Eleanora's friend, put his finger on the glass near the smear, and then, in a surge, all the passengers in the carriage rushed over to that side of the train to see what was happening. Prue did the same, and found herself between the Englishman's elbow and the cane of an Armenian clergyman.

Outside, soldiers in a strange uniform were in a circle around a man on the ground and great boots were kicking deep into his stomach. His head was twisted towards the train and Prue saw his tongue shoot in and out of his mouth each time a foot touched him. The Armenian clergyman, disregarding Prue, pointed his cane at the Englishman.

'You,' he said. 'What is happening?'

'Devil if I know,' he said, shaking out his trousers, irritated, finally registering Prue, his eyes opening wide as if surprised to see an English child next to him even though she had been there the whole time.

A procession was coming into view. Prisoners, shackled at the ankles. Exhausted, dirty, stooped. Prue had never seen men like these. They were local, she guessed, villagers. No women. They were being herded along by a couple of the soldiers wearing the curious uniform made up of revolver belts of Wild West pattern and large-brimmed hats decorated with scarlet ribbons. The prisoners trudged slowly past the man on the ground, they were carrying something over their shoulders. Not a cross, surely? Not a pilgrimage, something else. The purser shoved his way through the aisle behind Prue now, a Turkish-looking official, letting out a whistle each time he moved.

'British *gendarmerie*,' the purser said, whistling and breathing near Prue. 'They've caught an outlawed criminal. They do this to show everyone what manner of men they are.' He wiped his hands on the red velvet waistcoat of his uniform as if to clean himself. 'But it is unnecessary. We already know what kind of men they are.'

The Englishman would surely speak to her now. He had looked at her. *Now, I exist.* But no. He closed his eyes, as if to shut out what was happening. A man on horseback emerged alongside the weary, walking prisoners, also wearing the odd, semi-official hat. The Englishman had opened his eyes and straightened his back and Prue saw that he was staring at this man on the horse.

The prisoners did not look up from the ground as they paraded past. They did not see the faces at the windows of the train, gawping and gaping. They were carrying a ladder, propped on the shoulders of four of the men, and strapped to the top of it was a body. She guessed it was dead, because she didn't think otherwise the arms and legs of a body would jangle at such an angle. She had never before seen a dead man. She wanted very much to photograph it.

When it had all passed, the Englishman took his belongings, including the birdcage, and moved to a different carriage without saying a word.

The driver waiting for her from the Hotel Fast was an ancient English serviceman called Gibbons, decked up with war decorations.

'Collecting one more,' he said, not offering to carry Prue's knapsack. Two minutes previously the platform at Jerusalem station had been a blur of suits and robes and sun helmets, the floor covered in packages and luggage largely made up of bundled sheets, but in an instant it had all vanished. Now the light was fading, Prue was hungry, regretting the whole film she had used on the Mamluk tower which was just that: a tower, surrounded by nothing. The driver gestured over Prue's shoulder. She turned. Here came the Englishman walking slowly towards them. She had been correct then. She knew it.

'Hello,' he said, as if he had not stood next to her at a window just half an hour ago. His travelling coat was very crinkled. 'I'm Flight Lieutenant William Harrington.'

'Yes. I guessed who you were on the train,' Prue said. Gibbons took his suitcase without saying anything and moved towards the dust-covered Crossley.

'I'm Prudence Ashton,' she said. 'You will be working for my father.' He did not reply and so she continued, 'Eleanora told me about you. You're the bird-catcher.'

The man – William Harrington – jolted at that, which was a satisfaction.

Sharing the back seat meant both of them having to cling to the handles inside the door to avoid being thrown into one another's laps as they bumped along the road.

'How is Eleanora?' William Harrington said finally, it was obviously a tremendous effort.

'She's well,' Prue said, deciding to say no more and to remain mysterious to punish the man. Then, mischievous, without looking at him, she said, 'You know, of course, she is married to the great photographer, Khaled Rasul?'

The man coughed, nodded, said nothing more. Prue watched him stare at the bare rocky landscape that quickly changed into grey stone houses on either side of the road. He was very pinched and thin-looking and he kept cupping one of his ears with a hand. Did it feel significant, his arrival here? Most people – she had discovered – gave it great symbolism, arriving in Jerusalem. They had planned it and read and dreamed and thought about it for such a long time before coming and they all seemed to have such hopes about the famous city and when they got here it was never quite what they were looking for. Maybe, for him, just as it had been for her, it was like any journey: exhausting, tedious, difficult.

'Why did you let that canary go?' she said. He sniffed, looking displeased at the question, and then sighed. 'I bought it for Eleanora in the market in Cairo, but then it suddenly seemed not quite the thing.'

They sat for the rest of the journey in silence. Prue pulled from her knapsack the piece of paper that Ihsan had given to her. It contained a list of character shapes and their meanings which she was in the process of memorising under the cover of Arabic lessons. She held the paper in such a way that the men couldn't see it.

Finally the motor car splattered to a stop. Prue folded up her paper. There was the sign saying Messrs COX & KINGS Shipping and Travel Agents nestled in front of the Hotel Fast and standing under its awning was her father, wearing, as he always did, a white suit and a fez, flapping a fly swat around his face. Next to him was Frau Baum.

'That,' Prue said to William Harrington, hoping to shock, 'is my father's German lover.'

'Oh,' he said, eyes widening. She then twisted her neck to look further along Jaffa Road and saw Eleanora coming along the street. The low winter-afternoon sun shone into her coat so that the tips of the fur looked like fire.

'There,' Prue said. 'Eleanora.'

'Hotel Fast,' the driver said at the same time and William Harrington let Prue get out first. She waved at her father and his lover and at Eleanora heading towards them as they waited to welcome the new arrival, but Prue did not stop. She swooped past and although her father called something out to her, she did not catch it, and she carried on regardless. When she looked back at them from inside the hotel, they had forgotten about her already.

Shoreham, 1937

The man at the door is dressed like London in a crumpled but expensive suit that no Shoreham man would ever wear. I pull back from the gap in the wooden door panel, stand perfectly still as he tries the handle. His voice easily penetrates the rotten wood.

'Mrs Piers Miller?'

Oh do bugger off. Astonishing, how quickly that name has dissolved. *I am Prudence Ashton again. The person I was before Piers, the person I am afterwards.* I can hear his feet shunting loose shingle about and then I remember. It's the journalist who tele-grammed in advance. I ignored it and now, here he is. Touch my lips: no lipstick. Touch my head: hair still in curlers, under a scarf. I force my shoulders to drop, open the door. With his back to the light I can't see his face, just a tall person and an inconvenience.

'Mrs Miller, hello.' His foot is over the threshold before I say a word and he peers past my shoulder into the fishing hut that is my studio. 'Interview with the *Burlington* magazine? I understood from my assistant that it was all arranged.'

In the centre of the hut behind me, propped up on two railway sleepers, is part of the main sculpture I am working on for Margot's exhibition: a vast lump of Maltese limestone, a broken saint that I just doused with a bucket of sea water, the remains of which are pooling along the grooves of the wooden floorboards. I do not want him to see it.

'I don't think so. I mean, I received no exact confirmation.'

A seagull waddles towards us, opens and closes its mouth, begging. The sea-wind makes its usual effort to deafen and blind.

He steps back, makes a business of looking at the papers in his hands, flapping a copy of the *Burlington* as if it proves a thing. Behind him the tide is out, the sea filthy. I scan the coastline for Skip but can't see him. The man's manner suggests: Well! I'm here now, come from London. Perhaps? Might we? A nervy little punch in the air. I sigh, pull my cardigan around me.

'Would you wait here while I pack up?'

'Of course.'

I close the door on him, walk to the limestone, spread out my palms flat on its damp cool surface. It is particularly frustrating because today, after weeks of being frightened and preternaturally tense about it – Margot giving me the heavy lean to finish, sending daily letters of enquiry, evading my requests to be ignored until I'm ready – today, something in me shifted, or at least began to, and finally I am less afraid of this intimidating lump of stone.

I poke my finger into the back of Billy's work boot and heave it off, then the second one. I've taken to wearing his thick boots in the fisherman's hut, his socks too. I don't mind a man with feet the same size as me; a man the same height as me. I squeeze my own shoes back on, pull off my headscarf, quickly prise out the curlers, shake out my hair.

Ignoring his *So kind of you, terribly sorry to bother you, thank you* as he tries to keep up, the pebbles and chalk unsteadying him, I beckon him into my chalet with the half-thought: was Skip wearing his woollen cardigan this morning? The wind is nasty today.

The chalet's name Cecilia was carved into a piece of driftwood and hung up by owners long gone. This sign clatters in the wind day and night. I should take it down, but never do. I slam the door behind us.

'Take a seat. I'll make tea.' I will not be friendly but I can be civil. I clear Skip's cuttlefish bones from the only chair that isn't broken and fill the kettle from the water butt. His breathing is shallow. I can smell him too: aftershave, tobacco, something medicinal. The windows are splattered with spray, the sea-light shows how slovenly we are, how lax I am as a mother.

'I'm very grateful,' he says again.

'Yes. Well, one cannot say no to the *Burlington*.'

He is much too tall to fit into the room and can barely get his legs under the table. Skip's collections of whatnots are everywhere: whelk shells, crab bones, chalk. The usual stink of seaweed, or sea-rot. Everything damp and one of my brassières is poking out from under a cushion. Cecilia was once a disused railway carriage, now extended into a haphazard, wooden one-room home. Along the inner wall it is still possible to see remains of the velvet lining that long ago studded carriage panels. I thought it romantic when I was first shown it by Billy, my landlord – now my lover, though quite how it has happened I can't exactly say – but it was summer then. Not a whiff of the red slimy seaweed to come, no foreshadow of the months of low-hanging sea frets. I push the brassière down the side of the cushion and can see him getting his face ready to pretend that Cecilia is quaint and that there is wisdom in attempting to build a home for my son out of rotten wood on shifting shingle.

'We should begin, then?' I want to hurry him on. I run my hands over my yellow dress, which is not particularly clean, and sit in the unstable chair opposite him, ignoring the bowl of shrivelled apples in front of us.

'Yes. Indeed.' He writes in his notebook so that I can clearly read: *Interview with Prudence Miller, 4th October 1937*.

I look at him properly for the first time. He has a rash, or a skin condition, quite severe, along his neck. Old scars, probably. We all have them. In a sense he is generic, like any of the men from the art world constantly courting my errant husband, Piers. All the same: gallery owners, critics, dealers, journalists, their little beaks opening and pecking to be fed. It occurs to me: is Piers behind this? Is he affiliated with the *Burlington*? Sending a stranger to harass me in the guise of an interview is just the sort of thing he might do and this man is everything I have left behind. He is all the people at the exhibitions and the endless London noise, eyes too close to my face in the upstairs snug at the Chandos on Trafalgar Square or the Pillars of Hercules in Soho. He is the swinging lanterns in the Wheatsheaf on Rathbone Place where I once took my clothes off to an audience of six drunken, revolting Surrealists; all the men watching, including Piers, shouting *Bravo Bravo Encore Encore*. Piers had been blindfolded for the evening, so he wasn't even looking, the fool.

'You are newly arrived in Shoreham, I understand?' the man asks. His face is not open, somehow; he doesn't quite meet my eye.

'I've been here just a few months.' My throat is tight.

'Life is rather different down here, I imagine?'

'Indeed.'

He holds his pen over the paper but writes nothing. He shifts in the chair. 'What is the piece you are working on at the moment called?'

I answer to the effect that I keep changing my mind, which is not the same as saying I haven't settled on a name. The name evolves. Sometimes it is *Stairwell*, sometimes *Spiral*, sometimes *Axis Mundi*, and then I think: less literal, or even, more literal and I just want to call it *Hanging Stairs with Saint Helena*. It has an accompanying piece, currently called *Hanging Men*. I have been working on the exact angle of the head in relation to the rope, precisely how it looks when a person has been hanged, but I don't mention that.

'I read that you brought limestone from Malta, is that true?'

'Yes. I did. My father was stationed there and he arranged for various broken and disused saints to be sent to me. Malta has a remarkable number of unwanted saints.'

'Was it difficult to organise?'

'Not at all. They used them as ballast for the boat, and so they didn't even charge. I had to pay to get them here from Portsmouth, though, and that was a huge sum. *That* nearly sank me, as it were.'

'Why did you choose sculpture?' He looks like a dog trying to understand, head tilted, ears up.

'Oh. I was smuggled into classes at the Slade. My husband encouraged me, but soon I was working on my own. As a child, in Jerusalem, I fell in love with stone.' I give him my dazzling smile, because I can do all that, if needs be. He has still written nothing whatsoever in that notebook of his.

He leans forward and looks directly at me. 'When were you in Jerusalem?'

'When I was eleven. Not for very long, half a year, but it stayed with me.'

'Where did you live in the Holy City?' I pretend I haven't heard. The old feeling is creeping up on me, as if he is wiggling his finger where I don't want it to be: inside my ear, in the inner part of my wrist, high up inside my thigh.

A string of shells clatters against the window, making us both jump. The wireless, balanced on top of a milking stool, crackles and then returns to its sleep. Each question from this man is a jab at my chest. *Journalists. Questions.* An insolent woman reporter asked me similar prodding queries in the middle of the New Burlington Galleries exhibition last year, when the furore was still ongoing – talk of the town, Surrealists offending everyone, Constructivists sulking, critics looking for unsavoury information to justify their columns, rallying against the Decay of Civilisation and the Degeneration of Art – and Piers, frothing and fizzing because he was in the wolf's mouth of it all, forced me to sit up on a stage in the draughty hall on Endell Street and talk to the press. The *Daily Mail* called me 'disgusting' that day. I really did not want to be there and a woman in a red pillbox hat persisted in directing her questions at me, ignoring the men. *You're often making houses in your work, but they are always half-destroyed or ruined. They look like something made in secret, out of shame. Houses that might blow away. Is it a territory you are marking out?* 'Possibly.' (How am I supposed to answer that?) *Do you feel like a little girl, playing with furniture, when you create these homes?* 'Possibly.' She continued. *You are young to have achieved such success, what are you working on now?* On she went, provoking me, even though it was obvious I wanted her to stop, until finally I stood up and shouted: HE HUFFED AND HE PUFFED AND HE BLEW THE HOUSE DOWN. I climbed down from the stage and left. Nobody followed me, not even Piers, the treacherous beast.

'Miss Ashton, you lived in the Hotel Fast in Jerusalem?' His words bring me back to Cecilia, and today. At first it seems a perfectly normal thing to say. I almost nod, but then a tightening feeling as if a thread is being pulled in and out of my skin.

'My married name is Miller. Why did you call me Ashton?' We are both silent. Through the inadequate walls of Cecilia it is possible to hear the itchy sea. The kettle lets out its fierce whistle; how we so often rely on a kettle to rescue us. It is almost four so I pull together tea of sorts. I am English, after all. I open a tin of stale biscuits, manage to find a dry cake and lone jar of jam, pile it all on to a tray, with a dirty knife and two chipped plates, appalled at myself, but there we are: he was not expected. Unsurprisingly he takes nothing to eat. Without smiling, I pour the tea, look out for Skip, but I still can't see him.

'I read that your father died last year. I was sorry to hear that.' I stare at him: what is this?

'Yes, well. It was sudden.' I refuse to look at him. The *Daily Mirror*, when reviewing my piece in the Beaux Arts Gallery exhibition, called me 'delicate', 'fragile', 'pretty' and 'daughter of the civic adviser and architect Charles Ashton'. They did not comment on the art. The long grey beard of my father comes to my mind, and I am wearing, as it happens, a necklace he gave me many years ago. A filigree-silver chain whose links spell *I give you the end of a golden string only wind it into a ball it will lead you in at heaven's gate built in Jerusalem's wall.*

'I'm sorry,' I say. 'I'm not sure I caught your name.'

His face erases its previous expression, allows a new look to break through, and it occurs to me that we are alone; he might do anything. I keep a hammer near the door. It is three, four steps from me. He extracts himself from the table, goes to the window.

'Shoreham Beach,' he says, as if talking to himself. 'Bungalow Town, is it still called that?'

'By some.'

He turns to look at me and I fancy I can see his soul for a moment blinking at me, but I don't really believe in souls. Not exactly.

'Who are you?' It has not gone unnoticed that he hasn't given me his name, and the door handle twists, then in comes Skip smelling of rain and salt. *Eeeeeeeooooooowwwwww*. He circles me, flying his cuttlefish aeroplane in an arc, *eeeoooooooooww*. He stands dead-still when he sees the man. His bright red hair around his white moon-face never fails to make me want to draw him to me.

'Mummy, there's a dead seal cub on the beach.' I put my hand out to touch him but six-year-old boys are mercurial, he slithers behind me, tugs at my hand, pretends to ignore the man although this is all a show for him. He comes very close to me, eyeball to eyeball: 'There are ants in its eyes.'

'I really don't think there are seals in this part of the Channel.' I get up to close the door and lean back on it as if keeping out demons. I give Skip a shove which is really a kiss and he throws himself down on the floor next to the wood burner, the soles of his feet unspeakably filthy. I am washed over with guilt. I was up with the light this morning, my head clear and correct for work-ing, and so I banished him and told him to amuse himself until I was back. He looks up over his shoulder at the man with undisguised dislike. *I feel the same, my darling. I do.*

'Actually, there are seals,' the man says, still looking out at the sea. 'I was at school not far away and we used to see them in the winter time, flipping, bellies up.'

'See,' Skip says, his expression towards the stranger changing now, affinities switching. 'I told you.'

'Forgive me,' the man says, looking down at Skip's feet. 'Does he not need shoes out there?'

'Won't wear them, I'm afraid. He's a barbarian. A fully initiated inhabitant of Barbary.' I smile, loosely in the direction of this intrusive man but not for him, for the love of my boy.

I sense the man looking at me and as I live almost exclusively on cigarettes, tea and toast I am very slender. I must look half-feminine, half-wildwoman of the beach and, surprisingly, I have a pang for the old days of Schiaparelli dresses and evening gloves. My stockings have wrinkled up at the ankles again, my hair is not very well-set.

I set about stacking up the cups and saucers. 'I'm afraid I haven't been much use to you at all and I suppose you have the long journey back to London ahead of you?'

Smile bright. Go away. Write what you like about my work. I don't care. I pick a thin branch from the wood basket and poke it into the wood burner. The man straightens himself, becoming formal and cold.

'I would like to talk to you about a friend of yours from Jerusalem. Ihsan Tameri.'

'Oh?'

Various words chime in my mind: Ihsan. London. Photograph. *Dear Ihsan.* I catch a sideways look at my face in the mirror on the wall. I seem strained, not like myself.

'How do you know Ihsan? And anyway, you haven't told me your name, exactly. Is Ihsan in trouble?' I try a smile again but my face breaks into pieces of clay.

'I'm afraid it's rather worse than that.'

I try to remember when the last letter from Ihsan came. *Dear Prudence*, ah habibti, *it is so windy today, the window frames clatter, the doors have to be stopped with large pieces of rock to prevent them from bishing and bashing. It is as if something wants to take the Old City and fling it into the air.* His letters have always been full of weather, inside and out. Weather and dreams, nothing practical or real; wishes and yearnings, but when did I last hear from him? A fair while back, a couple of years. I have been wrapped up in Piers and Skip and working. Art makes a person selfish. The man pulls away from the window as if stung by something.

'I'm staying at the Warnes Hotel in Worthing rather than go back up to London. Might you come tomorrow at three?' He has tired eyes. 'There is something very specific I need to talk to you about.'

He moves a foot, one at a time, backwards and forwards on the wooden floor.

'Can't you just talk to me about it now?' And then I see what made him jump: Billy, bent over his bicycle which he is leaning against the clattered old fence in front of Cecilia, wearing fisherman galoshes, wiping the rain from his hair as he stands up with his wide-fisted hand that always makes me think of shovels or spades.

'No, tomorrow is better.' I can picture this man in his private moments, smearing off shaving soap, tasting blood on his tongue when eating a steak. My body is perfectly still, defiant. I am safe with Skip here, I could flog a lion to protect him, and now Billy is outside the bones inside me lighten.

'Under the Warnes Hotel there is a cave, a bomb shelter,' Skip says, twisting his head round and staring up at the man.

'Really, who told you that?' I say.

'One of the pilots at the aerodrome.'

'When do you talk to the pilots?'

'Mummy, don't be silly. I've spoken to lots of pilots at the aerodrome.'

'I flew planes once upon a time,' the man says, close to me now, and then he puts his hand in his pocket, takes out a shilling and offers it to Skip, like a tooth plucked from the sand.

'Oh no,' I shake my head, but Skip springs up, all surliness gone; bribed and easily won he snatches the coin.

'Come to the Warnes with your mother and I'll ask the manager to show you the smuggling caves.'

Skip, coquettish, smiles, 'Oooh, yes please.' He puts his hand around my waist, squeezes me, the masculine possessiveness that little boys display with mothers. I touch Skip's neck, his ear, lightly. The man pulls the collar of his coat up around his face.

'I will wait for you at the Warnes at three.'

He opens the door before I can question him further and steps past Billy, mutters a low *Good afternoon*. Cecilia expands as soon as he is gone and then Billy comes in and fills it again, eyes wide with questions.

'Who was that?'

'A journalist, wanted to interview me.'

I want to go to the window to watch him walk away, but I don't. My thoughts are shuffling about in parallel: Ihsan, at a party in Jerusalem, dancing with Eleanora in the middle of the dance floor, nobody else near them. Then: a series of balconies, rooms, doors, corridors, and the image of a man, tall and thin, skin very tanned, scowling into the light, like the unsettling feeling of trying to catch a memory provoked by looking at an old photograph.

'People know you live here already?'

'Looks like it.'

Billy scowls. 'You said you didn't want none of that no more? That's why you're here?'

I put my hand on his swollen lip. Billy Ludd. My boxer. His face even when not damaged from fighting is a gift for a sculptor. His skull seems to imprint itself outwards into his skin and it is easy to imagine my hands on the bone of him, manipulating the texture of his face and rearranging it from inside. I have these odd, dissembling thoughts possibly because I am yet to see him without a bash or bruise. There is always a spread of red or yellow-purple skin contouring his face like a map, or a swelling on the forehead that is sensitive if I press my finger on it. When I kiss him his saliva has a metallic taste of blood. When I hold him he flinches.

He moves into the room, but does not settle. He turns around as if things have been stolen or shifted, as if something is awry. 'Did you talk to him then?'

'A little bit, but then I asked him to leave.'

'But why tell him anything?' He goes to the window, stares out.

'To get money for the art pieces, it's something I have to do sometimes. Publicity for Margot's exhibition. They like to buy my secrets.'

He looks at me through his bruises, through his damaged bones. 'Do you mind giving them? Are they real ones?'

'Billy,' I walk towards him and put my hands on his back, 'when I tell them my real ones they never believe me.'

Skip jumps up on to one of the chairs, stands in the manner of a nobleman surveying his lands.

'A bloody shilling, Mummy.'

'Don't swear.'

I walk over and catch Skip's hand and squeeze it as adults will do to find reassurance in a child's hot little palm. It lasts an instant, and then Skip is off, bouncing on the chair, admiring his coin, *it's enough to go to the flicks in Brighton*, and then he is flying away from me. Billy remains at the window, ignoring us both. He has taken up the stance of a male of the species warning off predators: legs slightly apart, fists rolled up into little balls, an expansion of the blood vessels under the skin of the neck, fingernails digging into the flesh of the hand.

It is the low moment before dawn and there is no colour. The room hangs as if it is a still picture on a silent-movie screen. *Skip*. He is still asleep. I can see his foot dangling from his cot-bed. The smell of Billy is still on me, as is the memory of his hand on my stomach, almost a bruise left behind, but he has gone. He never stays the whole night. I want to get up and put the wireless on but I am pressed into the blankets, almost as if there were a weight on me. The creaks in the wood are the normal ones of the wind trying to move the house and the seagulls tap out despair on the roof as usual. I am sure there are rats in the cavity below the floorboards, but that is nothing new.

I doze in and out of sleep, each time falling into a lucid dream of a room where my husband, Piers, opens the doors of a balcony – it is our suite in the Russell Hotel – and looks at me before stepping off into London air, either to fly or fall. I turn on to one side, bring my knees up towards my stomach and, as I do, the face of the man, the journalist, the intruder, flickers like a magic-lantern projection. Then it is clear. My mind has finally shuffled through all of the cards. It is the pilot, William Harrington, a man from my past, much older now of course – I know him. I knew him. *I would like to talk to you about a friend of yours ... Ihsan Tameri.* And there is Ihsan's face, at the top of a stairwell, looking down at me, young, rubbing his hands together and laughing. He is standing next to Eleanora Rasul. They are speaking, laughing about something, but I can't hear what they are saying. Eleanora's lips are very red. She has around her neck a charm in the shape of a silver canary. Then a new room. I am posed in front of a fireplace, wearing a white dress. I am being drawn. Like curtains. Like a pencil.

The Warnes Hotel, Worthing. Have I been there? No, I don't think so. I don't like hotels, avoid them these days and stay far away from their disconcerting, transitional rooms. Long curtains and doors that click shut, and lock. Mirrors that lie. When I wake properly Skip's eyelashes are close enough to tickle my own eyelids. He is crouching over my face, inspecting me.

'I thought you were dead.'

'No.'

'You looked dead.'

'I am definitely alive.' My bearer of gifts, he uncurls his palm. In it, a perfect starfish, still moving.

'Where did you get that?'

'Found it.'

My brute with bruised elbows and blinking eyes, I stroke the pure, soft, freckled skin of his face and then he pulls away, goes to find a cup to fill it with water, to house his star and keep it alive.

Jerusalem, 1920

Willie was conscious that in civvies he looked not quite. His suit was ancient and he was skinnier than he used to be so the shoulders hung badly. He took one step towards Eleanora but stopped and stood like a man at the wrong wedding.

Her name was Mrs Eleanora Rasul now. He must remember that.

There was perspiration on the top of his lip, he could feel it. They had all been summoned to be a part of Charles Ashton's photograph, an image for posterity: the team responsible for Jerusalem's aesthetic and architectural redesign to be recorded and preserved. It would be sent to *The Times*, read by everyone at Ashton's clubs in London, at the Travellers, the Royal Geographical Society, and so forth. He touched the scar that travelled from his chest to his neck. Eleanora had her back to him, was crouched over her camera apparatus. Her dress was belted and from behind her rather boyish figure looked unchanged despite the years. Desire ran through him, made him contract his tongue, wipe his forehead. It was still there; undiminished. He walked towards her, lighting a cigarette.

'William Harrington,' she said in a voice from the past, standing back from her equipment, and he could not work out her expression at all. 'Are you ready to be photographed?'

He stepped back and lit his cigarette clumsily. He hadn't meant to swoop in so close where he couldn't see her properly. She gave him a sarcastic look and then began fiddling with the slides on the camera. *There is her neck.* Words came to his mind. Property. Ownership. Mine by right. He saw them stamped in red ink like a librarian's date on a thin stretch of her skin.

'Ah, ha.' It was Charles Ashton, looking absurd in a fez. 'My top-notch squadron.'

His mother had written, *Willie darling, honestly it won't do, it really won't, SUCH an inappropriate marriage, her mother is beside herself. And ... well. What got into her? You have always been close, darling, and you are near – aren't you? – Cairo is not so far away. Do what you can,* and this cause had glowed through his veins for weeks, an opiate flushing through his visceral system. In his last days in Cairo he had taken to imagining Eleanora buried under great piles of religious stones, or crushed beneath photographic equipment, or locked up in an old house. He thought vaguely of dust, a donkey, of water-bearers; it was difficult to see Jerusalem in any other light. Always she was on her back, one arm over her eyes. There were variations: her lips parted, the top of her dress falling open. Well. Willie had every intention of releasing her from the sordid situation she appeared to have arrived at.

And yet, here she was at the Fast, in charge, ordering them around for the photograph, her long hair cut short and sharp, worn like the hair of city girls of London which really was not how one imagined her. They were to be photographed at the bottom of the central staircase of the hotel. Willie stood behind

Ashton. Two other men were positioned like angels on either side of Ashton's shoulders.

'Welcome, welcome everyone,' Ashton said. 'You are gathered here, my team, because I would like to introduce you to one another. We have the technical surveyors: draughtsman Mr Manamanam and surveyor Mr Prushansky.' The angels nodded, twisting their heads around to smile at Willie.

'For the artistic vision of the city, shall we say, I am employing Mrs Eleanora Rasul, wife of the eminent photographer Khaled Rasul, and a wonderful photographer in her own right.' Eleanora squinted up from the camera and gave a wave, letting her arm hang in the air for a moment and then drop, apologising in its manner for her not being her husband.

'And this is my pilot, Lieutenant Harrington. Wonderfully experienced flyer, we are just waiting for the craft to arrive from Cairo and he will be able to assist Eleanora in taking aerial photographs of the city.'

Everyone looked awkwardly at one another. 'Modernisation! Reparation!' Ashton declared, and when he had finished this odd little outburst he signalled to Eleanora.

'Remain still, gentlemen. Look at the camera, Charles, please,' Eleanora said. Time was suspended as everyone waited for the photograph to be taken. Then they were not to move as she wanted more than one version.

She was older, of course, but still with a fragile quality. He was relieved that her face was not tired or crushed, or, worse, strengthened. He liked in women something of the swift with a broken wing. For her part, she hadn't flinched at his scars.

Looking at her, Willie remembered a day aeons ago when they had climbed the highest sycamore on her father's estate, hunting the elusive bird of their imagination, the golden oriole. She had paused, resting her head against the trunk. There was dew on her cheeks and arms and he could see the shape of her small breasts against the fabric of her dress. Her father's voice came through the woods, scaring birds. When he saw them, up in the tree, he began to bawl and Eleanora pushed herself backwards. Her fall was not graceful; she cracked through numerous branches before reaching her father's feet. She did not break bones but was twisted all over, ankles and wrists. Later, when he climbed through the window to see her in her bedroom she was angry with him, unfathomably, as if it were his fault.

When the photograph was done, Willie sidled next to her, coughed to help his voice sound casual.

'How did you learn all of this?'

'Photography, you mean? I was hired because I knew nothing whatsoever about it and Khaled wanted an assistant who would do what he said. Later, as you know, we married.'

She wasn't looking at him. She found ways to look everywhere else. Smiling then not smiling.

'And do you do as he says?'

'Mostly. I took to the darkroom like a … well, like coming home, I suppose. It sounds silly now.'

He had no idea how to respond to that.

'Surely you need help carrying those?' Around her feet were the scatterings of photographic equipment.

'Ihsan is here,' she said. 'He sometimes works as an assistant.'

For the first time Willie noticed an Arab man, about the same age as himself, leaning just inside the arched doorway wearing shoes made from exceptionally bright white leather, then Charles was upon them, clapping hands on Willie's shoulders, tugging him away from Eleanora.

'I expect the aircraft to arrive at Kalandia airfield in about three days,' he said.

'Righto.'

Willie looked at him. Was Ashton a man to take seriously or not? Willie was undecided. Ashton had not served in the war. He was already too old. He was famous as far away as Cairo for being *the Ingliz touched* who travelled everywhere with a fly swat and for wearing a fez in the most embarrassing manner of an Englishman who described himself an *anima naturaliter Levantina*. At his first breakfast in the Fast Willie had been waited on by an astonishingly beautiful serving girl and Ashton, coming into the dining room just then, had instructed her to stand rigid in front of them both as he pointed to the exquisite fourteenth-century cross-stitching on the fabric that encased her breasts.

Willie had been in Jerusalem for four days now, and so far, the only instructions he had received from Ashton were: *make yourself comfortable, get to know the place and don't listen to anyone who tells you Jerusalem is good for nothing but a bath and a train out of here.* When he looked back, Eleanora was leaving with the man with white shoes and Charles was drifting away. He had travelled all of this way, expecting what? More, he supposed. He pressed his feet into the hotel carpet.

In his room that evening Willie sat naked on his bed listening to the odd silence of Jerusalem towards the end of the day, rolling one of his tight little cigarettes. He liked to smoke this way, waving the red burning tip in front of his face. Most cities come alive at night, but not here. It locked doors and slammed gates as soon as dusk fell. Jerusalem was very different from Cairo, the filth and vastness of which could swallow a man and enable him – even a foreigner – to be lost and invisible for days. Here, he had the sense that everything was visible, witnessed inside the walls. He had no inclination to explore the streets and instead resolved to wait, so far in vain, for Eleanora to contact him. The Armenian concierge brought whiskies to his room; discreet, professional, a gentle tap on the door every hour to see if Willie needed a refill.

He was unsettled, now he had time to think about it, at the thought of that disturbance on the train outside Jerusalem. He had experienced hallucinations before – malaria rages, days spent watching flies crawl from the eyes of pretty nurses – but this wasn't mind trickery. It had been McLaughlin on that horse. Known as Lofty. Willie had last seen him in Salonika five years ago; they had not parted well.

As a schoolboy at Lancing College, Willie had experienced a series of vivid fantasies in which a man, for some reason Italian, would magically arrive at helpful moments and offer to be his *intermediario*. This middle-man, a fixer or wizard, would plant himself between Willie and the rest of the world and sort every-thing out. He charmed the loathsome housemaster, tricked bullies, coaxed his father back from his ships, and then, when his father's presence was altogether too much, cast him away again for four years and a day. At some undefined point, though, the *intermediario* had disappeared. He simply never returned, leaving Willie to navigate the large world alone. Lofty up on the horse had not noticed him inside the train but it was then that the ringing which Willie often suffered from, deep in his ears, began, though he had not been surprised; travel usually did this to him.

Willie ran his hand along his leg, scratched at a mosquito bite on his knee. He remembered too the face of the odd little English girl. Her hair in plaits; terribly plain and dour-looking. *Eleanora told me about you …You're the bird-catcher*. It was her name for him from childhood, a secret game, and the child's face was sarcastic.

Jerusalem.

His letter of application to Ashton had been quite the moving piece about the new perspectives; a different way of seeing the earth from above which changed everything. He had with him a mosaic of images promised to Ashton, photographs taken from the air: Villa Cisneros, Cape Juby, Casablanca and swathes of the Sahara. What they heralded, he believed, was a new way of seeing. Of *looking*, a relief from the tyranny of roads and horizons. There was no vanishing point; the rules of perspective were quite scrambled. Well, anyway, so he thought and if he looked at them for long enough he might be able to fly again. He had omitted one detail in his application to Ashton, namely that he hadn't flown for six months. Nor had he mentioned that if he so much as approached an aircraft he pissed himself: a trickle of urine down the leg whenever he heard the revolutions of the propellers. Even, sometimes, if he simply caught a smell of oil.

Draining the remains of his whisky, Willie stood near the window, at an angle so that he need not bother dressing but could watch the city outside. It was almost dark. He could see the wide, dark sky above the Old City and there was altogether too much of it. It went on and on. It needed containing. For the first time, doubt, regarding his mission. He had come to take Eleanora back, but it hadn't occurred to him, when plotting all of this, how she might look amongst these Jerusalem stones: as if she belonged here, in all the dust and crumbling brick, as if she had no intention of ever leaving. He was the one who was out of place.

He sniffed, shivered. Put his knuckle into his mouth and bit it, hard. He waited. Finally, the message came. She would come to the Fast in the morning.

Jerusalem, 1920

To escape the Church ladies who congregated in the lobby of the Hotel Fast with leaflets, Prue avoided the central staircase area and took the back stairs, hopping in twos, fours, sixes, eights. Down the bare steps she went, along a low-ceilinged passageway that smelled of mice, dragging fingers along the Jerusalem stone walls – a mixture of pink-grey grit and ash – until coming to the entrance of the court-yard garden. Here, in this secret, enclosed part of the hotel, Prue installed herself in a gap between a well-worn wicker chair and a large ceramic pot which housed the trunk of a palm whose upper-most leaves poked high above the hotel roof and settled down to spy.

She had overheard Eleanora arranging to meet the pilot here this morning. The waiter with the three gold teeth walked past, looked down at her, and said nothing, walked on. The hotel staff tolerated her because of her father, and because she was English and the English did odd things, which (so Ihsan had told her) the Jerusalemites, on the whole, tolerated.

She opened her knapsack and took out her best fountain pen, and a book plucked randomly from her father's bookcase:

The History of Architecture in all Countries from the Earliest Times to the Present Day. She dabbed at the first page of the book, smearing ink. It was a new nib and she hadn't got it right yet, it was still too scratchy. Her hand did its usual involuntary twitch and a blob of black bubbled out. Her fingertip stained, she wiped it the width of the page, obliterating printed words, and then she heard Eleanora's voice.

'Will this do?'

'Perfect,' he said.

Prue tucked her feet in, feeling clever, but was quickly thwarted as they took a table on the other side of the courtyard.

Every now and then Eleanora's laugh shot out. William Harrington coughed regularly, an explosive splutter, followed by wheezes, but otherwise it was difficult to hear what they were saying. Finally, she risked peeking. They were arranged *à deux*. The pilot's long legs stuck out of the side of the table and ash fell from his cigarette to the ground. Eleanora was wearing her green shimmery dress with tassels along the hem. Prue knew from previous examination that each tassel had a beaded eye sewn on to its end.

On seeing Eleanora properly, Prue darkened. When they were last together they had quarrelled. Or rather, Prue had tried to but Eleanora muttered *silly child* and dismissed her. The disagreement was about how to photograph a dead bird, of all things. Eleanora's husband was away and she had taken to asking Prue to join her for what she called *Tramps with Camera*, usually just outside the Old City walls, or towards the top of the Mount of Olives cemetery.

'I've found an organ,' Eleanora had said, crouching in tufty grass, her finger touching a bloody little mass. 'It could be a heart, or a tiny liver?'

It was next to a recently disembowelled sparrow and Prue had not wanted her to touch it so they could photograph it as found. In the manual that came with her Kodak there was a section on 'Snapshots': when making instantaneous pictures the object must be in the broad open sunlight, but the camera should not be. *Take the photograph to capture the moment. Take the photograph as you find it.* Prue had quoted this, but Eleanora disregarded it and held up the bird-carcass by its scrawny foot, ruining everything. Prue had picked up the lung, or heart, not at all revolted by its sinewy feel, and held it in her hand. There was a dot of blood from the bird on Eleanora's cheek and this was when Eleanora had said: 'An old friend of mine has written that he's coming to Jerusalem. Lieutenant William Harrington, to work on this project for your father.'

Prue still had the bloody stuff in her hand. She dropped it, rubbed her palm on her dress, knowing the stain wouldn't come out in the laundry. She saw, then, that it would have been a useless photograph. Not enough light, or contrast, or context.

'So I'm afraid I shan't be able to do these walks any more,' Eleanora had said, and began packing up her equipment. 'But you're working on your Arabic with Ihsan, are you not? So you'll be quite all right, Prue darling?'

They had walked back to the Hotel Fast together, tired and Prue had the very great sense of having been dropped. She recognised the feeling. Her mother used a similar tone when she got out the 'good' knives and forks because there was a visitor for dinner, a man Prue did not know, and as a three at the table they would eat fish, slowly pulling bones out of heads, until her mother said *Go to bed, Prue* which translated as *Go away, Prue.*

She peeked again. He was leaning towards Eleanora, sipping tea. Now, Eleanora's voice came clear and bright.

'Charles Ashton's daughter, Prue? Yes, she's a dear thing. He summoned her from England but appears to leave her adrift to do what she likes, with no programme whatsoever. She's heartbreakingly awkward. I sometimes have to rather shake her off.'

The man responded in a low voice, and they shifted, ankles crossing, tassels quivering, the eye-beads revolving, looking for the sky. More cigarettes were lit.

Heartbreakingly awkward. Prue wrote it down. Was that Eleanora's way of telling Prue that she knew she was spying? No; she thought not. In the margins she wrote: 'I am like a pigeon with a sore foot, or one of the pitiful kittens poking in the bins. I am Prudence Ashton. I came by boat. I was sent for. My mother was not.'

She felt a great lurch, as if the entire hotel was about to either collapse or set sail. Prue put her hand on to the floor below to steady herself, but the imbalance came from inside, not the building, or the bricks, or the earth, or the floor of the courtyard of the Hotel Fast or the bottommost deck of the SS *Aronda* which was the boat that had brought her from Portsmouth to Port Said. Eleanora and the pilot moved slightly, their chairs shunted closer to one another. She could not hear them again.

When he spoke his hand moved sideways in the air near Eleanora's face, as if cutting something.

Prue put the cap back on her fountain pen and then took it off again and wrote: *One should never tell anyone anything, or give information, or pass on stories.* An elderly Spanish man on the SS *Aronda* had told her that. *Telling is a gift and a gift leads to betrayal.* Then the flapping began, not just in her fingers, but in her wrists, fingertips, judders all the way up to her elbows, so that she had to squeeze the skin on the back of her hand to stop it. Once, a long time ago, her mother had asked if they could sleep together and climbed into bed with her. A new sister had been born, but then immediately died. Prue had curled up next to her mother's warm skin under blankets, hoping that when they woke up the next day the alarming fact of the dead sister would be forgotten, but her mother did not stay very long in her bed. She complained because Prue's hands flipped and flapped as if they confused themselves with wings and her mother left her alone. To stop her twitching, difficult hand, Prue lay on it to force it to be still, but it didn't work. It shook all night.

Later, Prue waited for Ihsan in the street as agreed near the gates with the blue lions on the pillars and when he came, late as always, he took her freezing gloveless hands, held them tight and breathed on them. He led her towards the narrow passage with the stone stairs, up to his *oda*.

'I haven't been in here since we last visited,' Ihsan said. He heaved open the wooden door, agitating the air which seemed full of pollen and spiders. He had explained the first time she came: it is the custom for men here to rent a space, one or two rooms away from their family, for relaxation and peace and study. She had been here just twice before, for Arabic lessons, and she liked the sense of being let inside the Jerusalem stone walls, rather than her usual feeling of being a foreign insect landed on the wrong flower.

The building was south-facing and Ihsan opened the blinds so that the light came in. It was cold. There was a fireplace, but no firewood. It was Ihsan's habit to always have with him sweets and, humming, he arranged a line of glistening nougat and baklavas across a table and then surprised her by opening a bag and pulling out firewood and tea supplies. This building had been the Commissariat offices during the war but neglected since the English came, so Ihsan said. There was a low sofa along one wall, otherwise the room was full almost entirely of books and paper. Purple cushions on the sofa were embroidered with silver stars. The more Prue looked at them the more the stars seemed to move about in their purple sea.

As he lit the fire, Ihsan chatted about friends and cousins, people she had never met, never would, but still, she liked to hear about them. *Hadid is a disgusting scavenger. He dredges through the belongings of old mothers and aunts who have been left after the war with no sons to protect their useless crates of family treasure. At this moment Hadid will be shouting: Ihsan, you bastard, where are you? You promised to help me clear out the house of Umm Diabis Abbud.* Prue smiled at him. *Dear Ihsan.*

'Help yourself, little bird.' Ihsan gestured to the sweets. This was what he called her, or the Turkish word, *kuş*. Swallowing a chewy baklava she went to the window and looked down on Jerusalem. The fire was getting going finally and she watched Ihsan's back as he crouched in front of it, blowing gently to encourage the shy flame.

'So, did you do your tasks?' he said, when done. He patted the sofa, indicating that she should sit down. There was a creaking noise in the bowels of the building. They were both quiet. A sound of keys, a man's shout, a door slamming and then silence. She found in her bag her notebook and searched for the paper she had transcribed for him.

Originally, Ihsan had been instructed to teach Prue basic Arabic, which she had requested to learn as soon as it became clear that her father had no plan whatsoever for her time or education. She campaigned to learn photography from Eleanora and Arabic from Ihsan. They worked once a week at the Fast, unless Ihsan was busy at his Al Muntada literary meetings or assisting Eleanora – he seemed to be involved in lots of different activities – but recently they had put the Arabic aside to learn shifra code, which could not be discussed outside of 'these walls'.

Trying not to show that she was feeling important, she pulled out a list of alphabet characters. Her favourite was *thā'*. It meant the choice part of anything, which seemed to her the perfect expression: *I'll have the choice part of this or that, please. The choice part of life.*

'Open it up,' he said.

She flattened the page on her knee, ran her fingers along the characters. Admittedly, she did not yet have them all in her mind.

jīm, a strong camel
ḥā', a stout woman with a sharp tongue
khā', the hair on the anus (when it is thick and long)
dāl, a fat woman
dhāl, cockscomb
rā', tiny ticks
zayn/zāy, a man who eats a great deal
sīn, a fat meaty man
shīn, a man who often has sexual intercourse
ṣād, a rooster that wallows in the dirt
ḍād, the hoopoe when it raises its head and cries
ṭā', an old man who often has sexual intercourse
ẓā', a woman's breast when it swings
'ayn, the camel's hump
ghayn, a camel reaching water

fā', sea foam

qāf, a man who can do without other men

kāf, a man who settles affairs; a chaste man

lām, a greening tree

mīm, wine

nūn, a fish

hā', a white mark (on the cheek of a gazelle)

wāw, a camel with a great hump

laam'alif, thong of a sandal

yā', direction, aspect

She also brought out the page of coded writing she had been working on. Ihsan took it. The shifra scrambled the Arabic. She was using the pictures to remember the key.

'Shall I read it?'

'Of course,' she said, although she blushed. Some of her drawings were very shaky. There were some characters – *khā'*, for instance, or *shīn* – that she could not look at without dying inside with embarrassment. She had not attempted to write them out yet.

'I shall translate it back to you,' he said, and sprawled himself on the rug on the floor so that the backs of his legs were close to the fire. Prue, sitting in the heart of his sofa, pulled a blanket over her. It smelled damp but she ignored that. His voice was sing-songy.

My mother was taken through a door, and I was left with four boxes: books, wooden ponies, pine cones, paper dolls, sketchbooks, skipping rope. The house we lived in was covered in flint, a useful substance traditionally used in weapons, the tips of arrows.

Underneath that house was chalk, also a useful substance, for writing with and crumbling. This part of England is built on chalk. There are similarities between chalk and Jerusalem limestone.

'Wonderful,' Ihsan said, tapping the side of his nose and looking at her. Then he put the piece of paper on the floor and turned on to his back. He was always flipping around, springing up and jumping on furniture, not at all like anyone she knew (by which she meant anyone English), and now, from lying flat on the floor he hopped on to the back of the sofa and looked down at Prue with eyes full of something she did not know how to read.

'You are doing well. Better than expected. It is interesting to write about your mother. In truth, all stories begin with the mother.'

Was he laughing at her?

'I like that the code means what I write is secret,' she said and smiled at him.

'Exactly.' He touched his moustache.

'Well. Secret from everyone but you of course.'

'Yes, but I don't count. You can trust me on that.' He closed his eyes.

After a moment Prue wondered if Ihsan had fallen asleep in this position, squatting on the back of the sofa. His eyelashes were very long; she leant forward to really look at his face and then his eyes opened a tiny bit and she jumped backwards.

'Let me tell you something, Prue.'

'Yes?'

'A word is treachery, sweet English child. Every word, a written letter, a character. Be careful what you write. Before the end of the war I used the shifra code to write about Cemal and my father. I did not write of the mother.' He laughed and then suddenly looked at her very intently.

'Have you done any more of the colouring in for your father's maps?'

She had told him, last time, about her father's plans for the city, and how she had spent an afternoon helping him shade the areas which he called zones. *Thick-shaded area: Jewish. Light-shaded area: Christian. Dots: Muslim. Tiny crosses: Armenian. Industrial area: slanted lines on a red background. Business and residential: slanted lines on a white background. 'New Military Area': a grid.*

She shook her head. 'No.'

Ihsan sighed and slid down into the sofa; he tugged Prue so that she came forward, her face close to his, noses almost touching, and she could see that in his brown eyes there were flecks of a lighter brown. His breath covered her skin.

'I don't understand the English,' he said, 'and I don't think I ever will. Your father, forgive me for saying this, has been appointed as civic adviser to a city he knows nothing about, has not lived in for very long and does not understand. He talks of the unsanitary maze and tangle of streets but, as always with colonisers, even the ones who truly believe themselves liberators before the killing starts up again, they do not take the time to listen. They make their plans before they have even lived here.'

Prue pulled back from Ihsan; she did not understand what he was saying.

'I think his main intention is to create a garden; there's nothing so bad in that, is there?' she said.

'Your father wants to bring a garden in, and trees. This city is abominably *dry*, I heard him say. And I said: You are aware, I am sure, that it is against the Quranic law to plant trees in public thoroughfares?'

But then Ihsan's face changed and he caught her hand and held it. Without realising she had obviously been flapping again. The skin on her palms was red-hot, prickly.

'I am sorry, dear Prue,' he said. 'I do not criticise you and I don't mean to speak ill of your father.'

She pulled the moth-nibbled blanket up to her chin. Prue had spent the long journey from Portsmouth to Port Said worrying about whether she would recognise her father, but in the end she had known him immediately, when he came into the room in the Casino Palace. She was quarantined for a week in Port Said on arrival due to a fever, and when he was finally let in – the last time she had seen him was when she was three – he sat on the edge of her bed and without asking permission took her sketchbook from her, and flicked through the pages.

'These are rather good.' Prue had flushed all over. 'Rotten about this illness. Not much of a welcome, hey? Bad luck.'

Not a single person had explained to her why, one rainy Thursday afternoon, her mother had been taken to a hospital that was not really a hospital called Graylingwell, in Chichester. Or why a woman, standing at the black gates of this Graylingwell place, had offered Prue a handkerchief with an embroidered cockerel in one corner and told her to keep it for the drying of tears. What tears? Was she supposed to be crying?

He had shifted about on the bed, was trying to be kind, she could tell, and then Prue remembered something her mother had said about him: when he is sitting down, he wants to be standing up. When he is standing still he wants to run. Your father: he is always travelling in two directions at once.

'We'll be living in the Hotel Fast in Jerusalem, until we can release the scoundrel Canon Brown from his villa which will be ours.' He had explained: the Canon was supposed to have vacated his villa in the nearby village of Lifta several months ago but he was touring with his suitcase harmonium and a copy of *Hymns Ancient and Modern*, carousing and wassailing the villages, and nobody could make any contact.

'Once he returns we'll ask him to hand it over and make us a home, but there are papers to be signed, as you can imagine. I hope you will be comfortable enough?'

She had nodded and he had pulled from his pocket a small neat sketchbook and showed her drawings of his own, his large hands turning the pages, his nose red at the tip.

'This is my sketch of the Via Dolorosa,' he said. He flicked through the images: the West Wall of Jerusalem. The Well of the Magi. Maps and maps. The Dead Sea. Hebron. Mount Nebo. Kerak. Jerusalem from the Skull Hill. Damascus Gate.

'You will see soon enough the charms of Jerusalem.' The fan on the ceiling above them span and for a moment she had thought it was a shot bird, falling towards her bed. 'And the wonderful work we will do here.'

'Yes, Father.' And she had said it; it was real. Father. At this point there had been a little cough from the other side of the room.

'Ah, forgive me, I have not introduced you. Prudence, meet Frau Baum.' From the wall where she had been hiding, or disguising herself as a curtain, emerged a petit woman wearing a feathered hat. She had a bright red mouth.

'Welcome. Welcome.' The woman was dressed in black with a collar also made up of feathers so that she looked like a person in costume. She came in close, smelling of acids, lemons it might have been, and placed her cold hand on Prue's forehead as if she were blessing her. She handed Prue a box covered in blue paper and tied with string.

'A small present, and you should call me Elspeth. You must be very tired after the illness. Was it a terrible passage?' She had a strong foreign accent.

Prue hadn't known what to say. What makes a passage good or bad? The companion had ignored her and played whist with a group of American women. She had befriended the ship's mouser cat. *This isn't the children's boat but it may as well be*, an old woman said, whacking at Prue's calves with her stick for running on the deck. Prue spent the evenings alone in her cabin. There had been one particularly stormy night and she had been sick.

'It was fine.'

Frau Baum and her feathers leant towards Prue's father, whispered secrets into his ear and then left the room, giving a wave. Alone again. Explanations were clearly felt needed.

'You will like her,' he said. He patted the bed. Prue pulled herself up a little, wishing she wasn't in bed, wishing her hair wasn't stuck to the side of her face, wishing she were dressed and presentable and clean.

'Yes, Father.' *She said it again.*

He cleared his throat. Frau Baum was a German who had returned to Jerusalem after admissions had been relaxed. *They were all expelled, of course, during the war*. She was civilised and discreet and it was a thrill not to discuss the war with her. Actually, it was a thrill to – he paused – be friends with a German. Did she, Prue, feel strange about this? (No, she did not.) Good. He continued to talk, about things Prue did not really understand: the problems of Palestine, of which she was wholly ignorant, his

42

plans for the city, which sounded complicated and brilliant. Prue's fingernails picked at the edges of the present that Frau Baum had given her but she felt she could not rip it open yet.

'How is your mother?' he said, getting round to it finally and not looking at her but at a discoloured square on the wall where a picture must have recently hung.

'She is not very well.'

'Yes. They wrote to me about this.'

She waited for more; he was silent for some time and then he said, 'I remember you so well, as a three-year-old, unstoppable hiccups and red cheeks.'

Why did you want me here? Why was I sent? He didn't answer the question but she was misremembering because she had not asked it out loud. When he left her in bed to organise their transfer to Jerusalem she had opened the package from Frau Baum. It was a bronze rabbit statue, with one ear bent forwards and the other upright, and she had put it on the bedside table in the room and did not remember to bring it with her to Jerusalem.

'Prue? Little bird?' Ihsan was waving his hand at her. He gestured all around the room. 'The hours I slogged in this very building working for Rusen Bey,' he said. 'Almost transferred to the Suez to fight the British and now here I am with you, little English girl.' He sprang down on to the floor again.

'So, tell me about this new pilot from England. Does he talk about his plans, will he fly?'

Prue was surprised that he was interested in the pilot. *Eleanora's pilot.* She did not particularly want to talk about him.

'All I know about him,' she said, black mood descending, 'is that he is an old friend of Eleanora's.'

Ihsan's eyebrows shot up at that.

'Father is bringing in an aircraft sometime next week and he will fly Eleanora around so she can photograph the city.'

'I see,' he was looking closely at the expression on her face, 'and are you not going?'

'I am positively disinvited.' She felt full of shadows and corners where thick emotions were sheltering and it seemed that Ihsan liked to shine lights into these places.

'I believe,' she said, and then lost courage to continue.

'Yes?' said Ihsan lightly, as he jumped up and retrieved the plate of sweets from the table.

Her eyes wide, mouth dry, Prue said, 'I believe he has come here to steal away Eleanora.'

There. She had said it. She thought of the bloody little heart she had held in her palm, and the way Eleanora had turned from her, no longer interested.

Ihsan, who was, Prue knew, very old friends with Eleanora's husband, did not look shocked, as she thought – perhaps hoped – he might, but he was staring at her. Really looking at her, until she blushed at the attention. She was amazed at herself, for saying it aloud, and it was ... what was the word? ... *satisfying* to have said it. Her father, when talking about Eleanora, said: 'I don't know what it is about her, but she just has a ray. A bright ray.' *Do I have a ray?*

Prue went to her knapsack and pulled out her Kodak. She waited for Ihsan to say something but he was staring into space. When Prue first met Eleanora, during her first week in Jerusalem, Eleanora had given her a present: a seahorse, suspended inside a crystal paper-weight. *Oh it is just something I had, I thought you might like it* and Prue had been so moved that she could barely say thank you. She took it back to her room that night and held it up in front of the candle flame. The seahorse inside shimmered. Its long snout and heraldic fins were pristine. It was perfect, with its blur of horse and insect and sea, and with that gift Prue had fixed herself on to Eleanora, like a puppy who hitches all its luck on to a new owner. She had felt them: real little hooks flying from inside her, catching on to Eleanora's skin, her hair, eyelashes. Nails.

'Will you do something, dear Prue?' Ihsan was still looking at her.

'Yes?'

'Will you slip into his room, this pilot, and bring me what you can? Any identification, or books? It will be useful, to understand why he is here. His ... intentions regarding our lovely Mrs Rasul.'

Prue was rather taken aback, but she hid it quickly as Ihsan turned and squeezed with his forefinger and thumb a tiny dancing fly that had landed in her hair. The nicest smell of the baklavas and rosewater came from him. Her hair was always straggly, in a mess, plaits coming undone. Great embarrassment; one of many she had.

'I know that Eleanora loves you the best, dear Prue. I understand that. She loves you better than this pilot.' Prue tapped fingernails on her knee to stop blushes; he could read her mind too easily. She picked at the frayed edge of the rug under her feet, dared herself, and then did it.

'I have a question for you, Ihsan.'

'Go on, little *kuş*.'

'Why does Khaled Rasul go away?'

'He travels for his work, taking photographs of our great lands.'

'But his photographs are usually taken in the studio.'

'Well. He has other work, too, why do you ask?' And then Ihsan sighed. 'Khaled is my friend since we were children. I have

45

known him for ever, but I say to him, you keep going to Damascus, wherever you are going, looking for a Syrian unity, you leave your wife alone too long.'

From outside a long hoot from a motor car, voices, a squabble in the street followed by the loud braying of a donkey reminded Prue that she was not in England but Jerusalem. Often, she thought: is this real? She was unsure.

'I shall help you get to the bottom of it, do not look so worried.' He took both of her hands and squeezed them. 'This is what we must do: you get me what you can from his room. That will be a wonderful place to start.'

She was unsure; she frowned and then stood up. She was too tall for her age; she was like the trees, knobbly and bony.

'We must be on Eleanora's side, surely? We must do what we can to protect her.'

Yes. That was true. He stood up too. 'Also, but only if you feel like it, dear bird,' he smiled, 'if you can let me know a little more about your father's plans for the city, these ideas of areas, these crosses and dots, that would be so wonderful too.'

'Of course Ihsan. If I can.'

'We should both get ready for the Pro-Jerusalem Society party this evening?' He did not look enthusiastic and then he laughed at her. 'The English always looked so worried.'

'I don't like it when you do that,' she said, knowing she was coming across sulky.

'What?'

'Lumping me in with "the English".'

Ihsan looked perfectly handsome in the half-light and she couldn't work out if he was laughing at her or not but his face was serious.

'I have given it much thought, actually, and I do not in fact consider you English.'

'Oh?'

'You are nothing like the men in Governance House, you are different. Perhaps it is your Irish mother? Who knows, but I feel it.'

Prue knew that this statement was illogical. She had been born in a boarding house in Torquay, which was very much England, but still, she warmed when Ihsan spoke to her this way. It *steadied her*. She felt as if she had been curled up on a magic carpet and whisked to Jerusalem. The word sofa, Ihsan had explained to her, derives from the Arabic *suffah* and what comes to your minds in London when you think of Arabs? The sofa, the bed, the day-bed, the carpet, the flying carpet, the place of dreams, the closed palace ... and he had laughed in a way she did not understand. *You think we are sleeping*.

Rubbing the metal case of the Kodak and twirling the tiny winding spool on its top, she dared herself to ask him if she could take a photograph, but in the end was too shy. Photographing a person was capturing them, like one of the singing canaries in bamboo cages in the souk. Instead she took a photograph of him in her head, and added details that made no sense: him holding a caught fish, standing next to a boat, or on a bridge, smiling, waving.

Jerusalem, 1920

'The problem with Ashton,' Eleanora said, using a cool formal voice as if he were a visiting vicar being given his supper, 'is that he thinks of this place, Palestine, the Promised Land, whatever it might be called, as an absence. He sees a piece of desert or fallow land and thinks there is nobody here, but in fact it's deeply populated and controlled. It's the great flaw in his plan.'

She was pointing up to the ramparts next to Jaffa Gate, protected in fur, her hair glowing.

'What does your husband think of him?'

She jolted at that, her right eye closing for a second, and looked up to the sky, as if seeing something secret in the distance that would be forever hidden to him.

'My husband has been gone a few weeks now, but Ihsan tells me he is due back.'

She put her hand to her lips as if to silence herself and Willie had no idea what to say. Something lifted inside him: *My husband has been gone.* Then sank: *due back.*

'He didn't tell you himself?'

'Let's go into the souk,' she said, stopping questions.

Eleanora slipped in front of him into David Street where they plunged into the most crowded part of the market. It was just the same as the Cairo markets: like being guided into someone else's nightmare, like being led into a trap. She turned to wait for him and he was felled, again, by her particular, stalking beauty.

'It's so confusing to have you here,' she whispered as he came near, but immediately they were separated by a flow of pilgrims. The cobbled steps of the marketplace became very steep and the soles of his boots could find no purchase as the path dipped. The buildings around them leant close together as if exchanging secrets. As they passed stalls selling holy water he caught hold of the sleeve of her fur coat.

'What do you mean your husband left? Where did he go? Where is he now?'

Her eyes widened, thoughts passed through them, but he couldn't read them. 'Khaled said he would be back, but he explained nothing. He did not say when or what he is doing or why. He asked me to trust him.'

'You don't have any idea where he is?'

She shook her head. 'I asked him, what is this, you are feeling more Arab? Is this nationalism? You hate the British? You must explain it to me, but he wouldn't.'

It was an offence to Willie that Eleanora was buried under the stones of this city. *City*. It was a medieval prison, a locked-up fortress; it was a child's drawing, an illustration from the Bible that they had been dropped into by magical forces. It was an *unreal city*. She was ahead of him again, trailing her hand against the edge of the stalls that lined the passageways, and the information that she had just given him – anti-British, gone, husband – ricocheted in his mind. But really: what the fuck is she doing here? What he meant, although he did not quite formalise the thought to himself, though the charge and momentum of it was there, vivid as a fresh scar – and he certainly knew about them – was, why is she wedded to *one of them?* His English sensibility was vivified, it was indignation. There was, underneath it all, outrage.

This part of the city was a place of stairwells and low doors, webs of passages continuing to spin onwards. They were flanked by pilgrims and conveyances of nuns marking their slow steps along the Via Dolorosa, a cloying smell of incense around them. Eleanora waited for him and when she took his arm he could see that something in her shifted: when she spoke it was the old, familiar Eleanora and he tried to hold on to the flow of what she was saying, but it was like holding water in his hands.

She was conscious, she said, that she was failing her husband. She should be immutable and fixed, steadfast. Unquestioning, but dear God, all those afternoons with Khaled's family. His mother and sisters openly staring at the foreigner as if she was a fairy in a picture brought to life. Khaled's sister patting her stomach, her arms indicating the rocking motion of babies. After weeks of intolerably awkward company in the houses of Khaled's family she began to walk over to the German Colony. For a while she helped the missionaries at the American Colony with the orphans but their hopeless wet eyes and neediness depressed her. She spent time with the English wives even though she knew they gossiped about her for marrying an Arab. Khaled started to ask, why do you go to those people?

'What did he mean?' Willie asked and she pulled away from him.

'He meant the British, and their confounded social expectations, and everything, class, I suppose, the prison of my home – which you, more than anyone, know about – all of that. Why was I walking back into that place?'

Willie tried to keep hold of her arm again but she found a way to shrug it from him.

'When I became friends with Storrs's fiancée, Lucy, he was furious.'

'Why?'

'He's the Military Governor. Khaled objects to his ways of … imposing authority. And to Ashton's ways of putting a British stamp on Jerusalem, too. He is cross with me, for working with Ashton.'

Then something further in her fell down and she turned.

'This city is exhausting.' Her lips parted, she had a gap between her two front teeth which she had hated as a child and the unexpectedly vulnerable look whenever she opened her mouth always surprised him.

'Ihsan said there is a woman who lives near Herod's Gate who believes she is being followed by a floating pair of hands. It's all rather hysterical. Khaled calls it the Jerusalem sadness, but anyway: this is where I live.'

They stopped and the sign KHALED RASUL PHOTOGRAPHY STUDIO was bright yellow with blue lettering and the woodwork surrounding the entire window-front of the studio was painted indigo blue.

'Do you live above the studio?' He was unable to connect this place with Eleanora.

'Above it, below it and also the house next door. They are connected into one house. It is usual to have passageways between houses here.'

He watched her unlock the ancient-looking wooden door with a large metal key.

The studio was dark and smelled of rosewater and limes.

'The maid Samia will be about.' It was a warning. She was formal again as she allowed him into this strange world she inhabited. Walls lined with shelves full of props for photographs, piles of dresses, costumes and fabrics. Willie examined a paper calendar hanging on the wall at an awkward angle:

Jerusalem
Sunday 28th March
15th of mart 131 Ottoman Fiscal
I Jammadi Awwal 1333.

She saw what he was looking at.

'They can't even agree on the time here.'

The opposite wall was covered with photographs, largely of entrances and doorways, a basket seller up under an arch.

'These are for the European and American pilgrims. The flocks must be white. The women at the well must wear shawls; fishermen cast their nets nicely in the dawn. Everything biblical. A rabbi looking wise and ancient, a water carrier. They sell terrifically.' She smiled. 'Not too much modern Jerusalem, not too much truth.'

She moved deeper into the studio, towards a door at the back of the room, and beckoned him. 'Would you like to see the darkroom?'

'Of course.'

———

To be closed in this space with her electrified him but he suppressed it, swallowed it. She flicked on a small red lantern so that the room was like the inside of a fireplace. Then she lit a bigger lamp. A wire was stretched across the room and clipped on to it were several photographs. Below them on the work surface trays of chemicals were lined up and around the edge of the desk glass bottles glinted. Willie listened to her breathing. He examined the photographs hanging in front of his nose. The first was of two young Arab women, as always with girls, a beauty and a plainer one, though they both looked shy and sweet.

'I must say,' Eleanora said into the strange red-black light, 'my advertisements in *Al Karmel* have turned out to be a marvellous hit. Fourteen sequences of photographs as a result. The Moldchadsky family. The nurse from Akka, the cousins Laila and Leyla. Dimitri and his mother and her dogs even – can you imagine? – yet it's these two girls that I like the best. I'm going to use them as hand-maidens for a new Moses picture, if I can get their mother to agree.'

In the closed dark space Willie, aware of her enthusiasm, held his breath and remembered them both sitting as children in the bottom of a wardrobe at Pentrohobyn eating hot scones that she, fearless, had stolen directly from the ovens.

'Photographs are always taken in studios here – the Krikorian rooms or the Garabad studios – with all the fuss of a great big entourage, a family and dressing up and props. Nobody before has ever taken photographs of Jerusalem people in their own homes, in intimate settings, by which I mean,' he sensed her smiling at him, 'of course, women.'

Despite the dark we could read her handwriting on paper in front of him: the same as it always had been. Mad and looping. Unrestrained.

She was acting . . . *properly*, whereas he needed to address everything. The whistle began, deep in his ears, his old problem. Then, out of nowhere, as if she heard it, she said softly: 'Was the war terrible for you? I noticed the . . .'

'Scars.'

'Yes.'

'My observer Mackie was eaten by flames, but I am alive. As you can see.'

He regretted saying it instantly, flippant and cold like that, and then, an inappropriate thought: if Eleanora were ever to see his body she would be repulsed by it. He pressed his palm against his ear, because what he struggled with more than his shrivelled skin, was the quinine-induced mosquito hum of tinnitus which came and went, maddening him with a zzzuzzz and hissss deep in the canals and runways of his ears. Like a moth trapped in his head. Or boots walking through his brain. Today it was the worst type, whistling.

'What are these?' he said to make that subject disappear and it took a moment for him to realise that the images in front of him were highly contrasted fragments of the girls: cheeks, legs, parts of faces, shoulders. They reminded him of a risqué jigsaw puzzle that his uncle brought home one Christmas, a French madam blowing a kiss, her leg kicked backwards and her breasts riding high.

'Experiments, with long exposure.' It was a series of square-format photographs that were all, to varying degrees, blurry.

'That's Ashton's daughter?'

'Yes. She was helping me. Ladies only.' There was Prudence, looking ethereal, frowning at the floor.

'Good God,' he said, looking at the next photograph, this one of Eleanora. 'It's as if all those years haven't happened.'

It was Eleanora sitting on a chair, her feet together, hands folded on her knees, and it seemed she had taken herself back to an exact point in time.

'That's you as a child.'

She seemed pleased, but also a little embarrassed.

'Yes. I do suppose that is what I was intending.'

Willie was standing very close to her now and he touched the skin on the back of her hand briefly; she did not pull away.

He took her hand now, held it fully. She continued to talk to him, in a whisper. *Injuria*: a wrong. The wrongs of time. The wrong time. The longer the shutter stays open, the flesh fades, the edges are blurred, transparent, and they disappear, can you see? The camera captures not the girl but the amount of time it looked at her. It captures time. She pulled abruptly away from him, turned to the door, opened it so that light conquered the black room, and walked out.

Willie leant against the work surface, the ringing in his ears so high now that there was an angelic quality to it. Further along the worktop near the wall were more photographs arranged in a sequence. Landscapes of Jerusalem. He glanced at the closest image: a line of soldiers wearing sun helmets, British-looking. Willie picked it up. A village in the distance, the sky full of curled smoke from a blown-up house, a soldier looking pleased with himself.

'What is this?' he called out. Eleanora turned and squinted over her shoulder.

'One of Khaled's, I think.'

There were four or five pictures underneath this one, they appeared to have been taken the same day. Eleanora had moved further into the other room. Willie gathered them up and slipped them into his jacket pocket then quickly closed the door behind him.

Tea was served by the highly disapproving Ethiopian maid Samia. Willie sat mute; Eleanora talked, almost to herself, about the particulars of the house. Like many of the old houses of Jerusalem, four or five hundred years old, the central living space had two staircases, one burrowing downwards towards dark kitchens and utility areas and the other spiralling upwards towards roofs. A flight of stairs. She had never before thought of stairs in terms of movement. On the table in front of them was an incongruous marmalade cake. Finally, she stopped speaking and stared at the complex woven patterns in the rug beneath their feet. Peacock feathers entwined around pomegranates.

'Houses bury one,' she said after a long pause. She did not look directly at him but more vaguely around the room.

'I often feel I am suffocating here, just as I did in Wales.' She gestured to a sideboard which stretched the length of a wall, topped with tureens and etched crystal fruit bowls. Samia could be heard moving up and down steps. Willie rubbed his hands together with impatience. How could Pentrohobyn Hall, with its rooms and corridors, parlourmaid, kitchenmaid, cook, groom, nanny, chauffeur, the French governess, the gardens and all of that, be similar to here? On the wall was a portrait of a handsome young Arab in an ornate walnut frame.

'Is that your husband?'

She nodded, frowning at him. He stood up to inspect. Younger than he had imagined, a moustache, confident clear bright eyes. Willie's mind hovered around the vicious sting of the fact that she had not refused all other men for him. She had run off and married a foreigner. It was too ludicrous, but he could not stop looking at Rasul's eyes.

The face of Eleanora's father came to his mind – its purple nose with broken veins – and he could feel even now his hand on Willie's shoulder. There was unspoken history between their fathers. *Old bastards together*, was how Eleanora put it. One was indebted to the other in a complicated, long-standing connection which resulted in Eleanora's father paying for Willie's school fees at Lancing College, insisting Willie summer with them at Pentrohobyn. Willie never knew the whole sum of it, but he suspected it was something to do with Eleanora's mother who died giving birth to her.

The condition Eleanora's father, for reasons of his own, put on the payment of Willie's school fees was that he serve in the army for a minimum of three years and so, aged sixteen, Willie had joined the 1st Life Guards. He was moved to Windsor, then to Knightsbridge where he caught measles but survived, and then, in 1914 when he was nineteen, he was finally discharged by purchase and free from the army by which he meant free from her father.

Returning to Pentrohobyn, Willie had bribed a stable boy for a ladder and climbed up to Eleanora's window. He brought with him a box and in it a very bright yellow shining shivering thing: the golden oriole. To him, the implication of this gift – never mind the daring climb into the bedroom window which if her father knew would result in him being scalped or whipped across Wales and England too – was obvious, but her face had been pale when he'd rapped on the glass. She let him in, of course, in the old way, but she hurried back into bed. Did not smile, or welcome him.

That year she was engaged in silent, mental warfare with her father. She refused the debutante rounds, claimed to be too ill to go to the balls. She shrieked when she touched Willie's gift of the oriole because it was stuffed and she'd thought it real. He had got it from the taxidermist in Shrewsbury. She went off to Switzerland soon after, and what kind of joke was played on him by the fates that two months later war would be declared and his military discharge annulled? Reinstated immediately, promoted to 2nd Lieutenant by October of that year, whisked far away from sycamore trees and yellow birds.

He wrote to her, a few months or so later. *It meant marry me, that bird. Did you not realise?* But he never knew if she got the letter. Her old devil of a father might've interfered with the post. Lying on a bunk on a deployment train he'd told Mackie about it. *You gave her a stuffed sparrow?* Golden oriole. *Fucking finch, you stupid fool.* That the war had taken him away and brought Khaled Rasul to her was – Willie turned from the eyes looking at him from the photograph – unbearable.

She was still staring at the carpet.

'Come back to England with me.' He swung his arms around the suffocating room. He looked at her face, uncertain.

'We can arrange it, now the war is over. There are things that can be done.' Everything in him was alight as he spoke, as if each bruise he had ever received through his life, each blow and burn and peeling of skin returned to remind him he was made of flawed flesh.

There was a framed picture of Pentrohobyn Hall on the sideboard. Because she hadn't answered he walked to it to compose himself. He loved that house; perhaps more than she did. To her it was simply a prison.

Willie tried to put Khaled Rasul's face out of his mind, but he could not stop himself imagining the man's fingertips touching Eleanora's collarbone, squeezing the white skin of her inner thigh. She still said nothing. She was not going to answer him. His thoughts filled then with an unwanted vision: Eleanora and Rasul in a vast, four-poster bed, arms and legs wrapped around one another. Rasul's hand on her small white breasts, with him, Willie, sitting transformed into some foul bird, a parrot or vulture, perching above them, peering into their marriage, like a man peeking up a woman's skirt, stealing intimacy as if intimacy itself were morphine.

'I must go.' He stood up.

His instinct was to make his way down towards the kitchen where surely there would be a back door? It was difficult to tell in this house of burrows and tunnels. He moved through a door but instead of a stairwell he found himself on a square rooftop where a washing line stretched from the wall to a wooden pole. A plate covered with the ends of old cigarettes was balanced on the wall and beyond he could see roofs of other crushed and close houses, lives lived on top of one another.

She came behind him. 'Don't leave, it is just rather a surprise.'

Surprise?

He heard her swallowing, fighting with words, but still: nothing.

'I need to go.'

She led him towards the door that took him back to the souk and as he opened it she gently touched his back.

'Soon we'll fly together, take the photographs for Ashton?' She spoke in a thin voice, he barely heard her.

Then she said, fake and bright, 'I'll be at the party tonight. You can't escape me, now you are here in Jerusalem.'

He looked at her. She gave up attempting to lighten things. She was close to him, at the door. He thought for a moment that she was going to embrace him. Instead, she leant her head back, tipping her chin up.

'If I gave myself to you now, you would throw me away,' she said.

'No,' he said. 'That is not true.' He stumbled into the Christian Quarter and turned into the first passage available, a steep, narrow road with a series of steps so shiny they looked as if they had been polished with the purpose of making a person slide. Carved rosaries of varying sizes and colours were for sale on both sides of the steps. He tried to imagine what it must be like to imbue faith in wooden beads on string. The walls around him concealed numerous monasteries and churches and it must have been the turn of an hour because bells struck, loudly ringing, out of synch. It was as if he were in a cog in the centre of the invention of time. He turned into an even narrower passage where birdcages were for sale, rows and rows of tiny prisons, and the sound of the canaries and chaffinches singing for freedom combined with the whistles in his head and the bells of time and noise became all that there was.

Shoreham, 1937

There is a mermaid outside Jimmie's Tea Rooms on the New Shoreham side of the harbour. Disturbing, almost obscene the way she beckons the children, with her chipped nose and voluptuous form, and when a tuppence is rolled into the slot where a mouth should be she releases a mechanical tune. Skip is in love with her yellow falling hair. He stares at her flawed, peeling face, begs for pennies to bring her to life, and he must be thinking of her now as he curls in the heart of my bed, because he is quietly singing her song. *Swimming in the brine her figure was divine ... she had a yen for all the sailors ... she had a most immoral eye... they called her Lorelei.* I will let him fall asleep where he is and move him to his cot-bed later. I shuttle around Cecilia, pretending to tidy things up, humming lightly, so that he knows I am near as he goes down. *They called her Lorelei.*

I promised Billy that I would not go to the Warnes Hotel, and so I did not go, but I did not tell him about the telegram that was delivered by the churlish, black-haired son of the postmaster who threw it at my doormat. It might easily have fluttered away to become seagull food if I hadn't seen him do it.

I WILL BE AT THE WARNES TOMORROW EXPECT YOU AT THREE
AND DAY AFTER UNTIL YOU COME URGENT AND IMPORTANT
REGARDING IHSAN TAMERI.

I slipped this unsettling message into an old copy of *Vanity Fair* that has somehow travelled with me from London and it is there now. Lying flat. Making no sense.

I dress carefully for Billy, glancing out at the last folds of the day's light into the sea, but what I'm really doing is looking out for William Harrington and wondering why he is here in Sussex. It is as if he has slipped through a cut-out hole in time, like the paper dolls I used to clip from the back of the draper catalogue, leaving the silhouette of a little girl, fallen backwards. Since his visit I have intended to write to Ihsan and yet I haven't begun the letter. It has been three days now. Might he still be there, at the Warnes? Surely not. Outside, the clouds are growing thicker until they blend into one flat, fading sky.

Skip watches me dress, sleepily, stomach nicely full after drinking his milk with the last of the dripping on toast. I am getting better at this, the feeding. Since leaving Piers I am marooned, financially, on gifts doled out by Piers's father, the earl. He deposits monthly cheques – not vast amounts, enough to feed the boy, essentially – and because I couldn't possibly afford to run to a woman I have learned how to cook a potato. Slicing brown carbuncles, washing off pig manure, cutting into the waxy white tuber.

I did cook once before coming to Shoreham, of course. I was wearing, I remember, a vivid blue taffeta silk dress at my friend

Marguerite's house in Mayfair and we were drunkenly concocting a surrealist soup we intended to serve to the down-and-outs at the workhouse. Onions, carrots, sequins from an old hat and diamonds plucked from Marguerite's dress. Piers's friend, Harry, cut his finger and let drips of blood fall into the mixture, shouting, as he did so, *Ripen! Ripen! Ripen!*

Skip's head is lolling. I turn off the lantern next to the bed but leave one glowing on the table near the mirror. We do not have curtains, just badly hung drapes, old dust cloths once used for covering my sculptures. There are many areas of domestic housekeeping at which I am failing, curtains being the merest tip. Fighting sleep, Skip demands that I tell him a rabbit story.

'Not tonight, lovely.'

I look at the clock. Billy is coming at seven. I pull the curlers from my hair slowly, liking the release and spring. Shortly after my arrival at Shoreham Beach, Billy, my self-appointed protector, gave me one of his hand-tinted promotional photographs: long shorts, fists wrapped in white bandages, his lips a shocking red. It had been hard not to smile, but I could see he was serious about boxing so I thanked him politely. On the back of the picture it said 'Bombardier Billy'. He stands out, here, but is accepted as one of the town's own. Unlike me. When I walk past the wide-hipped housewives of Shoreham cleaning their steps and windows they don't bother to tut-tut quietly.

I rummage in my wardrobe-trunk where not a single item is appropriate for Shoreham weather: ensembles, capes, collars, evening dresses, fox stoles, cashmere. I pull out a grey crêpe-de-chine dress, a sleek affair, almost like mermaid-skin itself, and a slip in a matching colour. Both are much too thin for this time of year, but there we are. All of my stockings are damp and so I lay them out in front of the wood burner to dry while I rub cream into my face without looking in a mirror. Finally, I dress, leaving stockings until last.

When the wind drops dead outside it becomes too still inside Cecilia and I whistle to cover it up. At odd moments I have the sensation that the weather is watching me here, waiting, as if planning a surprise I won't particularly like. On our first night, Skip and I slept together in the unfamiliar bed – I had not yet got the cot-bed for him – and all night the clamours and repetitions of the sea wove through my dreams. There would never be silence here, I realised. Not with the wind and the sea and yet, despite that, the room could be still. No Piers: that was it. No thick hanging golden curtains tied with a tasselled rope. No sounds of the light tingling from the room-service trolley, none of Piers's friends banging on the door at three in the morning, drunk from a night at the Midnight Follies cabaret at the Metropole, stinking of champagne and vomiting into the azure-blue flowerpots. I sit on the bed next to Skip for a moment and play with his hair.

'Can we take the train to London, Mummy?'

'You'd like to?'

'I would.'

'To see Daddy? I'm afraid he's not there at the minute, darling.'

'No,' he says, brave, turning into the blankets, eyes drooping now, 'I mean, not particularly. I would just like the train ride.'

'Well I am sure we can do that.' He puts his head on my knee and I sing to him, my own version of 'Scarborough Fair', with the herbs mixed up, rather tailing off at the end until at last he is asleep. I put another blanket on him so that he has two, make weak Indian tea, drink it. There is a scratching noise at the bottom of the door, claws, snuffling. I open the door, let the sea air flap in and I kick at whatever it is, feel the live edge of it against my toe. There is a scuffle, a noise that is carried off to the sea. I shut out the weather again. When I glance back into Cecilia all I can see is mess. Every drawer in the chest in the corner is open and emptied. An unpleasant stain on the floor next to the bed and Skip has left a bucket half-full of murky water in front of the kitchenette. I lean over and push a red-headed curl away from Skip's eyelid and begin to pick items up – his shorts, his socks, and the pile of newspapers he was using to make paper boats – but the disharmony of the room is too set-in and profound so I give it up, an impossible job. I have left Skip alone before in the evenings and, truth is, I am keen for a drink, but tonight there is a tension in me. It is string-like, a balancing. This boy of mine: made up of fingernails, freckles. When worrying he counts on his fingers for reassurance, or arranges and counts the pebbles or balls of chalk in front of him, over again, his fingers tapping a rhythm of his own. Moving up and down a secret scale. Over the top of my dress I wear a white cape. I put on siren lipstick, but leave off evening gloves. Whatever I wear here I am overdressed.

When I told Marguerite that I was leaving Piers and leaving London and leaving her and the art world and everything to do with our life as it was and taking Skip and going to a place called Shoreham-by-Sea she had laughed and laughed into her apple martini. *You have never lived in small-town England, my dear, wafting, as you were, across the shores of Empire. You do not know closed-mindedness. You don't know what you're letting yourself in for* and I blew a line of smoke towards her crushingly beautiful green eyes and said: 'But, darling, it cannot be worse than this.'

'You look a picture,' Billy says as I open the door and pull him out of the bad-tempered weather.

'We'll go to Flo's Club, shall we?' He looks over at sleeping Skip and nods.

'Why not?'

I walk over and kiss Skip, leaving a red stain on his white forehead, take Billy's arm and we step out together. I am a better person – will this convince me? – if I take certain moments for myself rather than give them to my son. What I mean is: I am a better person *for Skip* if I have a drink on this blustery night with Billy rather than stay in here and watch him sleep and listen to the rain.

The wind batters against us as if it wants to punish us but I'm grateful because it takes all of my concentration to walk and it is not possible to think or feel guilt in the whirlpool of gust. The signs of the neighbouring chalets – Kangaroo, Puss-in-Boots and Angel – clatter and hammer in their brackets. It is not all bad, the feeling of walking along shingle with a man made up of strands of muscle coiled like fishing rope, a man with a strong thirst for ale which he can handle well. The sea near us is a dead-black, and Billy is quick to pull me closer to his side.

'Come on,' he says, 'into the warm.'

The door to Flo's Club is secured with extra chains to make sure the wind doesn't carry it away and Billy, ever gallant, holds it open for me. It is Saturday night. The room is heaving with red-faced fishermen, ex-servicemen, harbour rats, spivs from Brighton. The air is cider, salt, sweat and the musicians on the stage are being applauded, fists banging tables, wolf whistles hitting the roof; the band dismantles itself for an interval just as we squeeze into a table in the corner. Billy's hand is on the small of my back and every man in the room stares at me.

'Everyone's looking at me, Billy.'

'Of course they are, don't get a woman like you in Shoreham that often.' There are hurricane lamps dangling from ropes lashed to the ceiling beams and they swing madly. The wind can be heard whipping at all the flags and sails across the harbour so that it feels as if we are on a boat. There is an air, somehow, of anticipation and, once we are settled into our seats and Billy has greeted everyone he has to, I tap his arm.

'What is everyone on this spit waiting for?'

'A war,' he says, 'or a storm.'

'Oh, that.'

'Not just that. It's more than that.'

'You think?'

'Front line of the country, lovely. We are the unprotected.' He waves, in the general direction of France. 'They aren't on our side, are they?'

He is an expansive person to sit next to. His breath smells of tobacco. A boxer. What would Piers say? I have a feeling he would approve, might even envy him, or me. Billy is half-gypsy, half-fisherman, as far as I can tell, and appears as lawless and ungovernable as the dog breeders or the cockerel fighters, the pawnbrokers and crooks of Brighton. The usual rules of society do not apply to him and this is how we cross over, as it were, because in England I have always felt out of step with how to do things or what does or does not do. This is what Piers and his friends thought so fantastically idiosyncratic about me, thinking me hilarious fun. *Original.* Out-of-step. They thought I was playing, or acting, at being clueless in that way.

Before long, the woman who I presume to be the club's namesake, Florrie Forde, walks on to the stage and leads a song. 'Down at the Old Bull and Bush'. Her voice oppressively shrill.

There's a little nook down near old Hampstead Town ... The fishermen clang their tin pint jugs on the battered tables ... *Come, come, drink some port wine with me, down at the old Bull and Bush* ... *Hear the little German band* and at the word 'German' the room roars up and there are chants of 'No!' The men around us have red eyes and flayed skin. I sip my cider and am in love with them all so much that I don't remove Billy's hand from my knee.

'If war happens, we'll be the first to be gone. Either bombed or evacuated, but anyway,' he says, my philosophical boxer, 'Churchill knows what he's doing. There won't be a war. Half the men in Brighton and Worthing are fond of old Hitler anyhow.'

I touch the yellow kiss of the bruise below his eye. I like the lines on his face, the non-London look of him; the way he said, 'So you're an artist?' And it neither impressed nor scandalised him. A man brought up to use his fist to punch and knock out a person for money does not tend to judge others. I cross my legs, let his hand rise further above my knee until his fingers trace the edge of the lace trim of my chemise. I speak to Billy Ludd as if he is my doctor. As if he is the psychoanalyst that Piers took me to: Mr Ridgeway? Mr Raymond? The one who tapped his long fingers and breathed heavily as secrets bobbed up like apples in a barrel. Only, with Billy, I put my ailments freely on to the table, allowing him to give his halfpence even though he is not qualified to talk about trampled minds.

'No more visitors today?' he says in a break in the music, sipping his cider. I shake my head.

The man sitting next to us slams his pint jug down on the table with a bad-tempered clatter. The stage-lights are dimming. A spotlight shines on to an invisible ghost centre stage, and the drinkers hush as they will do before the hypnotic power of a shot of light on a wooden floor. I shrug at him. I like this place, but the wind is like bad memories coming in before the dawn and I think of Skip, tucked under his blankets. How much of this wind would it take to fly Cecilia away, like a child's toy house in a gust?

A woman, clearly steeped and soused in Sussex cider, is coming towards us. She has trouble weaving her fruitful hips through the men and tables and she looks like a goddess coming out of the sea, only, as her face comes closer, I realise that she doesn't so much. Her skin is haggard and her features unbalanced, as if she has been knocked about here and there and healed incorrectly. Her long brown hair hangs in her eyes which are red and blurred-looking.

'Billy Ludd,' she says. 'Are you planning on getting Walter a present?' It is the first time I have seen Billy looking ruffled; his neck has thickened, veins show. He stands up, pulls himself away from me, whispers, 'Just give me a minute.'

The woman looks as though she might throw a glass at me; I can see she wants to. She is bigger, stronger and fiercer than me in every way. I can't stop staring at the red knuckles on her hand as it presses on the table, but before she does anything Billy steers her towards the bar where they stand together and shout out what they need to. I look away and their words are hidden in the music. This is the balance of things with Bombardier Billy and me. Truly, I don't want to know, but I can see how he is holding the top of her arm and I understand well enough that grip and what it means.

———

At Cecilia, Skip is snoring, his arms flung above his head, his forehead covered in a layer of sweat even though it's draughty. I ask Billy no questions, but it is clear from the way he lingers that I won't be able to shake him tonight, even though I am quite in the mood for my sketchbook, for drawing out night-thoughts. This is the first time, then, I've had the old sensation I remember from Piers, of not being able to move the man out of the room when I want to work. A thwarting, I suppose. Piers, naked in the large room at the Russell Hotel, slamming the door to the private bathroom and saying *it's mine for the night to work, you can piss in the vases, there are enough of them* and in the morning him emerging with nothing to show for it.

I can see there is no choice but to invite Billy in; he clearly doesn't want to go home to his wife, if he has one, or whoever it is waiting for him. Amazingly, the wood burner is not quite out; a sole ember still swells in the heart of the ash as if exemplifying stubbornness and the room is almost cosy. In the warmth, I forgive Billy for the way he held the arm of that woman. Or, rather, I put it out of my mind and send it off to sea. Billy carries Skip to his cot-bed and it is strange to see a man other than Piers holding him that way, Skip's legs dangling as if made from rags.

'You're too slim, girl,' he says. 'Need to eat more potatoes.' I can't tell if this is desire or disgust. I am not as slim as I would like, in truth. He is close, full of nascent intent, the skin on his nose greasy and red from cider. I undress self-consciously in front of him, still shy, with my back to him, taking the dress off so that I am left just wearing my chemise, wondering if the beads of my spine show through the fabric. 'Won't you tell me your secrets then? Instead of a stranger who'll print it all out in some magazine,' he says into my neck.

As if you're not a stranger, Billy.

I let him handle the bone and edges of me, ribs and spine and wrists and neck, and I talk, because I like to talk under blankets with skin expanding all around. Sometimes, I tell him, in Jerusalem – because it is a place that has come back into my mind, like a bottle bobbing a return on a wave – I was woken in the night by beautiful music. Sa'id playing the oud and my father singing in Arabic until he got to the rude bits, which he sang in English, and it usually meant they were having a party in the room next door. I would creep out of bed to watch. The corridors of the Hotel Fast were long and red and the rooms were all the same. I liked to step into the corridor, look down from one end to the other and then return inside. Then do it all over again. My father's room was next door to mine, and there was an interconnecting door, always locked.

I remember women from the Consulate – French, English, Americans – in long dresses, dancing to music played on the gramophone. At one party I was carried to bed having flopped on the coats and Eleanora came in and sat near me. She put her hand on my forehead, leant down so I could smell her perfume and the Turkish cigarettes she smoked. I was sure, then, that it was the same smell as my mother.

'Keep talking,' Billy says, thumb under my jawbone and finger across my lips. My father liked to draw and redraw cities, I said. Cities with high walls and bridges that stretch beyond horizons. Cities with amber pipes. With subterranean lakes. Cities with squares crossed by young girls with long hair. Walkways and ramparts, airfields and harbours. Maps and plans. He liked to make inventories of roads and coastlines and an emphasis on dwellings. There is a comfort in maps, he told me, in drawing a line around the outside of things, and I drew him a house. We should live there, I said, but he wasn't particularly interested. It was Ihsan I showed the plans to in the end.

'You London girls, you London girls,' Billy says into my hair and my neck, and I realise these names from the past mean nothing to him, he's not remotely listening.

'I'm not from London, Billy, I'm from nowhere.' He carries on, hands underneath my chemise.

'You girls from the city, then, you'll let me do what I want.'

In the morning I am bright and breezy and have decided: I need to know about Ihsan. Despite Billy's dislike of visitors, a little rebellion, begun in my stomach, is moving up. Why should I not go and see William Harrington? If he is still there, that is. Once memories are invited in, I can see, there is no putting them away again until their temperature is understood: are they warming? Or are they intent on tearing apart? Also: I haven't been able to work on my Saint Helena since the visit from the pilot. I don't know why.

'Skip, shall we take the bus to Worthing?'

'To the bunker at the Warnes?'

'Why not?' He hops up and down on the bed so that he is a blur of woollen cardigan and hair.

Skip draws snakes along the steamed-up windows of the South Downs omnibus. His cheeks bulge with boiled sweets the lady behind us insists on feeding him even though I have asked her not to.

'I can't wait to see the hotel,' he says, through the mouthful of sugar. The rain is set in, the sky a dispiriting grey. Bumped and jiggled along the winding coastal road, I concentrate on looking at the rain-splashed houses as we pass.

'I love hotels,' he says. Then catches my hand and squeezes it for attention. 'Don't you, Mummy?'

No. I do not like hotels.

'Of course, darling.'

Skip keeps it up the whole way: the Warnes has a famous smugglers' bunker, the treasures and the secret rooms. He's heard all about it, he will itemise the weapons of choice for smugglers: a musketoon, a blowpipe, a cutlass. I smile at him. I remember the hotel room at the suite in the Russell where the psychoanalyst, whom Piers had brought in for me, was waiting. I noticed he smelled of limes but I confused the word and said, 'You smell of lies.' This undid my plea for sanity in that moment, rather. I was in trouble for appearing naked in the lobby of the hotel. Piers gave him my notebook with sketches of spiral staircases.

What does the spiral staircase mean to you?

It is a point of tension. It's the way down below, but also the way up and out.

What does privacy mean to you?

Nothing.

How so?

I would like to make everything secret inside of me public so that there is nothing left in there, festering. That is art.

Do you think so?

I do.

Might it destroy you? What would be left?

Nothing: that's the point.

Skip rests his head on the glass and I take his hand; we are weary travellers as the road winds up and down its bobbing course on the rolling Sussex downs. His marble-blue eyes looking towards the sea but not seeing anything. I try to make a game of catching the names of the seaside bungalows as we pass – Will o' the Wisp, Sprite o' the Sea – but he doesn't want to play. Finally, we are ejected from the omnibus and here we are: the front at Worthing. A seagull pecks at a dead dogfish a yard or so from us and some-body has written in pen on a shelter wall I DID MY BEST OLD PAL.

The Warnes Hotel, surprisingly, is swarming and buzzing with activity, packed full with women waiting to be met by someone or other. The reception desk is unoccupied so I lean over and look at the neat, slanting handwriting on the Rooms Ledger. A quick scan gives a flavour of the hotel. The front doubles, rooms 15 to 21, are taken by Miss Alma Letts, Miss Rothwell, Lady Oldhan, Mr and Mrs Raybourne. A string of Misses in the front single rooms. Back doubles for maids and secretaries and valets of the occupants of the front doubles. There are several captains, and there he is: Lieutenant Harrington. Beneath him, a couple of Irish – McCallum, McConnaghan – and a Cohen, even a Schottlander. Indeed, foreigners in Worthing! It is nearly three. Skip is examining a full-sized knight's armoury on display and I have changed my mind. I wish, very much, that we had not come, and then I realise something that has not occurred to me before: I lived near here with my mother for a short time, when I was very young. In one of the many boarding rooms and lodg-ings we stayed in. Goring? Rustington? A Sussex nowhere place, with bleak grey drizzle every day and a chalky sense of the end of the world. Perhaps we took tea in this hotel? Perhaps there is a ghost of me here? A trace on the carpet? The doorman heaves open the vast oak door, there is a blast of sea air and through the crowding woollen-coated women I see William Harrington. He hasn't noticed us. He is ragged-faced, damp and harassed-looking and I squint at him, trying to find a thread, a context for him: next to my father in the meeting rooms? In the corner of a room in the Hotel Fast? Yes, it is him, I can see it now. How did I miss it? Though he is undeniably addled, aged. Then his eyes meet mine.

'Ah.' He pats his hair, tries to arrange himself from the disruptions of the weather. He scatters rain from his coat sleeve, his face is twitching on the cheekbone.

'Thank you for coming.' As uncomfortable as he looks, I feel as though he has won an imperceptible struggle between us. Skip smiles at him – thinking of more coins, no doubt, the mercenary little soul – and I am firm in my mind: tea, smugglers' bunker, ask him what this is all about and then we will be gone.

'Thank you for waiting all this time,' I say.

'Well. It is important. Can you bear the garden room, or would you prefer the restaurant? There is, of course, my room, but it might be a little small, and closed?'

'The garden room sounds just right.' We are polite now, a shift. We follow him through gilded arched doorways into a glassy, cocooned area where the murmur of female conspiracy can be felt rather than specifically heard and the sound of the rain falling creates a rattling sense of being trapped inside a tin. As we enter many curious and wrinkled eyes are cast over us. They are, I guess, the occupants of the single rooms of the hotel, most likely those without a sea view.

He fumbles about for a minute, looking for a suitable place to sit. I take a long breath and the women around us convey messages to one another, like shrimps disturbed in a rock pool. Finally, he chooses a table in the corner.

'Can I go out, Mummy?' Skip points at the garden outside; it looks like the worst, bleakest, English seaside sort.

'I don't know,' I take off my gloves and settle down in the chair. 'It might be for guests only.'

'I'm sure it's fine,' William Harrington says, 'the rain has lessened.' I shrug and Skip is gone. We both watch him stomping in the wet grass, bending down and examining the glistening red leaves of an acer tree, talking to himself.

He offers me a cigarette and I take one.

'I took the liberty of ordering a tea for us,' he says.

'Thank you. I worked out who you are,' I say. 'I didn't recognise you at first.'

'Yes. I thought you would.' Outside, a seagull lands on the grass, hops close to Skip and I watch him turn to look at it.

'What was all that *Burlington* business about then?'

'It was the only way I could get your address from your art dealer in London.'

I straighten my spine.

'I will be clear with you,' he lights my cigarette. 'Ihsan Tameri visited you in 1933, am I right?'

My body is perfectly still. He is talking about four years ago, when Skip was two. Piers was already sleeping with other women and it took every ounce of my being not to fling myself out of the window of the Russell Hotel every morning. I don't answer.

'I believe that Ihsan Tameri gave you something when he visited, and I need it.'

The waiter comes into the room, scanning his domain. I fold and unfold my peach-coloured gloves. I do not particularly recall anything; and then I do. Yes. *It's for another day* Ihsan had said, cryptic and mysterious, and I played along, caressing the sealed edge of the thick pink envelope that he gave me in London. I remember thinking that it still smelled of Jerusalem. Outside, in the sodden garden, a pigeon balances on the metal balcony behind Skip and advances with great purpose along the metal rim towards him; he now has a bird on either side but is looking into the grass, seemingly oblivious.

'I'm afraid I don't know really what you are talking about.'

My voice is a little loud, and the two women closest to us noticeably drop their own conversation and bow their chins in concentration. Skip is in the foliage now, crouched down, grubbing his fingers in soil. As the waiter takes the order William Harrington pulls out one of the wilting red carnations in a glass, pushes the green stem with his fingernails, returns it to its water. He smiles. It is possible that it is a disturbing attempt at a seductive coercion, but it falls flat. I am annoyed, suddenly, at the intrusion and this elusiveness, all the pretending to be a journalist.

'You're going to have to give me more information, or credentials. Is Ihsan in trouble?'

The two birds have stretched their wings and are advancing towards Skip, who is moving backwards, further into the leaves. William Harrington leans forward, towards me.

'I'm sorry to inform you that Ihsan Tameri is dead.'

I look at him, and then out at the garden. Those words, *Ihsan Tameri is dead*, momentarily have no meaning. They halt, in the air between us, as if each one is trying out a different position, manoeuvring itself in disbelief. I am disorientated, for a moment. The seagull is intent, I can see, on jabbing my son and I stand up from the table and go over to the window, slam my hand against the glass so that the spinsters of the hotel exclaim and flutter.

Skip spins round and looks at me; I beckon him in and return to my seat.

'How do I know what you are saying is true? When did he die?'

'Last year, an explosion at the Hotel Fast in Jerusalem.'

'An explosion?'

'Yes. Things are … tense in Jerusalem currently, as I am sure you know.'

I look at the man before me. His hand comes towards my arm and he touches it. Is he trying to threaten me? But there is something very broken about him, as if his internal clockwork had seized up, and this is difficult for him, I can see.

'I know you were … close,' he says.

'Close?'

'Ihsan Tameri looked after you, rather, in Jerusalem. When nobody else was particularly paying attention. At least, that is how I recall it. I may be wrong?'

I can taste in my mouth the sweets that Ihsan Tameri used to give me many years ago, pistachio-flavoured nougat with a secret ingredient which he refused to tell me, until one day he did. Camel hooves, he said, but don't tell anyone. Then laughed to himself, pointing at my shocked expression, squeezing my cheeks. *Look*, I remember him saying, highly amused, *look at your English little face.* My body feels as though it is lowering down, sinking with sorrow when I think of him.

Skip is coming through the door, back into the room, his cheeks bright red, lips wet, panting. He looks cross, accusatory. 'Did you see those birds? They were attacking me.'

'Yes, I saw just then.' I take Skip's hand. 'Did they hurt you?'

'Not quite.' He flops down, despondent, into a chair just as the tea arrives. It is an excessive affair. The lower tier of the cake stand is covered in tiny square sandwiches; the higher levels are layered in slices of quivering lemon meringue pie, two different types of sponge cake and a row of French petits fours.

'I bet you would like some lemon pie first?' William Harrington says to Skip.

'I would.' He looks at me, as if pre-empting that I am about to insist on him having a sandwich first, but I simply smile.

My mind is flicking, flicking: what do I remember about this man? He worked for my father? When nobody was paying attention to me? What does he mean? Ihsan's face the last time I saw him, a few years ago in London, comes back to me. I sit up. I cough. It occurs to me that I need not believe this man.

'I am terribly sorry, Mr Harrington. I'm afraid you haven't convinced me. Do you have more formal confirmation?'

Skip, whose mouth is as full as it is possible to be with lemon meringue pie, says something to me, but I have no idea what it is.

'I am aware it's probably a shock for you,' he says, not taking anything from the cake stand. I fold and unfold my gloves on my knee.

'What's a shock?' Skip says, swallowing meringue.

'The death of your mother's old friend,' says William Harrington, then he turns to me. 'I need the envelope. Will you be able to give it to me, Prudence?'

He was in love with Eleanora Rasul, I remember now, but then of course so was I. Why were we both drawn to Eleanora? What did Ihsan write about her? I can't recall. Not much, latterly. Ihsan dead? The weather in William Harrington's face changes. He nods at Skip.

'You look a lot like your mother did, when she was a child, I mean.'

Skip's eyes grow wider. 'Did you know Mummy when she was little?'

'I did,' Harrington says. 'Funny little thing, always scrabbling about under tables. She made friends with the wrong kind of people, although Jerusalem at the time was very confusing.'

I speak quietly to Skip. 'Eat it quick, darling, we have to go, something important has come up.'

I turn back to Lieutenant Harrington. 'I'm sorry. I can see that you very much want this envelope you speak of, but I'm afraid it is a long time ago. My life has changed hugely in the last few years; if I even have it – and I don't remember it – then I certainly don't know where it is.'

I take hold of Skip by the elbow, try to pull him up and away, but he scowls at me, squirms lower into his seat, staring at the cakes. He is now working on a piece of Victoria sponge. Harrington catches my wrist and pulls it towards him, looks down at it, with his thumb on the vein, and underneath, where Skip can't see, his nail is digging into my skin. Then he sits back, abruptly, and rummages in his coat pocket. His face exhausted, haunted. He pulls out a photograph.

'Do you recognise this?' It is a picture of Jerusalem where I lived with my father all those years ago. A black sign and the words HOTEL FAST in white letters.

'What is this?' I say, and the oddness of this man being here strikes me as so incongruous and unlikely in Worthing, with the sea whipping up into its angry froth, a place where everything withers not through violence or passion but through too much salt, and loneliness.

'How did you trace me here? Did Piers send you?'

He shakes his head. 'His Majesty's Service, it's all I can say. Ihsan Tameri gave you an envelope with photographs printed at the same time as this one.' He turns the photograph over and points at the small insignia at the back. *Khaled Rasul Photography, 1920, Jerusalem.* I push his hand away.

'Do please leave us alone, Lieutenant Harrington. There really is nothing I can do for you.'

'Take it. Perhaps it will trigger your memory. I need the envelope and the rest of the photographs. I am completely serious.'

I stand up; push my chair out of the way. We are going, I say to Skip with my eyes: we are going now.

'Ihsan used you, you know.' He stands too. He is smiling, and it makes his face look even more as if he is in a turbulent assault on himself.

'I'm sorry, what?' I try to ignore him, but I look up into his eyes.

'All that information you handed across to Ihsan. Did it never occur to you that it was useful?'

'I want to see the bunker,' Skip says, with petulant lips.

'Did you think he was your special friend?'

'I want to see the smugglers' bunker.' Skip's voice is whinier now, fortified by the sugar in the cakes, and I begin to gather my coat and my gloves and handbag.

'Not today, Skip. We must go.' The women in the room are looking at me, their eyes bulging slightly, thin lips being licked. Skip begins to cry out, loudly, and everyone openly stares. Harrington is frowning at me.

'Do you remember a room?' he says. 'Frau Baum, coming towards you?'

I grab Skip's wrist, haul him up from the chair, away from the table, through the hotel restaurant and out on to the street where the wind whips at us and we are stunned momentarily by the sunlight.

Skip cries, injured pride, injustice. *I wanted to see the bunker. It's not faaaaairrr.* I am sorry, I say in my head, tugging him towards the omnibus station where – miracle of miracles – an omnibus destined for Shoreham is ready to go.

Skip hops along the aisle, to the seats at the back, his face dark, his sulk deep-set. Then, dropping it all, as children can do, he springs to his knees to look out of the back window. It is only then that I see Skip is holding the photograph of the Hotel Fast.

'Why did you bring that?'

'He pushed it into my hand.'

'Is he following?' I say. We are the only passengers. He is bound to get on. He'll sit near us the whole way, trying to frighten Skip. I put my gloves on, take them off, put them on again and gaze out at the sea, which is devastatingly hostile-looking as the omnibus rumbles into life.

Skip at the back window says, 'No, he's not coming.'

He walks back down and sits next to me. 'Who is he?' Skip still has pie crumbs on the side of his mouth. I gently wipe them off.

'A madman. Don't worry about it at all.' I pull him close and he puts his head on my shoulder.

'Is he a detective?'

'No, I don't think so.'

'But he says he knew you.'

'Oh, a long time ago. So it doesn't really count.'

'He asked you if you remember a room, what did he mean?'

'I don't know, darling.' I look at him.

'Is he following us?'

'Don't be silly. I'm sure he's got much better things to do.'

We are as far as the Lancing part of the coastal road when he says, 'Stop it, Mummy.'

'What?'

'Your hands, you keep shaking your hands.' And I realise that they are doing something they haven't done for many years: an odd involuntary tremble, and the only way I can stop them is to press my palms together, as if in prayer.

Jerusalem, 1920

Willie stood in the corner of the ballroom and tried not to look as though he was seeking her out. Perhaps Khaled Rasul would be at her side tonight? And why not? It would be perfectly proper. Eleanora was right, of course. It was the party. He could not avoid it; Ashton would consider it unseemly if he did not attend. It was snowing outside and this did not cheer him. He stood near the window while the Pro-Jerusalem Society members were gathering and had the illogical thought that snow did not belong to this city. It belonged to England. Warsaw. Alaska. Not Jerusalem.

He was given a glass of red wine, rough as a dog's arse, but still he swallowed it in one go. He resolved to stay for an hour, find an excuse and then leave. A roll-call was read out: *Colonel Storrs, absent. The Mayor of Jerusalem, the Director of Antiquities, His Eminence the Grand Mufti, His Reverence the President of the Franciscan Community, His Reverence the President of the Dominican Community …* Willie rocked back on his heels, felt the equilibrium of his body stretch over its balanced point; every part of him was on edge.

His suit, as usual, was entirely wrong. His torso underneath it looked like a screwed-up piece of paper with white scars in crinkled lines across his chest and back and pointed scars – two fingers to the world, he thought of them privately – reaching towards his Adam's apple. He closed his eyes and was back in the cockpit: the dense cloud-bank that came from nowhere. In the white-heat of the moment when he realised his engine was on fire, instead of concentrating on the winking lights below, all he could think of was a manuscript he once saw which showed the logbooks of whalers. For each whale butchered that day there was a lovingly drawn inky woman, portraits of prostitutes, and that was how Willie saw death: inky women, the lull, the sinking. Sirens, he supposed. *Concentrate. Fuck.* When Willie opened his eyes he was being looked after by women with black-brown eyes whose names he never learnt and the pain from under his bandages was not stabbing, but pure, consistent. He swallowed a mouthful of the awful wine to shut down the memories.

Faces swam near him, like weeds coming up to the top of water after a disturbance, and he responded as required, nodding and agreeing, but perhaps he was giving off an unsociable air because no one stayed with him for very long. Arabists and archaeologists swooped this way and that, everyone with the starry look of people recently in snow. The roll-call for the meeting continued: *His Beatitude the Greek Patriarch, His Beatitude the Armenian Patriarch, the President of the Jewish Community, the Chairman of the Zionist Commission, Le Rev. Père Abel (Ecole Biblique de Saint-Etienne), Captain Barluzzi M. Ben Yahuda, Musa Kazem Pasha el-Husseini (the ex-Mayor of Jerusalem), various members of the American Colony, various members of the British delegation (including Lt Col. E. L. Popham)...*

'What is she doing?' A woman was talking to him; one of the indistinguishable European archaeologists in a large hat with blue flowers on it. She was from a village near Ghent. He forgot her name the instant she told him. She was pointing at Prudence Ashton and tutting. Willie looked. Charles Ashton's daughter, in her white party dress, hair in blue ribbons, was crawling on her hands and knees beneath the white starched cloths of the large circular tables that were lined against the wall. Each was topped with an impressive vase filled with lilies.

'An odd little child,' he said, thinking aloud, and the woman agreed with him.

Eleanora came in then, alone, looking very thin in a long white dress, with a cluster of white jasmine flowers in her hair that might have worked on a girl of sixteen, perhaps. He felt disloyal at that thought, but when she turned he saw her dress was backless and she wore a long string of beads which trailed down her spine. Blood fired around his body, as if setting the edges of his scars alight, and when she met his eye it seemed to him that she knew she had this effect on him. She shimmered, a low smile. The music in the room was too loud and from the periphery of his sight he was conscious that Eleanora was weaving her way towards him, but just as she came near Charles Ashton swooped on her and took her arm.

'So pleased you're here,' Ashton said. 'No Khaled still tonight?'

'Not yet, I'm sorry, just little old me.'

'Well we are much the better for it.'

'You've got the great and the good, Charles, congratulations.'

A newly arrived German architect, Herr Kaufmann, was introduced and then he and Ashton were tugged towards the stage. Willie lit Eleanora's cigarette and smoke encircled them like a magic cloak. They stood together, very close, both looking directly ahead at Ashton who was waving a pointer stick at maps hung behind the podium in the manner of a public-school teacher.

Eleanora used to prowl Pentrohobyn Hall like a thief, unafraid of the dark. An acute sense of social inferiority, a worry passed on by his mother, meant that Willie was overly concerned with manners and pleasing people from a young age, whereas Eleanora, spoilt little madam of the vast Pentrohobyn estate, ran everyone ragged. From the very start she impressed him with her badness, her ability to steal, lie, climb and throw, but this was when they were children, before her father locked her away. Before she used silence as a protest, and was not allowed to read or write, was given crochet to do. He remembered her indignation. Willie was the only person allowed in and he smuggled her Greek textbooks which she grabbed off him in a fury.

The entire room, he realised, was looking at him. He was being introduced to the company. He bowed and received applause although he did not know what for. He forced himself to listen. Ashton waved his stick at a large rectangle on a map which had been coloured in green.

'Lungs. What is needed is a park system, based on a similar model used in Ruislip.'

Ruislip, England. In Jerusalem? The unspoken question – is he serious? – hung in the air.

'There is a swathe of more or less open land between a mile and half a mile deep that I have designated park area from Mount Zion, through the village of Siloam and the Garden of Gethsemane, to Mount Scopus in the north-east. The bulk of the land will, it is hoped, remain under *fellahin* tillage or even in its present wildness.'

'Is it wild?' someone, possibly Captain Barluzzi, shouted. 'No land belongs to nobody. Not even here.'

Ashton ignored him, and on stage – trim, compact, debonair, loud – he looked wily, focused.

'Advancing the walls, increasing the gardens, accenting the stonework, a tremendous sequence of open lands, spaces and parks – gardens! – which will isolate the Holy City, formulating the importance of it, the sense of it as ...'

'One might,' Eleanora whispered, 'consider the foolishness of an English garden in a desert perhaps?'

Ashton began a curious intoning, as if praying, rocking on his heels back and forth. *The place where a great city stands is not the place of strech'd wharves, docks, manufactures, deposits of produce merely* ... Everyone in the room looked awkwardly at one another. Finally, when it became clear that he had finished, hesitant laughing and music began. The concertina player stared at the ceiling as he pressed his buttons, the violinist kept his eyes to the floor as his bow flickered up and down. Standing near the stage, looking at Willie, was Ihsan; and when their eyes connected Ihsan turned quickly away.

'El ... Ellie,' Willie said, using her childhood name, but a woman's hand came between them, splitting them apart. She was introduced, a Miss Lucy something who spoke in a sarcastic, high, daggered voice, but Willie did not respond to her because through a gap in the crowd he saw Lofty. McLaughlin. He was aware of Eleanora's cool stare on him.

Lofty hesitated on the threshold of the doorway to the ball-room, wearing the full-uniform get-up, two revolvers clearly displayed on his belt. In his hand a black baton. It was the Irish weapon, Willie recognised it, the shillelagh, and in his other hand a Turkish-style whip. The music stopped just as Lofty came in and so the atmosphere shifted; glasses could be heard chinking and voices echoed. Willie watched as Lofty made his way quickly through the room, clearly heading for Ashton, who looked up at that moment from talking to one of the deans from the School of Archaeology. Lofty's mouth close to Ashton's ear and then both men glanced around the gathering.

Something was happening. Willie instinctively looked around for Eleanora, but she had already drifted away from him, with the woman, arm in arm, towards the doors. Lofty and Ashton were turning, necks twisting, as if looking for someone, and then Lofty's strong Irish voice, shouting, 'Evacuation. Evacuation.'

Everyone in the room stopped talking at once.

'Out. Get out: unexploded hand grenade.'

There was an odd little pause, immediately followed by a confused clamour for the door; the room seemed to tip, to be swooped upwards. Ladies squeaked as they shoved past, Willie saw Eleanora herded along; she was stretching up, looking over her shoulder for him. A clearing materialised around a green device on the floor.

'You,' Lofty said, catching Ihsan's white-suited arm as he moved past him. 'Arab. Lie on it now.' He gave Ihsan a fierce shove towards the grenade. 'Lie flat on it.'

'Old boy,' Charles called out in protest. 'He's a friend of ours.'

Willie, propelled by instinct and training rather than thought, dived forward, picked up the grenade and threw it at the window. It exploded on impact, glass showering everywhere, there were cries from the men and women still running from the room. Willie stood near the unexpected cold air and examined his palm. Only then did he shake. He had thrown grenades many times, but had not before picked up a live one. Ashton was upon him. *Good God, man, I don't know how to thank you.* Other voices, fingers on the skin of his hands; he was being congratulated and patted. Hotel staff peered down through the smashed window.

'Nobody hurt,' someone called out.

Lofty still had his hands on Ihsan's collar, as if readying for a dance or an embrace, and Ihsan, with his judgemental glasses, was staring at the Irishman. Lofty's eyebrows so fair they were white and the skin on his face sunburnt: they made a strange couple, standing close enough to be almost embracing, and then with no warning Lofty punched Ihsan directly, in the stomach. Ihsan let out an *ouf* sound and folded in on himself. Willie caught his arm and stopped him from reaching the floor. From behind, Ashton's voice.

'Really, Lofty, was that quite necessary?'

'This is an outrage,' Ihsan said, puffing out the words. Willie supported Ihsan as he straightened leant against him for a moment. Willie could feel him panting and he felt a corresponding gesture, a pushing back towards him. Then Ihsan stood up, still clutching his stomach, but if Willie expected a thank you it was quickly quelled. A black look from Ihsan, and Willie saw that he was being blamed in some way. Lofty, who was picking at his gingery eyebrows, scowled, and looked as if he might be considering another punch. Willie caught his eye. His breath stopped. He must remember him? But Lofty's gaze moved immediately on. He was turning towards Ashton, and beginning to rant and rail: 'You can't catch a rat unless you've got bait.' Ashton put his hands out like a preacher to calm everyone and then span around.

'Where's Prudence?'

Willie noticed a movement from behind a curtain near the window, an impress against the thick weighty fabric. He walked over and poked his head round the thick mustard-yellow velvet. The child was on the floor, knees under her chin. She was whispering: 'I am Prudence Ashton, aged eleven. I travelled by boat. I was sent for.' Willie knelt down. She did not look at him, but continued her low song.

'Prue?'

She blinked at him. He did not know how to talk to children and she made him feel particularly awkward. 'The concertina player tried to convince me to come with him, behind the stage. He kept insisting, but I wouldn't, and then finally his friend came and pulled him away. They ran through that door there. He hurt my wrist, he was pulling it, but he wasn't unkind, that was the strange thing. I didn't know what to do.'

Willie took her wrist and there was a light red mark on it. 'Come on,' he said, and took her cool, pale hand, gently tugging her from behind the curtains.

'She's here,' Willie called. Ashton was without his fez for once so that the bald top of his head was exposed and looked rather shimmery. 'I think someone tried to take her.'

'Oh, Prudence,' Ashton rushed forward and was upon his daughter, 'but who?'

'No,' Prue said, 'he wasn't taking me. He was trying to help me.'

Lofty was gone. That was just the sort of thing he would do: charge in, demand an Arab lie on a grenade and then disappear. Ihsan had been helped into a chair and was swearing in five different languages.

Ashton stretched his back and let out a groan. 'What a business.'

'What happened?' asked Willie.

'Lofty had a tip-off, dear boy,' Ashton said, his hands shaking. 'Goodness, I need a drink. It was supposed to be an assassination but they muffed it.'

'But who?'

'Don't know: could be the Arabs or the Jews. They both have grievances against us at the moment.' He pushed his hand on his chest, above his heart. 'To be frank, it could be the Greeks or the Armenians or the French or the Syrians for that matter too.' Then he drew himself up, as if to bring himself together. 'You have to hand it to Lofty. He's irascible, but he's bloody good.'

'No. I mean, who was it aimed at?'

'Me, old chap,' Charles said, letting out a wheeze, and he pulled Prue towards him. The room was completely empty apart from one of the hotel boys standing in front of Ihsan with a glass of water, being shouted at.

Jerusalem, 1920

Prue longed to photograph the dead pigeon on the kerbside but her father strode on; they were late for the service at St George's. He had demanded she accompany him as Frau Baum did not want to come. *I circulate! Keeps everyone happy! Haven't been for a few months!*

'Chop chop, come on,' he said. 'Morbid child.'

Two security men had been allocated to him since the incident of the grenade: a large Englishman who walked behind them saying nothing, and a thin native *gendarme*, who skipped about in front, scanning windows and buildings and the sky. Somebody had attempted to kill her father. She held that thought, like a caught butterfly, and wondered at it as she tried to keep up with him. Were people, hidden behind the shutters and windows, ready to throw more bombs at him, at her? It gave her an illuminated, excited feeling, as if she had been lit up as a target. Her father was wearing his bright white suit and fez as usual and every passer-by looked at them, but were some of those faces hostile? The sun was behind them so that their shadows stretched, making their legs tremendously long and their heads tiny pins. That is me and that is him. Turn a corner and the stick-men shadows were obliterated.

At some point during the previous night, Prue had dreamt about rats: a long tunnel, and the sense that they were there, rather than actually seeing them. Since the grenade blew apart the windows of the ballroom there had been men busy all over the hotel, hammering, chipping, stomping about. Her room, which had always felt unsafe, like a boat, felt even more so now. Last night, something strange had happened.

Her father had knocked and come into her room. *I'd like to draw you, Prue.* His words hooked her out of sleep and fished her to the surface. She sat up in bed, blinking at him. He was holding his drawing things – charcoal, thin pencils – and two fluttering candle lamps which he arranged on the table. He used his architectural papers with scraps of plans on them, but turned on to their backs for blank clear sheets. He asked her to sit on the chair in front of the window shutters. She did exactly as he instructed, rising from the bed slowly, shivering.

'Arrange your hair that way,' and she pulled the rope of it over her shoulder. He sat on the edge of her bed and began to sketch her, making quick furious marks with an irritable expression on his face at first, and then slowed and drew in a softer way. As he drew it seemed to her that she was turning to stone. When he lowered the page she saw versions of herself. Lips. Neck. The cross of her foot over her ankle. Then he stopped abruptly and stood up.

'Thank you, Prue,' he said, as if she had fetched him his dinner. He took his drawings with him, but left the charcoal, and walked out of the room. Over breakfast, and now, on the way to the church, it had not been mentioned.

———

Her father was by far the tallest man in the congregation and Prue was conscious of their foreignness in this church more than elsewhere in Jerusalem. Here, Englishmen dressed in military attire ruled and strode about in charge and rolled their eyes at the Turks, even though Ihsan said that Turks was the wrong word for them. 'Your eyes are the colour of water,' Ihsan had said, and she supposed they were. She wished her eyes were brown, her lashes black. She could hear her father breathing.

'I have a penchant for architects,' her mother used to say, when she was in one of her shrill, bright moods. 'Oh yes! Architects! They come in and bring light into the corner of your broken bedrooms; they take a frame and readjust it, and they move the furniture. Lord knows, we need the furniture moved. Does a gardener always have a terrible garden? Weeds taking over and trees not pruned. Your father,' she would shout, 'always about to find a home, about to purchase a home, about to settle before moving on to a new project, and his wife and daughter are kept in rented rooms of interchangeable character in suspended places and how long are we supposed to do this?'

Prue flipped through the Bible as the sermon rolled on. What was the Table of Kindred and Affinity? Who could a husband's mother's brother be? And why did it need to be said that you must not marry your son's daughter or sister's daughter's husband? Letters from her father used to arrive with the prettiest stamps. Postmarks from Khartoum, Delhi. Prue collected the stamps in a special book, but where was that stamp collection now? At the end of the sermon was the singing, her father the loudest. *Hosanna in the highest!*

When the service was over she walked next to him, towards the bright light coming through the door.

'I was reading the Table of Affinity in the Bible, Father.'

'Oh?'

'Yes, and I was wondering how … Frau Baum fits in, to the table?'

He shook his head, as if the question had disappointed him, and did not answer.

'Tell me about our villa in Lifta,' Prue said, with desperation.

He smiled, sniffed, the tip of his nose very red. He looked down at his lapel where a purple cyclamen was drooping and nodded to a passing woman.

'It is a simple place, a village home. There is a *youk* carved from the wall. There are white walls, without much decoration, although near the fireplace there is a silver dagger hanging. But there is something special about it, Prue.'

'Oh?'

'The floor is tiled, in the main room, and they form a circle in the dead-centre. On the full moon in August a line of light hits the centre of the circle, perfectly. Just that night, that year. For a few minutes. You could live your whole life there and never know.'

When? She was about to ask, when would they go there? But it was too late; a man pounced on her father as they walked out of the church, speaking in a fast voice of terrible attacks, a flare-up and a fight in a private café near the Schmidt Building.

'Urgent message from Cresswell, Charles.' The man waved a telegram.

'Read it for me, would you? I haven't got my reading spectacles.'

Prue put her finger on the crumbling cracked surface of a gravestone which read REST WELL, ELIAS POLAND, 1888. Listened to the man's quick clipped voice.

More news of McLaughlin and the Palestine police: unspeakable behaviour. Charging through the district like the wrath of the Lord, shooting it out through the foothills, taking prisoners and doing sickening things to them in the name of British supremacy. Complaints from the District Court. Urgent action required. Can't emphasise enough. Cpt. CC.

'Captain Cresswell ... Prue, dear, can you make your own way back to the Fast?' He turned away from her before she even answered, and the two men leant towards each other like old trees against the wind.

Prue walked slowly through the Old City and it seemed as though it had all been rearranged, as if for a trick. The entrance to the gate walls was surely further to the east than it had been yesterday. The haberdashery had swapped places with the little hole-in-the-wall bakery. She drifted past the Notre-Dame Hotel and the French hospital, past the small Arab cafés, and did not realise at first that the hooting and honking and calls from the street were directed at her: she was in the way of everybody. She left the main roads and went down into the narrow streets of the souk.

Two Arab children were playing in a stairwell, the younger boy hopping from one step to another and leaning forward to tug on his elder sister's hair. The girl was ignoring her brother, twirling a piece of rope, dreaming her own dreams. Imagine if Prue took the small boy by the hand and simply led him off, away. I'm your new sister, she would say, and they would make their way to the villa with the magic tiles and live there with fifty grey kittens for company. Brother and sister looked up at her then and, like all the children here, they did not smile, just stared, half-threatening and half-inviting.

Prue walked on, pretending to be unconcerned. Loneliness crept through her body, the way sun bleeds across the carpet in the morning, forcing you to wake up. Then Prue saw Eleanora, in her fur, turn into the passageway ahead and walk towards her. She was with the pilot and they were not quite arm-in-arm but leaning towards one another, not looking up. Prue stepped backwards and folded herself, quite neatly, cleverly, into a Bedouin rug that was hanging for sale. She watched their feet pass. 'You can't imagine …' Eleanora was saying, but the rest was muffled. Prue touched the rough textured Bedouin rug with her fingertips and listened to their voices disappear. When she stepped out again they were gone, into a deeper, more hidden part of the souk.

They had looked very close. Seeing the two of them gave Prue a cold feeling inside, as if part of her was freezing up, and Ihsan's words came to her mind. *Bring me what you can? … It will be useful … intentions regarding our lovely Mrs Rasul.* Now was a good time, given that the pilot was *categorically not* in his room at the Fast. She ran, darting along the cobbled streets, flitting past the stands and the stalls, through Jaffa Gate and towards the hotel which, as usual, looked like a ship coming into harbour rather than a building on dry land. The whole of her body was concentrated on the task in hand. Her good work for Ihsan.

In the lobby she composed herself. It was surprisingly easy to convince the woman at the front desk. Lieutenant Harrington's in the restaurant with my father, he just asked me to run up to his room and get his watch for him. Voice light and swinging, and she was lucky because it was the young receptionist, not too worried about details. The key came towards her, dangling on its large wooden peg.

The lift doors opened like curtains on a stage, the corridor was empty. She looked left and right before knocking and letting herself into the pilot's room. It was not as big as her father's, who had an entire suite, but it was much larger than Prue's own room and it was a surprise to see that he wasn't particularly orderly. Half-drunk whisky glasses were scattered about, and clothes in untidy piles, which was not how one thought of a pilot. A dirty handkerchief on the chair.

Prue sat on the bed, felt the sag of it underneath her and breathed illicit air. Now she was in here she was unsure what to look for, what to take. What did Ihsan want? What had he said? *Will you slip into his room … bring me …* What was it? *What you can … any identification, or books … to understand why he is here.* She thought of the shifra code. A rooster wallows in *dir*. A hoopoe cries. What details are meaningful and what are not? On a kneehole writing bureau was a drift of papers, rubble from pockets. A black suitcase was on the floor near the window. Prue rifled through the possessions but found nothing particularly interesting.

'Must you always creep about?' her father had said to her once, when he found her under a table. 'Do you know Garo the concierge calls you the Little Witness? Always behind curtains and under tables writing your notes.'

Little witness. Little spy.

At the bottom of various receipts and envelopes was a blue cloth-covered book. PILOT'S FLYING LOGBOOK. Tucked into its back page were documents, some photographs, and attached to it was a typed piece of paper. IMPORTANT NOTICE. AN AIRCRAFT CRASHED THROUGH YOUR CARELESSNESS OR DISOBEDIENCE WILL DIVERT WORKERS FROM

BUILDING FIGHTERS AND BOMBERS TO REPAIRING TRAINING AIRCRAFT. This would do, she would take the logbook. Underneath it was Hotel Fast headed writing paper and in light blue fountain pen the words *Eleanora. Oriole.* Prue ripped the page off and took that. She dropped down to her hands and knees and looked under his bed, but there was nothing there, just dust and a musty smell.

She ran to her room, put the stolen items under her pillow and then bolted downstairs to return the key. The receptionist barely looked up when she handed it back, but Prue jumped when she realised that Frau Baum was standing near the concierge's desk, flicking through the telephone message book. Her tortoiseshell perfectly round glasses slipped down to the very end of her nose. Prue turned, thinking she had not been spotted, when she heard Frau Baum's voice.

'*Konfitür*, from my home. Would you like it?' Frau Baum was holding towards her an attractive, glistening little jar. The gloopy substance inside the glass made Prue think of poison.

'Oh no, I couldn't possibly.'

Frau Baum looked very slight and feathery, as if she might take off and float amongst dust mites and loose thoughts. Then Prue knew what would really impress Ihsan.

'Would it be possible to go to Father's desk and get some of his large architectural paper?' Prue asked. 'I had this idea I might do some drawing. Some big paper would be useful.'

'Of course, come on.'

Prue followed Frau Baum up the stairs, into her father's room which he evidently, boldly, shared with Frau Baum because her possessions were everywhere: archaeological books on the desk near the window, hats and scarves on chairs. She supposedly had 'a little room' elsewhere in the city, but Prue knew that she in fact mostly lived here. She heard them at night, laughing, or the tap tap tap of the typewriter, interspersed with conversation.

'I'll leave you here to get what you need,' Frau Baum said, in her weightless, soft voice. She drifted off to the larger room so that Prue was standing alone in front of her father's things.

The contrast between her father's desk and the pilot's little kneehole could not have been more pronounced. This bureau was huge; it smelled of beeswax, ink, polish. It was covered with various large maps of Jerusalem and over the top of them, on thin tracing paper, were sketched alternatives: a repaired wall, additional stairs, extended ramparts. His handwriting was very neat. Covering half of the desk was a large roll of architecture paper. The top one said: *Plans for the Demolition of the Clock Tower, Jaffa Gate*. Prue pulled up the page and looked at the one below. Her father's notes and drawing above had been done with a sharp pencil and the indents were clear. Carefully, she tore out the blank page underneath, rolled it up into a narrow tube. She listened for Frau Baum's movements, but there was no noise. The desk was so intimately her father's that standing near it felt like standing inside his arms. Prue touched the brass paperweight. She touched a candle holder. She touched the handle of one of the neat little drawers on the bureau, and tugged it open just to feel the slide of it. Inside, she saw her own girlish handwriting. A small pile of letters. Seven, to be precise, a letter a week since she'd been here, written dutifully to her mother. Her father had collected them from her but, evidently, he had not posted them. Prue pulled out the top one and saw that it had been opened, neatly, a sharp slit, the sort made by a paperknife. She looked on her father's desk, and there was his bone-handled letter opener. She put her finger inside the envelope, and pulled out a page.

Dear Mummy

*I am spending most of my time at present sitting on the roof of
the Hotel Fast. There is a splendid view. I am not entirely sure if I
am supposed to be up here, as I found the entrance at the top of the
staircase that the maids use, but nobody else seems to come. From
here I can see all the farmers going about their work, with carts,
coming in and out. There are many animals in the streets here. You
would think nothing of seeing goats walking along, donkeys, ducks
and chickens.*

Prue put the letter back in the envelope. The watch that her Uncle
Horatio had given her as a leaving present was too small; the strap
gripped into her skin and it had been irritating her for some time.
Now, at this instant, she couldn't stand it for another moment.
She poked her finger under it, to find space, as if she could stretch
leather, as if she could force it to fit properly and not hurt her, just
by touching it, but it did not adjust.

'Jerusalem, is it?' Uncle Horatio had said to her when she had
been sent for. He had stepped in to look after her in the short
interim between Mother and Father. 'Very odd place. Positively
stuffed with earnest European women, pilgrims, missionaries,
archaeologists, charity workers and religious zealots, shuffling
about in stones, or whatever their religion might be, no children coming from those women, no men wanting them. Be
careful you don't become one of them, Prue. You promise me?'
He had repeated it, over and over, 'You promise me? You promise me?'

'I promise.'

'Write to your mother. Promise?'

'I promise.'

Prue pushed the letters back into the drawer and closed it quietly. She called out a thank you to Frau Baum and did not wait for a response before rushing with the roll of paper out into the corridor, where the doors were all the same and led to nowhere and the carpet was thick, but not comfortable.

Back in her own room, Prue shivered, but could not sit still. She paced like a dog marking out the borders of its own territory, but no matter how many times she did that the room did not feel safe.

Outrage. At being a child. There, on that very bed, the Prue of the first few weeks of being here had sat writing the letters to her mother. Naive little descriptions of her first trip to the market or the Wadi al Jouz, or the Mount of Olives cemetery. Already, she was not the same person she had been in the first week, in the second week. Already, she understood Jerusalem more. It was not just a market, religious walls; the stones here – the rocks, she had been collecting good ones and had a row of them under her bed – the limestone here was alive. There were different types of stone, of colours. Ihsan had explained: royal stone, sweet stone, Jewish stone, red stone. Nari. Kakula. She could not possibly have known the names of the stone or the feeling of holding it, the reds and pinks in her hands, at the beginning when writing to her mother. Now she was different. She had even asked her father several times why her mother had not written back and he had replied that perhaps she was too ill. Uncle Horatio had looked at her sadly when she left. Perhaps he had known that her letters were not going to be sent.

On top of her red embroidered bedcover Prue spread out the stolen spoils of the day. She unpeeled the architectural paper. The pilot's book. His letter page. She was good at stealing things; it felt good to be good at something. She could do that at least. The front half of the pilot's book was a log, of flights, times, distances. At the back, though, were sketches. Birds, dragonfly wings and aeroplane engines that looked very technical. She almost liked him a little, when she saw the detail in the dragonfly wing. There were photographs, but they made no sense: swirls and dots and shades and shapes, but then she realised they were pictures from the air; they were beautiful. She would like to discuss them with somebody.

She went to the window: flying, falling, she thought. Almost the same.

Here was the city. A long way from the sea. How grey it always was, the sea, and how much she missed it, and how sad it was that she spent her time sneaking and stealing, but there it was. Prue did not know who bestowed talents, who chose pursuits, or why a person became good at this one thing over another. In one of the first letters to her mother she had described how she had accidentally opened a large linen closet, thinking it was a doorway to a back staircase, and inside a woman was asleep in the pillowcases. When she saw Prue the woman jumped up and said, 'Shalom, shalom.' She had black hair and was quite young and looked terrified. Prue said, 'Do you speak English?' 'No.' 'French?' She nodded. In faulty French the young woman pleaded with Prue to forgive her for being asleep amongst the sheets. She was a Polish DP. A displaced person, come to Jerusalem on the promise of a room, but when she arrived, it had been let, or stolen, or burned down, or had never existed. Prue had not known what to say, had closed the door. She had written to her mother about the stairs going up and up in Eleanora's house and how Ihsan had told her that Jerusalem is a ladder, an axis mundi; that it leads to a blissful place. I wonder why, she had written in that letter which was never sent, if Jerusalem is a city that reaches the sky, why can you not see up? Why did the closed tunnels and stairwells of the Old City shut her down when she thought of it? Why was there no sky?

Jerusalem, 1920

Whisky: burnt honey, wasp's feet, the sticky gum from a chestnut tree. Willie held the glass up in front of the candle and the honey-red liquid glowed like love. He was sitting in a comfortable chair deep in the furthest recesses of the Hotel Fast bar. In front of him a couple danced, a European-looking fellow with his hand on the bare back of a woman in a long evening gown, her head resting on his shoulder. They were swaying slowly and everyone was watching them. The musicians were playing a tune from another place, another time, and he was four, possibly five glasses in. Ashton had confirmed it: the plane was being flown into Kalandia airfield tomorrow. He was to fly; and there was the trigger near his thigh: he was a six-year-old boy again, almost wetting himself in terror.

Willie drummed his fingers on the paper in front of him, closed his eyes. He held a gnawed pencil in his hands. He started to sketch, absent-mindedly, drawing from memory the partridge, that very English bird. He had been such a keen birdwatcher as a child, he could remember its call: *chu chu chu ka che che*. He punctured the paper, a row of tiny bullet holes, and the bird became

Eleanora's body: the angular shoulders and her wrists. Then he wrote:

> *Extinguish my eyes, I'll go on seeing you.*
> *Seal my ears, I'll go on hearing you.*
> *And without feet, I can make my way to you,*
> *Without a mouth I can swear your name.*

The barman placed another glass in front of him, looked down at the poem. 'Rilke?' There was a lull in the music; Willie nodded.

'Break off my arms, I'll take hold of you,' the barman said, in German. 'You speak German?'

'A little. Schoolboy stuff.'

The barman, Theodore, was the half-cousin of the Hotel Fast's owner Albrecht. It used to be German-run, but of course since the British, they were expelled, only returning now. In broken sentences Willie and Theodore spoke in the private space of this language, beneath the rolling tunes from the concertina and violin, about changes coming to Jerusalem, settlements every-where, tents being pitched across the valleys and *wadis*, problems at Haifa, at the ports, adjustments in boundaries and borders and walls. There was a claustrophobic element to Jerusalem, perhaps because it was a city of walls. A city crushed under its own history, and yet as soon as he arrived it was oddly familiar, and almost sleepy or dreamlike. People from one's childhood appeared. People one had met along the way, and done terrible things with, seemed to be here. The significant English public schools were all repre-sented. The religious groups had startling names: the Myrrh Bearers, the Everlasting Faces. It was the most famous city in the world and yet somehow it felt like a village from one's past.

Willie glanced across the bar. Sitting alone at a table with a nearly empty glass in front of him was Lofty. The large hat, a fist on the tabletop, a glazed, distracted, half-drunken expression, and Willie felt as if he were buoyed in the sea, as if he had been bobbed up, taken down, surrendered to a blue-green liquid lucidity, but when he looked again, it wasn't Lofty. It was another *gendarme*, red-nosed, drunk, pulling off the wide-brimmed hat, his face fleshier than Lofty's. He was seeing things tonight. The barman, Theodore, drifted back to his work, smiling, nodding.

Salonika was a long time ago. He was now in Jerusalem. The war was over.

If he did remember, if he did, then what would he say about it?

Men, dying not from bullets, but from mosquitoes. One morning he had found the body of a young Irish fellow with a length of barbed wire wrapped around his own neck: suicide, to avoid another dose of the malaria fever and everything that came with it: delirium, madness. None of the regiments in and around the Birdcage of Salonika were prepared. Not enough quinine, barely any nets, tents full of men ripping into their own skin, shouting out to be shot and put out of the cycle of recovery and fever again, a spiral down to the bottom of a deadly well.

Lofty was there with Willie. He had been held back from the recently relocated 10th Irish Division who had been sent off to take part in the Palestine campaign and he was the maddest of them all. He'd had five recurring bouts of fever and each time he came round a strip of his soul had been removed and he was even more deranged. He insisted he was fit for service; the medical reports said otherwise. He grew violent. He was strapped to his bed, considered too dangerous to transfer either to Palestine or home to Ireland. His wolf-howling could be heard across the mosquito-ridden swamp valleys so that whenever anyone walked near the tent that housed him they would say, 'Somebody put that man out of his misery.'

But he made one final recovery, and he talked himself out of the medical tent, in the Irish sing-song way, gift-of-the-persuasive talk when there were new nurses who didn't know the rules. He stopped howling, looked almost normal, and finally, due to a shortage of men, he was sent up as an observer on a plane that had been scouting across the border, in the same convoy as Willie. Both planes crashed, and Willie's own observer, Mackie, died. Lofty's pilot was dead, and then the two of them were captured on the Bulgarian side.

Willie lifted his drink to dampen the memory. The dancers in front of him were still shunting slowly in their personal constellation.

In the holding room in a Bulgarian sanatorium another Englishman next to Willie had lost an eye. *At least you've got the other one.* Fuck off, he said. Rightly. Three Englishmen captured. They were treated quite civilly. A Sopwith down, two-seater, and the scout, earlier. Flames, blackout. This part of Willie's story is burnt out now. Each nerve end shut down. Close it. Close it. Again and again the click that happened just before the rev counter crawled back. The engine making a noise an engine should never make.

Bulgarian nurses with brown eyes put cool cloths on his face and spoke soft words he could not understand. After some time, the Englishmen nodded at one another. *Bad luck.* No one particularly felt like talking, sores under bandages unbearable, transitioning from painful to itchy, how much of him was burnt off? Was there much left? Lofty was three beds down and didn't say a word at first. Something had happened to his head; lost his memory, lost his mind, lost his sight. Just simply lost. That was all Willie knew.

'We never tire of having English guests,' a man said. Light German accent, not Bulgarian, bolt-straight neck and eyes that got straight down to the paper-heart of things. It was the famous Eschwege; was he being sarcastic?

They had all heard of him: Eschwege. He was legendary, even on the English side, known for his impressive side-slips, spinning earthward, transforming his machine into a fluttering leaf heading to dry land and then abruptly changing course. He had personally claimed seven victories to date, including Flight Lieutenants Ingham and Maxwell and others from before Willie's arrival. He visited them in the sanatorium each afternoon; cordial, polite. Lofty said nothing, did not even respond to a greeting. The blind boy was losing the sight in his second eye and he had begun to gibber, talking to his mother, calling out for his girl.

The nurse worked silently when she peeled back the bandages on Willie's chest, fingers like rain on him, burning rain. She was the one who came at night, too, with a glass of water, when nightmares turned him inside out. Some days passed, time was rearranged, impossible to keep under check, and when he woke Eschwege was sitting next to him.

'You can walk soon?' Eschwege said, in English.

'I don't know.' Willie looked at him, repeated in German: 'I don't know.'

For fifteen minutes they had talked; Willie did not know what about, now. In German, light discussions, perhaps about birds. Yes. It was. Eschwege had on his knee Willie's logbook.

'It survived?'

'Your whole bag did: cigarettes, camera, logbook, found some distance from the craft.'

Eschwege had examined the drawings in the back of the book – Willie was remembering, now, as the whisky slid down his throat, as the woman swayed her snake-back next to her dancing partner – and was talking about birds. Pelicans. Did you know there are pelicans? Near the Kalochori lake. Dalmatian pelicans.

Another whisky. Pelicans.

Did Eschwege talk to Lofty? Willie did not remember, but Lofty was always there, lying on his back, snoring earth-shatteringly loud snores, and then sometimes whispering to himself, but saying nothing to Willie.

Finally, Willie was able to move, although purple-black clouds came into his vision with the pain: were they inside his eye? Or his eyelid? Or in front of him, hovering in the air? He was helped to walk by the older nurse. He was taken into a room. It was empty, just a table and three chairs. No window. It was deep in the sanatorium and on the table in front of him he saw his own reconnaissance photographs laid out in rows of four. They had developed the film. The door opened again, and Lofty was brought in, shuffling. A young Bulgarian officer offered them cigarettes; they were not treated badly.

The two men were left alone.

The Irishman did not seem badly injured on the surface, but there was something wrong with the look in his eyes, one of which was seeping at its corner. He did not wipe the moisture away from his cheek. He kept whispering: 'Crack skull of it, and blood coming out. There is a steam and a release of air when somebody dies, each time is a thrill, slightly different from the last. Not thrill. That's not it. It's a softer sense than that: a pulse in the guts, the sun too bright. Each time, a hit in the blood, a shot, like the morphine tried that time in Holborn, sweet little knee to be sitting on ...'

'Whatever they ask, don't tell,' Lofty said, audibly then: the first time Willie had heard him speak out loud since being in here. There was a smell in the room which made Willie think of rain, of dead-weather days when there is no point in going outside, and yet this room was beyond weather.

'Do you remember that girl Ana?'

'What?'

Willie had turned towards him. Lofty looked clearer-eyed now.

'You don't remember? Near the White Tower.'

The smoke on Willie's breath filled the room around him and then dispersed. A memory: drunk, a deeply, deeply drunk night. Several soldiers, and Lofty must have been with them, in a brothel near the White Tower in Salonika. Sticky retsina. *You can get anything you like here, for silver. Children sold for the price of tea, women by the handful, a fistful of hair, blood on the nostril. Dead bodies too, if you wanted it, if that sort of business is your liking.* A girl. Either Greek or Turkish or Serbian, Willie couldn't tell, and she walked directly towards them, wide-eyed with black hair. She was very young and when she reached their table she looked first at Willie, and then Lofty. Willie had been so drunk the world was frozen, the hard dirt floor welcoming. He couldn't walk. He was dragged into a room with Lofty and another man. Bouzoukis playing, then faded. Small room, thin bed, a chair against the wall and a picture of Santa Maria hung unevenly. He could remember that. Oh Mary. Oh Hail Mary. Sitting on the bed, staring at the floor, was a child. She was ten, he had thought (she was younger, he knew). Lofty took her first. Willie concentrated on leaning his head against the wall. The other man – it could even have been Mackie, was it him? – took her next. Then they pulled him over, out of the nausea; he had vomited the retsina against the wall, made a map of the British Isles out of the putrid substance.

His turn. He did not ask her name. He was immediately powerfully aroused. Below him, she looked even smaller, as if she were made of hollow bird bones. She had dark circles under her brown eyes. She made no noise when he pushed inside her, just as she had made no noise with the other men. He was not gentle, but he was quick.

How had he forgotten this? He had not forgotten this, he had run through the corridor, out on to the Salonika street, carrying with him a moment of judgement that would fix itself, like a tick bedding down and feeding at the still point of his life. I did not hurt her. I only did it because I was there; I did not plan it, it is not in my nature. This is what he told himself at the time and then he shut it away.

'I don't know what you are talking about,' Willie said. He looked at Lofty: was he all there? He could remember Salonika, but his eyeballs rolled backwards so that they were mostly the whites of his eyes rather than the iris. Eschwege came into the room, then, alone. He nodded, smiled, closed the door. Thanked them for being there, as if it had been their choice.

The camera film that they had developed on Willie's behalf was of a series of aerial photographs relating to the port of Kavala. They were laid out in formation.

'The English are going to attack Kavala?'

Both men said nothing. Eschwege shifted his chair slightly, turned it away from Lofty, towards Willie. He lit a cigarette and smoked it slowly. Nobody spoke for some minutes.

In German, Eschwege put a proposition to him: you explain what you were doing with all of the photographs and I will release you. I will also release your comrade, if you would like me to. Eschwege moved the photographs around as he said this, re-arranged them in lines, the top to the bottom, these five here, these five there. Kavala. Willie pulled one of the photographs towards him: a landscape of trenches, dugouts. The photographs made the destruction, the modern world of intolerable suffering that all sides are forced to endure, look like, what? Like an ancient earth-work, like layers of agricultural development, like a series of hieroglyphs, like tattoos drawn with ink and compasses by bored little boys.

'Yes,' Willie said, in German. 'The spies have informed us that there is a German submarine laying mines and there will be a bombardment. Or at least, that was the plan before I went out on the reconnaissance flight.'

Lofty, whose chin had lowered, whose eyes were rolling, raised his head: looked directly at Willie. Coughed. Did he speak German? His blue eyes were red and swollen around the rims. Eschwege moved slowly around the room, and then he opened the door and said something in rapid German to an officer outside.

When he came back in, Willie, not looking at Lofty, in faulty German, talked him through the information, each photograph. He gave up more than Eschwege asked for and when the German left the room again the Irishman finally spoke out:

'You are a fucking treacherous cunt.'

Willie said nothing. Eschwege came back in.

'Thank you,' he said, and they were both returned to the sanatorium. Eschwege, Willie saw, did not respect him for talking. He saw him as a weak man. He was a weak man. Back in their beds Willie did not look at Lofty; he concentrated on the ceiling, on the open sores on his skin.

But he was wrong about Eschwege; he kept coming back to him, sitting next to his bed, and talking. They drank decent coffee for several days and then, his bandages refreshed, his wounds cleaned, he had been taken in a wheelchair out into the harsh Greek sun. Lofty had been removed several days previously; Willie did not know where to. The blind boy was also gone.

In the wheelchair he had been loaded into the back of a Bulgarian truck, along with Eschwege, and they had been driven to the lake. After so many days in the sanatorium the wide shimmer of the water hurt his eyes. He could see innumerable mosquitoes dancing on the surface. The Greek wind was blissful.

'We could track them,' Eschwege said.

'What?' Willie had been confused. Track the Germans? English? Irish? Bulgarians?

'Pelicans. But what am I saying? You are still immobile. I think we will content ourselves with watching.'

They sat in a small camp, with several petty officers in attendance, on the stony shore of the lake where miniature grey crabs moved sideways from one rock to another. Willie had waited for Eschwege to ask him the inevitable question: why have you given me this information, betrayed your country? The question did not come, apart from in Willie's own head. Why had he? He had no defence. Other than it was that or surrendering to death.

No way out, or up, less a travesty of King and Country, more a suicide note. It was, he had thought, near the insect-laden water's edge, because he had wanted to run the blade of a knife along his own white skin. It was a dark memory of Eleanora: her father, catching him in the corridor one morning by the elbow: 'She is not for you.' The betrayal of a country is nothing compared with human travesties. Shame moved through him; the sense of smashing things, of talking too lightly, of losing her because of war and the hollow despair of never being enough for her, leaving everything else meaningless. The pelicans came, as if performing, and the two men watched the inelegant flops of white underbelly on to water, the magnificent stretch of the wing. That evening Willie was transported to the barbed-wire edge of the Birdcage and thrown back to the English side, complete with his bag, his logbook, his camera, his freshly bandaged body. They had taken most of the photographs. Left him with twenty. He never knew why.

Willie had reported it, but what he said, of course, was that he had been forced. Threats, candle flames next to eyelashes, cigarettes above the face, bright, glinting knife blades. He did not mention the lake; he certainly did not speak of the pelicans.

'May I?'

Willie looked up from the hotel paper before him and the doodling pencil that had completely scrawled out the Rilke quote and the partridge, sketched something remotely like Eleanora's neck, and then begun a pair of pelican wings. In front of his table, blocking his view of the bar, a man was bending towards him like a poplar tree. Willie's stomach contracted with irritation; he should've taken the whisky up to his room.

'Go ahead,' he muttered, without enthusiasm. Willie squinted: it was a familiar jawline. 'I know your face but you'll have to help me out.'

'Lancing College.'

'Of course.' Yes, he did know him. Had known him. 'Wicker? Wickers?'

'Wicklow. Augustus.'

'Forgive me, brain shot in the war, as it were.'

Wicklow arranged himself on the opposite chair and Willie tried to recall what he knew of him. A great tedium always came over him when confronted with grown men wearing the tie of his old school. It was impossible not to be immediately reminded of the flying buttresses of the old Gothic building that pierced the clouds on the top of a wave of South Downs. Smells came back: spotted dick, cold tea, cut grass and behind the smells a half-resurrection of childhood fears: a hunger that would never abate, endless nits in the hair, getting lost and never finding a way back.

Wicklow ordered a gin and bitter from Theodore. Judging by the shimmer of his shoes and the sprightly look about him, it was clear that he was earning more money than Willie, or had at the very least emerged from the war the victor, possibly even a hero, certainly in charge of his own navigation.

'Do you have a wife here with you or are you alone?' Willie said.

'Fly solo, indeed.'

Willie wriggled in his chair, crossed and recrossed his legs. There was a discomfort about this place; different to Cairo, where comfort could always be found.

'What are you doing here?'

'Field research,' Wicklow said enigmatically.

'Are you staying at the Fast?'

Wicklow didn't answer and Willie sneaked a look at his watch. It was nearly midnight. Wicklow began to chat, amiably enough, about life under what was still military administration in Jerusalem. *Have you met Captain Mackay, the new British Inspector of Antiquities, yet? He'll call in on you soon, no doubt. Major General Sir Louis Bols is here too. You'll be hearing from him* and Willie really had no choice but to surrender to the company. Without warmth, they remembered old acquaintances; Harold Piffard in particular, the crank in the sheds at Old Salt Farm, inventing more and more elaborate flying machines, clapping wings on to the most dubious-looking birds. It was Piffard who had created the Rumpety, a queer contraption made up of wires, cloths and sticks. Willie had asked to be his apprentice.

'I can see how you ended up being a pilot,' Wicklow said, 'and you were in Salonika, Cairo?'

'That's right.'

'Herr Slonimski is about to begin.' Wicklow nodded in the direction of the concertina player who met Wicklow's eye, and continued to play. It was so dark now that it was difficult to identify the shapes against tables, the spine of a chair, the shunting of a man's back, an arm that might hold anything: a gun, a loaf of bread, unwanted gifts. The music was tender and disturbing and Willie drained his glass. This would be the last one.

It occurred to him that Wicklow was very briefed up on the comings and goings of Jerusalem; he watched his old school friend rub his moustache and constantly look over at the musicians. Willie reached into his jacket pocket and pulled out the photographs he had taken from Eleanora's darkroom.

'What do you make of these?' he said. As he did so, he noticed the curtains behind the stage flicker. There was a bulge, which stopped for a moment, and then filtered along the web of fabric. A bare foot poked hesitantly from the bottom of the curtain and he saw Prue emerging from the edge of the drape, wearing a white nightgown. She came out from the side, crouched for a second and then jumped off the edge of the stage. Nobody else in the dark bar seemed to notice her.

Wicklow rubbed his moustache as he held the photographs up and examined them. He sniffed, took out a cigarette and lit it without offering one to Willie. The top photograph was of the line of soldiers wearing sun helmets.

'Rasul's?'

'Think so.'

Wicklow placed the photograph in front of him and picked up another one, realising something he hadn't noticed before: that there was a line of corpses on the ground, five of them.

'Do you know McLaughlin? Lofty?' Wicklow asked.

'No,' Willie said, the lie making him lick his lips. Wicklow looked at Willie steadily.

'That's him.' He put his finger on to one of the photographs. Willie looked down at it. In the distance it was clear that a village had recently been bombed or shot at; there was a cloud of dust in the air and three men were standing in a row on the edge of a precipice. In the corner of the photograph, a man was lying on his stomach over the wall, his head hanging down; and standing over him, one boot on his back, pointing what looked like a gun, though it was not clear, was Lofty. Willie recognised the shoulders, the shape of him.

'I've heard Khaled Rasul will be back soon,' Wicklow said, not looking at Willie. Willie took a sip of his whisky.

'He is a good man, but he is involved in a project. I understand. He's rather got it under his skin that Lofty is up to ... no good.'

'Well, judging by this picture, he is up to no good.'

Wicklow wrinkled his nose. 'It is true he has methods. Rasul has been following Lofty around, photographing him. He's built up some what you might call revealing pictures.'

'Well I can quite understand it,' Willie said. 'His behaviour is appalling.'

Wicklow's eyes narrowed. 'Dear boy, do you know how many members of the British *gendarmerie* we have? Eighteen. Eighteen British, half of them Irish, in charge of a few hundred of the local men. There is a limit to what can be achieved. In these circumstances I think he does very well. The people here see Ashton and his superior Storrs as in charge. As *responsible*. For everything Lofty does.'

There was silence.

Wicklow tapped his watch. 'I rather thought you might be in a position to talk to Eleanora about her husband's photographs. To help him be convinced to stop taking them?'

Willie coughed. 'Why would you think that?'

The dancing couple were sitting down now, heads close, arms knitted. Willie turned to look across at Prue again. She had flattened herself against the wall and was moving, slowly, around its edge. She looked like a ghost. Why was a child, in her nightgown, free to roam a bar like this? She was holding her doll by its hair and, for a moment, she looked at him. Then she was gone through the door. His stomach made a loud and disruptive growl, the result of downing whisky with no lining of food. A surge of nausea. Something happened in his eyes: they gave up the ability to focus. His body was fading.

Willie turned to ask Wicklow what he knew of Ashton and his daughter, and another question surfaced beneath that one: How had Wicklow known Willie was in Cairo, and Salonika? But Wicklow was gone, and had taken Rasul's photographs with him. Theodore smiled, nodded at Willie as he stood up and made his way from the table. Steadying himself. He had not drunk like this for a long time now. Like the old days of Shepheard's or Groppi's in Cairo. Like the bar at Lake Prespa near Salonika.

Shoreham, 1937

When Skip was a baby, just six months old, I handed him to an Irishwoman who was sitting on a bench at Victoria station with her own three children. I had been watching her smiles, her continued kindnesses towards them: dabbing running noses, pulling them into her bright, patterned dress and squeezing them. I held Skip out in his bundle of blankets. Perhaps she thought I needed a hand with my tickets or my luggage because she automatically took him from me, pulled the blanket down, peeped and ahhhed at his face. When I asked her to keep him I believe she thought about it for a moment and something in me lightened, but then she frowned at me, gave him back.

Here comes Mrs Deal along the shingle path, laden with parcels, wearing a yellow mackintosh which even I might say is very bright for a vicar's widow. The only woman in Shoreham who speaks to us and whenever I see her I have the same terrible thought: she lost her only daughter to tuberculosis, and this after losing her husband too.

I wave at the window and call out behind me, 'Skip, it's Mrs Deal.'

He is curled up in the chair near the wireless, reading his bird book, whispering under his breath: *raven, jackdaw, nutcracker, magpie, hooked bill, webbed feet, posture upright*. I open the door.

'Not stopping,' Mrs Deal's voice is high and piped, 'but the postmaster's boy asked me if I would bring you these.' A postcard and a letter.

I am embarrassed because I am wrapped in my nightclothes – a flimsy negligée – with mascara on my cheek, eyes glued together, hair good only for bird nesting and I wonder if I smell of sex, but then I remember that I did not see Billy last night. I look at the clock; I can't believe that it is eleven in the morning. As well as the post, Mrs Deal has a bag of fleecy white Shetland wool which she shows me with pride.

'There's some spare, if you'd like to try your hand at a shawl?'

'Knitting is not quite my thing, Mrs Deal,' I smile.

Skip jumps up. 'Is it from Daddy?'

And it is. The postcard is from Piers. On its front is a picture of a cat, sitting on a wall. It is stamped *Paris* and the message is: *Yearning to see you both! Here, then Stockholm, Venice, back 14 Nov when we WILL TALK. Kiss beast for me. Piers*. He writes notes as if everything that happened between us didn't happen. I put it on the table message-side down, intending to put my teacup on it later, but Skip hovers. No choice but to give it to him and the way he follows the curve of his father's handwriting with his finger, tracing the marks, wishing him here, makes me feel very tired.

'You will stay for a minute, Mrs Deal?'

Her eyes are all concern. I know I am a mess. I slept badly after the visit to the Warnes. Mrs Deal, who is a person who watches one closely, examines my face. She is a very thin woman, with rather a hunch in her shoulders as if she is fending off trouble through the curve of her back, much too ready to please, a teeny bit interfering, but kind, so kind. She picks up a tea towel and immediately is off, rubbing at cups and making tea, owning and stamping all over the cupboards and claiming my kitchen for herself as some women cannot help but do.

'I won't stay long. Just a quick cup.'

She sets the kettle on the hob and I wilt on to the chair; my head is a raging, banging drum.

'You seem always to be coming to my rescue, Mrs Deal.' She makes a tutting noise of dismissal and smiles at me.

'How is that map, Skip?' She is the type to speak to a child as if he is another adult.

'Rather well, Mrs Deal, would you like to see it?'

'I certainly would.'

Skip unravels his *Map of the Entire World* with great ceremony. It is made up of any paper he can get his hands on which is then carefully hand-stitched by himself, using my thickest cotton, so that what he has, now, is a quilt made of paper and Skip talks Mrs Deal through the contours of his invented land. When I first met Mrs Deal it was the same: no judgement, just a clear white kindness, like a child who suddenly hands over her toy or half of her food. Skip and I were caught in a hailstorm and the sting of the sharp white stones made him cry. She opened the door to her chalet and summoned us, *Quick, inside*, ushering us through to a warm, comfortable-looking front room where it appeared there was a tremendous sort-out of wardrobe in process because all the chairs and any imaginable space were covered in piles of men's jackets.

'I'm sorry about the mess in here. We're considering some bits and pieces for the Distressed Gentlemen's collection in Brighton.'

She did not introduce herself, but shooed a cat and moved heaps of tweed out of our way. The room was crammed with nursing chairs and books, everything swathed in a yellow or green or golden velveteen. She wrapped Skip up in a blanket, gave him a hunk of bread and even rummaged in a drawer and produced for him a box of tin soldiers. I was surprised when tears came up, pricking the rims of my eyes. I suppose I was sentimental over the kindness, or the homeliness of the room; the Michaelmas daisies in glass jars on the window ledge. She gave me a handkerchief with no fuss. *It's your house: the sense of home. I can't begin to explain to you why it makes me so sad.* And she had said: 'I'll tell you a secret: oh, I run the various societies, and I am always very busy with my projects, but I don't belong in Bungalow Town.'

'How wonderful,' Mrs Deal is now saying to Skip. 'Talk me through it.'

I listen to Skip explain the shapes, scribbles and textures of his never-ending map and it astonishes me that the names come from places in my own life, mingled with his. I suppose they are words that have always been familiar to him, spoken in a thousand conversations around him since he was a baby. He runs his finger along the key which I wrote out for him, under his instruction. *Cecilia. Shoreham Harbour. The Redoubt. The Hiding Place. Jerusalem. New Shoreham. The Island. Beach. The Hotel Fast. The Russell Hotel. The Aerodrome. London Bridge. Norfolk Swing Bridge. River Adur.* His own personal geography.

'This is the river,' he says and his face is bright and wide.

'What is this?'

'The road of towers: a bell tower, a clock tower and The Tower.'

'Excellent. I've always thought there should be more than one tower to a town.'

I can see that the letter beneath the postcard from Piers has Margot Eaves's handwriting on it. It will be another pep talk. Mrs Deal is still looking at Skip's map. She has exactly the right way with him, in tune, not patronising, and I am grateful.

'Would you like to see my new pet?' Skip says to her.

'How intriguing,' she says, 'what can it be? Yes please.' Looking pleased with himself, Skip moves to the door.

'Put your wellies on,' I say. 'It had better not be something disgusting.' He raises a mysterious eyebrow and then runs out of the door. The shells clatter to remind me of their existence. I look out at the sea: along the peak of the shingle a row of gulls stand aimlessly. Far out on the horizon it is possible to see a fret gathering.

'He's a treasure,' Mrs Deal says, soft and low.

'Mrs Deal, can I ask you something?' I feel, without quite knowing how or why, as if we have something in common. Loneliness, probably.

'Of course, dear.'

'We went to a birthday party not so long ago.' I rub my forehead with my palm and she nods at me, all encouragement, setting down the teacups. I let her mother me.

'It was a celebration at the fishermen's club for a little boy called Walter. They rolled in a large barrel and released marbles; all the children ran running and chasing them but Skip wouldn't play.'

Mrs Deal smiles at me and nods. Go on, go on. The barrel lid had been pulled off and out poured unimaginable numbers of cat's-eye marbles. Blue swirls and white swirls, cat's eyes and dead-black ones clattering across the wooden floor. All the children at the party ran around, screaming and trying to catch as many as they could. A cake was brought out, seven candles blazing, and the birthday boy made his wish. Billy had forced us to go to this party, even though we did not belong there. Not a single one of the sour-faced mothers spoke to me. Skip, too shy to catch a marble, went outside alone. A moment later there was a shout and I ran out. A group of children were laughing down by the shore and Skip had been pushed into the water, only as far as his ankles; his shorts had been pulled down along with his johns so that his bottom half was naked and boys were flinging globs of river mud at him. The ringleader was the birthday boy, Walter. I ran into the estuary and dragged him out, yelling at the children who disbanded as soon as I appeared. All I say now to Mrs Deal is:

'It didn't work. We did not integrate very well, and I am not sure that Billy understood.'

'Billy is a hothead, and you know – I suppose? – that the boy Walter is his son, though he never married the mother? But he means well. He is kind, I do believe that.'

I look at Mrs Deal to see if she is speaking in a malicious way, but I don't think so. It is just a clear, helpful imparting of what I should have guessed and what I suppose I was asking her. Yes, Billy was standing behind the boy Walter as he blew his wishes into the world. What was it I said to my own father? *I'm averse to the thought of children growing up and all the adult relations around them being a lie.* Look at me now. Straightening her glasses, Mrs Deal pours the tea, and we drink it in silence. I pull Margot's letter towards me.

'It is from Margot Eaves. She wants my work for her exhibition.' I rip it open and it is just as I suspected. There is a cut-out piece of text from a magazine and a picture of me but I am not interested in reading it. I let it float to the table but Mrs Deal says, 'May I?' And she reads it aloud:

We might say that the work of Prudence Miller née Ashton allows us to look at things a different way. At first we feel we are being put in a room with a photograph album of her life. The staircases of her childhood, the self put forward through the spiral shapes, a prism of her existence to date, her time in Jerusalem, her training later at the Slade. Perhaps in the end there is no mystery to her because she takes the intimate and puts it outside. It is possible that people have missed the significant dimension to this work ...

'Oh I do insist you stop, Mrs Deal.' She smiles at me and continues to read it to herself. I go to the window to watch the idiotic gulls.

'I told her, I can only work if she leaves me alone.' I think of William Harrington; a cold feeling comes down on me.

'You know,' Mrs Deal says, almost shy. 'I would really like to see your work. I walk past your fishing hut every day and I wonder.'

I pause and resist; it is not the best time. I am rather struggling with it all. I've lost my own thread, I've been interrupted. Thoughts of the past have tripped me up, but something in me drops because she is the closest to a friendship I have here and, although Billy is soothing in his way, I miss the company of women.

'If you would like to, of course.' She looks so pleased. We wrap ourselves up in our coats and then run against the wind which is determined to force us in the opposite direction. I call out for Skip in case he is close, but he is not. He is probably over at the café or the fishermen's jetty. Gulls bob on the waves like paper boats.

I have always hated anyone coming into the rooms where I work and am tense as Mrs Deal takes it all in. Like everyone who enters a sculptor's studio I can see she wants to touch things. She picks up my favourite mallet, its handle so well-worn that it is perfectly shaped to the curve of my palm. The dust cover has fallen from the main piece and she stares at it. I lean against the door and light a cigarette, feeling shy and idiotic and exposed, but I'm surprised how it looks. Positively dramatic, much better than I thought it was yesterday.

'Is it a saint?'

'It was originally a Saint Helena, from Malta. I had it shipped here. It was much damaged, they were going to destroy it. So I am enhancing it, changing it.'

'It's very beautiful.'

'Thank you.'

The face, and most of its head, has been toppled off. Not by me, but at some point in its tenure as a saint on the roof of a church in a fishing village. Mrs Deal walks around it.

'May I touch it?' she says.

'Yes. By all means.'

I have kept the main form and sweep of the stone, the swirl of the robes falling to Helena's feet, and in various places limestone corrosions have created holes, the largest the size of a fist; in other places smaller, like honeycomb. For the past few weeks I have been extending the hole in the centre of the saint, where her stomach should be, and have carved a curl twisting through the middle. It resembles the twist of a spiral staircase, although it is still crudely hacked and needs much work. It is layered: the original sculptor, then the weather, neglect, erosion and now me.

It is strange material, this Maltese al-Tanka, an in-between stone that is neither European nor Levantine. It feels as though it is alive and, here again, it brings with it a memory: Piers sneering, not understanding why I liked its decomposing, fragile element. I don't know why Piers was so resistant to this project. This is when he began to interfere heavily with my method, wanting me to work from drawings when I preferred to respond directly from the material in front of me. I did not have a plan, and this offended him. Make your own work, I said to him, because his rages were coming more regularly since he had stopped pretending to make his own work, his dabbling with painting, his poetry, and his vague attempts at photography. He was entirely focused on me and what I was doing instead, until suddenly he wasn't.

'What does the staircase mean?' Mrs Deal asks, but I don't answer. This reworking of Saint Helena has been a tapestry of doorways opening up into places I did not want to remember, but without opening them, it seems I can't finish. Mrs Deal looks at another partner piece I have pushed against the wall. For this I have submitted plans to Margot but haven't begun it properly yet. It will be two men, hanging from their feet and suspended from a staircase. I want the heaviness of the stone to be contradicted by the lightness, the oddness, of the floating men, but I tell Mrs Deal none of this. She is quiet, as people often are in front of large pieces of stone, shrunken, humble even.

'You are welcome to touch it.'

She has bony fingers and ragged nails which she pokes into the honeycomb holes. Each chisel-shave a moment I have pushed Skip away. I lean outside the door and throw my cigarette into the shingle. On the highest tideline, where cracked oyster shells and fishermen's ropes are straggled in a stripe, there is a layer of thick curly red seaweed and I have a superstition, I don't know where from, that red seaweed is unlucky. Skip comes up the beach, dragging his bucket.

'Oh Lord, what is it?'

'Look.'

Mrs Deal stands up, next to me, and watches Skip stagger towards us. Inside the bucket, clinging to the sides, are eight starfish.

'Hinges the fisherman said there was a colony washed up, hundreds of them the last few days.'

I put my finger into the water and touch the half-slimy, half-noble creatures. Skip's eyes round with pride at his haul. Mrs Deal, admiring the magical starfish, smells lovely, of lavender, rose, older-lady soap. *Lavender's blue, dilly dilly*. I used to sing that to Skip when he was three, four months old, in the days before I walked into Piers's studio and found him with his face buried deep in the groin of one of his students. His hands on her thighs looked like starfish too.

We say goodbye to Mrs Deal and I help Skip to roll up his paper world.

I am sure that the seeds of my son's love of maps were sown years ago by my father when he laid his own maps out across the marble floor of his house in Malta. We visited when Skip was two, perhaps three. The trip was a disaster: my father hated Piers. Piers hated him. I didn't want to be there. Skip cried for his nanny whom we had foolishly left behind in London, and was cross with me because I did the bedtime business all wrong. My father, however, adored Skip. As soon as they met they touched each other's faces, explored eyes and ears and hair. My father sat him on his knee and talked him through the contours of his maps. *This is the famous city, Alexandria.* The Corniche, the Great Harbour, the lake, the municipal gardens, the line of the coast, and I could see Skip thought he had the power to draw all the cities of the world in sand, with a stick, and then knock them down and destroy them if he wished, and probably he could. Skip's fat little two-year-old fingers danced over the pages in awe.

Your mummy used to help me with my maps, shading and drawing and colouring.

I realise, now, that this was the last time I saw my father before he died. It was the first time I had returned to his house after leaving when I was eighteen. Not much had changed: large shutters, maids to wipe surfaces, drivers to transport him, gardeners to bring the roses to bloom, housekeepers smoothing down the beds, mopping the clean marble hallways cleaner. Piers and I were engaged in a harsh, wordless battle which expressed itself in movement – namely, one person coming into the room and the other one leaving – and I also avoided being alone with my father.

Of course, he had a mistress. On that holiday I had told him not to bother introducing us but I kept seeing her out of the corner of my eye: an impressively exotic-looking woman who was only about four years older than me. Very thin and dusky, her hair covering her face as if she had something to hide, and indeed she did. She was married to a diplomat on the other side of the island. This woman, I remember, was always leaving through the gate, or closing a door, or driving away in a small green convertible sports car just as we arrived back at the house.

It doesn't take much for the familial edges of your life to fall apart. I distinctly recall thinking that in Malta, Piers furious by then with me for not being what he wanted. What did he want? A *poupée*? A doll to bend over? To walk behind him? I occupied myself by exploring the villages, looking at the saints carved from the limestone of Malta, so soft it almost crumbles into nothing, quick to corrode and yet strong, and lovely colours too, a blackish dark hue or a light yellow. This was one of the things that infuriated Piers. It enraged him. He was a purist: use the Italian marble, not this crumbling chalk, as if I was sullying him or his reputation by wanting to work with this al-Tanka, the hybrid stone. It was on the final night that my father finally spoke to me, alone in the corner of his vast living room.

'I know you are angry with me,' he said, 'but what I don't know is why. And why wouldn't you let me introduce you all to Tessa?'

'I don't know,' I said. 'I wouldn't mind if we acknowledge it, but you expect us all to sit and pretend she's your "friend" and lie about it to Skip.'

'He's two. What does it matter?'

'It matters because it's the message you are sending him. That it's normal to lie.'

'Some relationships are complicated. They don't need to be spelled out to a two-year-old.'

'I'm averse to the thought of children growing up and all the adult relations around them being a lie.'

'So it's about you. It's not at all about Skip, or whatever moral stance you are taking.'

'It's all combined. We'll obviously never agree. You just take things as you want them.'

It was too thorny to unravel. He had always had a mistress, and thinking about them I tended to spiral back, to old thoughts, of living with my mother in guesthouses, whilst he was away, with whoever. On our last evening my father and Piers made an effort with one another, buoyed because they knew soon it would be over. Drinking whisky together, looking out over the balcony, speaking in a manly fashion of manly things, legs apart, jaws raised, the bright fishy smell from the Mediterranean floating through the window. My father invited Piers into his studio. Inside there was a single canvas in the middle of the room with a portrait of the exotic-looking mistress, naked, blackest black between her legs. He had always sketched, but now apparently he had taken up painting.

'That's Tessa,' he said.

Piers looked closely at it, and then called me in, said he admired it. I could tell from the silken feel of his voice that he was genuine. Then my father, drunk, pulled out all of the initial drawings and sketches that he had done in preparation for the painting and laid them around the floor.

'She looks a little like your mother Isabel.'

I hovered near the door. Their two backs crouched together, peering at the various drawings of a woman who almost looked like my mother and in the half-light of the evening they did not seem like fully formed human men, but rather creatures who fed on the skin and bodies of women. They leant towards each other and their shadow was a two-headed beast. What was confusing, though, was that I wasn't sure if I was offended that it was not my body painted or posed in front of them, or if, once, it had been.

———

I climb on to the bicycle that Billy left on my veranda; I am going into the New Shoreham town. Skip wants to stay here with his starfish. I blow him a kiss, but he is oblivious, too wild and free for kisses now. When I look back over my shoulder at him his head is bowed, almost as if praying, although I know him to be a heathen.

Shoreham village has a post office that doubles as a bookshop known enigmatically as Ships and it is the centre of all local knowledge and activity. I cycle across Norfolk Bridge towards it, cursing the fact that the rain never stops in this part of England. It swells from the Channel and dampens everything like wet blankets. Soggy, dripping, I enter the dry capsule of Ships. It is one of those post offices that sells a little of everything: flypaper, eggs, cigarettes, envelopes, castor oil, panama hats, canvas shoes for children. A coughing noise comes from the counter in the corner of the room followed by banging. The postmaster is beckoning me.

'Hello?'

'You are the new lady in Cecilia, am I right?'

'I am.'

'Mrs Prudence Miller?'

'Yes, yes.' There is a concoction of familiar smells in the shop: paraffin, sulphur, coal smoke, something recently baked, Clorox.

'Mrs Miller?'

'Yes?'

'I heard that your friend Billy Ludd was in a fight last night.'

'Well, I'm afraid he fights for money.' I shake the rain from my hair, impatient at this intrusion, and turn to look through the items on the shelf, having completely forgotten what it was I came in for.

'No, I mean in the street, with a man.' I sigh. Billy's bruises when they come are like changeable maps.

'But who was he fighting?'

'I believe, according to Mrs Radcliffe's son who was there, that it was the journalist who was staying at the Warnes in Worthing. The one who telegrammed you about an interview.'

Really. The sense to which one's own business is discussed in this town, the sense to which every single person does not even attempt to hide their interest in one's affairs, the evidence which clearly shows that the postmaster openly reads – *and discusses the contents of* – all telegrams that come through him is truly quite astounding. What's more, there was a sneer with which he had said 'your friend Billy Ludd' and it hadn't gone unnoticed. Whatever Billy says, of discretion, and all of his creeping out of Cecilia at dawn, it is very clear that the whole town knows of our liaison. My ears, cheeks, neck and chest burn and I have a strong desire to shock him, this vague gentleman, with white hair, so overly concerned, so knowledgeable about affairs of my life. I have a compulsion to undo my dress and let it drop, to take off my scarf and wrap it around his mouth and yank back his head and to either kiss him or slap him, but I don't. I leave and the bell on the door rings like an angel falling to its death as it closes behind me.

I walk over to the mermaid outside Jimmie's and rest my hand on her head. I can't exactly explain why I dislike her so. Perhaps I am jealous because Skip loves her.

A boat is coming into harbour, and even though I am staring right at it, it takes me a moment to work out that it is Billy waving from the prow. I wave back, although no mechanical tune comes from me, and he signals for me to wait for him. I watch him clamber out of the boat, exchange a few words with the fishermen and then come towards me. I am used to him looking a bit swollen or walking oddly as if creaking after one of these fights of his, usually near Horsham, or Crawley, in male theatres that I have no interest in visiting, but this is different, I can see even at this distance. This time his face is a red mess and the entire right eye has disappeared behind a huge swelling, bloody and seeping. My hand is on his face as if I might kiss him there and then, even though the woman who gives out the milk tokens near the school is watching us.

'What happened?'

He takes my hand. 'A fight, you know.' I tug him towards me, away from the edge of the harbour water which laps darkly.

'But the postmaster told me it was the man who came to visit me.' Billy scuffs at the quayside with his feet.

'Nosy bastard,' he says, and glances over at men from the boot factory walking past, all looking at us.

'I found him near your shed, Prue, trying to break in.'

'But I was just there now, with Mrs Deal. I didn't see any sign of anyone breaking in.'

'No, he was just about to, I think.'

I put my hand on Billy's cheek. The scarlet parts of his bruises meld with a thick yellow middle. The rain intensifies, and so we move from the harbour edge and stand under the awning in front of Mr Snelling's butcher's shop where an entire pig hangs from a hook in the window; its back looks human and beneath it, as if in mockery, is a tray of pink-purple sausages.

'Listen, I should have kicked him in the head and thrown him in the river. I knew I should've. It was my instinct to, but I let him live.'

Billy kicks the pavement with his foot as if trying to damage his own toe, scuffing chalk. Skip asked me recently: *Do you know what chalk is made from?* What? *It's a soft, white limestone,* he said. And what is that? *It's made up of fragments of an unimaginable number of skeletons of sea creatures.* Clever boy. *Think of that, Mummy.* Billy pulls a black leather wallet out from his pocket.

'This fell out in the fight, though. We got his papers. He's not a journalist at all.'

'I know,' I said. 'He's someone I ...'

'He's a Ministry man.'

I take the wallet from Billy and open it up. Inside are identification papers – Lt W. R. Harrington, Ministry of Information – and folded behind is a pink official envelope of the sort that office secretaries use to exchange internal mail. 'Thank you, for trying to stop him. I'm so sorry.'

He squints out at the river. 'What is it he wants, this man?'

'I'm honestly not sure. He gave me a photograph; he wants the other ones that came with it. That's all I know.'

I think of what Mrs Deal said about Billy being the father of Walter. Why had he not told me this? I have never been able to determine the shifting sands of trust. I sometimes believe that we are designed to betray the people we love, just as sometimes we hand everything over, like a bright unclipped purse, or a secret part of our body, to a stranger.

The river has changed shape with the rain and the tide is moving in quickly so that the mud banks are disappearing and soon the path closest to the river's edge will be covered in water. Billy tells me the full story: he was on his bicycle last night, it was dark and the sea was crashing; he was heading to Flo's Club when a friend of his, Sam, shouted that there was someone near my studio with a piece of wood. Together, Billy and Sam ran towards my hut, past Cecilia in fact but did not want to alarm me. The man – Harrington – was wearing a long overcoat and had picked up a large piece of driftwood and positioned himself so as to ram the door. Billy had called out and told him to stop but then, as Billy approached, with no warning the man had swung round and quickly begun battering at his head with the wood, several blows. Billy, despite all of his fighting experience, had not expected it. The man had then run off along the spit, and it took Sam a moment to get Billy up. They chased the intruder, calling out for back-up from Flo's: Hinges and the others. Four of them all together rounded up on him near the bridge. They circled in, and then he'd pulled from his pocket a small pistol and pointed it directly at Billy. Everyone stood still. The man had then calmly got into a black car that was wait-ing very close and had been driven away.

'Driven away? With a driver?'

'Yes, think so. Let's go into Snelling's,' he says, 'and we can work out what he wants.'

But I resist. There is a shift in the sky as the rain shower lessens. Clouds rearrange themselves, swap places, move up and down. Egrets stalk the riverbank like detectives looking for clues and the sun breaks through the cloud and highlights the harbour section of the river. I feel as if I'm meant to be somewhere, meant to be doing something. Mr Snelling is coming to the door. Billy has known him since childhood; old comrades.

'Where's Skip?' Billy says, turning around and looking at my legs, as if he might be hiding behind them, as small children do, but Skip is too big for that.

'At Cecilia.'

'Alone?'

And this is when I call his name, Skip, but all I hear in return is the inane seagulls crying out for food.

Jerusalem, 1920

The next day was difficult for Willie: the sky big and blue and there was no wind. In short, perfect weather for flying. The vista looked like an open book, pages flat, trees popped up.

'Ellie,' he said, 'can we stop for a moment?' The whisky residue was painful. It was possible that he might be sick.

'Yes, I'm parking it over here anyway.'

There was a sign saying 'Forbidden' in four languages but they drove through regardless. Kalandia was a bleak, military airfield with limited resources. Like most airfields, in reality it was nothing more than a grubby expanse of land. The watchtower was manned by an old Effendi-type who peered at them suspiciously but, after checking paperwork, nodded them through. As they drove through the gates, Eleanora turned and looked over her shoulder. Another motor car was coming over the hill behind them and the black silhouetted heads inside bobbed as if on sticks.

'Here's Ashton, coming behind us now.'

The sky swelled as if expanding. Willie automatically patted his jacket pockets for his cigarette case but it wasn't there.

Eleanora drove to the edge of the airfield and brought the car to a stop. A sparrow landed, briefly, on the bonnet of the car, then flew away.

She turned to him.

'What is it, Willie? Are you all right?'

He looked up at the cloudless sky where he knew images would begin to flicker, and indeed they did. Mackie's face on fire. Other friends now dead – Simpson, Roberts, Hamilton, Jones, Whitby, Osborne, Turner – all burnt like crackling pig skin on an open fire. He put his head into his hands. He could feel her looking at him.

'Listen.' He turned in his seat and looked at her properly. 'I haven't been able to fly.' His tongue felt as if it were covered in a thick, rough substance. He was sweating. 'I don't know if I can fly. Something – happened, and since then I just can't.'

Eleanora's hand touched his neck, traced it down to where the white shiny skin of the scar made its point around his Adam's apple.

'Because of this?'

'This ... I could fly again after this. It was more recently.' The earth around them was rust-coloured. 'Fact is,' he said, ears red and cheeks on fire with shame, 'I've been grounded ... for more psychological reasons.'

He looked over to the olive-tree trunks, searching for a way to convey his bravery, because he needed her to know he could be brave. He had flown such a number of planes, had safely landed planes that had almost fallen apart in the sky, their storage batteries flung out of holders, the ribs of the wings ungluing in mid-air. He had looked all around his blasted room that morning for his logbook to show her the flights – though how that would help he didn't know – but couldn't find it. Whisky in the brain. She took his hand. He couldn't stand her concerned expression.

'Well, I really rather think Charles is expecting you to fly,' she said. 'What do you want me to do?'

'Just stall it a little. I can recover my nerve, I am sure I can.'

'I'll think of something.'

'It is me who is supposed to rescue you,' he said. 'Not the other way round.'

'Rescue me?' She looked away from him when she said this. A feeling of physical longing, a magnetic impulse to stretch his hand out and touch her, so vivid and intense it shocked him.

'You should be my wife,' he said. She turned; he couldn't read her face. He had said it now, so he continued. Reckless. 'You married the wrong man. In the wrong city. I will always see you as my wife.'

There was a circle of fire around her, like those camping-trip games, making a fire ring up on the South Downs, gathering dry bracken and hopping in and out, feeling the flames kiss the hairs on the leg. He wants his wife: nothing immoral in that. Khaled Rasul's face comes to his mind, but he blocks it. The circle of fire. He wants to tell her, everything. What? (A little girl called Ana? No, never that.) Spirals of confessions, as if she were a priest. Confessing what, exactly? Original sins. In Cairo he had been taken to the Lieutenant. Reported for drinking on duty. Hands shaking. Eyes red. Talking nonsense. *You need a rest, Harrington. Grounded. Think about alcohol, Willie, and what it is doing to you. But it is not just that. You need to think about how you – what? – approach the world. Think about it. See it.*

He was Category V. Discharge from draft: persons found to be totally and permanently physically or mentally unfit. Somehow, this had not filtered to Ashton. Jerusalem a backwater. The war over. Coming here had meant he hadn't had to go back to England, in disgrace.

He had loved flying, but in the end it was a terrible loneliness and a contradiction. When he was called up for a flight he would sit in the cockpit feeling as if he had an attack of the flu. Or as if his bones had walked a thousand miles. It was his body's way of telling him not to risk it again, he supposed, and each flight, every single one, involved this internal battle. It made no difference if he was flying with a co-pilot or solo and on his last flight in Cairo he had flown drunk, blotto as an owl. Forced landing. The machine on the ground, taxiing, a ditch, struts of the under-carriage snapping, whole thing over, on its back. Angels: *Bring me my bow of burning gold. Piss.*

The surgeon: you were born under a lucky star to have survived twice.

I beg to differ.

'I can deal with Charles,' she said, and she pulled out her lipstick, reapplied it slowly. He was horrifically cold. He shivered all over and looked at her. She was always turning away: caution and grace, but where was the substance of her? He couldn't hold on to her. She was like smoke.

'Here it comes,' Charles shouted, pointing his fly swat up at the sky. Frau Baum next to him, both shielding eyes from the sun. The aircraft was a Sopwith Strutter, a two-seater. It looked like a gnat in the sky and came towards them like a bad memory in the night, descending quickly.

'Nice landing,' Charles applauded.

The pilot emerged in full Sibleys, climbed out and saluted them, his face bright from exertion and success. To make matters worse, it was a chap Willie had once met in Cairo. A young Etonian with a bright-blond moustache, eyes red and bloodshot from the flight. Willie let Charles, Frau Baum and Eleanora surround the pilot, shake hands, clap him on the back, until it was no longer possible not to walk forward and arrange his own face as it should be. He couldn't remember the man's name but he blustered through it. Ashton was at the aircraft, touching its nose, stroking the propellers. He called over to Willie, 'Have you had a look at it yet? Bloody beauty, what is it?'

Willie spoke without looking at it, 'Sopwith. Topnotch.'

Anderson.

That was his name; it came to him now. Willie had spent an evening with him in Shepheard's once, talking the ears off one another all night, competitive bad-taste jokes. Ach. Have you heard the one about the faithless widow? Ach. Heard the one about the dead brother? Anderson eyed Eleanora professionally, up and down, a once-over, registered a glance back to Willie. Willie turned away from the group, looked over at the watchtower.

'Charles, a terrible thing,' Eleanora said, pulling off her sunglasses, opening her eyes wide. 'I had a problem with my camera equipment, it was all in a dreadful muddle, so I couldn't get it together accurately, so difficult without Khaled. Ihsan and I have been going through the studio, and well, it's all rather a mess, and I'm afraid to say I haven't been able to rig up the camera for the photographs from the aeroplane in time.'

Ashton flapped at the air. 'But, my dear, we've been looking forward to this day so much. Reconnaissance. A clear, bird's-eye view. A different sense of the horizon – so humbling, to see the earth below and the city we exist in so small. I've been desperate for it, I really have.' He gave her a disapproving look. She sniffed a little.

'Will you forgive me, Charles?' Eleanora said, and Willie could see she was making herself as bright and charming as possible and he knew what that comment about her husband must have cost her.

'I will have the equipment ready soon, I promise,' she said.

'Might you go up for a spin for the hell of it?' Charles asked Willie, capitulating.

'No,' Willie summoned a calm flat voice. 'I'll wait for Eleanora. No sense in wasting fuel.'

'Oh well, rather a blow.' Ashton put his hand to his forehead, shielding off the sun. 'That's that then.'

Frau Baum turned to the pilot and said, sweetly, to move things on: 'Anderson, so you flew against the Fokkers, did you?'

'I bloody did.'

Night of bombs, near and far. Called out of bed at five, patrol the skies, ended up feeling sorry for the Huns, God help 'em, having to fly a Pfalz! Willie, unable to listen, walked over to a cedar tree on the edge of the airfield, leant against its trunk and attempted to get the noises in his head straightened out. Now that the immediate threat of having to fly was gone he thought the ringing in the ears might fade, but it did not. In fact, it grew worse. A clamouring, a rushing. *I soon heard I was getting another piece of ribbon for my efforts* ... He was grateful to Eleanora, but mortified. Willie scraped the palm of his hand against the tree bark and propelled himself forward to them.

'Blow it,' he said. 'I will take her up for a spin regardless.' He walked towards the Sopwith and patted the wing, ran his hand along the nose and the long slicing plane of one of the propellers. He looked over his shoulder at Eleanora whose eyebrows were raised.

Ashton smiled. 'Hurrah, old boy.'

'Willie, why don't you wait until we have all the photographic equipment in place? It will be better, I think?' Eleanora said.

Anderson had white-blond eyebrows that moved ferociously as he spoke.

'Might be an idea to give the beast a once-over from a mechanic, though, eh?' He looked doubtfully towards the desolate watch-tower. Eleanora shook her head slightly.

'My dear, you do not need to worry,' Ashton said, seeing Eleanora's face. 'He is the best pilot in the region, I have it on the utmost reliable authority.'

He has invented that. He wants to believe that.

Willie squatted beneath the undercarriage of the Sopwith pretending to examine it. The sound in his ears was the same as a ground-strafer; it was all one, a roaring. Eleanora came behind him and crouched down, close.

'There is something wrong with my eyes,' he said, wiping along the lower rim of his right eye.

'It's called crying, Willie.'

She took his hand, held it against her lips. He stood up. He looked at the sky and the bright sun. It was nearly noon, he guessed.

'I'm coming with you,' she said.

He helped to fasten her in first, her long thin legs folded neatly underneath the seat. The mount where the guns were usually positioned was there, but no gun. She would have her back to Willie and look at the places they were flying from; he would be staring into the future. Anderson stood near, smiling, smug and knowing. He knew what flying a girl in the sky meant and his smirks irritated Willie whose eyes were now dry.

'Be good to be up in the air again, heh?' Anderson said, and leant forward, gesturing over to Eleanora. 'Impress the lady, eh?'

'Better than sitting around here all day,' Willie even managed a smile and climbed into the cockpit. The sky was very bright; Anderson moved backwards away from the machine.

'Feeling all right?' he shouted over his shoulder.

'Yes!' Her voice in his ear. I'm giving you my life, she was saying by flying with him. To drop, to land, to carry; to do with what you like. He pulled his goggles over his face. He put his right hand on the stick, left on the throttle. He was shaking, but curiously, his ear-whistles had stopped.

As the Sopwith lifted there was the inevitable trigger in his loins, but perhaps because of Eleanora's proximity he controlled it. The fear did not go – it expanded, through his stomach and oesophagus – but when fully airborne he settled into a feeling of pure tension that at least was consistent. His skin, his muscles, his skeleton were all electrified by the sensation of flying again. He wished he could touch Eleanora, or ask her: what do you make of the clouds up here? The world is different, is it not? The sky around him, left and right, but he did not need to look for enemies here. He remembered how Knefler, one of the German pilots, would use the light from the sun as a shield, and how he had learnt that trick from him. That was the stupidity of it: they taught one another the techniques, and she was with him, behind him. He could no longer call out to her, she wouldn't hear him.

The land shrank beneath them. He checked his rev counter, all well, apart from his turbulent stomach, and it was difficult to hold back flying memories. He recalled sitting in a hangar on the Cairo airfield waiting for one of the men, Whitby, to come back. Whitby had been called on duty to fly to Haifa and had been gone for five hours when he should have been back in three. Willie didn't know him, particularly. Had only spoken to him once, an abstract conversation about how he liked to eat his baked beans cold rather than heated up. Told Willie that it used to annoy his wife dreadfully. Willie had replied, Why did you eat baked beans with your wife? Oh I don't know, summertime in her family's cottage. No cook about. She thought them rather common food so it was a bit of a joke. That was the only exchange of words Willie had ever had with Whitby but he never came back. Five hours became twelve.

Concentrate: he was looking straight ahead now. The explosion, the hollow dense heart of it. Flames through the floor, through the cockpit, a tunnel of cold air, the sky not sky but a ceiling, a trap.

This was not now: this was then.

He did it. (Smoke in his lungs.) Not now. (Mackie's face on fire.) Not now. Through it all: Eleanora.

Willie's landing was nowhere near as smooth as Anderson's drop had been. At the end of it, engine shuddering, he climbed out of the Sopwith and turned to help Eleanora. Her face was flushed as she pulled the goggles off; she smiled, shook her hair. He immediately asked Ashton for a cigarette.

'Good stuff. Think of the photographs,' Ashton said. 'How did the Holy City look from up there? A heavenly perspective, eh?'

'Amazing,' she said. 'Changes everything.' She had understood exactly. She was holding in her hand her camera, a snapshot brownie; she handed it to Ashton.

'Do take a photograph of us, Charles?'

She beckoned Willie to stand next to her, looking at him with clear eyes.

'Closer,' Ashton shouted. Willie's hands moved around her waist, the slimness of her body sending an electric shock through him. She was smiling towards Ashton. When she was concentrating, in her darkroom, with her slides, with the chemicals, bringing the images to life, he knew she must look like that: fully applied, attentive. She was a person who could make everyone around her disappear, who became only herself. She owned light, controlled it, and he guessed that each morning began for her by looking at the sky without fear.

They waved goodbye finally, Willie shaking off Anderson who wanted to come back to the bar, and when they walked towards the car he said, 'I'll drive?'

'All right. I thought you might have had enough steering of machines today?'

'Feel like it, if you don't mind.'

He became brighter in the eye, sharper in the ear and drove as if he might continue with Eleanora onwards to Ramleh or Baghdad or Baalbek or even Constantinople. The vegetation around them was wintry, but a few green stalks were coming up through the rust and the yellow colours. She was struggling with her scarf around her head, and turned to him, shouted over the wind.

'I loved flying.'

'Of course, you were meant to fly.' On the dip of a hill he increased the speed slightly.

'You weren't nervous after all?'

'Not when it came to it.'

'Slow down?' He stopped the car, abruptly, and did not bother to pull over and park. It was possible to see the stretch of road leading down through the valley and onwards to nowhere. There was no sign of any other motor cars; not a soul in any direction around them. Finches hopped near the side of the road. They sat silently for a moment; his hands on the steering wheel looked to him like dead birds. Then he took hold of her face and kissed her. There was peace, for a turn of the world, but when he looked at her eyes he saw all of her bad dreams. Her fingernails scraped along her dress, as if she wanted to scratch at herself. Part of him fell away with desire, but, underneath it, surprisingly, there was resistance in him. He did not want to be lost in her. Her cheek rested on his; he could feel the light breath from her nostrils.

'You were stupid to come here,' she said.

'Was I?'

She sighed.

'Look,' he started, 'whatever it is that is the trouble, your father, and worries about what they'll say at home, me, any of it, we can arrange things. I'm confident that –'

She put her hand on his mouth. Stopped him talking.

'Khaled wants a child, but I was serious when I told him that I do not want children. He won't accept it. That is where we are.'

She said it calmly. Willie knew why she was frightened: her own mother had died giving birth to her; what bigger haunting is there than that? Why would she possibly want to re-create the same risk? But what did this – Khaled not accepting – have to do with him, Willie? She was shaking her head, turning from him, back towards Khaled Rasul, a man who lived inside a walnut frame, she was climbing back inside a photograph. He opened the motor-car door. 'What are you doing?' she said.

'I'll walk.'

Two minutes later she drove past him. She did not slow down or look at him. His feet very quickly objected to the walk; his shoes too tight, the air cold, sharp. His knees cracked and it seemed to him that he had always been walking towards Eleanora, only to walk away again.

London, 1927

My new husband is naked as a baby, his penis soft and reduced almost to nothing. He puts his hand on the windowpane and looks down on London as if he is a giant who owns it, as if the bridges and the cobbled stones and the ships coming along the Thames from India and China and Russia all belong to him. He tells me that men in the square are hanging trails of lanterns from the plane-tree branches because soon it will be Christmas.

I am still wearing last night's evening dress which is ruined from wine and other substances. I feel as slippery and as manhandled as a piece of leather. It is a new feeling, having been rolled about as if my body is made of modelling clay, my lip bitten as if it were food, my hands squeezed until the skin wrapped around them is white. I lie back on the vast and endless four-poster bed near the long tall windows of the hotel room and it is just like looking out of the porthole on a boat. I think of the tremendous things I am ready to do. My empty stomach contains a feeling of urgency, a pressure: London! Begin! How, though, to begin? And begin what? Piers is making a business of dragging furniture across the thick carpet and something in my chest lowers.

'This is where the donkey will look best, Prue. Closer to the window. You need light to work.'

What he calls the donkey is a narrow wooden bench with a sloped edge for life-drawing students to lean on. It was stolen by Piers and his friends from one of the St John's Wood life-drawing classes that many of the Slade students attend. I am not enrolled at the Slade, I am too young at eighteen, but Piers smuggles me in to lectures and twice I have been asked to sit for the professor they call Tonks but both times I said no. *Keep it up*, Piers said. *Being aloof increases your mystery.*

I close my eyes. I was asleep but he woke me up. He is tapping the table impatiently, wanting me to rise, to start. He has laid out thin blue hotel letter paper and put a box of sharpened pencils on the floor. He wants to prepare the perfect surroundings for me, he says, the *exactly correct conditions*. He sets me tasks, little exercises designed to open up a room in my head and produce the contents, on a plate, for him. It started as a game, before we were married. Draw with your left hand, write before you wake up properly, don't think about it, and just see what comes out. Art, Dear Prue, Art. But now when he arranges the room he does it without looking at me. He focuses fully on what he is doing, scraping the large heavy curtains back so it is lighter. He gets a twitch below his right eye when he is like this.

My name is Prudence Ashton. No it is not.

My name is Prudence Miller.

The only way to bring him back to a good mood is to look inviting on the bed. I shift so that I am a roll of up-and-down curve and look over at him. I think that he is going to join me and slide his hand behind my neck, but instead he jumps quickly on top of me before I can move, each of his knees pushing into the side of my chest. He does not have much hair on his body. He is smoking a Spanish cigarette.

He is drunk, I see now. The buildings outside the window are London-grey, a dream colour, the same as the inside of a Whitstable oyster. Last night we went to a lecture by the sculptor Gill and I listened to his long and mesmerising explanation of working the chisel directly on the stone. No pointwork, and if you work with heavy granite, he said, you feel heavy in thought, emotion. If you work in lighter stone, you feel lighter. In the corner of my vision I can see the glow of the cigarette end, a red coal, a snake's eye. It sparkles as air is sucked through it. It comes closer.

I have been taken up – that is the way they phrase it – by Piers's set. My unknowing ways entertain them. I understand the codes of international colonial living – the servants, the driver, the cook, the gardener, the natives, the rulers – but in London I have no idea *how things go* and they mistake my endless faux pas for subversive deeds and find me a hoot.

I wriggle under Piers's knees, push my nails into his skin. I've had enough of this game. There is something unwise and destructive about his face, and yet beautiful, with his sloppy contemplations which suddenly transform into an intense concentration, an insistence on everyone in his orbit doing exactly as he wants, a despotic domineering quality.

'Get off me. You're drunk.'

He says nothing but squeezes his knees tighter against my ribcage. There is this new look again, he is staring at me but doesn't really see me. Or what is it that he sees? A physical entity, like a doll you might pull around, tug legs off, discard.

'Move, Piers, come on, I can't breathe now.' I hit his knees. He is shaking his head, lips loose and wet. I am not laughing.

'You didn't do the drawings yesterday. You didn't give me any more work.' He takes one long inhalation of his cigarette, moves his face towards mine.

'I couldn't come up with anything.' The more I squirm beneath him the heavier his weight. The glowing end of the cigarette dips between us. Ash falls on to my lip.

'Yoo-hoo.' There is a banging on the door. It is Marguerite, coming in without waiting to be invited, which is her way, and Piers leaps off me, stag-like and supple, and I see that before he turns around his face has a sarcastic smile. He puts his cigarette out on the rim of a vase full of dead Christmas chrysanthemums. I tug the sheet up around me.

Marguerite, wearing brightly coloured stockings and a dress that looks Grecian in its flow, loosely belted, and covered with a bright blue gypsy shawl, brings outside smells into the room. I have been in here for days. Weeks. Centuries. Food comes. Weather outside changes. It is not fresh air that she has brought in, just a different version of stale air. Marguerite looks at me and then quickly away.

'Please don't just walk in,' Piers shouts in mock-horror, taking his time to clamber across the floor towards his dressing room. I sit up, exposed in the bed, trying to remember how badly ripped or stained the dress I am wearing is. Piers moves slowly; he has a long thin, perfect streak of a body and he likes eyes on his skin. Marguerite watches Piers. She lets her hand, with its own cigarette, drop. Her mouth open slightly, she brazenly looks at him and the question rises up in me: have they slept together? And I know: of course they have.

'What do you want exactly, La Margarita?' Piers calls over his shoulder. Marguerite stands at the mantelpiece, quite still, as if half with us in the room but half elsewhere. She told me one night as we drank schnapps together that Piers had had a particularly terrible time during the war and that it had done something awful to his mind; burnt out a hole in it, she had said. Like a cigarette burn. She had caught my hand, that night, and rubbed it with her thumb and told me not to let him tell me what to do. I was not interested: in her rub-rubbing the skin on my hand and looking at me oddly. At her warning, which I took to be interference.

'It was really just to say that Herbert Read has invited us all to dinner. He is keen to meet *la petite fille*.'

Piers, trousers on now, doing up his button, spins around and seems to snap out of his half-cut morose fug.

'Really? Margarita. That is rather brilliant of you, how did you pull it off?' Now he is all warmth towards her and gestures towards the fireplace where, with his thrifty nature despite his comfortable circumstances, he has installed a tea-making rig on the hearth and, so far, the maids and the room-service waiters have turned a blind eye.

'The inestimable Herbert Read,' he says, clapping his hands lightly. 'Only the most powerful man in the art world. Will you have tea, dear? We rather lost track of time and I am guessing it is elevenish?' He looks around the room as if for confirmation. He has forgotten that he smashed all the clocks up in here when we first moved in.

'I don't think so to tea, do you?' She laughs, a brittle yelping laugh, and puts her hand to a silver charm that hangs around her neck. I can't see what it is, just the glint of it. 'He's taking us to the Savoy. Nine on Friday.'

She looks over at me, suspended in bed, and there is my old doll, Lulu, at the end of it, making me feel even more as though I am their child. Looks between parents that mean something but I am not sure what. I don't know why that doll is there. I haven't seen it for a long time. Piers must have moved it from my trunk. When Piers first introduced me to his friends he led me through a crowded room one evening in a flat in Chelsea to a corner where we could speak privately.

'I want to show you something,' he said, and opened his book. In it were drawings, or doodles rather, all very similar: heads stretched, eyeballs, layers of faces, and twisted bodies. They were dolls, I realised. Some with extended heads, or twisted necks. They had a similar face, eyes wide, far apart.

'They look like me.'

'I drew them five years ago.'

'What does it mean?'

'It means I imagined you before you came. Or it means we were meant to meet.'

That was it then, the perceptible shift. A change in the way they all treated me; less like open game, less like a stray foal in the oddest dress, with the women wondering: did she actually mean to put that hat on her head in such a manner? They began to talk to me as if I were fragile, difficult, vulnerable, as if I had come back from a long voyage on a steamship with an incurable disease that had no clear symptoms. Mostly, they saw me as Piers's property. He laid down his claims and without discussing it, just by default, I moved to his bed and as it was his father, Earl something or other, who was paying for everything, he asked everyone to leave apart from me. He cleared them out. GET OUT GET OUT GET OUT I'VE HAD IT WITH YOU PAUPERS AND SCROUNGERS AND ARTISTS

DISPLACED LEAVE US IN PEACE. Shortly afterwards, very drunk, we were married by an easily bribed official in Hackney who had never seen as much money in his life as the bundle of notes that Piers forced into his palm, and Marguerite was always there, shimmering, moving as if ice skating. She picks up the doll and examines it. Puts it back down on the bed, gives me another look, training her eyes on me as a dog does, lowering the head, telling me to stay, telling me to run. I half-expect her to bare her teeth.

As soon as she is gone Piers points towards the donkey. 'Now, draw. Get up,' he bangs his fist on the bed, 'get up, get up.'

I ignore him, turn over. London. Piers. It is the one place my father, with all his Englishness and his rearranging of cities all over the world, has never lived or known. Piers is sitting on my back, his hand on my hair pulling it up so that my mouth opens involuntarily. I let out one gasp, thinking this will be sexual, but before I can respond he has pushed my face deep into the pillow. There are bright lights crossing on the inside of my eyelids, and I heave my spine, push against him, but he doesn't move his hand.

His voice has gone sickly sweet. 'I want to see what comes out of that beautiful little mind, that's all. Draw, or write then.'

When he lets go the air comes back at me in a rush, and I push him off, furious. I jump from the bed and go to the window, rubbing a tear from my eye so that it is not crying, just part of skin. His words follow me around the room like a snake. *I understand Herbert Read is a literary as well as artistically minded fellow.* In the mirror I am a wreck; I look like a broken bride. I peel off the evening gown and change quickly into a simple green dress, my skin tense, not looking at him or listening to him, but it is pointless. My attempt to punish him falls flat as he is unaware. I lean against the donkey and take a pencil.

~~Dear Father~~
~~Father~~
~~Dearest Father~~
~~Father~~

Piers comes behind me, making me jump, and whips the page from me, screws it up.

'Good Lord, not that.' He gives me another sheet of paper. 'Tell me.' He needs these stories, as much – maybe more – than he needs drink. He has a knife and he weasels out parts of my mind. If I tell him a dream he writes it down. If I doodle on a writing pad, staring into space, he whisks it from me. He returns, hours or days later, and shows me his own working of a drawing or painting and it is always based on something I have done. He takes my notebooks and turns them into his own. I refuse to look at him, but I draw: a snake creature with feathered edges, a curling tendril swirl, I do what he wants, let it come automatic and unthinking, the loops and the edges, the words and the scratches, and as I do, he disappears, the city disappears, the sea and the boats and the sky disappear, I am at a still-point inside myself, the unsafe feeling calms, fades, I am balanced.

He takes, and he takes them all, as if they feed some hole in the centre of him.

The only painting he has done recently which does not originate from something I created was still a portrait of me, although not completely realist. I am standing next to a bicycle on a Bloomsbury square, wearing a long blue dress, looking down at the ground. Perhaps the expression is furtive, distrustful, as if any morals I might have had have been laid out to be picked over by birds. There is a figure behind me, leaning against the railings of the gardens, a person in a black coat, who is obviously intended to have a menacing presence, a threat. A crouching, creeping, following person and I assume it is him, Piers, putting himself into the picture.

I move over towards the fireplace and put both hands on the mantelpiece. At first, being the intense object of his focus, his attention, was wonderful. I felt bathed, wrapped up, as if I had been tucked into bed with my shoulders covered and my toes warmed, then examined, understood, observed. Now, I am getting rather tired of being told what to do. I look up at the large, alcove-arched ceilings and remember how, as a child in Jerusalem, I wanted more than anything to go up in an aeroplane and fly above buildings that were empty. To see what the world must look like from above. It seemed to me that a person who can look down on the world is free.

'Here is what we are going to do.' Piers, fully dressed now, is walking around the hotel room with the rigid neck of a sergeant-major. Sometimes, I can clearly see the soldier rather than the artist he purports to be. 'I am going to my studio and you are going to *work*.'

The word *work* has become a threat from him. For days he has been telling me about his new studio on a ground floor with four tall windows that open out on to a garden where rabbits hop. 'You would like it,' he keeps saying, but he doesn't invite me there.

'I am going to the studio,' he says again, as if he is offering me a gift.

'Surely I could come and work alongside you?'

'You work better alone. I work better alone. You know that. I need you to not be there, it's too distracting. I will be ... two days.

I have put all the food over there.' He points to the bureau which is really a disguise for a liberally stocked drinks cabinet. There are three netted bags and I can see oranges and cake and sour bread and jam. He went out and shopped for all of this early this morning while I was asleep, bringing it back himself rather than having the packages delivered.

Then he takes me to bed. As if sealing something in his mind, but the sex is different. It's too tender and careful, less calamitous than usual. Normally we fall out of bed. Bump noses. Sneeze in faces and fall asleep halfway through when drunk. He wants to gaze into my eyes, wrap his fingers around mine. It makes me queasy and when he's done I turn on my side, eroded by the empty feeling after sex that did not quite meet in the middle. He tiptoes around the room, as if I am a child having an afternoon nap, thinking I am asleep. The door clicks. One, two of his footsteps outside the corridor and then nothing.

I immediately sit up. A pigeon flutters on to the balcony, its grey scraggly wings dragging in a pool of rainwater that has collected there. It has a gammy, revolting wound at the end of one leg in place of a foot and it hops and balances awkwardly as it bows to drink from the puddle. I hear another door slam and click locked further along the corridor. Something propels me to the window, I open the balcony door. That at least is not locked, and I look down at the street. Piers, pretending to be a socialist, eschewed his family's insistence of a personal valet, but somehow within the web of political reconfigurations – confused and contradictory at the best of times – agreed to retain a driver called Barnes and his Buick. Barnes is standing with the door open and Piers is striding across the street towards the vehicle. I put my hand on the balcony railing and watch them. Piers leans close to Barnes talking about something and then he turns and waves. It is Marguerite, walking quickly, muff in her hand. She must have been waiting. They slide on to the back seat together.

I come back inside the hotel room. The door to the corridor is locked, although I could of course shout. Bang on the door. Someone would come. I sit on the floor with my back resting on the bottom pane of the balcony door. I press my palms into the fluff of the red carpet. Stretch my toes so they are flat. There is something not quite right with my breathing. I lie down, head on the carpet, and I stay there.

Piers told me that he first saw me in the bookshop on Charing Cross Road. My face flushed, peeling off my goatskin gloves and looking very queer, but I didn't notice him at all. I was watching the bookseller, with his neat beard and his little puffs on his pipe. My skin felt as if it was on fire, I wanted to be entirely stripped of all clothing, as if the feeling of silk or cotton on my body was torture. This desire to release myself from hats and gloves and scarves and coats kept overtaking me. In the bookshop, my cheeks were blazing. I knew I must move and I made my way to the door but another woman was coming in. Roughly, rudely, I barged past her, out into the despicable London rain, though I welcomed it because its coldness cooled my skin.

I crossed Charing Cross Road and later, Piers said, he and his friend Marcus ran to keep up with me and I was almost hit by a fast omnibus that I had barely noticed. I ducked under the Hercules arch into Greek Street. Walked, fast, to Old Compton Street where I paid a penny to a hand in a slot and descended steep steps which smelled of urine. A penny cinema.

The film was Alfred Hitchcock's *The Lodger: A Story of the London Fog*. On the screen, a man with a black hat and a bandanna around his mouth arrives at a London door. The landlady opens it; behind her a staircase winds upwards, perhaps leading to heaven. I remember that my body was hot, my skin still on fire, and with my eyes on the screen I undid the top button of my blouse and then quickly, in a flurry, undid the rest. I leant down and unfastened my shoe buckle. The sensation was similar to a small sip of brandy: peace, for a second, and then an immediate need for more. As I rolled my left stocking down, I was aware that two men had sat close to me; one on the row of seats behind me, the other two seats along on my row. I did not particularly care. I removed my right stocking. I was not afraid of anything. I glanced at them. They were quite handsome – at the good age, twenty-eight or similar – with sharp straight noses and arrogant eyes and mannered collars and I knew their type: the men who want to impress one another, who live for the posturing and the flippancy. I had their complete attention. I wouldn't quite say that their mouths were open, but it was close: a hypnotism, a transfixed extended moment of time controlled by me. I turned to the man sitting closest to me.

'Please, take me out of here before I remove all of my clothes and am arrested.'

Greek Street was full of the drunken and the loud, a crush of men rubbing up against one another and shouting for more drink. Tarts blinking from doorways eyed up the two men walking either side of me so that, oddly, I felt protective of them and glared at the women to scare them away even though they were ten, twenty years older. It was dark, but the rain had stopped. I asked the men to buy me a paper bag of chestnuts and they did. I knew by then that they would do whatever I told them but when we reached

Shaftesbury Avenue it was as if I had emerged from a dream because all of my strength dropped away and I was exhausted. I hadn't eaten for such a time, not a meal – my father had disowned me for coming to London and refusing to live with his sister, but I did have a small income from my mother's family, £150 a year – and the chestnuts felt like globs of earth in my mouth. In the glare from the street lamp on a shop window-front I saw myself splintered, because the glass was not flat, distorted, and I took one of the men's arms to stop myself from fainting. They introduced themselves. Piers. Marcus. Well-spoken. Clean ears. Bright eyes. All their teeth.

'I've lost time,' I say. 'My name is Prudence.'

'Don't worry, Prudence,' the one with fair hair said, 'there is time at the hotel. We will show you.'

My hipbone aching, finally I get up from the hotel-room floor. Piers has gone with Marguerite, this is all I know. I am not sure how long he has been away. I go over to his typewriter on the table and pick up a page.

> ~~You can't xxxxxx find a lonelier creature than a married person turning the key in the backdoor, last one up, shushing the house hand taking hold of the toe and anklexxxxxxxxxxxx but doesn't wakexxxxxxxxx~~

I screw this page up and then take off my clothes and run a bath and even though the water is cold I get in, and sit shivering, my skin puckering, my heart nearly fading, until something in me propels me to get out.

I escape the room by climbing from my balcony across to the next balcony and asking the woman inside, who looks rather shocked, if I can leave by way of her door. Her mouth swings open like a fish, but she lets me through. I am still wet, from the bath. In the corridor I walk along thick carpets leaving padded prints. I do not take the lift, but rather the stairs at the end of the corridor. In my head a looping refrain: Upstairs and downstairs. And in my lady's chamber. Whither shall I? Whither shall I wander? A hotel man, the concierge or perhaps just a waiter or a kitchen person, comes towards me, surprised.

'You can't be here, madam.' He has an accent; he does not know where to look.

'Where are you from?' I ask him.

'Italy.'

'Ah.'

I push past and then I am outside.

'Madam,' the doorman shouts.

It is raining; a taxi splashes along Russell Square, past the dripping, spacious doorways of each tottering Georgian house. I stand at the edge of the kerb. People are gathering. Madam. Madam. Barnes, who is back, leaning against his car and smoking a cigarette, drops it on the pavement and rushes towards me. He takes off his coat, covers me, bats away the doormen and outraged gentlemen and ladies who have congregated on the steps of the Russell Hotel in horror at my nudity. I feel Barnes's hand on my back, pushing me into the back of the Buick. I sit on the leather seat, shivering inside his coat, grateful.

Barnes, in his driver's seat, looks at me in the mirror with astonishing professionalism and waits for me to speak.

'Would you mind taking me for a drive, Barnes?'

'Where to, Mrs Miller?'

'I'm not sure.'

He waits politely for a moment, and then says, 'Would you like to go back up to your rooms?'

'No. Definitely not.' He nods. 'To be perfectly honest I would be grateful if you would just drive. It doesn't matter where to.'

'Into the city or along the river?'

'The river sounds like the perfect plan.' I am grateful for him, and ashamed – although I never have been before – of the hours Piers makes him wait around for us.

He drives. I say nothing for a long time. His coat is scratchy on my skin. I lean forward.

'Did you take Mr Miller somewhere this morning, or yesterday, or whenever it was?'

He is alert. 'Yes, ma'am.'

'Where did you go?'

'An address in Pimlico, ma'am.'

'Pimlico? Marguerite's ... I mean, Mrs Alva's house?'

Barnes's ears immediately go a bright red, and he makes an actual sound of suffering which he attempts to hide with a cough.

'I'm terribly sorry,' I say. 'I will ask you no more questions. Forgive me.'

I am quiet for a long time, and we wind down towards the river. It is pleasant to look at the buildings on the opposite bank. In the rain-light they appear as if covered in silver paper. The road along Embankment is busy with traps and cars and omnibuses so that we move slowly. There is an enormous amount of traffic on the water. A large container ship creeps forward like an iceberg, and behind it barges look as if they might be sunk under their cargo of coal; a steamer comes too and in between them all smaller fishing and sailing boats, just like toys. We pass London Bridge.

The Buick edges towards the docklands where City men in their bowlers are not so much in evidence. We reach Trinity Buoy Wharf where we do not get out. Barnes stops, turns the engine off. I open the door and the air from the river comes in, smelling of the sea rather than the city. I point out to Barnes the cormorants hanging up their wings like vampires drying their cloaks, and then I ask if he will drive us back to the Russell and if he would be kind enough not to mention all of this to my husband, and he agrees to both.

But everybody else in the hotel has spoken to Piers and now I have been kept in this room for days. Similar to the times he locked me in to take the drawings or scraps of writing, but now he comes with fresh fruit and strokes my head and tells me to sleep and not to fret or strain or worry. Marguerite arrives and brings with her a doctor, Dr Ridgeway, Dr Radway? He is thin-faced and looks like a squirrel. *When the compulsion comes, don't do it. Think about doing it, run through it in your mind, slowly, controlling it, and then the desire will pass.*

I say, 'What compulsion?'

'To be naked in public. How do you feel when you take off your clothes?'

'Safer than with them on.'

After the doctor has gone, they sit around my bed, talking about a mini-exhibition they are organising for Piers's work and mine. A Greek art buyer is interested in buying some of my photographic pieces.

'Which ones?'

'Those dust pieces,' Piers says, 'remember?'

As if I have lost my memory. As if I am an old lady. He is referring to a series of oblique close-up photographs of large pieces of glass covered in dust, entitled *View From an Aeroplane*, and indeed they do look like aerial views, with swirls and lines and abstract shapes. Glass plates I left under the bed to accumulate dust. Similar experiments are happening in Paris; Rrose Sélavy, they say, as if I am meant to be impressed.

They bring in another man: Sir Herbert Read.

'We were meant to meet at the Savoy?' I say.

'No matter.'

'I'm not looking my best.'

'Never mind that.'

He asks me to explain: it's the snapshot. The ready-made. The arbitrariness. That's what they want. Snapshot. A long-lost memory of my Kodak Eastman (what happened to that?) and a bird on the ground. The freckles on Eleanora's arm, the fact that Eleanora, remote, untouchable, was an inexplicable complexity at the heart of my travels. I don't tell them, but from the bed I feel the curtain edge move. I am sure that there is a creature in there, something breathing quietly.

'Where on earth did you find her?' says Mr Read. He has taken his hat off and balanced it on the edge of a table; I am worried it will fall.

'Let Prudence tell you the story.'

I shake my head. I am nervous in front of this powerful dealer of art and maker of artists' fortunes who is looking at me in bed. I listen, as Piers tells him about the night of *The Lodger* in Soho. Sitting around me, they all drink drink drink to my health and future. I lie on the bed and pretend that I am asleep until I am.

Jerusalem, 1920

Ihsan found Prue standing at the point where David Street became the Street of the Chain. If she stood here for long enough she might exist, like a stone lion statue in the heart of an Italian square. She had read of such a square somewhere along the train-tracks of her life and there was always the temptation to be magical and believe that such a place had been spread out like a painted set, just for her, that she had invented it. But really, she knew well enough that the places of the world existed whether she was in them or not.

At the end of each day the Holy City shut down like a toy put back in its box. It was as if all the doors and windows were slamming and closing in front of her.

'Prue?'

Ihsan was tightly wrapped in a thick coat, his face half-covered with scarves. The temperature had dropped further. She hadn't seen him for a few days and he looked a little odd. Not quite himself.

'What are you doing?' he said.

When she saw him the part of her that was keeping her balanced on the ground snapped and she swayed. Ihsan took off his coat and put it over her and it was only when he did this that she realised that she was freezing, out in the cold air wearing a thin dress, not even a cardigan. It was windy, as well as cold. Since being here Prue had become frightened of the wind. She felt it might carry her away, or blow her apart.

'Come with me. Walk to warm up.'

They walked quickly, in silence. Out of the Old City, out through Damascus Gate, and along the Nablus road. Her nostrils were sore. Ihsan was clearly on his way somewhere. She should make a polite exit; she knew as they walked he was thinking up ways to deposit her somewhere, just as everyone else did. Today, however, she had no pride.

'Wherever are you going, Ihsan? Can I come with you?'

He frowned and tried unsuccessfully to hide it. Normally she would let Ihsan be, knowing herself unwanted, but today, without understanding why, she was frightened of being alone.

'Of course. You come with me.'

There was a blue gate on the curve where the Nablus road climbs up the Mount of Olives towards Mount Scopus. Ihsan banged out a coded knock on the door and they were let inside by a man with a birthmark across the whole of his right cheek. The steps were steep and lined with tall, well-established cedars, like a scene from a Germanic fairy tale rather than a desert-dwelling garden. At the top they were met by a man whose mouth dropped open when he saw Prue at Ihsan's side. In Arabic, he said, 'You can't bring an English child into the house of Abu Swayy, you louse.' Her Arabic was shaky, but she worked out the essence.

'Is Hassan Fahmi here?' Ihsan said and then Prue, who was looking at the floor, heard him say in Arabic: 'There is method. She brings us information from the *Ingliz*.'

The man called Hassan Fahmi was brought to the door and she stepped away a little to let them discuss whatever it was they needed to without her listening. She counted to ten to stop herself from rubbing her nose, and also to stop herself from crying which she seemed to be on the verge of doing. A robin sat on the bottom branch of the cedar but it would not look at her. It would not come close.

Ihsan turned to her and said quietly, 'Prue, this way.'

There was a wide entrance-hall area, and everything inside was made from the pale grey-pinkish Jerusalem stone. Groups of men stood in clusters of three and four, talking. Ihsan whispered to her, 'It is the Al-Muntada Literary Club.'

He steered her through a dark hallway, past a door which opened out on to a stone-floored kitchen, and round into a spacious living space. There were sofas along the edge of the wall and chairs arranged as if for a meeting or a talk in the centre of the room. Ihsan took her to one of the sofas and told her to sit.

'Here is my friend, Saliba al-Jouzi,' Ihsan said, and a man with beautiful shimmering eyes looked at Prue as if she were a rodent.

'What are you doing?' He spoke in Arabic.

'She was with me, today, she wanted to come. She doesn't understand it, don't worry.'

'You idiot. Get her out.'

Prue looked at Ihsan's face. He was surely regretting bringing her now. When he came close she whispered, 'I'm not sure I'm welcome, Ihsan, perhaps I should go?'

'Come, come. Don't worry, they are ignorant and foolish.'

The coffee boy came forward and took orders and then there was a cheer. The eyes that had all been looking at Prue turned away towards doors which led through to yet another room, and a balcony which opened up over the whole city and let in a bright harsh breeze. Ihsan squeezed her hand.

'Just wait here, dear Prue, you will be quite safe. I will be back in a moment.' And he stood up and went towards a small group of men on the balcony.

It was a room full of men. They were mostly the same age as Ihsan, or younger, but there was one boy who was maybe just two or three years older than her. He looked at her, but he wasn't interested. He turned back to the man next to him, a father or an older brother or an uncle, who put his big hands around the boy's shoulders and he was pulled deep into the heart of their group and crushed by hands and arms.

She listened to the men laughing. She tried to identify the boy's name because the older men joked with him often. Yusi, Yusa, Yasa, Yusef, Yaacoub, it could have been, but then she thought that might be the name of the older man after all, and in fact the younger one was called Isaaf or Issa. The older man kept touching him with a glorious straightforwardness: the younger, the elder; the protected and the protector. Twice, the boy looked over his shoulder at her, but he always returned to the men he belonged with. The conversations across the room appeared to get louder. People were both looking at her and ignoring her.

When Ihsan came back he was as ruffled as she had ever seen him. His face looked hot and he sat next to her, letting out a strange noise: *ouf.* He took a deep breath, patted his knee with his hands as if to say: we are here now. He told her the names of the men on the balcony: al-Jouzi and al-Nashashibi. Many of the men had begun chanting.

'What are they saying, Ihsan?'

'The Balfour Declaration is a lie and a trick! Unity for Syria!'

Prue's eyes opened wide. There was a man leading the talks on the balcony, quite short, with his back to her. He was surrounded by a group of intense-looking fellows.

'What are they saying now?'

'A future of blood and the treachery of the British.'

You shouldn't have brought me here. Though she knew it was she who had clamoured to come.

A man entered the room and several people shouted out, 'Welcome. He is back, thanks be to Allah.' The new arrival was immediately swept into the centre of things, people clapping his shoulders, taking his hand and kissing it. He scanned the room. When he saw her, his eyes widened a moment and then he glanced at Ihsan and nodded. The chanting on the balcony continued and then the man was walking towards her. He must be coming for Ihsan; but no. He was looking at her. Prue's spine tightened. *Treachery of the British.* When he reached Prue he knelt down on one knee and she was sure she might let out a whimper.

'Hello. You're the daughter of Charles Ashton?' he said in sing-song English.

When she nodded he said, 'Can you give this to your father for me?'

He handed her a flat piece of card. It was a photograph, printed on shiny paper and pasted on to the card, and the image was of a courtyard, with a door in the background. On the floor were six children's bodies, and next to them was a man with a broom, smiling at the camera. The child closest to the camera, she could not tell if it was a boy or girl, was naked and had a black mark, a stain, which Prue guessed was blood, across its chest. The eyes were open but it was not alive and then she realised that all the little bodies laid out in a row in the picture were dead and the man who was standing near them was laughing.

Ihsan sat up and said something in quick, ferocious Arabic that Prue did not understand. Prue's eyes burned.

'No,' the man said to Ihsan, but in English, holding his hand up. He turned to Prue: 'I want you to take this to your father, and say that we hold him and Storrs responsible for authorising these killings.'

The way he talked was very soft, kind almost, so that his voice did not match the words he was saying. Ihsan put his hand forward to take the picture away, but Prue stopped him.

'She is just a child herself,' Ihsan said, in Arabic, sadly.

Looking closer, she saw it was a boy. 'How old is he?' Prue said, her finger on the image of the child with the stain on his body, circling around the eyes and their strange look. The man in front of her shifted, his knees creaked a little. He looked down at the picture.

'I imagine he is six. Something like that.'

'Is he dead?'

'Yes.'

Prue looked at him. 'I will give it to my father.'

'Thank you.'

Prue looked at his face, and then she knew who he was, from the picture in Eleanora's room. It was Khaled Rasul. He turned abruptly to Ihsan, speaking in very fast Turkish, rather than Arabic, so that she couldn't understand. Ihsan was rubbing his hand over and over his lip and finally Khaled Rasul walked away, towards the balcony, and as he did so there was a cheer.

'We must go. I was stupid to have brought you here.' Ihsan pushed Prue quickly through the door, and the men around them appeared to be laughing. Prue searched the room for the young boy with his father but they had all moved out towards the balcony to join in with the rest of the men who had begun to chant.

Because of the very cold weather many places were closed but a small café run by a Christian from Smyrna was open. Ihsan ordered tea and then began to apologise to her, over and over.

'Don't worry, Ihsan. I didn't feel unsafe.' This was a lie. She added, 'I shan't tell my father, please don't fret.'

But Ihsan's anxiety did not diminish; in fact it grew as they drank the tea. Morose, he sighed.

'You must get rid of that picture, Prue. It is best if you give it to me. I really don't think you should give it to your father.'

It was resting on her knee. She had no intention of getting rid of it, but she nodded and then she said, 'I shall keep it, but I won't show him.'

'No. I must take it.'

She shook her head. 'I won't show him or say anything about the meeting.'

There was a cluster of Carmelite flowers in a vase on the table, most nearly dead. Ihsan saw her looking at them and picked the one remaining fully alive bloom, letting a drip of water from the stem fall on to his sleeve. He stroked the lilac cross-shape of the flower as he regarded her. She thought he was going to pass it to her but he didn't. There was nobody else in the café apart from them and the owner had disappeared. The table was not quite straight, so that one of her knees fitted under it and the other was wedged.

'Ihsan, what did you mean when you said I bring information, there is method?'

He looked at the table and then down at the floor. There was a pause.

'Can I trust you, Prue?' he said, with a solemn face, talking quietly.

'Of course.'

'I asked you to bring me some things from the pilot's room?'

'Yes.'

'It is for the cause of Great Syria. We have discussed this.' She glanced down at the image on her knee: the flap and bruise on the small ribcage, the marks on the skin, the blurred imprint of a bullet in the shoulder. The strangeness of a face that looks asleep but is not. The sharp-looking bristles on the broom near the bodies. Who was the man, pushing their bodies with a broom? Laughing?

'Is my father responsible for this?'

'I'm afraid … he is. He has been sending his policemen in advance of land surveillance operations: surveys on who owns what, intelligence on the smallholdings, the *moshavot*, the *fella-hin*, and if they don't comply with this information gathering, then there is uproar. Fights. As you can see.'

Prue longed to slide under the café table. The cloth was thick enough to conceal her completely. Down there, might it be possible to stop time, or rearrange it at least, so that it did not stomp forward but curled instead, in spirals, or wound around ladders? Back to a place where mothers were not lost, fathers were not found; where time was not something you move through but something you look through. Like one of Eleanora's camera lenses. Like opera glasses.

'Ihsan, do you know anything about the assassination attempt on my father?'

'My dear, I was in there! That terrible man … If you want to play detective then I think you should have a look at the musicians who play in the Fast.'

He sat up. 'Are you hungry? Do you need to eat?' She shook her head. 'There is something in your face that reminds me of the hungriest days, the bad days when Jerusalem was starving. When the price of food was tremendous, when rations were impossible, when one couldn't get shoe leather or tobacco. Oh those days, those days.'

She said nothing; she had a feeling that little speech was not natural. An act. He touched her hand.

'Prudence. You seem … a little … unprotected.'

Her eyes were throbbing. He rummaged in his pocket and pulled out his small notebook with the leather cover, and gave her his fountain pen.

'Use the shifra code and write down what is worrying you.'

He watched her write, he had taught her well. She was quick, quite fluent now that she had been practising; it was so clear that he could read it upside down. What she wrote, in code, was: my father stole my letters, he did not send them to my mother. I am not sure who to trust. Ihsan read the words swiftly and he seemed not his usual springy, bouncy self today. He was calmer; sad even. He rummaged in his pocket and pulled out a tiny pipe that he liked to smoke rather than cigarettes, and he looked at her with an expression that she did not understand.

'I have this for you, Ihsan.' She dug her hand into her bag and then put the book she had taken from Willie's room on the table.

'What is it?'

'It's his pilot's logbook.'

Ihsan picked up the book, and gently turned the pages. Inside were columns and lists in William Harrington's handwriting.

'How interesting. Read it to me?' he said, handing it back to her. Prue looked up at the motionless fans that hung over their table like a threat. 'If you want. "A2. Take-off. Landings. Emergencies. Medium turns."' She stopped. Ihsan's eyes were unfocused, a little dreamy.

'Does it say where he's flown to?'

'Algiers – Gibraltar – Rabat – Gibraltar – Algiers – Elmas – Naples – Bari.'

'Imagine. All those cities: hopping from one to another.'

She continued to read. 'Drama – Salonika – Algiers – Tunis – Malta – Algiers – Elmas – Naples.'

Khartoum. Wadi Hafa. Amaza. Fayid. El Adem. Malta. Rome. Ishmailia. Bayid. Fayid. Malakal. Juba. Nairobi. Asmara. Castel Benito. Luqa. Port Sudan. Heliopolis. Mogadishu. Hargeisa. Mosul.

'Thank you, Prue.' He took the book from her and leant forward. 'It is for the greatest cause. You understand?'

'Ihsan,' she said.

'Yes?' He sometimes looked like a cat when he sat up erect. She had not given him the photographs. She had decided to keep them. Instead, she pulled out the large piece of paper from her father's desk. She had folded it up and carried it with her.

'What is this? Blank pages?'

'Look.' Once it was flattened, she took her pencil and very lightly rubbed it over the corner. The indented marks of her father's plans appeared, magical white lines in the shade.

'Now this,' he said, smiling at her, 'is extremely interesting.'

It was important to do it lightly; too much pressure and the indentation was lost. It was possible to see everything: the plan for the city, the notes, and the outlines. It was a design for Jaffa Gate. The words emerged. *Demolition of the Clock Tower, Jaffa Gate.*

'Our beloved clock tower?' Ihsan said, shaking his head. He began to talk in a different way. He got up from his chair and stood behind Prue as she continued the shading. *This map is more than a map. It is a change. It is a political statement. It is an intention. It is a way of altering a city and making it something other. It is a stamp. It is an outrage. It can't be allowed. It can't happen. What right? What consideration for an intervention like this?* Overlaid across the drawing of Jaffa Gate was a grid, and Prue could see that the world was built this way: stones, blocks, and laid-out maps. She was good at the shading. She even managed to bring into relief notes at the bottom of the page. *The Pro-Jerusalem Society recommends the demolition of the clock tower built during the mayorship of Faidallah al-Alami to celebrate twenty-five years' rule of Sultan Abdul-Hamid and designed in a 'Franco-Arab' style that is not conducive to the 400-year-old form of the Jaffa Gate walls.*

No. Ihsan stamped on the floor: was he angry with her? He was a small man, she could see, even though she was smaller, and when cross, when bouncing up and down in shock and outrage, he shrunk even more; he became slight, like the Arthur Rackham illustrations of fairies, and she couldn't be sure, looking at him, if he was a benevolent fairy or a malevolent one.

When she left Ihsan she had the feeling she had tipped everything out of herself, emptied herself of secrets and betrayed everyone around her. She felt the underlying unease, of which she had been aware in the Al-Muntada meeting, begin to increase and take over. All his words began to swing and judder in her mind. Who to trust? Her mother, Irish, always said this. Coming from Monaghan, which is as English as Irish gets, she said she was born confused. *I can't trust the Irish at home and the English hate me.* Prue's mind in circles, her father's face coming towards her in the room: Can I draw you, Prue? Then turning away again.

Prue had spoken to Garo the concierge once, about Jerusalem. He had a hare-lip, his top lip tugging upwards as if it had been threaded and the cotton was being pulled. She liked it. She had asked him where he was from, in her first week here. She could not ever tell, in Jerusalem, who was foreign and who native, whose family belonged here from generations and who was recently arrived. It simply was not possible to understand, from dress or skin colour or age or religious robes and hats or anything. It was the most confusing mix of people. 'Armenia,' he had said. 'We have been chased from our homes. The Greeks are chased from their homes. The Turks are chased from theirs. The Jews are chased from everywhere. The Arabs are chased from this land and the British are on the top of the pile.' He laughed when he said this but she had not understood the joke.

Without intending to, she had drifted towards Eleanora's road deep in the Christian part of the souk. The feeling of unease was more powerful still, and she was aware of her heartbeat, of the shape of her eyes, of her bones itchy, under her skin. But perhaps she had intended to gravitate towards Eleanora because it occurred to her that she wanted, very much, to see her. Before the pilot came, they had been friends. That was a true thing; Prue did not believe she had invented that. They had shared the baklavas together, drunk tea, talked. This and that. This and that. There was the paperweight, with the seahorse. It was just: the weather kept changing here. She must tell Eleanora that she had seen her husband. That he was in Jerusalem again. But surely she must know? He must have been home to her? They would soon be celebrating together and happy.

When she arrived at Khaled Rasul's studio she saw that Eleanora had taken down the picture of Damascus Gate that previously decorated the large front window space and in its place hung a print of a photograph from the time when Prue was 'assistant for the day' with the giggling Muslim sisters Lamia and Thuriya. In a vast golden frame, there was a picture of Prue. The label underneath the photograph said, *An English Child in Jerusalem.* Prue looked at herself. A serious face, miserable, even, and something in the way she sat that showed how eager she was to please, how desperate she was to be liked and how much she failed at that endeavour. She abhorred her own childishness. That day Eleanora had hired an Ottoman palace on Mount of Olives Street. It had a grand downstairs area, but on the upper floors it was shabby, the paint fading, and not much furniture. They used the largest room, with a great circular window and broken shutters. At first, the usual formal photographs of the sisters. Thuriya and Lamia had arrived wearing their best dresses, in the Jerusalem style with dropped hips and excessive buttons that did not seem to have button holes. Matching white stockings and black shoes. Lamia was prettier, taller, a pointed face. Thuriya had more of a square face, a natural scowl, but she was funny, silly, whereas Lamia was shy. They held carnations, which Eleanora finally prised from them, and after a while they had both become giggly, and Eleanora opened a bag: dressing-up clothes, stoles, furs, beads.

'Jump! Jump!' Eleanora had called out, her camera on the tripod in the middle of the room, taking photograph after photograph. Some were staged: stand here, stand there, sit here, and wear this. Prue sometimes assisting, sometimes in the photograph. Eleanora in them too, sitting on a chair, holding a cat up to her face, pushing her nose into the fur. She had dragged a table into the middle of the room and asked each girl to jump, to run, to move fast. She remembered Eleanora saying, 'Legs become simultaneously sculptural and architectural,' and Prue wrote it down: t-h-e-a-r-c-h-i-t-e-c-t-u-r-e-o-f-l-e-g-s. From all of those joyous, raucous photographs, Eleanora had chosen this sad one of Prue sitting still. Even though clothed, reserved, seeing herself in the window of the studio made Prue feel naked, as if she had taken off her dress and shoes, all of it, ribbons from her hair. She did not know why.

At the studio, the door was open but there was nobody in the front area where a customer, if he so wished, could come in and order a portrait.

Prue stepped inside. It was dark, and full of all the materials and clobber used for portraits. She moved slowly. She was creeping, again. She should call out, she should make it clear that she was there, but she did not. Instead, she continued, as quietly as possible, across the stone floor. She opened the door at the back and crept through into the house. She knew her way well enough. There was no sign of Samia but there was the sound from upstairs of things being shunted about. She moved up the curved stone stairwell that led to the main floor. She was four steps from the top. She heard the tingling of a bell. It was a fairy-like sound and then Eleanora's voice:

'The old kitchen bell, and what's this? An eagle?'

'Don't you remember it? It was the insignia on that great huge range in the Pentrohobyn kitchen. I prised it off with a knife once.' The pilot.

'You thief.' The bell was rung again. 'You kept these things all that time? Carried them with you?'

'Everywhere.'

Prue dropped down and sat on the steps. They couldn't see her and she was not sure why she didn't continue to walk up. She still had, clamped beneath her arm, the photograph of the dead child. She placed it beside her so that she could climb up one step, two. *Little spy. Creep creep.* Now she saw feet. The lion-shaped golden buckle on Eleanora's shoes and Harrington's bright black shoes, close together, facing each other.

'Ellie. It's clear enough to me. We should leave. Back to London and then arrange things from there.'

There was silence, then Eleanora said: 'It is not so simple, Willie. It is more complicated than that.'

'Well I don't see why. We can explain: you made a dreadful mistake.'

'Who says it was a mistake?'

'It can all be arranged, you cannot stay here.'

'It is not so easy.'

'I'm not saying it is easy, but –'

'It is not easy because Khaled's family's prayers and wishes have finally worked and, you see, I am carrying his child.'

Prue did not hear what his response was because she had already begun retreating down the stairs. If Eleanora caught her, sneaking, spying, she would despise her for ever. In order to leave the studio and house without them realising she was there Prue had to hold her breath until a ringing began in her head. She made her way to the door, and back through the front part of the studio as quickly as she could and it was only when outside again that she realised she had left the photograph on the cold bare steps.

Jerusalem, 1920

Prue was dressing for the evening meal when they came in: Frau Baum and her father. She thought at first they were going to say that war had been declared. They had the same look; she remembered it from when she was six: frowns, seriously sitting on the bed, shaking heads, but Ihsan had said if there is a war in Jerusalem then it was underground and that nobody was sure exactly who was the enemy, or who was fighting whom.

In the end, though, it wasn't that at all. They told her that her mother was dead. They took it in turns to sit on the bed and say the same phrase over and over. Your mother has choked on a piece of bread. She had accidentally swallowed a piece of bread the wrong way. The bread went down the wrong way. She had a terrible accident after eating a piece of bread.

'In Graylingwell?'

'In Graylingwell.'

Frau Baum was wearing a long tan dress and peculiar shoes for dinner, with a flamboyant hat with yellow feathers sticking out of it. This news had obviously come in at an awkward time, which was quite like her mother who would have been pleased to have ruined their party. Prue was half-ready, her woollen navy dress not buttoned up, her hair loose. She picked up her camera and turned it over in her hands as they spoke of bread, and choking, and looked serious. For a second in her mind she saw the letters she had written, in her father's drawer. She stopped listening and noticed through the window that there was something different about the sky.

'Is there a storm?'

They were both silent. Her father stood up, his knees cracking as he did so, and went over to the long window-door that opened on to her small balcony.

'Yes, it's snowing,' he said.

Did you hear what we said? they began again. *She's dead. Bread. Choked. Swallow.*

So it was snowing again. The last drift had melted very quickly. This explained the oddness of the light, and then she noticed another strange thing: her hands weren't flapping. Prue went to the window, aware that she felt nothing. Apart from being quite light, weightless and unreal, but was that a feeling? Did it count?

Her father, standing near her, moved his hand as if he were about to touch her shoulder. In the end he didn't. *Dear Prue*, they were saying. *You will be feeling some shock.* They said other words. She couldn't make them out, exactly. There was a day, oh so long ago now, when her nurse was washing her in a horrible old bath-tub. The water was chilly and she was desperate to get out but then her mother came in. *Look at your hair. You look like a mermaid.* Her mother knelt down, and put her fingers in the water and tangled them into Prue's long hair. Prue's arms had been covered in scratches, long thick ones from the neighbour's dog who kept jumping at her. Her hands were sore from where she had bitten the knuckles to stop the flapping. Her mother had looked at the hands, looked at the sore patch on the top of her right hand and started to cry, without explaining why, and so Prue began crying too to keep her company.

The turrets along the edge of the wall on either side of Jaffa Gate were layered with a light sprinkling of snow. Snowflakes were coming in, through the walls, through the windows, propelled by magic, and entering her heart and settling.

It was Frau Baum, not her father, who said, 'Come away from the window, Prue. It is cold. Cold air.'

Prue turned. Perhaps now there would be a long boat journey with him? A house in England. A villa, even. There was a lifting feeling inside her, followed by shame and a conscious putting out of her mind a very vivid hallucination of her mother's face.

'I suppose we must go back, then? To England.' Prue's knowledge of death was limited, but she knew about funerals, was vaguely aware of arrangements. He stood up straight, ran his hand over his beard, his long fingers stroking himself.

'I've just spoken to Isabel's mother by long-distance telephone from Governance House,' he said, now holding together troubled hands as if asking for forgiveness. 'The funeral will be soon and it certainly can't wait for us to make the six-week journey. In which case, we shall not leave immediately. We will go in a few months. Later in the year.'

Frau Baum looked at the floor. Prue wondered where the handkerchief that the woman at the gate of Graylingwell had given her might be, the one with the cockerel. Frau Baum, whose face displayed the most emotion of anyone's in the room, came forward with her long thin fingers covered in large stone rings and wiggled them near her as if she were about to touch her but Prue flinched and the fingers retreated.

'Prue, dear. Would you like something to eat? Or some tea?'

She shook her head, saw them giving one another significant looks. It was now or never; they were more likely to be nice to her now than at any other time.

'I don't like living here, Daddy,' Prue said, fast and in a rush. 'In the hotel, I mean. Can we go to the villa and make a house? Or return to England? I really feel ... I really feel ... that I must have a home.'

There was silence. Frau Baum let out an odd noise, almost the mew of a cat, and turned to Prue's father, whose elbow, as usual, she was holding but this time she spoke in a more forceful voice than normal.

'She is right, of course, Charles. I agree with her. She needs a home.' Prue was grateful; she almost smiled at her. Her father knelt down in front of her in an almost ceremonial manner.

'It is true, darling,' he said, 'that we need a settled place for you to live. I shall do my utmost to arrange it. This nomadic life is no good at all.' She realised that he was leaning down in such a way as to produce the least crease to his silk suit. There was a long pause. Finally he said in his deepest voice, 'I have made a decision not to cancel dinner tonight because I am not sure it will achieve anything ... for us to sit around being gloomy.' He burrowed about in his pocket, found a handkerchief, dabbed at his eyes. 'It will be helpful simply to carry on. Rally troops, keep the side up.'

'If you don't want to come, my dear,' Frau Baum said in a rush, 'I will stay with you?'

'Oh no,' Prue said, uncomfortable at the thought of being locked in this room with her, despite their recent exchange of smiles. 'It will be better for me to simply carry on, just like you, Father.'

He smiled at her. 'You are a strong little soldier.'

Prue did not bother to respond to this statement. They moved, together, like swans turning on a lake.

'You will let us know if you need anything?'

'Of course.'

When they had gone Prue stood in the centre of her hotel room. She let her hands do their flapping – violently, ferocious – and when that was done, and the muscles inside her were calmer, she dropped to hands and knees, then down on to her stomach. She shunted herself forward, made herself flat enough to fit under the bed. When she was right in the heart of the dark dust-space, she closed her eyes. She would like proof that her mother was dead. Perhaps it was a lie? A trick. She would like to see a certificate of some sort or another, a stamped piece of paper, perhaps even the telegram? They had not shown her this. Her mother had been ill for a long time; she had not been particularly kind to Prue. She had slapped her, several times – many times – across the face. She had pulled her hair, ignored her for days, left her in rooms alone, not returning until hours later, but she also remembered moments of love, before she was ill, even afterwards. The long stories she told. Mermaids. Sea creatures. Lost sailors. Usually stories to do with voyages; the sea. Prue closed her eyes, touched a scab on her elbow and began to pick at the edge of it. For tea, often, they used to simply have a boiled egg and a slice of cake and her mother would say, 'Look at us. Tea, egg and cake.'

'Now,' Prue said to herself. 'Now you can cry.'

But she didn't. The scab was not quite ready; it stuck, wetly, in the middle. She scratched around the edge of it, eventually fell asleep.

She woke, but did not want to eat. She opened her knapsack and looked in her purse: just enough money for a film at the Zion Theatre.

Jerusalem at night was cold and still. The Zion Theatre was still playing *The Blue Bird*, a film that had been showing for as long as she had been here, and it was about halfway through but, still, the man in the ticket booth let her in, smiling as the *piastres* landed on his palm.

The Zion Theatre wasn't a real cinema. It was a large shed which her father had told her had been rented from the Armenian Orthodox Church and it was cold enough inside for her breath to make clouds. When she had seen the film previously it had been accompanied by musicians, but now all that could be heard was the squeaking wheel of the projection machine.

Prue sat down near the front, the only person in there. It was at the point in the film where the children had been trying to find the Blue Bird of Happiness and had reached the Land of the Unborn Children. Ghostly, floating children in white veils filled the screen. *We are waiting to be. We can't choose our fate.* It was difficult to tell the difference between the film and her thoughts. There was a girl in a theatre in Jerusalem watching a girl looking for the Blue Bird of Happiness. All the girls merged. Were any of them alive? Inside Eleanora was the beginning of life. What was it like? A little soul, like the ones on the screen, veiled ghosts, or was it like the first flicker of a candle wick immediately after being lit? Was it like the fireflies she chased one summer, running in long grass, crushing snail shells under her feet?

The theatre doors behind her opened and let in unwelcome cold air. Footsteps made their way along the wooden floor slowly and rhythmically. She tried to see who it was without obviously turning her head. A man wearing a hat, but not one of the large black Hasidic hats, the name of which she didn't yet know; nor was it a bowler like in London, it was something wider-rimmed.

And then: the man did it. An entire theatre to choose from, but he sat directly behind her. As close as it was possible to be. Smells of tobacco and meat and another familiar scent? Horses? Prue pushed ankles together; her toes were cold, he was breathing in thumps. The words on the screen said: Find the Soul inside Your Home. We are waiting to be. *We can't choose our fate. We are the unborn.* The man behind her leant forward, so that the combination of horses, the outside, man, grew closer. She lowered her chin. Looked very carefully, studiously, at the screen in front of her.

There were fingers on her neck: rough, calloused. She rubbed the leather tips of her court shoes on to the wooden-planked floor, body stiff. Tips of fingers at first, pressing, and the slide of a hand. He did not push hard, but his hand was so big that it covered much of her neck and he cupped the whole of it. Just for an instant. His breath touched the curled ridge of her ear which was exposed because she had tucked her hair behind her ears. Then the hand let go. Prue turned round. It was a wide-faced man, with a large bulging nose.

'A gift,' he said; he reeked of drink, she recognised that well enough from her father's parties: wine, cider, whisky. The acrid breath. In front of her face he dangled a wriggling, squirming pale brown mouse by its tail. It folded its body up, curled into a ball, its feet near-transparent pink.

'Would you like it?'

She nodded automatically and held out her palm. The man gently lowered the mouse on to her hand and as soon as it touched her skin it became calmer and sniffed the air, as if to see who might make the next move. It sat perfectly still as if under a bush, as if deep in a hole, listening to the outside world and making a decision not to venture out there.

'He's trained,' the man said; he had an accent. 'Watch.'

He pulled a peanut in its shell from his pocket and made a clicking noise with his mouth. The mouse immediately sat up, span around and raised itself up on its back two feet, its front feet in the air.

'I can't take him if he is yours, and trained,' Prue whispered, wanting it more than anything else in the world.

'Just make the clicking noise, feed him a peanut, and he will be your friend.'

The man stood up. From where she was sitting he looked as large as an oak tree. His hat was like a cowboy's. He rummaged in his pocket and pulled out the packet of nuts in a paper cone and gave them to her, tipped his hat, and then walked off towards the door. His boots were huge. He made her think of a Chinese emperor.

After he was gone, the mouse quivered and then was startlingly still, as if waiting for her to decide its fate. She considered her pockets. There were two in the pinafore on the front of her dress;

they would be big enough. She dropped the mouse into the left one, a little disturbed by its closeness but not wanting to let it go. A mouse from a Chinese emperor, a gift; and then she remembered, with an obscure feeling of guilt, that her mother had been frightened of mice.

Jerusalem, 1920

Eleanora pushed past him into his room and closed the door quickly behind her.

'Really, Willie, you look awful.' Her fur coat was covered in melting specks of snow. She pulled her gloves off and threw them on to his bed.

'What time is it?'

'Four in the morning,' she said, putting her purse on his desk.

That explained the odd dawn light. His room was all bed, all mirrors, angles. The stark reality of her in his room was like an obscenity. He could see her too clearly, but also it was as if she were disfigured. He sat up in bed and blinked at her.

'I can't work out who I'll be safe with,' she said, wilting on to his bed.

'Not many people can at this time in the morning. What the devil did the receptionist say when you walked in?'

'I just strode past. You should lock your door at night, you know.'

And then, as if those words were a tremendous exertion, she folded in on herself.

'Khaled?'

'He is in Jerusalem.'

Willie floundered around for his cigarettes. Found them, lit one. She had not taken the fur off. It was just like her to come, like this, in the night. It was a surprise, the irritation he felt. A contradiction, but there was an electricity to her that meant she would never be considered, rational. She would not wait until nine in the morning to drop in, for instance.

'What are you doing here then?'

She was standing at the end of his bed, looking at him, and it was only then that he realised she could see it all: the scar tissues, the contours and swirls and ridges that made mountain-range lumps, the dips. The mess of his body. He pulled the covers up to his chin.

'He's in Jerusalem,' she said, 'but he's not at home, I mean ... he came, but he went.'

'Where has he gone again?'

'He's obsessed, with this man, McLaughlin. He is photographing his actions; he says they are abominable. Which is all well and good, and I am sure that is true, but the thing is: he just keeps on leaving me.'

'Lofty,' Willie said.

She gave him a strange, hopeless look, then came closer to him and sat down on the bed. He smoked. Underneath the sheet his scars flared and he lurched inside with a nervous, nauseous feeling. She pulled the edge of the sheet down and touched the dead skin that covered his collarbone. It was an effort not to flinch and a bright truth in his mind slotted into a gap in the matter of his brain that had been waiting for it: he would never again be able to make love. It would not be possible to be touched again. He twisted away from her.

Her hand dropped and she flipped open her purse. 'Can I photograph your hands?' She pulled out a small camera.

'Well I don't see what that's going to achieve.' Her face was concentrated; she seemed to mean it. He saw that her hands were shaking as she fumbled with the clasp on the camera and a flicker of irritation filtered through him, to have been so caught off-guard. To be frank he would rather be asleep, or fucking her. He did not wish any part of him, in particular his skin, to be photographed.

'Please?' Her eyes were hooded, deep-set. As a child this had made her serious, as if always frowning. Now, it was more wistful. Her face looked quite red, uncomfortable; she had a hot uncertain air about her, but still she spoke as if she was offering him something. He understood that she was trying to be open to him, in her own way.

'If you like.' They were ugly enough to him.

'There. Put them on the table under the lamp.'

He laid his hands flat as directed and watched her face; she tried to smile at him when she met his eye, but the expression was more of a wince.

'Don't squash them,' she said. 'Arrange them as if they are naturally just there.'

A natural pose was difficult to maintain. Noises from deep in the hotel could be heard: kitchens waking up. She took ten, eleven and then twelve photographs until he said, 'Did you know when you were training with your husband that you would be taking photographs one day of another man's hands in the middle of the night?'

She paused, and lowered her head. He saw that her eyes were wet. He snatched his hands away from her.

'Well I suppose this brings things to a catalyst, rather?'

Then, out of nowhere, she said, 'I liked your father.' All the past came down on them like a lingering smell and he was inclined to throw the ashtray at her. He did not want to talk about his father. She sat there, on the edge of his bed, a sharp intense light around her, a crackling, and a bad twitch.

'I was always trying to run away from Pentrohobyn, do you remember?'

'Ellie,' he said. What he meant was *shut up*.

'You're a foolish idiot for coming here,' she said gently. He moved towards her and they sat next to one another on the bed, formally now, upright, looking like orphans deposited in a dormitory.

'Do you remember,' she said, her voice cracking, 'I can write backwards and forwards, equally with both left and right hands, and the nuns at my school thought I was a child of the devil for this skill?'

'Oh yes. I remember that now.'

'Well. Perhaps I am a devil after all. Those nuns were right?'

'I don't think so.' All the tension through his body was concentrated at a singular point in his temples; very soon it would – he knew – move deep into his ears and begin the torture.

Her hand pulled away. 'Khaled has other things on his mind. Revolutions, but it doesn't mean I don't love him.'

The dawn light ripened. Was she a magic-lantern image, of everything he wanted, but couldn't touch? He wanted to understand a definite thing about her. Might he ask if she was happy? Was she happy?

You can be happy with Rasul?

No: he would not ask that; why would a man ever ask a woman that? She didn't belong here, though. She needed to be in the vast Pentrohobyn, with its corners, its fallen rooms, its lofty arched ceilings, its leaking, peeling, struggling wooden beams, running and running from room to room in a dress.

'What kind of bloody man doesn't come home to his wife first and foremost?'

'He said that he is staying away to protect me, that he brings danger. He is not here long, then going again. It will all make sense, eventually, he said. And then, I'm sorry.'

They were both silent. Something in Willie throbbed, but he did not know if it was his heart or head or loins.

'Don't worry,' Willie said, 'because we can find a way to be together.'

'I can't see you again, you understand?'

They had both spoken at the same time. She looked at him and shook her head. Crack in the room, crack in the day, as if it was all just a scene in a painting and someone had slashed the canvas with a knife.

'Tell me, Eleanora. Why did you come here, to my room, tonight? To tell me you love him and don't want me?'

'I don't want this child,' she said, putting her hand on her stomach, 'and I don't want him to know.'

'Does he know how your mother died, Ellie?' And she turned quickly and stared at him, pushed a stray hair from her forehead. 'What I mean is,' the ears began, the moths in the ear canals, the tremulous bells, 'you could explain?'

What was this? He was helping her explain to Rasul? A wretched taste in his mouth. She shook her head.

'I don't understand any of it,' he said. 'Tell me, then.'

So she told him.

It went like this: the story of Eleanora Roberts and the famous Khaled Rasul. The unlikely love. Photograph the space. The thing that exists between earth and sky. That is what Khaled told her when they first worked together in the darkroom in Zürich. She had looked down towards earth, then up to the sky. How does the thing integrate into the sky? What is its relationship with the sky? Find how the light builds architecture.

Khaled taught her about light, layers, fragments. About keeping the shutter where it is, stepping into the picture, stepping out of it again, how to walk, to look, to keep walking and looking, to see the entrance and to look again at the entrance. Khaled Rasul was an enigma; this concentrated person, this self-taught photographer from a biblical place. *Nobody comes from Jerusalem. Who comes from Jerusalem?* She had, of course, seen pictures of the Holy City. It appeared to be an endless web of tunnels and arches, doorways and stairwells. Later, she understood his obsession with framing things.

'That isn't a real place, you can't be a real person,' she said.

'It is a real place and I am from there,' he said.

As well as teaching her about light he taught her how to waltz. They danced in a club called the Dead Cat, as if he didn't come from Jerusalem, as if she didn't come from Wales. Pentrohobyn, to be exact. He said it like a dream, a mystical otherness, as far from the desert as it is possible to get. Rain, clouds, the flint and the chop. Ferns. Clay and limestone. 'How magical,' he said.

'But I'm not really Welsh,' she explained. 'My family are English but live in Wales. So the Welsh hate us. The English hate us. We are in-betweeners, but we own a lot of land there.'

'Let's waltz, and not think about land?'

'Let's do that.'

Khaled worked for his photography master, Keller, who was employed by Louise-Elisabeth de Meuron to take photographs for Eleanora's father of Amsoldingen Castle. Its curves, its cellars, its garden were all of a style that her father craved for Pentrohobyn Hall. When she had heard of this project she begged to be allowed to go, to learn a little about photography. Her father was *sick of her*. He walked out of the room when she came in. He was appalled at her refusing the debutante balls. She assumed he would say no.

'These are not the times to travel.'

'Switzerland is neutral.'

In the end, her father had agreed, but only because his brother was travelling there, and because he was exhausted with thinking about the problem of her and, yes, it might be better for everyone if she went to Switzerland.

The journey was uncomfortable. Awkward for both Eleanora and the resentful uncle who had not welcomed the company. He deposited her at Zürich and she was left to become the assistant's assistant. Keller couldn't stand photographing Swiss castles. He would rather be photographing soldiers. A war was coming. It made him sick to be photographing crumbling castles. Madame de Meuron made him sick.

Eleanora sat on Willie's bed as she told him this story, speaking into the air between them. He tucked the sheet around him further to cover his flawed, revolting body. On the wall opposite, a framed illustration of a series of medicinal plants native to Palestine. *Inula viscosa. Foeniculum vulgare. Urginea maritima.* He stared at them, to avoid roaring.

'And you were gone, Willie. To fly. Off to Greece, or other places.'

'To war, Ellie.'

'Well. Yes.'

What he felt as she spoke was: a terribly empty, hollow feeling. An inside-out undoing.

She continued:

Eleanora Roberts and Khaled Rasul waltzed at the cabaret and drank most evenings with a mime artist who was often accompanied by an odd woman who claimed to make love to parrots. By this time, military officers moved in lines with beautiful women in their arms. They danced, sang, drank jugs of beer. Eleanora picked up a button she saw fall from an officer's coat sleeve once and put it in her pocket. When the third of their friends, a painter called Stael, and his model were both killed in an unexplained incident near their studio, Eleanora said, 'Can we go to Jerusalem now, to the house you told me about? The one that your family have owned for generations and generations?'

Khaled said, 'Maybe, maybe soon.'

He tried to convince her to come dancing with the parrot lady who lived in the same building as him, who kept summoning him down at midnight. 'Come down,' she would say, and Khaled always went to her as if towards a magnetic pull. 'Let's drink.' He hadn't drunk under the Turks in Jerusalem, he hadn't drunk all his life and so he was making up for it now.

'Why not come dancing?' he asked Eleanora.

'I don't like the soldiers. I don't feel safe.'

Zürich is neutral. They said it again and again. As neutral as Wales.

'What would make you feel safe, Eleanora?'

'That you will love me for ever, that I have enough food, though I will remain thin, that I am in a library surrounded by books, the pages are curled and the ceiling is covered with maps, the blue lines on the maps link from one page to the other and there is no separation, no end to all the countries and connections in the world, and men in overcoats following orders they don't agree with will not kill tiny children.'

Khaled had looked strangely at her and then he had laughed.

'I don't want to bring children into a world where soldiers kill them.'

Khaled continued to look at her, with his odd expression, as if trying to understand what language she was speaking, even though, as he told her so many times, with his secular education at one of Jerusalem's best schools he spoke English better than the English.

'Also, I don't trust the parrot lady. There is something about her shoes, they are boots. Men's boots.'

Khaled continued to leave at midnight, disappearing through the door, moving, slipping out slowly and then running down the wooden stairs, but then one night he came home and fell headlong on to the bed. His face was swollen; she crouched over him to examine his cheek. When her finger touched his skin he groaned. This was when he'd said: 'It is time to leave. I have a letter from my aunt's cousin. She has died; the house then, despite the family moaning about it, is mine. It is full of cousins and uncles and family but he will remove them, and it will be for us, if we want it. Our own studio. I will not be conscripted if I am married to you.'

'Oh, let's go, let's go.' Because the officers who danced scared her now. The one who had dropped his button made a point of catching her eye.

'Yes. We'll go to Jerusalem, but first we must marry.'

That was how she explained it. Willie lit a cigarette. Her face was hovering in front of him. Her skin pale and bloodless and it occurred to him that she always looked like a daughter in a state of mourning.

There was a night, Eleanora continued, in the room of one of the artists on the run from the front line; several men, many of them French, an aristocratic French prince of something or other, Poles, Lithuanians, Hungarians, and lying on the sofa in the centre of them all was a young woman from Skopje. The men were taking it in turns to stroke her ankle with just one finger. First an elderly Frenchman, his knees snapping as he crouched down, and then a younger man, an Austrian with a bald head and pointed beard. Eleanora sat and watched; the girl's face remained still. She was older than Eleanora but not by much, perhaps twenty years old, and of a higher social class than all of the men. She was unmoved, if her face were to be read.

Eleanora had leant towards Khaled and said, 'That would be a photograph.'

'I was thinking the same thing.'

'I hear you are going to Jerusalem,' the woman from Skopje said, her thin voice rising from the heart of the chaise-longue.

'Yes.'

'I too have been promised rooms there. On Saint Francis Street. I feel the breath of war on our necks here.'

'Then we shall be neighbours,' said Khaled.

Eleanora finished her story. Her hand was resting on her stomach. 'And now we are here.' Was that the end? Where did she go from there? He looked at her, and then down at her hand. They were silent. Then she made an exasperated noise.

'I need your help,' she said, staring at him with red eyes. 'You are the only person I can talk to about this, it is terribly *haram*. I've tried all the usual things: jumping off the bed, steamed onions.'

Reeling, dying inside from the story of how she fell in love with a photographer from Jerusalem, Willie didn't know what she was talking about.

'If I have this baby I will die,' she said simply.

'You don't know that. Just because of your ...'

'I do.'

The whistling in Willie's head changed tempo, became more of a thud.

'I'm sure there are potions, but how do I get them here? Mohammedan doctors? Can you imagine?'

It finally unravelled in his mind what she was talking about.

'Darling Willie,' she took his hand. 'You have to help.'

'What? I don't have the remotest idea how to.'

She took off her fur coat. The blue dress she was wearing underneath had buttons along its front. She stood next to the bed and looked down at him. Underneath the sheet, the dead tortured skin on him came alive: nerve endings forcing their way through. With shaking fingers, she began to undo the buttons above her navel. She opened five or six and revealed the pure white area of her delicate stomach.

'You need to hit me here, as hard as you can, as terribly as you can. I am so sorry to ask, I know it's dreadful, but you can do it for me.'

The sinking inside him was exactly that of realising the cockpit is on fire; that he himself was on fire.

'I'm sorry?'

'It's the only solution I can think of.'

All the days of their lives strung together like beads on a wire, entwined. This was something entirely different.

'I'm not sure I understand.'

She said nothing.

'Eleanora, I absolutely refuse, I just ...'

She did not move; her hand hovered in front of the fabric of her dress as if she were showing him a wound of her own to match his scars, but all he could see was the skin he had thought about all his life. She looked like a statue, apart from her shaking bottom lip.

'You are my only hope, the only possible solution.'

'It's not possible. I just couldn't. I couldn't.'

'I know. I know, darling, but I am asking you, it is the only time in my whole life I will ask you to do something like this for me. I am begging you.' Her face, high up at the top of the syca- more tree all those years ago; the soft cry she made when she pushed herself back and allowed herself to fly.

'I need to think about it,' he said, sinking backwards into the bed. Wishing he could continue to fall.

Shoreham, 1937

Billy is standing in front of me, speaking, but I can't hear the words. All I can think of is Skip crouched over his starfish.

I forced him to leave his father. I did that. I packed the clothes into the little brown suitcase, told him that his toys would follow, in a trunk. That was a lie. I stole him, bundled like a package, away from Nanny Jones, who loved him. Loves him. Away from Piers, who loved him. Loves him, and I thought I had enough love to fill the places of all these people?

Billy, with his large fat fingers, tugs me out of the rain and into Alfred Snelling's front room. The butcher himself emerges from the back of the house, his apron covered in blood-red finger marks and purple smears.

'You're a pretty sight,' he says. At first I think he is talking about me, but he is looking at Billy's bashed-up face. I turn, to have another look at the damage: my fault. The right eye got the worst of it, swollen, purple-black, and when he manages to open the eyelids, inside the eyeball is scarlet.

'Who did it?'

As Billy tells Mr Snelling the story, I see in my mind the image of a seagull, black-eyed and devious, picking at Skip, tugging his cardigan with its beak, using its feet to pick him up and fly away, the opposite of a stork: a child-stealer rather than a baby-deliverer.

'Listen, Prue, what does he want?' Both men look at me.

I cough, and then answer. 'He had a few more questions, and then he was after papers relating to an old friend of mine, a photograph in there.'

'A friend?' I remember now that Billy had mentioned a ministry. A Ministry of what? Information? Intelligence? Mr Snelling, who hasn't invited us to sit down, goes to his rocking chair and flops into it while we both stand, bowing, as if the ceiling is lower than it actually is. There is a line of framed photographs along the mantelpiece, all droopy-eyed dogs apart from one at the end which I guess is a freshly married Mr and Mrs Snelling: him looking pinched and spivvy, her face apprehensive, as if worrying about the conjugal night to come.

'Will he be back?' Mr Snelling says. 'That's the question.' They send a signal to one another, a masculine code which I try to read: we'll get him. Revenge will be ours. That sort of talk. As foolish as it might be to build a home out of sticks on a windy beach, I realise now that it might be even stupider to seek out a safe haven in bed with a man who smashes up bodies for a living.

'Prue?' Billy says.

I jump as if pinched.

'Oh God, Skip. I don't think I should have left him today, I'd better go back to Cecilia.' I push my way towards the door, just as Mrs Snelling comes in with a plate of scones. *Sorry. Sorry.* Outside, I squint into the Shoreham sky. Run over to my bicycle, Billy is calling from Mr Snelling's door, but I don't listen. I give him a wave. Fly away.

I cycle as fast as I can over the bridge. The river below is a silver path and further along the banks of the Adur terraced houses peter into sheds and makeshift lean-tos for horses. The air smells very strongly of salt and I try to remember what Skip has told me about his perambulations, the roaming and exploring I have allowed him to do. The tide is low; my fingers on the handlebars are numb.

Hair in my eyes, the rain has finally stopped. I cycle towards Cecilia which sits like a gingerbread house by the sea being nibbled by beach mice. He is not on the veranda and why would he be? Sitting there like a boy in a storybook, waiting for me to come back? A bucket full of starfish gasping their last breath. I throw the bicycle on to the ground, panting a little from the exertion of pedalling. I put my hand on my chest and wonder at the choice I made, coming here with Skip. All the stack of twiggy choices, piling up together, making kindle wood, useless moves in life. Pointless. Dry old sticks. Every day adding up to be good for nothing, apart from setting on fire. Turning to smoke.

In Cecilia the blanket from Skip's cot-bed is on the floor. The perfect white balls of chalk that he spends hours arranging and rearranging into specific constellations in front of the wood burner are in position. I pick up Mrs Deal's long-ago-drained teacup. Put it down again. Skip is often out alone. No need to worry. Really, it is no different to any other day when I banish him to play, to roam, to do whatever he does, to fill up his hours until I have finished working. Yet the feeling is there; a mother's instinct if one believed in such a thing. I open the door and stand again on the veranda. The light from the sea is glaring, harsh, as if actively wanting to inflict eye-trouble and slices of headaches. There are children on the beach, further down towards the shoreline, huddled together by the chalk boulders, and I run towards them. The crunching of my feet on shingle alerts them to me while I am still quite a distance away and they spring up like puppies on defence, watching out. They are poking sticks into a found-thing, but Skip is not with them, I see that at once. They all look up. Three wild boys and one scraggy-haired girl, guilty as cats caught scavenging in a bin.

'Have you seen my boy?' They flinch and lean together to hide whatever it is behind them and shake their heads, saying nothing. I glance away from them, along the beach. The clouds in the sky are low and heavy-looking.

'He was collecting starfish, in a bucket.'

'We dipped him.' It is Walter, and I step closer, crouch down to see him properly. He seems surprised at this sudden concentrated attention and his lip curls a little, his head pulls back away from me, the wind takes his light brown curls and flaps them about his face. It is not hard to see the combined traces of Billy in his eyes and the straggle-haired woman full of cider in the club. He is the same age as Skip. I suspect he's not the only one of the children of Shoreham who has had a go at damaging my son.

'When?'

'That was yesterday,' the girl says, the eldest-looking one, and she – I can tell accurately now – has the freckles of the woman but not the sharp jaw of Billy. It has clearly been a while since any of them have seen a facecloth. 'Today, I mean. Have you seen Skip today?' They shake their heads, the whites of their eyes bright. I can see they are lying, or hiding something.

'What is that, behind you?'

'Nothing.'

The wind comes up, and carries a rancid smell. I push the girl out of the way and they all spring backwards as if connected. In a gap between the chalk boulders there is a coil of grey matter and for a moment I think it is Skip, crushed like a crab, but then I see that it is a baby seal cub, its face half-eaten and pecked by gulls and the chalk beneath the blubber of it stained pink. So he was right, seals can be found here.

I turn from the children and look inland, ignoring their whispers and sniggers behind me, ignoring the narrow-eyed stare of the eldest girl who has the most fearless expression of all. I look down again at the seal cub and jump backwards. Something is eating it, from the inside; its skin swells outwards.

'Well, if you see him can you tell him I'm looking for him please?'

I tramp back across the shingle and pause for a moment, looking up towards the row of seaside chalets and the railway carriages. I call him again, but the wind simply gives his name to the sea. There is a sting, on the back of my head. I turn; another sting on my cheek. They are pelting me, with sharp pieces of flint. A shower of them now and I put my arm over my face, move backwards, the little stinging flicks against my ear, against my neck, vicious and horrible.

Up on the higher shingle path Billy is sheltering his eyes and looking in my direction. He must have followed me. He waves, beckons, and I think of mermaids and of sailors gone awry following the wrong signal. I run towards him, the boxer. He touches the blood on my face. 'What's this?'

'Your son, Walter.'

Billy's eyes widen a little at the words *your son*, and then he looks down the beach at the cluster of children.

'The naughty little blighter,' he says, but I shake my head.

'It's all right.' I want to say: *you don't have to explain anything to me, Billy.*

'I can't see Skip.' I put it lightly, and turn a circle on the shingle, as if to prove that my son is not in any direction. Then the shadows of Billy's face change and I realise what he is going to say. I think of the shilling Harrington gave to Skip. I shake my head, look all around as if another person might come out of the mist and put a stop to bad thoughts. Listen! I want to shout at him. He will be close by. Billy looks at the sea, as if he is listening for a particular sound, but it's not there. He can't hear it, and neither can I.

'I'm sure he's close by,' he says. His tone not convincing.

I stand on tiptoe, my ankle wavers on the unsteady stones. 'Skip,' I shout into the beach air. My hands drop by my sides.

Mrs Deal is walking along the shingle path, and has turned towards us with a concerned look.

'Mrs Deal,' I say. 'Oh Mrs Deal, have you seen Skip?' She picks her way across the stones and the sea cabbage and squints towards the sea, glances up to the heavens. When she reaches us her eyes widen at Billy's wreck of a face. She shakes her head.

'There's a policeman waiting for you at Cecilia,' she says. 'I thought I'd better come and find you.'

'Police?' Billy tenses, being the kind of man who avoids the police if at all possible. I move forwards quickly, but there is a rush of blood in my head. I have always been apt to lose my breath and fall out of my body, to faint at unfortunate moments. I've always thought it is a preservation technique: I'm not sure I want to be here, I shall tip myself away, blur myself out, but right now I do not want blackness, I want to be clear, and present. Billy takes my hand and the rough touch of it brings me back. It is impossible to run very fast on a slope of pebbles; together we move slowly away from the sea.

A policeman in his smart helmet and boots is standing next to the wall along the edge of Kangaroo, the bungalow next door. When he sees us coming he stands up straight. He addresses Billy instead of me.

'Afternoon.'

We all wait in a row, an unnatural group, looking at one another.

'Is it Skip?' I say. The policeman tilts his head at me and then gestures to the door of Cecilia. 'Is this your house?'

'Yes, come in.'

Inside the small space we all awkwardly try to arrange ourselves around the corners of my bed and table. There is a slippage in time, it seems. This day isn't proceeding as it should. I see in my mind Skip, ducking my blown kiss as if avoiding a dart and running on to the beach in ragged clothes. Was that this morning? Another day? Looking like a nomad, like a gypsy child. When did I stop dressing him properly? But I already know the answer: it was when Nanny Jones stopped dressing him for me. One of our first nights here I took Skip out on to the beach to see the shooting stars; it was the end of August. He crouched next to me, scrunched his feet in the pebbles, and took it very seriously. He did not speak and stared up at the sky. *You're breathing too loud, Mummy, I can't hear the stars.*

They are all looking at me. Mrs Deal, Billy, the policeman.

'A message has been sent for you.'

'What?'

The policeman steps forward as if he's about to deliver a lecture.

'We just received a phone call at the station saying you are to come to the aerodrome immediately.'

'What?' I say again.

'Is it the journalist man?'

The policeman shakes his head. 'Nope. Actually, it's an instruction from London. Government officials. You are to be escorted to the aerodrome and the message is, and this I confess I don't know what it means so I hope you do, "bring what has been previously requested".' And then the policeman shrugs again. 'All I can say is, it comes from *high*.'

'High?' Mrs Deal says, scoffing, as if she can't remotely take him seriously.

'They are sending a man down, he should get here on the four thirty-six, we'll have a car waiting for him. He's coming to meet you, Mrs Miller.'

They all look at me, and I have finally got the breath in my lungs and throat to quieten down, but a new, different sort of gulping for air is rising up in me.

'Is Skip at the aerodrome?'

The policeman looks confused. 'Skip?'

'My son?'

The policeman reads through his notes. 'I'm sorry, madam, I don't know anything about your son.'

Billy takes my hand. 'My guess is, he'll be there.'

'Taken, you mean?'

'I don't know.'

Skip and I often go up the hill together and look at the roofs of the hangars and the airfield behind. There you can see the tips of the wings of some of the parked planes that were fighters in the war but are now used for joyrides to Hastings or Lydd. Skip has always been obsessed with aeroplanes. He makes them from paper, from wood, from sticks. He flies them, he crashes them, and he dreams about them, he draws them. Yes, I think. It would not have been difficult for Harrington to convince Skip to join him at the aerodrome, where it is always chilly, where the field is prone to flooding.

'But what is it you are supposed to bring?' Billy asks, as if I understand why this is happening. As if the holes I used to make in wax, when I was first learning to sculpt, the finger-poked spaces inside the creamy substance, somehow provided a gap-space that linked one part of my life with another. I glance over to the little bureau which rests against one of the remaining original carriage panels. On it is the Hotel Fast photograph. Mrs Deal, in her bright clear voice, takes over.

'I suggest this,' she says. 'I stay here with Prudence and help her find whatever it is this man, or the Ministry, wants. You gentlemen wait outside until we are ready to leave?'

'No,' I say. 'We should go straight to the aerodrome and find Skip.'

The policeman flaps his notes in the air. 'It does seem important. Whatever it is you are supposed to bring.'

'I don't care about that,' I say, turning to Billy for support, but Billy is agreeing with the policeman, I can tell from the expression on his face. Even Mrs Deal concurs.

They go out, closing the door gently, and the sea behind them is still there, even though Skip is not, and I can hear Mrs Deal rocking on her heels, moving herself forwards and backwards like the tide. I turn quickly to her. 'I'm just going to grab anything, Mrs Deal. I need to find Skip.'

I go to the wardrobe-trunk where I keep my suitcase full of papers. I can hear her thinking what to say to me, rubbing her dry, weathered hands together. There have been many times in my life when I have looked at the disarray around me and wished, truly wished, I could keep my own affairs in order. Even my sketchbooks and notebooks which are very precious to me are in a muddle, many of them lost.

'Do you think this fellow will have taken Skip roughly, or just talked him into wandering off?' Mrs Deal says gently, still with that dry hand-rubbing, still moving backwards and forwards on her heels.

'I don't know.' It is as though there is a hand around my throat, squeezing. *A bloody shilling, Mummy.* 'I suspect he went along with him happily.'

'Really?'

'I have a feeling he would go anywhere with him if he offered him a coin or two.'

Mrs Deal stands uncertainly near the door.

'Perhaps he's angry with me?' I say. She doesn't answer, because she is Mrs Deal. She is tactful, thoughtful, aware.

I haul the ancient, battered suitcase from the back of the wardrobe-trunk. It is a repository for all the paper of my life and I am appalled at the chaos of it, the disorder of it. I am the only person I know who lives like this. Even Marguerite once showed me her photographs of statues she had taken over twelve years and they were beautifully filed: an angel in Berlin; *Victory Horse*; Rome; Giuseppe Verdi; *Head of a Girl*; Gore Hotel, London ... all neatly dated and logged. It was odd how her delicate handwriting did not connect at all with the unhinged look in her eye. I heave the suitcase on to the table.

'The past weighs a lot, Mrs Deal,' I say, not sure whether I am making a joke or not. Mrs Deal is now quietly tidying, picking up Skip's clothes from the floor, and if she replies I don't hear it.

I do not enjoy looking at artefacts from my life. Old letters make me sad. Photographs are worse. Inside the suitcase is a tumble of matter from my past and the first thing I pull out is a black, rectangular photograph album. On its front I have written SKIP – *FROM LIFE*, my brief attempt at photo-documenting him as mothers should, an experiment that lasted six months.

A photograph of Skip and Piers sitting in front of a pair of beach huts; a seaside holiday when Skip was about three years old. They aren't touching but they are mirroring each other, toes poked under sand, chins tipped.

'I shouldn't have made him leave Piers,' I whisper. Discreet Mrs Deal pushes the broken chair under the unwashed table.

When Skip was not quite walking, but dragging himself up on chair legs, I had no choice but to bring him into the studio with me on Nanny's days off. I was carving with wood. Teak. Carving was the only time I was happy, trite as that sounds. The studio was full of scraps of materials, and mess. Unlike the rooms that Piers chose to occupy which were empty and austere (producing nothing, it turns out). As Skip grew bigger I found every opportunity to pass him over to anyone who would have him, but there were times when there was no choice; I couldn't find a stranger's arms to put him in so I would put him under the table. Leave him to play. One day he tugged at a cloth and pulled it and a sculpture called *Form*, made from crisp, pure white marble, fell and shattered.

I shouted at him. He wasn't yet two. Fat little wrists, rolls of skin under the chin. He took refuge under the table, his eyes uncertain, but then he was convinced it was a game and began peeking out at me, peepo-ing. He found a small mallet and threw it at my toe. I pulled him out, my body red and snapping; I held him by the top of his arms, gripping him, and screamed at his little moon-face. I smacked him with my palm, and then I kept hitting him, so that he was crying harder. I hit him perhaps three, four times in all.

He crawled away from me and curled up under the table, crying to himself, sucking his thumb. I went back to the carving I had been working on. There was a rushing noise in my head, loud enough to cover up the noise of him, like the sea, like a tidal shift. I was made of stone myself. I had no remorse, and then there was a crash. I turned. Skip had crawled out again and pulled a dust cover from the tabletop and on it a box of nails had fallen. A cascade of sharp little nails. Red marks all over his skin where the points had landed, had poked in and fallen off.

Mrs Deal behind me coughs. I flick through the loose photographs, the letters, the envelopes, and the detritus. There is a jumble of photographs below the album and I pull out one that is printed in a larger format. It is a portrait of me, aged seventeen I think, sitting on a chair. I don't look very comfortable. I push it back down towards the bottom of the suitcase. There is a note from Marguerite – *Dearie, dearie, might you wear diamond earrings and tinted ostrich feathers tonight* – and then I find it: the pink Jerusalem envelope. I grab it. What's in there? Photographs, a few letters, the smell of the past. I don't care: he can have it, this man. I grab the Hotel Fast photograph too.

'Oh, Mrs Deal, I've got it. Let's go?' I already have my trench coat pulled around my shoulders. I tighten the belt, as if trapping myself in, and knot it.

'Good, good,' she says behind me.

As we step outside Billy and the policeman in his bobby's helmet and shiny buttons are smoking cigarettes, deep in conversation. A waxy black police car is parked further along the road and the ladies in Kangaroo are peeping and pointing at us. There is an odd feeling to the weather, as if energy is being gathered and drawn upwards from the sea into the sky. The policeman beckons us towards the car.

From the back seat I can see Billy has a ladder of moles along his neck that I have not particularly noticed before. I look out of the window for Skip but there is just an empty beach. Far out at sea it is possible to see a fret gathering and the feeling of Skip not being with me, right next to me, in my sightline, or with a part of him touching me, is like a belt tightening around my stomach.

It does not take long to drive to the aerodrome. Billy jumps out of the car before I can even move, runs around and opens my door as if he is a chauffeur. His bruises look dramatic in the clarity of the strange, bright light. He takes hold of my hand, and I'm grateful, because the fainting sensation is here again.

'That fret will stop any flying at least,' the policeman says. I look up at the sky. It is grey, the clouds low. The part of my palm that touches Skip when he is asleep in my bed burns.

Jerusalem, 1920

The lift was stuck, as it frequently was, wedged on the ground floor, and so instead of waiting Prue ran to the stairs. She wanted not to be in this building but out in the snow, although she was not dressed for it. As she rounded the final curve of the stairwell she stumbled into the back of a person who was sitting directly in the middle of the stairs. They were propelled forwards together, fast, so that she barely realised what was happening, and crumpled in a heap on a small landing. Prue's hair was around her face. There was a snort of alien breath on her skin.

'Oh I am so terribly sorry,' she said into the shoulder of the person wrapped around her, and that person unpicked himself and she saw that it was the concertina player who had tried to warn her, the other week, about the grenade.

He pulled himself upright, shook his head and groaned. He was tall, very skinny. Scattered all over the stone stairs in front of them were tiny green felt circles, and buttons, spikes of wood and pins. It was the inside of his concertina. The main body of the instrument case had fallen a few steps down.

'I am so awfully sorry,' she said again.

'Don't worry,' he said in English, but with a strong accent. 'I was repairing it, you know. I should probably have done it in a more sensible place.' He hopped down several steps and picked up the instrument case, peered at it. He stretched the bellows, held it to the light, ran his finger along the edge of the wooden case and blew into the bellows. Then held it all up to the light again. Prue helped him gather up the fragments that had spilled all around them, keys and pins; she did what she could, cupping her hand into a hollow and filling her palm with shapes that were like pieces from a puzzle.

'Is it ruined for ever?' She couldn't bear to look at it.

'Working instruments are always being patched up; they have long complicated lives, don't worry.' But his expression was a sad one. 'I have another one I can use tonight. Not as nice as this, but it will do.' He introduced himself. His name was Jacob Slonimski; he already knew her name, and that she was Charles Ashton's daughter.

'We've met before,' he said and she nodded, remembering his arm on hers behind the curtains. She blushed. He was silent, then, for such a while that she asked, rather desperately, 'Have you been a musician for a long time?'

He shook his head. 'To tell you the truth, I only learnt to play the concertina three years ago. When people don't like you and they chase you from everywhere, it's helpful to give them something they can recognise, or feel comfortable with. You know? A fiddle. A concertina.' He gave her a wry smile. It was always this way, here, she felt; she was always just one step behind what everyone else was referring to.

'Were you in a rush somewhere?' he said.

'Not really.' She pressed herself against the wall. Somewhere above them a door slammed.

'Prudence, I have something to say but you must keep it to yourself.' He was a few steps below her now so that they were almost the same height.

She nodded.

'It wasn't me who threw that grenade at the Pro-Jerusalem Society meeting, you understand?'

'Yes.'

'I just ... I knew it was happening and I wanted to warn you.'

His eyes were the same brown as a feather she once picked up and kept for days and days until it went the way of all feathers, stringy. Was he a person who wanted to kill her father? She now knew the word death in Arabic, Turkish, Spanish, and could write it in shifra, but what about the word kill? She didn't know that word in any language other than her own.

'Do you like living here in this hotel?' he said.

Why did people keep asking her this when she obviously had no choice? She replied honestly, 'I don't know.'

He scratched his chin. 'My advice, not that you are asking for it, but still, is never to put your faith in a house, or a hotel for that matter.'

She did not know what to say.

'Any building, I mean. They are all flimsy. We stuff them up with furniture and cupboards and rugs but they end up as dust, blown away.'

'Yes,' Prue said, trying to make her face look as if she understood because she half-thought she did. 'I can see that.'

They smiled at each other.

'Where do your family live, Mr Slonimski?' She became confused, self-conscious. 'Um, I mean, Herr Slonimski?'

He nodded. 'From a small town near a mountain but my family are no longer there.'

'Where are they now?'

'They went for a long walk through a forest but they had to keep going because a fire exploded and created a wall which meant they couldn't get back that way. So, since then, they have been trying to get back, but have had to go the long, long way round and it will take years.'

He was playing a game with her, she was sure, but his face looked serious.

'Do they send you telegrams?'

'No,' he said. 'But we have a clever trick where we can talk to each other while we are asleep in our dreams, so I can say, "Grandfather, are you well on that furthermost part of the forest, unable to get back?" And he can say, "I've been better, Jacob, but I've also been worse."'

'It sounds like a fairy tale,' Prue said and Jacob Slonimski rubbed his fingers along the concertina bellows and made them breathe in and out once as if letting out a sigh. She was still holding bits of broken musical instrument in her hand and she offered them to him and tipped them into his palm.

'Goodbye, Prudence Ashton,' he said. She waved, but he couldn't, his arms full of concertina. He continued downstairs as she went back up. As soon as he had gone she wished very much that she had thought of better things to say to him, talked to him more, and then she saw that she was back in the carpeted corridor she had just been trying to escape from. Defeated, she suddenly remembered that she had been requested at dinner and needed to go and dress.

———

Prue and Frau Baum were alone at the dinner table. They were in the largest restaurant in the Hotel Fast and Prue preferred the smaller, less stuffy one. She made friends with the restaurant kitten, letting it pat at the laces on her shoes, and looked over the table at Frau Baum's hands. She had rings on a finger of each of her hands that were made from something yellow that looked like a camel's eye. Prue kicked her foot and shook off the kitten.

'Do you have any news on Canon Brown's villa?' Prue said, picking up a spoon and looking serious, pretending to be a grown-up.

'Ah that. I wouldn't count on that.'

'Oh, why?' Secretly, under her blankets, Prue had invested a lot of time in imagining this villa, sketching what it looked like, dreaming of its doors and windows.

'Well, there are a lot of questions about who owns it. The Church pays a subsidiary rent to a Mr Platzer but he in turn pays a nominal rent to a wealthy Arab, El Hassan, who has a number of houses in that area of Lifta. It is very complicated.'

'Well,' said Prue, grateful for being spoken to as if she were an actual person, but at the same time nearly knocking over the glass next to her napkin, 'can't we just pay the rent required?'

'Alas not. There is an argument. The actual inheritance of that part of land belongs to one family but it is disputed because the old grandfather, despairing of his sons and grandsons fighting, has left the *wiq al fad* to the sisters. The law, however, states they are not eligible to own it and the canon is supposed to use it, but he doesn't, and so it goes on.'

'Why can't we live in another villa then? Must it be that one?'

'Not really my dear,' said Frau Baum. 'The Church that Canon Brown represents has an agreement with the British military that, in payment for another piece of land they have built a small church on, the civic adviser – your father – can use this as his home.'

The restaurant kitten, forgiving Prue for her change of heart, tapped her ankle for attention, and the waiter leant over and asked if they would like more drinks. Frau Baum shook her head.

'Besides, it is very charming. There is something special about that house. We visited it before you came.'

Frau Baum was trying very hard to be kind to Prue, she could tell, but for some reason Prue found it difficult to respond to her dryness and could not bring herself to call her Elspeth. Frau Baum looked towards the restaurant windows and was no longer seeing Prue. She was quite a mystery. Had she been married once? Before the war? Was she a widow, or a divorcee? What did Prue know about her? Only that she went on walks up into the hills beyond Jerusalem, moving stones around and analysing them, rummaging in dust, hunting down ancient pots, and that she liked to wear hats with black feathers sticking out of them. That was the sum of it. She was not glamorous, like Eleanora, and she had stolen Prue's father. She was not Eleanora, or her mother. It was simply that, perhaps.

'Ah ha,' said Frau Baum with obvious relief, 'they have arrived.'

'Darling,' Ashton declared, although it was not clear which one of them he was speaking to, 'so sorry we are late.'

He was not alone; there was an unknown man with him. Tall, balding, a clipped moustache.

'Prudence, this is Mr Wicklow, British Intelligence.' The man scraped his chair backwards. Beneath the odd bristle of his moustache, his teeth were very white and sharp-looking and there was an awkward moment when he should really have said something amusing, but failed to.

'Prudence has just been asking me about Canon Brown's house,' Frau Baum said, looking significantly at Ashton as the two men arranged themselves in their seats.

'Yes, where the bloody hell is he? He's buggered off into the interior with the keys to our house.' Ashton summoned the waiter and made a business of ordering the food.

Prue let the words dissolve around her. Why was she here, exactly? In this room, at this table? She had an odd feeling of floating. *It's always marvellous having dinner with Wicklow. He knows who every damn person in the room is.* Perhaps the things that were real – a garden in that grey place by the sea surrounded by stones when she was very small; a mother who sat on the piano stool and played alongside you – were not in the end real? *Well I know the notables. That blond man over there is Monty Parker. Old Etonian, son of a Cabinet minister in Gladstone's last government.* Prue looked under the table for the kitten. It seemed important to find it, but it had given up on her. *He's a flaming idiot. He is staying with a French couple, Roux and his wife, but do you see the man standing by the bar? He has been working for many years on the Book of Ezekiel. He has convinced Parker to help him find a cipher. He is extracting funds that Parker is bringing in from London. It's a tremendous con. Everyone knows apart from Parker who is panning all of his friends in London for the readies.* Her hands beneath her thighs were going numb.

Prue glanced up: through the arched entrance to the restaurant she saw Eleanora, hovering. Holding her fur in her hand, wearing a sleeveless piqué dress in a filmy coffee-colour that looked much too flimsy for the weather, and there he was: Khaled Rasul, next to her. Had she found the photograph on the stairs? Prue's hands were on fire beneath her thighs but she did not move them. She trained her eyes on Eleanora and Khaled as they moved slowly towards the table, Eleanora with a bright false smile, not noticing Prue. The whole world looked over at them: all the men in the restaurant, all the waiters behind the bar, the ladies being helped to their seats.

'Good evening,' Eleanora said. Her lips red, her neck decorated with a black choker.

Prue's father stood up and shouted, 'Rasul. What an unexpected but thoroughly wonderful surprise.'

Everyone was introduced to Wicklow who stood up and shook hands with Rasul and Eleanora. There was much clapping of shoulders. Rasul himself was collected, polite, Prue noticed; it was the Englishmen who were frothing over him. Prue slid herself lower in her chair and watched. Khaled looked like a king staring down at visitors from far-off lands. He was laughing in his eyes, Prue thought, and even though he was silent it was interesting to see the way the men – her father included – all turned continually towards him, directed all of their conversation and questions his way. She willed him not to look at her, and then of course he did. She slipped even further down in the chair, crossing her fingers under the table, hoping that he would not say anything to her father about the Al-Muntada meeting. Would he mention the photograph – the dead children, the broom, presumably used to roll dead children's bodies away? He had asked her to give the photograph to her father, and here he was, but Eleanora was tugging his arm and he turned away from Prue. Eleanora wanted the attention of the assembled company.

'Tomorrow I will be joining the American Colony photography department to take a new photograph of the bulrushes psalm. Would you all come? Make a day of it?'

Frau Baum interjected, 'Is that near Lifta?'

'Yes, I think so.'

'We've just been talking about that village. You could come too, Prue?'

Finally, the villa; she would see it.

'Oh yes please,' Prue said. She released her hands finally and lifted them up towards Eleanora, who was looking down at her with strange eyes. *The colour of water.*

'I would rather Prue did not come,' Eleanora said.

And it was Frau Baum who piped up: 'Surely it would be a shame to leave her out of it.'

But Eleanora had moved on already and was talking, in her most gracious, charming voice, to the man from British Intelligence, who was sitting perfectly upright, nodding back at her. Prue's right hand began a flap and so she curled it into a fist and the conversation rattled around her. *I would rather Prue didn't come.* Eleanora was not meeting her eye.

On one of their *Tramps with Camera*, before the pilot came, when it was just the two of them, Eleanora had told Prue a story. When she (Eleanora) was a little girl, in Wales, she had taken to feeding a crow that regularly visited a tree near the kitchens. She begged the cook for stale bread, then leftovers. She stole meat to mix in. She left the food for the crow under a beech. The same tree, every day. Eleanora was aged five, or maybe six. At first several crows came, then more of them, ten, fifteen. She continued to feed them and then one day there was a piece of glass left at the bottom of the tree. The next day a broken earring. The day after, a fragmented sliver from the inside of an oyster shell, and from them on they always left her gifts.

'When did they stop?'

'I was forced to visit my aunt, in Shropshire, for a month. When we came back, the crows were gone.'

And it was this story, about the gifts from crows, that had made a part of Prue want to attach herself to Eleanora and to cling there, hang on, whatever the weather, wherever Eleanora was going, even though Prue knew well enough that Eleanora pushed her off like a person who strokes a dog and then tires of it and shoves its snout away. Prue listened in to what Eleanora was saying to Mr Wicklow. 'Oh, Khaled wanted to have a word with you about something.'

Wicklow, smiling, stood up, 'Of course,' and together the two men went towards the bar and leant in close as old women.

'What are they whispering about?' her father said to Eleanora, openly annoyed at being excluded, but she just laughed, shrugged and patted him on the back.

When Khaled returned they took a long time to say goodbye to everyone; kisses, shoulder pats, nods, smiles, nothing particularly in Prue's direction.

'Well,' her father said when they were gone. 'The great Rasul is back. I shan't imagine our pilot likes that very much.'

Frau Baum stretched back in to her chair. 'Indeed,' she said, significantly. Then she glanced across the restaurant. 'Who is that over there, smoking cigarettes and holding a cane?'

Wicklow spoke up. 'That is Ragheb Nashashibi, ' he said, 'and in front of the Fast you might have noticed his green American limousine sat waiting; that is his Packard.'

Frau Baum moved closer to Prue, making an obvious attempt to include her in the conversation: 'The Englishmen who come here bring their feuds from boarding school. They like to employ members of the big Jerusalem families because they remind them of home. They are boarders, fighting over territory and Houses.'

Ashton glared at her but Wicklow merely laughed and then carried on talking to Charles as if the women had not spoken. *I'm going to slip off now. Have to go into the interior for the night.* Then he spoke in low whispers so that it was not possible to hear what he was saying. Prue, sick of being excluded from everything, put her napkin down.

'Father,' she said, 'do you mind if I leave you now? I suddenly feel like a rest.'

They all stopped and looked at her. 'Of course, my dear, if you wish.'

Frau Baum said, 'Would you like some company?'

'No, thank you.' Prue used her politest voice and counted to fifty before standing up. Her feet on the floor reminded her that the ground was stable and that there was an element – something flat, rock, and holy or not – that could be relied on. When she was out of their sight, in the reception area, she ran upstairs.

Once she had closed the door Prue stood in the centre of her room, breathing fast from the exertion of running. She had made a home for the mouse in an emptied drawer but it had lasted less than an hour before the creature escaped. The paper cone and a few peanuts were all that was left. She lit a candle on the dressing table and watched the flame flicker and dot for a while then she sat on her bed, feeling unsettled.

The room was cold and she remembered that her mother claimed to believe in ghosts. Used to see them in the gardens, own up to talking to them. Black thoughts were coming down on Prue, she rubbed her face with her hot little hands to stop them, but it didn't work. She recalled her mother on a piano stool, turning and saying to Prue, Who are you? Are you a little ghost, or a little devil?

The black thought was a realisation. Now her mother was dead it was likely – more than likely, possible – that Prue would never go home. The full knowledge of this cloaked her. If she had known this, when she was packing her things to come to Jerusalem, she would have thought about it all a little more carefully instead of just putting dresses and shoes in the suitcase. She might have brought photographs with her. Treasures.

Prue looked around the hotel room. It seemed she didn't have much to hold on to, apart from the fact that she felt distinctly unsafe, exactly as she did when she was being sketched, or photographed, or told to stand in front of a camera lens and be still. A horrible feeling, but it was at least familiar. Prue thought of Eleanora no longer wanting her; Eleanora with an unborn baby, a seed growing in her, her pilot friend, no room for Prue.

She had an idea. She shoved, with much effort, the dressing table into the middle of the room, taking care not to destabilise the flickering candle, and then she knelt in front it, as if for prayer. But it didn't work, because she was too low, so she pulled over the chair from the desk and sat on it. The growing seed in Eleanora was keeping her away. Prue concentrated: a wish. Real, vivid as possible, but she paused. Opened her eyes. In order for it to work it must be changed, transformed. One thing needed to become another.

She took a piece of paper from her notebook, held it above the candle flame and watched the edge of the page quickly curl, smoke, and then, panicked by the enthusiasm of the flame, blew on it until it was gone. Paper into ash to smoke. That would do.

She did not bother sitting down again, but stood in front of the candle and the singed page. She squeezed her eyes shut. She held her breath. In her mind she sang: *Begone seed, wash away to the sea, return my Eleanora back to me.* A childish, silly spell, but she repeated it again and again and then she changed it for a while, *bring my mother back to me*, until the clock let out its reminders and Prue shivered, hating the cold.

Jerusalem, 1920

The tap on the door was Wicklow, who amazingly appeared to be entirely dressed in Bedouin gear, the full regalia flapping around his head, his skin dusky and dark and his eyes desert-whipped.

'May I?' He stepped into Willie's room. 'Bloody hell, you look shocking.'

Willie had drunk a good deal of whisky through the small hours of the morning, but it had not eradicated the vision that was scraped into his mind like a tattoo: Eleanora, breaking like a crystal ornament over his fist. His skin crawled with shame and he could make no sense of Wicklow standing looking at him.

He had said he needed to think, but then Eleanora had returned again the following night, last night. After spending the day with Khaled who was asleep, she had said. She did not have much time.

'Tomorrow we are going to Lifta,' she kept repeating and Willie could not understand the reference.

'So?' he had said.

'Please. Please.'

Are you sure are you sure are you sure? Stand by the window, then. Be quick. As he prepared his hand and flexed the muscles of his fingers the thought of what he was about to do almost derailed him. Did she belong to him, or to Khaled Rasul? That is what he had wanted to ask, but then there was a sliver of consolation in the fact that Willie was the one who knew the truth, who was prepared to do this for her.

The first hit had been hesitant, although he could see from her face it still hurt. She had tried very hard not to cry, but it came anyway. Then he thought of Khaled Rasul opening her, pushing in, withdrawal, and the next punch carried in his knuckles very real intent.

He had wanted to stop, but she asked him to keep going, to be sure. When she fell, over his fist, it had been like snapping a flimsy piece of wood and saliva flew from her mouth and landed on his cheek. He had touched it with his finger and finally she staggered from his room, refusing to let him help her. Afterwards, he had vomited. His breath stank now, his teeth were furry. He blinked at Wicklow.

'What do you want?'

'Quick,' Wicklow said, not bothering to hide the fact that he was disgusted at Willie's state. 'Harrington, now: up to Ashton's suite, it's urgent.'

'Why are you dressed like that?'

Wicklow did not reply, and for a moment the two men, standing very close, opposite one another, might as well have been boys in the school refectory.

'Give me five minutes. I'll be there.'

———

In Ashton's suite Willie watched both men shed their various garments. Charles took off his linen suit jacket, exposing a lavender-coloured silk shirt with sweat patches. Wicklow was rapidly decanting from his dusty desert gear.

'Where on God's earth have you been?'

'The interior, obviously. Undercover last night moving through the villages outside Hebron. Had a tip-off.'

Willie slumped on to a leather chair and fumbled about in his trouser pocket for a cigarette. He squeezed the bridge of his nose and tried to focus his eyes on the men in front of him. Wicklow had the infuriating face of a man in possession of superior information, and he was clearly holding on to it, relishing the moment. Willie, although irritated by him, could not help but be impressed at Wicklow's seeming ability to disguise himself and go thoroughly native.

'Do you speak the lingo?'

'The dialects? Of course. Madani. Hauran. Ajloun. Badawi, language of the Bedouins.' Willie had meant Arabic, or Hebrew or Turkish. Ashton poured each man a glass of whisky despite it not yet being noon. Silence in the room, aside from the swallowing. The swill of the liquid in his mouth greatly vivified Willie; it straightened his vision and stabilised his blood.

'Well,' Charles said, finally dressed. 'He's done it now, the flaming idiot.'

'Who?'

'McLaughlin,' Wicklow said, 'who else?'

'I want the full report.' Ashton poured himself another glassful of whisky and drank it in one. He walked towards the window, and looked down on Jerusalem. Willie, if he could, would erase the night before. Instead he had done as she asked and now they could never go back.

'Of late,' Wicklow was saying, 'Lofty has become obsessed with tracking down and punishing a particular band of criminal outlaws who have been committing robberies and attacks along the Jericho and Jaffa roads.'

He continued with the full story.

The outlaws had been menacing everyone: shopkeepers, travellers and villagers. Lofty and members of the *gendarmerie* followed the trail towards Wadi Farrar but achieved nothing and returned to barracks frustrated.

The *gendarmerie*, just a few Irish and English officers in charge of a fleet of native officials, were in a confab about what to do when an elderly shopkeeper came up to the gates. His face a mess of bruises and blood, he had clearly recently been beaten and was in an agitated state. Through an interpreter he explained that many years ago he had stood bail for the outlaw in question, Mohammed Al-Din, but had never been paid back money owed to him. When the shopkeeper heard that Al-Din was running a criminal gang from caves between Lifta and Nebi Samuel, he had set up a meeting through contacts in Jerusalem's Old City and visited the cave to request at least part repayment. When the meeting took place, however, all he received was a beating. Because of this, he had told Lofty and his colleagues, he wanted to betray his enemy and was prepared to instruct the British as to his whereabouts, as long as he would be given a reward for his pains.

As Wicklow spoke, he wiped the stuff that formed part of his disguise from his face with one of Ashton's towels and Willie realised, from the shimmer of the white of his eyes, that he had used kohl in the manner of the women of the souk. The intelligence officer, now back in the guise of a slick, rather slippery Englishman, threw the towel on to a chair, stood erect and smiled. The transformation was impressive.

Willie didn't know much about the *gendarmerie*, apart from the fact that they had a reputation for vicious retribution. They were the muscle of the British administration and the colonial staff in Governance House, who did not like to talk about them much in polite society, preferring antiquities. The *gendarmerie* looked like a joke but apparently they terrified everyone.

'Are they under your command?' Willie asked.

'Storrs's, really, but I've been asking them to bring in the information about the specifics of land ownership in the region. So many wild, unmanaged areas.'

'So you are able to tell them what to do, what not to do?' Willie said. A wave of nausea, exhaustion, regret, despair; all of those threads, webbed together. Wicklow was watching him closely, his too-blue eyes on him, predatory.

'Yes. I'm authorised to do that.'

'Wicklow, how did you come across all of this information?' Ashton said.

Wicklow looked coy, and wiped his mouth with the back of his hand. 'That little tête-à-tête with Khaled Rasul at dinner.'

Willie pulled an uncomfortable cushion out from behind him and threw it on to the floor. He was surprised.

'Rasul?'

'Yes. We discussed those photographs you gave me, actually.'

'I don't think I quite *gave* them.'

Ashton, eyebrows raised, looked confused. 'Photographs?'

'Actually, it was Eleanora who suggested I talk to Rasul.'

'Eleanora?' A line of saliva from her lip as his hand punched deep into the softest part of her; it was an intimacy he did not want to remember.

'Yes, she was there.'

'Yesterday?'

'Yes, when I had dinner with Ashton and Elspeth.'

This was before she had come to his rooms in the night, then. Why did she not say anything about this? She had not mentioned Wicklow to him. Willie looked at the man, perky, punchy, in front of him. He said to the room, generally: 'I know him. I knew him, rather, in Salonika.'

'Who?'

'Lofty.'

Both men turned towards him. Wicklow's eyes narrowed. 'You didn't say.'

'No,' Willie said, casually. 'It took me a moment to place him. He's had endless rounds of malaria fever. He's a madman.'

You're a treacherous fucking cunt. Call yourself an Englishman.

Wicklow regarded Willie for a moment and looked as if he was making an internal judgement or mental cross-reference, then he continued with the outline of his report.

Lofty, being Lofty, did not promise the shopkeeper a reward for his information. Instead, he instantly handcuffed the man, mounted him on a horse. He was strapped on and told that he would be shot dead if he did not take them to the cave and that there was no hope of a reward. He was warned that if he was leading them into an ambush he would be the first man shot.

They all arrived at the foot of the Moab hills at dawn, and advanced slowly up towards what they thought was the mouth of a cave. As they approached, one of Al-Din's men came running and screaming towards the British, gesturing back into the cave and betraying his own leader: 'He is in there. Come and get him.' That man was shot through the back by Al-Din himself. Apparently, what then followed was, as Wicklow put it, 'a good old-fashioned shoot-out'. The native officer working with Lofty shouted for Al-Din to surrender but all he did was fire shots out towards them. They all took cover behind various rocks, having left their horses in the valley. The British threw a couple of grenades, a native officer had the idea of climbing up on to an outcrop above the cave; he crept above and then shot the outlaw in the head.

There was silence in the room.

'He was very well armed, by all accounts.'

'But what with?' Ashton asked.

'Two revolvers. A British service rifle, over four hundred rounds of ammunition and two more hand grenades in his knapsack.'

'So what is the situation now?' Ashton pressed both thumbs on to his eyebrows and rubbed the grey-white hair of them. Wicklow drained the last of his drink, and carried on.

'Discovering that the whole village was involved in harbouring the outlaws, providing bread, whatever they needed, Lofty has taken it upon himself to send out "a suitable message" to other villages who might consider similar activities.'

'Well, what does that mean?' Ashton said.

'Eleanora didn't know, but she said we must go. Today.'

'We need to do something,' Ashton said, 'before news of it trickles out and causes major rioting. We need to bloody stop him. God knows what he might do to the women.'

Ashton stood at the window looking down at the street with the air of a man not in a particular hurry. Perhaps he did not take seriously the comment about Lofty and the women; it seemed that Wicklow, perhaps, had some understanding of that. Ashton stiffened, then, and turned.

'Which village did you say?'

'Lifta.'

'But that makes no sense whatsoever; Eleanora has taken Frau Baum with her to do a photograph with the American Colony there.'

'Oh?'

A pain, in Willie's right eye, difficult to ignore.

'Yes. They wanted Eleanora to dress up the thing; you know, make it look authentic. Actually, come to think of it, it was Eleanora's idea. She convinced the Colony it would work.'

'Eleanora went, you say?' Willie said. 'Even though she passed on the message and knew what was happening nearby?'

Wicklow frowned. 'I would say she insisted, certainly suggested, that we go. Yes, come to think of it, I did hear her invite everyone to the photography excursion. Khaled himself was insistent too; they made rather a team.'

Jerusalem, 1920

Eleanora hadn't wanted Prue at the photographic staging of Moses in the bulrushes, but Prue was up and bright and dressed and foisted herself upon them, knowing from Frau Baum that a motor car was arranged to take them as far as possible and then they would walk, or travel on horses which were to be collected from a farm. Lars and his team from the American Colony photography department were meeting them there. Eleanora had raised her eyebrows when she saw Prue, but she had said nothing, and now, by late morning, Prue assumed she was allowed to be present.

Most of the snow was gone from Jerusalem, but there were still stubborn icy patches outside the city. There was birdsong all around but Prue couldn't see the birds to identify them so it was as if the trees were singing to themselves.

Prue wandered into the makeshift tent that Lars had erected. Eleanora was crouching near her Gladstone bag, pulling items out – handkerchief, pillbox, pen – and evidently not finding what she was looking for. They were on the outskirts of the village of Lifta, just west of Jerusalem. All Prue wanted was to see the villa. She had been promised a walk there with Frau Baum as soon as the photograph had been taken but it was all going on for an interminably long time.

'Prue, would you pass me that chair?' Prue did as instructed, moving mechanically. She was working hard to avoid looking directly at Eleanora, but it was impossible not to notice that there was something unusual about the way Eleanora sat herself down, heavier than normal. When she pulled out her compact, covered in filigree silver, Prue saw that she was shaking as she checked herself in the mirror.

Prue went to the edge of the tent and looked out. The two handmaidens were shivering next to a stream that apparently drained down from Lifta's spring in the Wadi al-Shami. Through the magic of photography this stream was going to be transformed into the Nile and the wooden doll that was currently poking out of the basket was Moses and it would be a joint bestseller for the American Colony and Eleanora. They would sell a million copies to the never-ending flow of pilgrims who came to Jerusalem look-ing for themselves and everybody would be happy. May a plague come down on you all, Prue thought: locusts and wasps and famine and thunder.

'I wonder, Prue, if you could pass me a drink?' Prue turned back behind her. Eleanora inside the tent seemed diminished, gesturing over to the water bottle that Frau Baum had left on the table near the haversacks.

'Of course.'

Prue gave up not looking at her and inspected her instead. Eyelids: purple-pink, vulnerable. Neck: wilting. Sweat on her face, she kept rubbing her forehead. Prue was about to ask: Are you all right, what is happening? But Lars shouted, 'Eleanora, where is the baby's basket?'

Prue replied for her, 'It's here.' She picked up the woven basket with the doll inside and went out to where Lamia and Thuriya, forlorn handmaidens, were waiting. Lamia was adjusting her sandal. Both sisters were wrapped in beige robes as they stood next to faux-marble steps which were tilting. Eleanora walked towards them, frowning, and went over to the tripod. She bent her head under the camera hood and looked down into the viewfinder.

'It's no good. It's not right.'

'Is it the light perhaps?' Lars, very serious, very concentrated, did not bother to speak to Prue ever.

'No, no.'

Prue watched it all in a ... what was it? In another place? Perhaps she was a girl in one of Eleanora's photographs, who had been left in a room with time moving, ticking, and consequently she was faded, blurred? Normally, like a family dog, she would hop under everyone's feet, become involved, position herself so that they must acknowledge her (and that way she would become real), but today she was on a high wall looking down at them and they were barely aware of her. The mysterious bird-voices continued coming from the dead-winter tree bark.

'I wonder if another handmaiden might help?' Prue was pushed into the scene and Eleanora leant forward and undid her hair. It was strange to have Eleanora's fingers moving her hair about, touching her scalp.

'Would you mind taking off your shoes?'

Prue was placid. They could do what they wanted with her. Barefooted, wrapped in a beige robe that swaddled her dress, she was put in front of the sisters.

'Stand there, and look down towards the reeds.'

'Yes.'

'You're right,' Lars called, his head popping up from the camera hood. 'That is supremely improved.'

Thuriya whispered behind her in Arabic that she was starving and that the *Ingliz* were raving lunatics.

'That is true,' Prue said. She did not feel like meeting the eye that was looking at her through the camera lens; instead, she gazed at the stones at the bottom of the silt water and wondered if they were red, or Jewish, or golden.

'We've got it, I'm sure,' Lars said, turning round and clapping his hands to applaud himself, but Eleanora was not behind him; she was walking back towards the tent.

'Prue,' Eleanora said, when Prue came in, looking for the white cheese and the dark Palestinian bread that Frau Baum had brought along.

'Yes?'

Eleanora was pale and then she came close to Prue and took her hands, both of them, and held them tightly. Eleanora's own hands were freezing. 'A little bit later they will all be going to Lifta. I don't want you to go.'

'But I want to see the villa. I am going up there with Frau Baum.'

'It's been arranged. For a reason. It will be dangerous; is there a way you can trust me?'

'Trust you, Eleanora?'

'With Khaled, they are going to ... it's your father, you see, and the things he does, to the people here, the things he allows.'

'Do you mean the clock tower?'

Eleanora shook her head, a dart of confusion on her face, and then looked down. Prue followed her line of sight. Blood was dripping over the lion-shaped buckle on Eleanora's shoe.

'Eleanora, you're hurt?'

They both stared at the gentle red dripping which did not make its way down the ankle and shoe with any urgency.

It's because of me. The curl of smoke and the wisp of paper.

Outside the tent, Prue could see that the sky was thickening into a violet shadow and Frau Baum was talking to Lars. She was about to call them when Eleanora let out a cry and fell forward towards Prue, who stepped backwards and did not catch her.

Prue ran so fast that she was almost flying, and by the end, by the bottom of the valley, she really was flying. She landed in a heap in a patch of browning snow and it took a moment for her senses to steady.

In front of her was a path. Frau Baum had said earlier that to get to the villa they would need to go down to the base of the valley and then follow that alternative path uphill. Prue wiped down her dress and walked.

Think nothing.

That did not work well. As she walked her hands hung down by her thighs. She was very quickly hot, no longer concerned by the cold, sharp air. After some time the path entered a dense area of elderly olive trees.

Here, the air had a displaced feel, as if recently breathed. The path was steep, the icy soil cracked underfoot. There were stone houses on a higher ridge, all made from the pale, nearly white Jerusalem stone. Prue glanced about, as if Canon Brown might have chosen today of all days to return to his house and was at a window, waiting for her. Her breath, as she walked, became rhythmical. Is a death a person's fault? For example: if her father had found a way to force her mother to go into the Graylingwell place and then, very soon afterwards, she dies, is that her father's fault? Or: if a person makes a wish, before a candle, and a baby does not become itself properly, instead turns into blood and drips away, is that the person's fault?

Prue carried on through a natural archway of trees and on the other side, in a clearing, an old man was working in a garden. He was digging a circle into the ground around the outside of a tree. Prue tried to remember from her *Leaves of the Levant* book which tree it was. Walnut, possibly, with the wide, wagging leaves, and she remembered that her father had told her that the word walnut comes from the Anglo-Saxon *wealh*, and that means *far away, foreign*, but what was it called here, in Arabic? Where it is not foreign or far away? She did not know and then remembered it. Wadi al Jouz near Jerusalem was valley of the walnuts. *Jouz*, but in Egypt it was the eye of the camel. The earth was frozen so each time the old man put the spade into the ground there was a cracking noise. He heaved and huffed too and if he was aware of her watching he didn't let on. Finally, she called out in Arabic: 'Hello. How are you? Do you work here?'

The old man stood up and regarded her for as many minutes as he liked to take. 'My family have worked on this land for ever,' he said. She could not tell if he thought she was impertinent or not.

'Is Canon Brown's house near here?' From his eyes she could see he didn't understand. Then she said, 'The man with the music, the musical organ?'

But she did not know the word for hymn in Arabic. Church-singing? The gardener was chewing something – leaves, perhaps – and he spat the leaves on to the earth and leant on his spade and looked away, at a sparrow which was near his foot, hopping, and then fluttered off.

He shook his head and pointed at some trees further up the hill. 'The music man has been living there.'

'Where?'

She turned away from him and through the branches, up on the higher path, there was a square stone house that looked as if it were mushrooming out of the limestone; as if it were made up of a million carcasses of creatures, crushed skeletons, and then covered with sand.

'My family's house,' he said.

'It's your house?' He nodded, and looked all around.

'My garden, my orchard, my wadi.'

'May I go in?' she asked, as politely as possible.

He shrugged and she was unsure for a moment what to do. Then, when he seemed no longer interested in her, she walked away but he called to her, 'There is a man in there, asleep.' He said it fast, in Arabic, so she asked him to repeat it, to try to understand. Man. Asleep, in the house.

'Oh. I see.' Though she did not. 'Thank you, sir.'

True, there were boots on the tiled floor, well-worn, massive and crusted around the heel. The fire had been recently lit but was down to embers. The house was warm, and Prue's fingertips and wet cold toes flared with the sudden change of temperature and began to prickle.

This was it: the villa.

Moving again, for the twelfth, thirteenth, fourteenth time, and her mother had said: 'Imagine a house in your mind and that is the one your father will build for us, eventually. You can trust in that one.'

Prue walked through the entrance into a room with low domed ceilings. It was smaller than she had imagined a villa to be. She bent down and undid her shoelaces. A relief to have her toes out. She rolled each of her wet stockings into a ball and stood like a goose asleep on one leg, rubbing one foot to warm it as she looked around. Could she live here? Indeed, she could. She moved towards the remains of the fire and held her foot in front of it until her skin speckled with a heat rash.

There was a sound. At first she thought it was the rush of her own blood in her head then she realised that it resonated through the bones of the villa. Hansel and Gretel came to mind: *Nibble nibble, little mouse. Who is nibbling at my house?* The noise was coming from the adjacent room. Prue walked slowly towards it, not nervous, but in an almost sleepy mode; empty of everything. In the bedroom, lying on the bed face-down, was a sleeping man, fully dressed, but with his boots neatly lined up on the floor beside him. With each rolling snore the mass of his large back rose, then sank, just as one might imagine a dragon asleep in front of a cave of treasure. Enormous feet.

Prue stood rigid. The room was full of his breathing. The walls and ceiling had been painted white. The floor was covered in native tiles. Were these the magic tiles? She crouched down and ran her fingers along the grooves between the squares. A cowboy-style hat and a revolver were on the chair next to the bed. It was the Chinese emperor who trained mice. She took a step closer, and then a step back.

Prue stood against the wall in her thin coat, looking at the gun. She had never touched one before. The volcanic snoring chimed through the room and she remembered the pressure of the man's fingers against her neck in the cinema. She turned and looked out over the hills. The *wadis*, they were called here, deep dry river-banks that led to nowhere; but there was no such place as nowhere, she knew that.

'Hello.'

It was the Chinese emperor. 'Wee little girl,' he said. 'Am I dreaming?'

Prue did not turn around immediately and she had an odd thought. *I am the ballet dancer in a jewellery box. Round and round.* When she looked he was half-sitting up and his large stomach hung in a way she had never seen before, dripping flesh. He smiled.

'Would you come here, lovely?' His skin was very bumpy-looking, as if each tiny pore was stained a light violet colour. Might she tell him that this was her villa, meant to be her home? A rested ship. He was patting the bed, his hands a blur. Pat pat pat. The walls were all around her and she stepped towards him, knowing she had no choice. Children do as they are told. Pat pat pat and the bed beneath him sagged, sprang up again. She was one step closer. He heaved himself up a little more so that the curl of flesh on his stomach grew even bigger and he rubbed his finger under his nose as he looked at her.

She was close to him and he had a clever way of twisting her wrist so that she was forced to bend towards him, even though it seemed he had barely used any strength at all. Then he lifted her with both hands over the top of him until she was dropped into the space between his armpit and the large, squashy, curve of his stomach. His skin had a smell: it was tangy, like sausages. She was lying on her back, now, like Lulu, like a doll, and his face and gingery beard and gingery moustache and white eyebrows and wide red nose took up the whole of the domed white ceiling.

'What have we here then?' His finger pressed the tiny dip where her collarbones met. She said nothing, just stared upwards, and then he sang a song. *Rest tired eyes a while. Sweet is thy baby's smile. Angels are guarding and they watch ov'r thee. Sleep, sleep,* grah mo chree. *Here on your mamma's knee. Angels are guarding. And they watch ov'r thee.* An Irish song, a lullaby maybe. Perhaps his mother sang it to him when he was little? Or perhaps he heard it in the bedrooms of his own childhood. She did not know.

Jerusalem, 1920

They travelled by horseback as it would take too much time to arrange any other transport. Willie was mostly silent as they rode. His horse was calm, a solid plodder. There was a daytime moon; he looked up at it, abstractedly. It was cold, but he was oddly immune to the weather. In the depth of the dry valley Wicklow pointed out a small encampment.

'There's the photographic expedition, but where will Lofty be?' Ashton said.

'They must have had the shoot-out the other side of the village, up there. Lifta is a little higher in the mountains. I doubt the American Colony people know a thing about it.' Wicklow threw the remains of his cigarette into the bush.

'Apart from Eleanora?' Ashton said. 'Elspeth is with them. I just can't understand why Eleanora would have brought her here.'

'Well, they look safe enough from what we can see,' Wicklow said.

'Yes,' said Charles, 'but I would rather they were sent back to the Old City immediately.'

Wicklow was in front, followed by Charles and then Willie. As they descended the narrow track, the horse rocked beneath him. There was an architectural element to the shape of a walking horse. He had forgotten that, the way the flanks shift up and down, the momentum of knees and rhythm of the hoofs, and he had an imprint of a memory: himself four, perhaps five, tugged into a farmer's yard, way out on the perimeter of Pentrohobyn Hall. Beyond the confines of that large house was wild-land, full of wet thorns, big brothers, boys from poor families. A farmer had been trussed up against a fence and whipped for treating his young black colt badly and a gang of boys were jeering. The colt was nearby, its muzzle tied tight against a post so that it couldn't shift or twitch and along its ribs four red stripes, slices. Willie's elder brother Edward, already sixteen when Willie was four, pushing Willie back. *Don't look.*

Transfixed on the lumbering movement of the animal, Willie closed his eyes so that he was not an undistinguished, unribboned pilot who could barely fly in a godforsaken nowhere valley. He was on different, softer land, where grass grew over chalk, where the hoofs of horses gave off a softer resonance, a place where the spectrum of colours was a shimmering green leading to grey. Not yellow; not this pink-yellow dust. Not this smell of – what was it? He honestly didn't know, couldn't identify it. He shivered. It was bloody cold. He was disturbed; it rattled him that Eleanora had spoken to Wicklow in such a way. He could tell that Charles was disturbed by it too.

As they got close they could see that Lars was waving both hands, but not in a friendly gesture, more along the lines of come quickly: trouble.

'Ashton,' Lars shouted, 'thank goodness.'

Ashton spurred his horse on and the filly let out a snort, a horsey breath of air.

'I'm afraid Eleanora is rather ill. Come.'

He was speaking to Ashton, but Willie also jumped immediately from his horse. He ran behind Ashton into the tent. Eleanora was wrapped in Frau Baum's fur and was shivering, sitting on a stool. Frau Baum was crouched in front of her holding her hands. It was only when she glanced up, at Willie first, and then at Charles, that Willie realised how much he had been dreading seeing her. He regretted everything. He looked away. The world outside, the valley, was mostly empty. He knew this. 'Oh, Charles?' he heard Frau Baum say behind him. 'What are you doing here? Never mind, we have to get Eleanora to the French hospital immediately.'

Willie turned back to Eleanora. He began to kneel down, but she shook her head at him, her eyes moved left and right: no, keep back. His ears in a thunder: drum drum drum. His arms hanging useless, he hovered and he stayed where he was as Ashton knelt down next to Frau Baum and took Eleanora's hands in his.

'Oh, Eleanora, my dear,' Ashton said. 'What is happening?'

Behind them, Wicklow pulled Lars from the group and began asking quick questions. Had he heard gunfire? Any disturbance? Lars shook his head. Any sounds of upset from the village? They hadn't actually gone into the village, but set up in the outskirts, here, as they could see. Wicklow was oblivious to the grey transparency of Eleanora's face.

'Can you carry her on your horse?' Frau Baum said to Charles. She indicated the puddle of red around Eleanora's feet.

Willie had not realised, it had not filtered through his brain what was happening, but now he saw the stained floor, the pale skin.

Charles said, 'There is something tremendously urgent, Elspeth, we have to go to the village and we will return immediately for Eleanora.'

Frau Baum's voice cracked. 'More urgent than this?'

'Lars can take her, perhaps?'

'Not you?'

'It is too difficult to go into, it's Lofty. There's trouble.'

Eleanora looked up then. 'Yes, Charles,' she said in a quiet voice, 'you should continue on up to Lifta.'

Charles frowned at her. 'Why, Eleanora, did you come here when you – ?' But Frau Baum stopped him speaking; the air around them felt warped.

'You too, Willie,' Eleanora said softly. 'You should go up there. I can go to the hospital with Lars.'

It seemed that there were hazards behind her words. Willie thought of all that he would do for her; all he would have done for her, if she had allowed him.

'Where's Prue?' Frau Baum said.

'She was here a moment ago.' Eleanora let out a small pant as she spoke.

Charles sprang up into the air, and Willie noticed something he never had previously: there was something odd about his right hand. Often he was wearing gloves, or long sleeves; his silk suits were specially tailored. The little finger on his right hand was slightly withered. His face was red with shock.

'Do you mean to tell me that Prue is here as well?'

Frau Baum, looking strained, glanced over her shoulder and then said, 'I suspect she's gone to find that villa; I had said I would go with her – you need to call her back, Charles.'

'Prue has gone that way?'

Wicklow stood behind Willie. 'Harrington, come.' Willie did not move. He was looking at Eleanora and something in him, something private and natural and childlike, was severed and died instantly. That was how it felt, a quick slice, an immediate death, because this display was her decision, it was clear to him now.

'I could take Eleanora,' Willie said, swinging round to stop his own thoughts, speaking to Ashton. 'You go on and I'll take her to the hospital?' But Wicklow stepped towards him.

'No,' he said, 'we all need to go. I think we had better go and find this old cohort of yours.'

'Yes,' Ashton said. 'Lars, can you take her?'

'Of course.'

Eleanora was not looking at Willie. What was she looking at? He couldn't tell; her eyes were abstract. The edges of her were blurred. Like those photographs she insisted on printing. The edges rubbed out.

Wicklow offered Willie a loaded revolver and he took it as their horses made their first philosophical steps forward. Willie followed the rhythmic plodding of Ashton's dark-brown filly, tensing the reins every so often. Each step felt like an unpicking from Eleanora. The scars on his body fired up, reminded him of their existence. The sight of Eleanora's blood around her feet was in his head; difficult to think past.

Wicklow relayed further information as they continued along the path. Canon Brown was dead. Shot in what might be called a small incident with one of the many false Messiahs that inhabited the desert. An English-speaking man, robed in white, stood preaching and carousing in the village square. It was illegal to preach, or to have any form of public gathering under the British military administration, and Canon Brown had walked up to the imitation prophet and politely suggested that he was committing an offence, trying to warn him. The man, who lived in his mind entirely in biblical times, addressed Canon Brown as a centurion: *What do you wish of me, centurion?* God knows, the worst of it was that he actually had followers and the crowd gathered around was tense. The followers, it turned out, were devout because a shot was fired and Canon Brown fell forward so that his head went into the prophet's chest.

Before long there were signs of the first houses of Lifta, a lone dwelling half-buried into the side of the hill.

'Which one is Canon Brown's villa?' Willie said.

'Not sure. I think it's further in.'

On a cold January day like this the land looked dead, but it was possible to see that the soil was heavily cultivated. Lines of dead thistles stood in rows. Prickly-pear cacti clustered around the large boulders of Jerusalem stone. They heard a banging noise, coming from further down in the valley.

Wicklow called out: 'Gunshot?'

Nobody answered. Ashton and Wicklow increased their speed along the central pathway which led along a crevice that wound higher and it was possible to see more stone houses sprouting from the hillside. Willie's horse objected. It did not want to go on. Willie pushed his ankles into its flank, he smacked the side of its neck, but the creature was stubborn and unresponsive. The olive trees surrounding them were ancient enough to have split and bowed.

'Come on, old girl,' he said, and jabbed his boot into the horse's ribs but the horse stayed firm. 'I sympathise, but we really need to move.'

Ashton and Wicklow disappeared ahead. There was another loud banging noise and Willie heard a voice behind him. It was Frau Baum, in her large black fur, running towards him, her cheeks red and her black hair blown out and unruly.

'It's that one,' she said, pointing towards the stone house up on the higher path. There was a pile of wood near the door.

'That is the villa Prue was searching for. I think you should look for her.' She was out of breath.

'Which house?'

She pointed once more. It was closer than he thought. Willie dismounted.

'But Eleanora, aren't you accompanying her?'

'Lars has fixed her on to his horse and they've gone. They'll get a cart or a motor as soon as they can. I just have a bad feeling about Prudence, you know?'

Willie did not care about Ashton's child. His horse raised and lowered its head rapidly. He did not know what to make of this woman always attached to Ashton, but something about her, her frayed manner, her bony fingers, the sense that emanated from her of clinging, made him pause. He nodded.

'Stupid beast.' He climbed off, tugged the animal towards a fence. He tied her up and left her bowing her head, looking for grass to chew.

'Eleanora,' he said, and then, 'is she going to be …?'

'She's in a terrible state.'

They looked at one another. He knew he was blushing – like an idiot – and he was aware that she was studying his face very closely.

She pushed her glasses to the top of her nose. She was about to say something; he interrupted her.

'Why did she bring everyone here if she knew there would be trouble?' he said.

Frau Baum's shoulders moved up and down in a shrug. 'For Khaled?'

The word Khaled echoed around the trees, bounced off the leaves and the dry dead bark. She pointed again at the house. 'We should look for Prue?'

The air outside the villa was heavy and dead, as if the wind had given up on it. Instinctively, Willie did not knock, but opened the door silently, with Frau Baum close behind him. He gestured for her to wait; it took a moment for his eyes to adjust to the dark interior.

It was a neat room with bare furniture. A peasant house, simple but attractive. It was warm. He was about to call out, but instead he moved towards a door in the corner which led to another room. She was there: Prue, curled on the bed like a small cat. There was an odd smell in the room, metallic. He looked down at the incongruous sight of Ashton's daughter sleeping in this room, but only then did he realise that she looked strange, her face white. 'Prue?' He went over to her. There again, that distinctive smell. He was holding the revolver but his hand was shaking. He touched her arm and, as he did, the whole of her body convulsed, shivered, and she drew her knees in closer to her chest.

'Prue?'

She did not respond. Her little dress was ripped, her under-clothes were twisted, she was exposed. He breathed in, closed his eyes.

'Frau Baum?' he called. He went to the door. Frau Baum was standing, with her chalky white face, painted eyebrows and dyed black hair, looking concerned.

'She's in there,' he whispered, and he shook his head, his mouth tasted bitter. 'I think she's been hurt.'

Frau Baum stepped past him into the bedroom. Willie went out along the wall of the house, his feet snapping twigs, until he found a small window and looked in. Frau Baum was crossing the room like a shadow-puppet in a children's story. She could be either the bringer of dreams and good fortune or the thief who steals something precious in the night. The scene was almost normal, a mother checking on a sleeping child. Willie glanced around. Was Lofty near? He shivered.

Willie watched as the child rose up, as if in a dream, and a moment later they emerged together into the cold air, Frau Baum holding both Prue's boots. Prue had Frau Baum's handkerchief to her face because she had begun, upon standing, to have a nose-bleed. Her dress, twisted around her body, reminded him of the sanatorium gowns worn by the patients in the military hospital in Cairo. The branches of the tree near the house creaked. Prue, coming to properly, was confused and began to cry.

'I'll take her back up,' Frau Baum said, removing her bear-fur and wrapping it around Prue's shoulders, steering her along the path.

'I spoke to the gardener, an Arab who has worked here for fifty years,' Prue said. 'Did you meet him?'

Willie heard Elspeth speak softly: 'No, he wasn't here.'

Willie was unsure what to do. There were rooks in every tree, it seemed, their confident posture an assault, their belonging an offence. He realised that it was snowing again, light hesitant snow, and when he looked up along the bank of the hillside he could see Lofty-shaped shadows behind every trunk. Trees, skeletal and unfriendly, and then a noise, cracking the sky in half. Clear, distinct: gunshot.

Willie said, 'Get her away from here, back up to the tent. I assume Lars didn't pack it all up?' Frau Baum nodded, and helped Prue past the prickly-pear cacti, the rooks in the trees. Willie, not bothering to get on the horse again, began to run.

The village square was surrounded by narrow streets, each with an arch leading over it, joining tall-built stone buildings to one another so that the dwellings appeared to be interlinked. There was tension in the air, like bad news, and the sky above was made up of snow colours: bright grey and sea blue. Groups of men and women stood around whispering, talking in low voices, women pulling shawls over their shoulders, shivering in the snow. At the northernmost point of the square a number of ladders had been propped against a wall of the modest mosque. On the opposite corner Willie recognised the backs and shoulders of Ashton and Wicklow in conversation with several men and he turned, walked towards them. Lofty was nowhere in sight.

Willie called out but failed to attract Ashton's attention. He could see in his mind's eye Prue's thin arms, bruised thick finger-marks at the top of them. He was in the heart of the square and as he drew closer to the ladders he saw that bundles were attached to each one. People in groups were looking at them and then away, pointing. A noise came through the air and coalesced into a sound he recognised: the women were crying.

'Charles,' he called out again, scuffing his boots. Wicklow and Ashton finally looked over at him, beckoned him towards them, and then he turned towards the ladders.

Now he saw that attached to each ladder was a human being. He stopped. Charles was shouting to him but he didn't hear the words. Each strung-up man was an Arab, presumably members of Al-Din's outlaw gang, and they were tied around their stomachs and necks with rope, like a gruesome tribute to Guy Fawkes.

He walked faster towards Ashton. 'Good God. Are they dead?' Ashton nodded.

'Shouldn't we get the bodies down?'

'About to, but they are convinced he is still close.'

'Lofty?'

Ashton's head lowered. 'I'm afraid so. He's overstepped the line this time.'

Willie looked at him, opened his mouth to tell him about Prue. Ashton's face, long, with its beard, its cultivated air, was surveying the square not in horror, but partly in admiration. For all of his projected artistry – the Arts and Crafts training, the jewellery making, pottery analysis, antiquarian collecting, the waving of his nets – who exactly was he? Yes, he was eternally sketching, drawing, painting, redesigning, researching, gathering, but what were his credentials, under it all, under the fez and the badly spoken Arabic? Willie understood then that Ashton had authorised Lofty to do what he did, but not only that, he agreed with it: with those men, bound on the ladders, dead.

Willie cast around, examining the village square and the quiet murmuring of people, and then he noticed a woman silently sobbing on the ground, being consoled by two other women. He looked at the spiral staircases in each corner of the square, leading out towards covered arches and passages that led in turn to the backs of houses edging into the centre of the village. Two men had been hung there. Necks snapped, swaying in the wind like

Christmas decorations on a tree. Nobody seemed in a hurry to get any of these men down.

A small dog, jackal-like with flat ears, kept sniffing and creeping towards the ladders but was shouted away by a sobbing and wailing boy who threw stones at it, kicked dust at its eyes. The dog would not pull back, though. It snarled and then barked properly, a high bark, insistent. It was interested in something on the ground. Ashton and Wicklow had their heads bowed, close together, and were talking to one of the elder Lifta village men. The man was rocking back and forth, shaking his head.

Willie stepped away from them, towards the dog. It was sidling forward and then springing back, giving low snarls. The boy continued to throw stones, but the dog was impervious. Once Willie was closer, he saw what the dog was trying to get to; he could smell what the dog was trying to get to. A pile of severed hands and feet, skin grey or bloody, covered with flies. The little boy was talking in fast Arabic, gesticulating, crying. Seeing Willie, he pointed at one of the trussed-up men. *Aba aba*. Willie put his hand over his mouth, because the sight of the fingernails, and the calloused knuckles and wedding rings on dead hands, caused his stomach to heave. A swaying, a sense that he might fall. The torsos tied to the ladders had their hands and feet hacked off.

The village elder was receding into a house on the edge of the square, and Ashton was now talking to another man; it seemed that he was pleading with him. Wicklow was standing erect, saying nothing; he met Willie's eye, looked away. Coughed.

The man Ashton was engaged with was an Arab, not particularly tall and with a small moustache. He wore a dark suit and carried a case. He pulled himself free of Ashton and walked to the dead-centre of the square. Willie watched; everyone was watching. Even Wicklow stood perfectly still, observing.

The man undid his case and took out a large, three-legged tripod, then he crouched down and opened another, smaller case. He positioned the tripod in front of the first ladder, where the strapped-up man's head hung forward, his mouth open, his tongue out. The blood from the severed limbs was black with ants. In no hurry, not speaking to anyone, he pulled out a slide from his photographic case and turned and looked up into the sky, as if assessing the light. He arranged his tripod as he wanted it, inserted the slide and took a photograph. He then continued to move, slowly, methodically, around the square. He took a photograph of each dead man on the ladders, including the two hanging in the corner.

Wicklow, his expression black, put a cigarette in his mouth, did not light it.

The man then moved backwards, to the western corner. He squinted. Wicklow was next to Ashton. Willie was near. He was photographing them. When he had finished he walked towards Charles Ashton, leaving the tripod standing where it was, but at the last minute he turned to approach Willie. Of course: it was Eleanora's husband. The stones beneath his feet crunched. He paused in front of Willie and took from his pocket a small flask. Unhurriedly, he unscrewed the lid and slowly drank. He then offered the flask to Willie.

'Water?' he said, in English.

Willie shook his head. Ringing in the ears. The dog began again, a more insistent bark; determined to get to the blood and flesh offered before it.

'Eleanora said she thought you would be here,' Khaled Rasul said. His moustache. His cool brown eyes. Did Rasul know what was happening to Eleanora at this moment?

'I thought it important that you be included in these photographs: the world will know, then, what the British are doing.'

Willie's hands were shaking. Wicklow stepped forward. He had, Willie could see, his hand on his revolver and a dead-flat look in his eye. The tinnitus in Willie's ears started to clamour, crackled through his head, drowned out the sound of the dog and the flies. Ashton gave Wicklow an alarmed glance and stood next to Willie, shaking his head at Khaled Rasul.

Willie turned to Charles. 'Your daughter ...' he began, but Ashton jolted.

'Good God, he's alive.'

They all followed Ashton's gaze. Wicklow, who had lit a cigarette, dropped it to the ground and with Ashton ran towards the body on the central ladder, followed by Willie. A dripping, sticky line of blood from the man's severed wrists had left two large scarlet circles. It was true: this man was twitching. A woman who had been silently crying suddenly shouted out, began screaming.

Willie searched in his pocket for his knife and climbed up on to the first rung of the ladder. In order to reach the rope around the man's stomach he had to lean in close. Khaled Rasul was next to them, photographing.

'Really,' Ashton said, 'stop it, Rasul, you are not helping.'

But he carried on. The shutter: click. The day: a dream. A photograph. Suspended in light, and what is not light. Wicklow caught the man as he fell. He was gagging, groaning, green liquid coming from his mouth. The woman ran over, collapsed on to him. Other men came forward. Voices rose in the air around them, as if a spell of immobility had been broken and the whole village, frozen in shock previously, was thawed, given permission to howl.

The body was carried into a house next to the bakery on the edge of the square. The room was filled with people and women came forward to bathe and bandage the wounds that were still bleeding ferociously. A woman whose face was as lined as the oldest olive tree trunks bent over the grisly fly-covered hands and feet, and called to the wife: *Which are his?*

Willie stood inside the door to the bakery where a group of people were surrounding the surviving man. His fear of Rasul was all-consuming. It shut down a section of his brain, reawakened it. Did Rasul know what he had done to his wife? At her behest. Those words in his mind. She asked me.

Eleanora said she thought you would be here. I thought it import-ant that you be included.

What did it mean? *Fuck. Fuck.*

Willie watched Rasul's quick, certain movements around the square, talking to people in the village. A woman, draped in black dotted with light snowflakes, stepped forward. She began a full-throated shout. His Arabic was shaky at the best of times, he was better with the Cairo dialect. She was holding her head between her hands. She was shaking her head. Then letting out a cry. *Ingliz Ingliz Ingliz.* That, he understood. It was a call of blame. Two younger women came forward, also wrapped in dark colours, and tugged her away, pulled her screaming into a door which was shut on the badness, on the tight air, on the ants turn-ing the red black.

Willie's hands were slimy, slicked with sweat. Rasul occasionally took out a smaller camera to photograph something. A box, which he looked into. He was not hostile towards the British, but he moved in a way that was ... what was it? Could Willie capture it? Defiant? He surged with a quiet power as he moved. That was the only way Willie could describe it to himself.

Ashton and Wicklow had both taken off their shirts and ripped them to be used as bandages on the man who was laid out on a bed, letting out gasps. A noble yet fairly pointless gesture at this stage. Too late. Too insincere. An elderly woman threw herself on to the floor in front of Willie and wailed; whether prayer or insult, it was filled with sorrow. Willie turned away from her, and saw Prudence walking across the square, her cheeks bright red and her hair blown awry.

'It's Prue,' he called to Ashton.

Frau Baum came running behind her, stumbling and reaching out for Prue, but the child hopped in front of her, tugged away.

'I thought you said Elspeth had her?' Ashton said over his shoulder, stripped down to his bare chest.

Did I say that? Willie ran back through what had just happened. I did not. Ashton had assumed. He hadn't asked about Prue.

The child was walking towards the ladders. The light was dipping now; the corner stairwells with their spiral staircases brought the edges of the village houses into relief. Prue stood looking at them, for a moment, and then swung around. She walked towards the two hanging men, whom nobody else seemed to be concerned about any more. She shouldn't see this, Willie thought. He stepped towards her. She should be protected from this, but then he stopped moving. She was not his child. It was not his place to help her. Ashton came to the door and squinted out into the light. His thin sallow chest very pale, his stomach a perfect round ball with a line of black hair down the centre of it.

'Where is she?'

'There,' Willie said. The small girl stood alone, staring up at the dangling, hanging bodies.

'Prue,' Ashton shouted. 'No, get away.'

A stream of crows, rooks, birds of all sorts, took to the sky at the sound of a gun being fired from just behind the trees at the corner of the square, and Lofty stepped from behind an outhouse. Several women cried in alarm and sheltered behind men. Khaled Rasul stood up and squinted towards him.

'Lofty,' Ashton shouted, and then the Irishman looked directly at him. 'What the bloody ... Jesus Christ, what HAVE YOU BEEN DOING?'

Lofty walked slowly, but at the sight of him everyone drew back, held on to one another, cried out. Prue did not look around; she was staring up still at the men dangled like autumn leaves. Lofty had his Turkish whip in one hand and a rifle in the other. A woman, kneeling in front of the ladders, saw him and began shuddering and screaming. Lofty held his rifle towards Willie's face. 'You,' he said. 'Make her stop.'

Ashton stepped forward. 'Lofty, old chap, things have got rather out of hand. I think we should ...'

'You,' he repeated to Willie. 'Get her to stop.'

Red eyes. Here they were. *Call yourself an Englishman.* Coming from an Irishman.

'Make her stop.' Lofty's rifle was trained at Willie. The circle of it, the central definition of it. The truth of the barrel of a gun at the head. Willie moved towards the hysterical woman and leant forward. *Stop it, stop it, stop it.*

'Get out your gun.'

Ashton, who had been wittering behind them – 'Stop, too much, Lofty, gone too far' – was suddenly still. Watching, as was Wicklow. Willie pulled out the small revolver that Wicklow had given him earlier.

'Point it at her.'

With shaking hands, Willie held the gun towards the village woman who was sobbing on the ground. She was about the same age as Eleanora. She looked up at him. Behind her the men were hanging from the ladders. The dismembered hands and feet were rotting in a heap. Wicklow stepped forward, Ashton stepped forward, everyone looked up at Lofty and there was a click, but not a gun. The compression of a shutter. Rasul had photographed it.

Lofty jumped a little at the sound of the camera, and swung around. Willie let his arm drop; the woman bent forward and continued to sob. Wicklow moved to her, said something, tried to help her up. Ashton, rubbing his beard, furious, began to shout at Lofty.

'What the devil, what the fuck, do you think you have been doing?'

'Oh, His Majesty's Service, Charles.'

At this, Willie watched as Ashton turned away and saw his daughter on the other side of the ladders, staring at them.

'Who left her there, on her own, in the middle of this?' Ashton shouted, standing half-naked, having dedicated his shirt to the wellbeing of one of the men barbarically attacked. He walked at first, then ran towards her.

You did. You did. You left her there. Willie looked up at the sky. There were no more snowflakes; it hadn't been a real flurry, just a few noble attempts, a falling for no reason.

London, 1933

Charing Cross Road, then Denmark Street, leading to St Giles, and of course it is raining. 'Let's walk, my friend.' He is shy: that is the central thing about him, I realise; the alarming thing. In person so different to the letter-writing Ihsan whose pen sings warmly: '*Habibti*. When it rains in Jerusalem I think of you in London ...'

'Are you hungry?' Ihsan asks, and then four footsteps later he asks me the same question and I say no, although I am, because who isn't hungry in London at this time? Everyone tired and looking for work. I am still living off the fat of Piers's family but the girls I know, the artists' models at Slade, and the tramps in the pub are always ravenous and I starve myself with them. It is a way of feeling part of things, I suppose, although with most of them there is a mode, a mood, a modern way of thinking which rather lends itself to the encouragement of self-extinction. I am wearing Piers's trench coat with long deep pockets. It is much too big for me.

'London rain,' Ihsan says, 'just as you described it.'

'I'm sure it's the same as any other rain.'

He stands in the street with his palms up and his lovely face directed at the sky, with his Jerusalem breath and his Jerusalem hair getting wet, refusing to put up his umbrella.

'No,' he says. 'It is different. You're skin and bones inside that coat,' he said, looking at me instead of the sky. 'Are you cold?'

'If you like the rain I want to stay out in it.'

'We make a good pair then, don't we? The baby is happy enough with the nurse?'

'Well, she's not really a nurse and he's not really a baby, he's two, but yes, he is fine with her.'

He takes my arm, it is the first time we have touched since he arrived, and before long, with the rhythm of our feet, we are moving in tune again, huddling together against the December cold.

'Jerusalem is such an unhappy city, Prue. It is a relief to be away from it.'

I don't quite know what to say to this. It is a city that has burned in my mind all my life, but I can't, in all honesty, picture it that well. I see twisted alleyways, endless stairs. I remember the coldness of the wind and a feeling of parts of it always seeming to change shape, a bit inconsistent, unsettled.

'I'm not here for long. Business for my family,' and he refuses to see any London sights, so I tug him towards the doors of Lyons on Tottenham Court Road, and after a moment's hesitation he comes in. The tea room is very popular, due no doubt to the rain, and it takes the nippy, tucked up like a penguin in her black and white uniform, a minute or two to find us a seat. In the end we are lucky because it is a table for two next to the window; we need not share and we can watch people scurrying past.

Ihsan looks distinctly exotic compared with the drab English faces staring gloomily into their cups around us, almost dandy, in a natty suit which is smart and yet somehow not the British style, and so quaint with his bow tie. As soon as the tea things are laid along with cake and a small pot of cream, the feeling between us is awkward and not quite as I'd wished. The waitress looks at him as if he is about to steal everything in the shop, as if she wishes to move the teacups away from him to keep them safe from his foreignness, but Ihsan doesn't notice or, at least, if he does he does not let on.

The sugar in the bowl in front of me has flecks of I don't know what in it. I cross and uncross my ankles. The rain has made its way through all the layers of my clothes, leaving me shivery. I play with my saucer, spill sugar, I'm unsure quite how to be with him. I have just spent fourteen days in a fury in the Little Antiques at the Slade, I have artistic pretensions that I would like to share with dear Ihsan, but the vast gulf of time passed between us is both resolutely there and also diminishing with each tick of the Lyons wall clock. Are we close? Are we intimate? I can't say. I have written to him, oh, I don't know, lines such as: 'I want to make art that captures the curve of light, that makes the person looking at it feel a sense of vertigo, and this is the one thing I feel to be true: imbalance, and the sense that life is always on the fine edge.' What I want to say is: 'I am trying to love and care for baby Lawrence, whom we call Skip, but the two things are incompatible. The child. The work.' Of course, I say none of this; I should make light chitchat about his family, about his business concerns, but I just smile and he smiles back.

We are shy because, even though we have written to one another over the years, our letters have never particularly dealt with real life or practical concerns. I find I cannot bring myself to ask him certain questions about his private life, such as: does he want a wife? Is he lonely? Does he still write poetry? Nor do I say much about Piers, or motherhood, because how can I even begin? I find ways to cover my face, lock my hand over half of it to block out my mouth and teeth, or lean on my palm, covering up my cheek. I am exposed in the window-light, opposite him; it is too much after all these years. I would have preferred to meet him in the dark.

At the Russell Hotel the doormen who look like the hatter from Alice in Wonderland swing back the large golden doors for us, raise their eyebrows at Ihsan's Arabness and the shimmer of his shoes. It is only four o'clock but, as it is London-winter, night is already coming. We walk into the lobby and Ihsan takes my arm.

'Would it be inappropriate . . .?' He looks shy.

'What?'

'To request that we go to your room, rather than sit in a public place. There is something I need to talk to you about. Is your husband there?'

'No. But he may be back at any time. It's fine, Ihsan, many people come and go through our room. Let's go up.'

The staircase winds upwards, the music in the lobby hums. Everyone I know lives in these halfway homes. This person has a cottage, that person is giving up rooms in Kensington, do you want to take over this room in the hotel? Everyone tramps from one abode to another, I really don't know why. Is it the nature of artists, or a lack of trust in buildings? Ihsan is chattering now as he did not do outside or in the tea room, ringing complimentary bells for every step: 'I always knew you would be elegant.' It isn't until I unlock the door, push it open and we are engulfed in the musty smell of hotel room, surrounded by the scattered mess of my clothing and underwear everywhere, that I feel the chaos of my life exposed.

'Forgive me, Ihsan.' I rush around the room, trying to clear things away.

He stands near the bay windows, looking down at Russell Square, and then glances around our suite. There is a piano in the corner which neither Piers nor I can play. The bed is vast and four-postered, the wardrobe even larger. My dresses, many of them given to me one night by an American heiress who couldn't be bothered to pack her bags to take them back to New York, lie in heaps about the room. As soon as the door swings and closes shut behind us there is an awkward electric jolt to the air. It is, after all, a hotel room and I find myself looking at Ihsan less as a person I have known for so long, more as a stranger. The age between us – once eleven and twenty, now twenty-four and thirty-seven – seems much less of a gap now.

'Where is your husband?' And I do not say *with other women, dear Ihsan.*

'He's working, I believe.'

He takes off his coat and walks over to the piano, putting his hand on it as if blessing it. 'Why do you live in a hotel rather than a home?'

'I don't believe in homes,' I say, hating myself for speaking like Piers, and walk out of habit immediately across to the drinks cabinet even though it is early. I turn, 'Would you like something, Ihsan?'

And he lets out a small giggle which is almost girlish. 'I would like a small red wine, perhaps?'

'That I'll have to ring for.'

'Where is the child?' He looks around, as if Skip might be hiding behind the curtains or under the sofa.

'They must be out for a walk. I'm not sure.' I have in fact instructed Nanny to stay away as long as possible. I didn't want Ihsan to see how clumsy I am with my son. I order the drinks whilst he is in the lavatory and glance in the bedroom mirror to see how I must appear to him. My teeth look big. I am tired. Piers is sleeping with a student called Camilla and it upsets my every waking moment. He walks around with large eyes as if always on the verge of a confession. Whenever he 'wanders' in this way, it is always me he eventually looks to for solace. I guessed about this new woman – or rather, girl, I imagine – but when he got round to the moment of telling me, transforming an anxiety in his mouth into words which I saw dissolving before they were fully formed, the confession was not what I had been expecting. Instead, it was resentment: for me spending all my time in the studio, for the focus I can achieve, for the buyers who come to pluck what they can out of my mind. Piers cannot make art himself. He can critique it, sell it, he has the most divine taste, he can talk about it, he is steeped in it, he wants nothing else than to think about it, be it, absorb it, understand it, but sadly, he cannot produce it. The night he fully realised this he cried on my knee like a baby. *Why?* he kept repeating. *Why?* I could think of nothing to say. 'Perhaps you are not prepared to expose yourself?' I remembered his nights of locking me in hotel rooms to extract 'material'. Those years. Bruised years.

To come to terms with his difficult struggle involved him going to bed with other women to help him navigate his way. Did I understand? Perhaps I do, but Ihsan does not need to know one jot of this.

I powder my nose, attempt to hide the shadows beneath my eyes, go back into the main room and pour myself a finger's width of whisky, knocking it straight back before Ihsan returns.

We settle at either end of the long green sofa with a reassuring distance between us, but he keeps glancing around the room; something about it disturbs him.

'Do you have anything here, of your own?'

'Of course.' I look about me. 'My sculpting materials. A few books.' There is on the table a book called *Unit One*. It has just been published by Cassell and sent to me. There is an entire chapter devoted to my work. I am between Wells Coates and Colin Lucas.

'I am in this, look,' I say, ashamed of myself. I was rather cajoled to be in there, but I realise that to a man like Ihsan, from a city full of stones and a family reaching back in time, the idea of living in a hotel is disturbing and I want to distract him. He opens the book. The illustration plates are black and white. *Duennas, 1931. Interior*, by Nash. Ihsan reads: 'Unit One is the name of a new group of English artists – painters, sculptors and architects ...'

'Yes,' I say. 'They all like to form clubs.' I force him to put the book down. 'I have a trunk and a suitcase of bits and pieces, nothing much.'

Ihsan puts his hand into the black leather briefcase he has been carrying around with him and I realise that it is so lovely to see his face, after all these years. It has a sadness to it, of course, as faces do over time, corroding, no longer fresh, but it is a sorrowfulness that doesn't need to draw in other people to exist. It is self-contained. I admire that.

He rummages about in the briefcase. I imagine myself touching his cheek; could I have loved Ihsan? I mean, married him? I have never articulated that thought before – how odd? – and as if I've flicked on a projector I can see a different life: living with him in a house in Jerusalem surrounded by pots of figs and geraniums. A scurrilous fancy flitters through my mind: this is why he is here? I am full of tenderness for him, but then it occurs to me that he has always held something back. His letters, yes, they have been full of yearning, but who does he spend his days with? What does he do? I think he is going to bring out poetry, and then my cheeks are red and my breath is short in my throat, because it comes to me: a declaration of love, *of course*. That is it. *Ihsan*. The curve of a different life shows itself to me, but it seems it is his job that is preoccupying him most. He takes out what he was looking for – papers – puts a package on his knee, folds hands over it.

'You know, Prue, that I am a clerk in the German Consulate in Jerusalem, working for this new consul, Heinrich Wolff?'

I compose myself. 'Yes, you mentioned it briefly in a letter, I think.' I smile at him. I am an idiot, of course. What was I thinking, a marriage proposal? I am already married. This is Ihsan.

'It is an awful profession, it should not exist.' He crosses his legs.

'It can't be that bad.'

'It is indeed that bad.' He flaps a piece of paper towards me. 'For instance, I have to copy out a page, and then record it, make sure there is a duplicated letter, make sure that is filed, make sure I know what is coming in and out, make sure it is in the correct place, labelled, dated.'

'There are worse jobs, Ihsan. Imagine if you work in a factory, making eyelets for soldiers' boots. That would be terrible. All day long punching the little holes for laces on boots.' I feel I can say this with authority because one of Marguerite's friends did a job like this, during the war, and her fingers were damaged and she almost went blind. So the story goes.

He leans forward. 'There is much strangeness.' He frowns. 'Things are very difficult.'

'What do you mean?'

'The new consul has to follow orders from Berlin. He has to check whether the German academics now taking the posts in Jerusalem are either Jewish, half-Jewish, a quarter-Jewish or, as they call it, Aryan.'

'Well, why does this bother you, dear Ihsan?'

'Because I am the clerk. I have to do the checking. You have no idea of the madness. I will describe it for you. Imagine this: Frau Lang is shouting at me. Wolfgang Lang is saying to me that his wife is Jewish-blood free. I say, I believe you, I believe you, but the consul says it has to be proved, these are the instructions from Berlin.'

'Well, how can it be proved? Is she Jewish?'

'It doesn't matter what you practise, it is who you are descended from: Herr Wolff is very clear on this.'

'It seems a lot of bother for what reason?'

'Who knows the answer to that, dear Prue? I certainly do not. Here is Frau Lang and her parents are Slovene, Izmirian, French and some unidentified Roman Catholic origin. So, you know what I must spend my mornings doing?'

'What, Ihsan? I am beginning to think you are right, this is a terrible job.'

'I must contact the officials in each of the cities that Frau Lang's grandparents supposedly lived in; I must attempt to collect documents from each town relating to these grandparents. I must send a telegram to each city, and then follow with a letter and, following that, a phone call.'

'Oh stop, Ihsan. You are giving me a headache.'

'My life is a headache.'

'But why do you work for the Germans?'

'They employed me because I am secular and I speak the languages.' He leans further in and lowers his voice. 'I have heard it is possible that soon all the German Jews in Jerusalem will have to change their name to Sara or Isaac and guess who will have to formalise the paperwork for each and every one of them?'

What he is saying is too fantastical; I do not believe him. 'That cannot be true.'

'It is.' He pauses.

'Did you know the pilot, William Harrington, was a fluent German speaker?'

This, a name from another time, and it is important that Ihsan thinks I am doing well. That I do not dissolve, like dust blown about in the wind. I want him to think of me as substantial, not silk. Not like a sliver of light. I am listening to his stories but the words aren't sticking to me, they are falling like leaves, other lifetimes and other people's problems, and none of it makes any sense. I want to make art and not think of the troubles of the world that only involve men in coats with shiny buttons, taking people to other rooms, taking them away, hurting children.

'He returned to Jerusalem this year,' Ihsan says. 'He is doing something for the British Consulate.' Ihsan holds his hands above the package on his knee and spreads them as if looking at his fingernails. They are immaculate.

'Oh? What was he doing?' I am trying to remember him. The Englishman who loved Eleanora, the photographer's wife. Of course, I hadn't forgotten him; I simply hadn't thought about him, specifically, for some time.

'Elspeth – Frau Baum – and I have become friends. She does wonderful work at the School of Archaeology and helps with some of the legation around houses. Who is entitled to make a home in a place, who owns a piece of land? Sometimes it is diffi-cult to say. Everybody is arguing about property, but she told me, and I will tell you, what he is doing. He is working for Wolff.'

'What do you mean?'

'He is based at the Fast, and this is agreed by his office in London, and he is overseeing the exchange of information regard-ing transfers of money via the Palestine-Anglo Bank. In other words, my dear, the British and the Germans have a fruitful co-operation and many agreements via Jerusalem on behalf of these people in Berlin we are now calling the Nazis.'

'Oh.' A pigeon lands on the balcony rail for a moment, bobbing its head and looking at me, and then it is gone. Ihsan's words curl around me, but all I really hear is that he is not telling me that he loves me and the skin on my chest is itching with embarrassment and the shock of what I had imagined. He looks a little disap-pointed in me. I haven't really risen to the occasion, and I try to concentrate.

'I'm not quite sure what this all means.'

'Well. Last month, he contacted me. He wanted to meet.'

He takes my hands, both of them, and pulls me towards him. His eyes are very strange; they are full of an unidentifiable emotion, as if there are secrets, but at the same time everything inside him is transposed outside and that causes him pain. I feel full of shame:

I have done everything wrong. I am an awful mother. A terrible wife. A useless artist. An unimpressive being. I want to tell him all of this.

'We met at one of the Arab cafés. He was agitated, in a state of anxiety.'

I try to listen, I really do. I haven't eaten for a long time, it might be days, and my stomach is flipping, turning, drowning, and an odd thing happens: the light, a dazzle on the floor, clatters from Russell Square, a crystallisation in my vision. I push my palms together to stop the flapping.

'What was wrong with him?'

'He talked about you. He was remembering you. I did not tell him that we write to each other, that we have always stayed in touch.' Pages and pages of letters I have sent to Ihsan over the years. All the strains of thoughts, and a horrible urge came through me, not to move, not to speak, but to pull back all the words I had offered Ihsan, all the crossings-over of intimacies. Sometimes I wrote in shifra, I was entirely uncensored, I spilled it all. There was a creeping flurry inside my stomach. He was, of course, such a gentleman in person that he would never refer to the transgressions, the tiny exposures which seem, now, like cuts made with a knife into the skin and blood offered up. His hands in mine felt like dry, crisp paper.

'He was convinced that someone at the Consulate, someone working for the British Government, was trying to assassinate him. He was paranoid, he looked very unwell. It was an extremely uncomfortable meeting.'

Willie Harrington in Jerusalem: the smell of burning, and a dog near a foot, sniffing it. Once you have begun to remember it is difficult to stop; one day from the past collapses into another.

Memory is not a stream of photographic images, it is flightier than that. It is the sinew along the edge of a bird's wing. It is a dangling bird's foot, the startling touch of feather-fur. The smell of burning again.

'He mentioned a day, with your father, and you. A trip to a village called Lifta.'

I stand up. I remember this: a long time before my father came back into my life and I was sent to Jerusalem to be drawn and ignored. A trip to the seashore with bucket and spade, an 'amusing summer day' with a neighbour boy whom I didn't like. He sat with his bottom in the dank wet sand, the sea so far out that it was hardly worth the effort of tramping that far. Sent off together with the boy I didn't like, or know. I am wearing an emerald-green dress. Go to the horizon, keep walking, walking and at the shore toes in, too cold, the boy scratching his head saying, 'Eggs in the hair.' I turn and look back, and they have gone, the mothers, gone. My mother gone. They don't come back to get us until the sun is dying.

Ihsan is looking at me. 'You don't want me to continue?'

'Of course I do.'

'Do you remember the day?'

'I remember dogs, burning. Feet?'

Ihsan nods. I think of the sea: of drowning, in large swimming pools in great hotels. The hotels I stayed in with my father, in those years after Jerusalem, always had swimming pools, on the roof, or in the garden, or sometimes deep in the bowels of the building, and I would walk down the long hotel corridors in the complimentary hotel gowns, almost naked under the robe, feeling both intimate and exposed. The pools were invariably empty and I would slip in, and as soon as I floated, buoyed by water, blinking up at the sky or the dripping wet ceiling, I would hear a voice. Always calm, sane, perfectly integrated with the flickering light reflections on the tiles and the sound of lapping water. Go down, it said, and so I did, swimming underwater with eyes closed until I nudged the edge of the pool, just as I imagine a shark might nose against the side of a boat. An unambiguous sweet voice that terrified me.

'Prue? Something happened that day? I wasn't there, of course, but you were, with Eleanora?'

'Yes.' Time slipping under me like a hand. Underneath me, on the sofa, is a fox-fur coat, draped over a cushion. It is one of my favourites, narcissistically I suspect; its colours match those of my own hair, a streaking, blended red-blonde. The light on the fur makes it look as though it is on fire.

Ihsan coughs. From inside his package of brown paper he pulls out a pink envelope and places it on my knee. 'I don't want to bring back bad memories, Prue, but you need to hold on to these. He wants these. He said whoever is trying to kill him wants these. I don't think they should be in Jerusalem.'

'What is it?'

'Photographs, by Rasul, printed in Eleanora's darkroom.'

Something in me wakes up: a click, out of the stupor of memories from too long ago. The sound of a bicycle bell from the street below pierces the room.

'Eleanora?' I say. 'How is she?'

His face comes closer. 'I did write to you about it, my dear, but she died, in childbirth, two years ago.'

'I never received that letter.'

'Oh?'

'Childbirth?'

'Yes, a late pregnancy.'

My hand in hers: her turning away from me. It was not her fault. It was because she wasn't my mother. I took the envelope from him and stroked it.

'Why are you giving it to me, Ihsan? I am not the terribly best person to give important things to, I feel.'

'Keep the envelope. It might be important, I don't know. There is something about that Harrington, he is trouble. I don't trust him. These photographs ... well. It is possibly incrimination.'

Gifts, I have come to realise, are curses. When a person hands you a mouse, or puts something in your pocket, or creeps into your room at night to leave something behind, it is not a gift, it's more often a stain. A blemish, a scar, and a reminder of something you work hard, very hard, at burying underneath other broken elements of daily life.

'What is it?' I tap on this envelope of his.

'Photographs, Prue, and some letters, but don't worry about them now it is better if you don't look. Just keep it. One day you might need it.'

He is being cryptic, and he is looking mysterious, and I half-laugh in my head at his ways and the pink envelope which smells of Jerusalem.

'And a few other papers.'

I am not at all sure. I put the envelope on the low table in front of us. You know, Ihsan, I was poorly for a while, and I saw a doctor. I told him about my dreams of bad weather, the snow falling down and collapsing a roof. The sea coming up and taking houses away. The wind blowing homes to pieces. He said, 'These fears are not rational,' and I said, 'Oh, they are.' And I thought: what kind of doctor cannot see that feeling terrified of houses blowing away is rational? Thoroughly logical. This is why children rail against adults, because their fears, which are real, are ignored and told to be wrong. Fear one: my mother is not my mother, she is a monster wearing a mask. Fear two: the hat stand is not a hat stand but a person standing in the room. Fear three: the house won't survive the night.

I don't want to talk to Ihsan as if we are strangers. I want to talk to him as a person who knows me, but I can see that if I really do talk it will come out too fast, and unhinged, or unmoored, however poetically it can be put. Ihsan is a person cloaked in the worries of a world that hardly exists for me. I am barely aware of it. The talk of bad times in Jerusalem and wars and pilots from the past impacts on me only as much as I worry about getting materials to carve, and whether exhibitions will be available, will still run.

We are awkward saying goodbye, but in the end I kiss his cheek, and he squeezes my hand and regrets that he has not met my son or my husband. He sets off to his business and his long journey back.

As soon as Ihsan is gone, of course, I open the envelope. Inside there are a few photographs of Jerusalem and I am surprised to see several letters or notes, written in my own childish hand. Not recent letters; these are old. I look at the date: 1920. The pages are largely unintelligible. Alien shapes written by me, and swirls and doodles, mixed in with Arabic, Hebrew, French, Turkish, even Russian words. I turn them over. Could I really speak all of these languages? Drawings of birds, a précis in French of a film called *The Blue Bird of Happiness*. Pages and pages written in code, and I remember it then, the hours spent learning it all and the thrill of being able to give a secret a form and keep it locked in a certain dimension; the exquisite contradiction of letting the innermost thoughts flow out through black ink, whilst trapping them into a private place.

I stand in the middle of the hotel suite, the room too silent now that Ihsan has gone. I should have asked him why he looked so sad, what he was going to do now; he should have stayed, met Piers, met Skip. Or I should have told him I loved him.

A cold feeling comes down on me. I run to the door to call him back in, to talk to him properly, in a less distracted way, to understand what he was telling me, but the long yellow-walled corridor is empty and smells, as usual, of recently boiled or steamed food. There is a hum coming from somewhere. I did not listen to him properly; I did not speak to him truthfully. My ears feel red and hot in contrast with the rest of me, which is cold, and I sit back down on the sofa and wish that Skip were here.

The papers in my hand are singing to me. They are covered in the furious telling of conversations retold to myself, scenes witnessed and spied, noted down for my own use. Each ink stain and smudge on these old pages brings up a feeling of loss, or regret, and finally I push them all back into the envelope and do not want to look at them any more. I will take the lot to the Thames, down on the sloping part of the bank near Battersea Bridge where I can follow the steps to the mud-banks if the tide is low and rip up the pages and give them to the herons to use as stuffing for their nests, or to the fish and eels to nibble.

It is Eleanora in my dream, in my sleep. We are at work together: a large project, the undertaking of the creation of an enormous family album made up of all the photographs that we have taken. It is a joint effort, a team endeavour, and we spend a long time arranging sequences, pairs, matching photographs. But! We can't agree: there is a problem. We are discussing montage. Selection. Which moment to be chosen and which to be left out. The book hung with photographs. A story for each one of them. But I haven't started yet. Eleanora is unholdable, drifting away from the scene of productivity, the work table where the photographs are all in the wrong order. The dream not really a dream, because I was awake. Piers creeping in. Opening my door. *You awake?* I don't respond. I fake a deep sleeping breath and hear an incomprehensible sound of pre-dawn birdsong outside. You're too early, I say. You're too soon.

Shoreham, 1937

There are three men in front of the entrance to the aerodrome and their words travel on the wind. 'I hate being out of London,' one of them is saying, 'in the scrappy parts of England. There is nothing more deplorable than the out-of-date dress shop of the provincial high street.' Another one says, 'Next door to it an emporium dedicated to the welfare and dressing of dogs.' Laughter. Billy coughs and they turn around. It is two policemen but in different uniforms, London issue presumably, and a man in a beige overcoat who immediately steps forward. He takes off his hat and holds out his hand. He shakes Billy's first, and then mine, introduces himself as Mr Wicklow, of the British Intelligence Service, and then glances down at the envelope in my hand.

'Is that what he wants?'

'Yes.' I hold it tight. 'Where is my son, have you seen him?'

'We think he is on the airfield.'

'Well, can we go then?' I look behind me; Mrs Deal has not come forward: she is standing next to the police car, looking uncertain. My tongue feels thick, as if fur is growing on it, as if it is swelling.

'I would be very grateful,' the man from British Intelligence says, 'if I could just have a quick look at the envelope, to verify.'

'No, I have to give them to him, to get Skip.' I stare at him.

'I need to look first.' The man, Mr Wicklow, though he is very thin, has a definite way of blocking my movement whilst barely moving himself. It is clear that he means whatever it is that he means. My ears are hot, tongue getting bigger, hands flapping, looking left and right and over towards the airfield for Skip. Billy puts his hand on my shoulder, but I shake him off, although actually I am grateful.

One of the policemen intervenes. 'It is three. He designated three o'clock, is that correct?'

'Yes, that's true.'

'We should go.'

Billy, I notice, is strangely quiet under this gaunt-looking man's self-imposed authority. We step together in a small troupe towards the Art Deco doorway with the long angular handles but then Mr Wicklow says, 'Actually, it might be better to go that way.' And so we move along the edge of the building towards an industrial gate. I look at all the aircraft dotted around the edges of the field, and as far as the perimeters which are hedged by wind-crippled trees, but I cannot see Skip. It is much windier on this side of the building.

'Where are they?'

'There, look.' It is Billy who sees them in the furthermost aircraft. 'In the Blackburn.'

We walk towards the aeroplane and I can make out a person in the cockpit and another behind him, much smaller, barely peeping over the top of the window ledge.

'Billy,' I say, 'you have to stay here and not come. I don't want Skip to see you.'

He looks surprised. 'Why?'

'In case, some of this, he has gone with him because of ... I don't know. You. Walter.'

'Me? Walter?'

I have the envelope and am about to run but Mr Wicklow stops me, pulls my arm and is surprisingly strong. He swivels me around so that I am facing him and this is when I realise that I know him.

'Oh,' I say, 'I remember you.' A lot older and thinner and greyer and looking as if he had hollowed out some bright shiny part of himself a long time ago. 'We've met before?'

He nods. 'We have.' He squints into the sky, and up at Lancing College on the rim of the curve of the downs, the spires of its chapel pointing into the cloud. Then he turns and looks out at the sea.

'My old school,' he says.

One of the policemen pipes up: 'The message that came through very clearly said, PRUDENCE MILLER ALONE BRING WHAT HAS BEEN PREVIOUSLY REQUESTED.'

Mr Wicklow stands still. He appears to be undecided for a moment and scuffs his brogues on the tarmac. I just want to get to Skip.

I look over at the aircraft, at the dot of black that is my son. Before the summer finished I tried to teach him to swim. I thought, if we are going to live by the sea, he needs to learn even though he had never seen the sea before. All the other children of Shoreham flippered like minnows and eels in both river and sea but Skip was afraid of the water. He stood at the edge of the Adur when it was high tide and shivered. He put his feet tentatively into the sea when the tide was far out but refused to go any further, until one hot September day I siren-called him in. I waded in first, held my arms out. Called him. He came. I told him to lean back, on my shoulder, and let me support him. His little body was tense; he resisted floating and thrashed his legs about uselessly. The sea water was cold in most places and then odd sections would be warmed by the sun. I found a balmy spot, and we bobbed. *See, relax, the water wants to hold you.* Seaweed, like a lick, around my leg and I let go of him, for one moment. He panicked, screamed and went under once, twice, his eyes stinging with the sea-salt. I hauled him back to the beach and he sat with his back to me. He wouldn't look at me and I knew from his shoulders and the tension in his arms that he was crying, in the dignified, private way of boys dealing with their own weakness. Afterwards, he said to me, 'You let me go.'

I ignore the men around me and run towards the aircraft which looks like an insane bird dreamt up by a child. I can hear somebody behind me, I assume it is Mr Wicklow, and I picture him clearly now, at the dinner table in the Hotel Fast, glancing around the room, knowing who everyone is. I am ten yards away from the aeroplane and I can see them: Harrington in the cockpit and Skip behind, both looking at me.

Skip is a happy little passenger. He does not look in distress, he is even smiling. He does not quite wave, but one hand raises and something in me falters because it is possible that he doesn't want to be with me, in this scrappy life that I have been trying to make for us on the beach. It is possible that Harrington has told him they will fly and find Piers. Or go on a fun ride, a trip to somewhere close, to Fairlight in Hastings. Or further, perhaps he has given him money or lots of chocolate or told him he is about to be whisked off to Mexico or China or a place where he doesn't have to be disappointed by me. It is possible that the hesitant hand in the air is a goodbye. I slow down and stand still. Then I hold up the envelope. Wave it.

'I have it,' I call. The wind blows my hair, makes my eyes water. 'This is it.' I shout out to Skip, I wave, and beckon, but Skip looks away, responding, I guess, to something that Harrington is saying to him. When he turns and looks at me again, this time he is not smiling.

The plane shudders into life; the noise of the engine is a vicious rattling that takes away all the air around us and slowly the propeller, which seems like two oars tied together on the nose of the plane, begins to rotate.

'I have it!' I am like an old woman who has picked up a fallen scarf. I have it, I have it. Mr Wicklow is behind me, his collar concealing half of his face, not running quite but walking very fast, and I am close enough to see Skip looking at me with wide eyes.

'Skip, darling?' I shout but I slow down again because I can't quite understand the expression; what is it: blame? I turn, hiss towards Mr Wicklow, 'What are you doing? Go away.'

But Wicklow advances quickly towards the plane and shouts, 'Harrington. Turn off the engine and release the boy.' It is almost impossible to hear him over the sound of the propeller. I am full of fury; this man from the Ministry of Knowing Everything, who is escalating this rather than letting me simply hand over the documents that I don't even care about.

Harrington looks down at Wicklow and I can see him shaking his head.

'Skip.'

I pull on Wicklow's coat sleeve. 'Are these papers more important to you than my child's life?' I shout through my hair which is being blown into my nose and my mouth, but the engine eats my words and sea mist has stealthily been creeping across the airfield and now hangs like a drape in the air. I tug again at Wicklow and he is surprised at this; I don't think people, perhaps women, touch him very frequently. The aircraft rolls forward and I run towards it, as close as I can.

Skip is not wearing goggles or even a hat.

Skip, darling. He is looking at me, his bright blue eyes, and I can see he is speaking to Harrington. Emphatic. The engine spluttering, the propeller spinning; something is happening inside that little space. The door is opening. It is Harrington, climbing down, in his dark coat, pulling his goggles off his face. *At least now he is out of the craft he won't fly away with Skip* and I know that my son is made of glass and so precious and I have smashed him, dropped him, left him, over and over again to work on carving stone, and my hands and my skin reach out to him. Harrington walks around the tail of the aircraft, slowly, seemingly in no rush. I don't like Skip being in there, with the rumbling, the spluttering. I look back; Mrs Deal and Billy and the two policemen are watching. Harrington then takes a step towards me and Wicklow.

'Do you have the papers I asked for?' he shouts.

'Yes, I have them,' and I wave the envelope, but Wicklow is next to me.

'It doesn't reveal anything we don't know, Willie,' he shouts, 'even if you do get them and destroy them. We've been watching you for years. We know you went over the line in Salonika and stayed with the Germans, exchanging information.'

Harrington lets out a bitter laugh. 'That is how you intend to paint it, is it?'

The engine and the propeller and the wind are like external manifestations of a migraine that simply won't go, and he looks at me.

'I didn't take him,' he shouts. 'He asked to come.'

'Yes. I can see that's true.'

Harrington gestures to me: come? The sea fret is in my eyes, in my mouth, and Wicklow has hold of my elbow; his fingers pushing into it, tight and crushing. I shake him off; agitation ripples through my whole body and I step towards Harrington. Skip is at the window, his nose flat on the glass, and he is waving at me, beckoning me. The entire fuselage of the craft is shaking. I feel as though I am caught in a drifted net, but I move towards Skip. Harrington takes my arm and pulls me, around the tail of the Blackburn, and I am pushed up, into the mouth of the aeroplane. I throw the envelope on to the floor. There is only one passenger seat; I wriggle under Skip, pull him back down on to me, on to my knee. The slam of the door.

'Oh Mummy,' Skip shouts, worried, excited. I squeeze him. I would rather die in the sky with you than leave you alone ever again, I want to say, but don't. Outside, Billy is standing next to Wicklow; they are shouting, waving arms. Harrington does not say anything to me; he is staring dead ahead, his goggles on, and the Blackburn is moving.

'Look,' Skip says. Billy and Wicklow are now in front of the aircraft, trying to block it.

'Where are we going?' I ask Skip.

'The Isle of Wight, I think.'

And the men must have jumped out of the way, because we are rolling fast along the airstrip now and when we leave the ground Skip says, not at all afraid, 'See, Mummy, we are up up up.'

With the sensation of moving upwards, I remember all the times when younger, in Jerusalem – and London too – of wanting to fly. Images of birds drawn in my books, feathers collected, all the dreams of falling. I take Skip's hand and we no longer look down but instead gaze out at the white, bright space around us.

There are two bluebottles flying in spirals around the room we have taken at the nearest hotel to the Sandown airstrip on the Isle of Wight. On the flight, I surrendered. Skip and I, with our faces to the window, looking down at the curl of the land and the white stripe where it finishes and turns into the sea: the face of the earth; this is what it was. The chalk we walk on. I was furious with the boy, but I was holding him, his grubby fingers on top of mine, and the sweat of him near.

'When we go up into the sky, the world becomes a map,' I said.

'See the world like a bird does.'

'That's true.'

It occurred to me that Harrington might kill us, crash us, or keep flying until we dropped into the sea, but he did not. He landed neatly at Sandown, and we were met by the airmen there with smiling faces, nods, signatures on papers. As if we were on one of Amy Johnson's joyrides.

'We should talk,' Harrington said.

'Did you need to do all of this? Just to talk?'

'I did. I'll explain.'

The hotel room is number seventeen and Skip, exhausted, is unhappy about being deposited in it.

'I need to speak to Mr Harrington, Skip. I would prefer it if you stay in here.' He is at the window looking down at Sandown, which, with its seagulls and sleepiness, feels the same as Shoreham.

He flops on to the bed.

'I should be very angry with you.' I bend down, hold him by the arms and look into his face. 'I'm asking you, please, stay in here.'

'All right, Mummy,' he says, the rims of his eyelids bright red, sore-looking. I close the door, and then I do something I could have hardly imagined myself doing before today. I turn the lock.

Harrington is waiting in the hotel bar in this shabby, desolate place. The owner ducks in and out to see what we want and to attend to other things, surly, non-communicative. The room is damp, the carpet a black-brown colour. The chintz is dusty. We take a seat near the window.

'Wicklow will be here soon,' he says, with confidence, looking out of the window at a view of blackening sky and the grey sea in the distance. It is possible to sense the weather out there, rather than hear it.

'All of that, for this?' The envelope is underneath his arm. He shakes his head.

'No. Well, yes.'

He orders us each a small glass of bitter. I want to make a joke: here we are again. Old friends. This is getting to be a habit. He coughs.

'This will sound very fantastical, but Wicklow has been authorised to "silence" me and so I needed to find a way of making it public, his insistence on getting hold of the remaining Rasul photographs.'

I have no idea how to reply to this, but he says it in a low voice, weary, not trying to make an impact or a statement. I watch as he opens the envelope, pulls the photographs out. The first is of the Hotel Fast, the same as the one he showed me earlier. Flags: the swastika, the British emblem next to each other. Cosy, friends, and I think of Billy: *half the fishermen in here are for Hitler*. And my father: his arms around Frau Baum. *Admissions relaxed, after the war*. Harrington digs about in the envelope.

'This is it.'

'What?'

'This is the one that Wicklow wants.'

I am distracted by the row of ceramic ladies perched along the mantelpiece and a smell of cooking vegetables coming from kitchens: cabbage or sprouts.

This photograph is of four men in a row: one of them, Harrington, holding a gun, pointing it down at a woman crouching in distress below. Behind them, bodies on ladders. I flip it on to the back; there is the stamp: Khaled Rasul Photography. The young Harrington, young Wicklow, my father.

'And here is the negative.'

I hold it up.

'British behaviour in Palestine – well, in particular the behaviour of the *gendarmerie* – has to be written out of history. There is a systematic cleansing. It is so tense in Palestine at this moment, the British are enemy number one, and these details are to be eradicated.'

There is a clanging noise, a bell from beyond the bar, a man's voice: 'Anyone there? Service please.'

'What we did. He wants it all destroyed. Ruins his plans for the next war that's coming. No schoolboys will have this little period of history beaten by canes into their brains.'

He looks out of the window again.

'They will be here, very soon. They will have flown behind us, no doubt, once they've had it radioed in and discovered where we landed.'

Outside: the sky, dark, as if frowning. His face has changed, and something occurs to me.

'I remember you coming into the villa on this day,' I say, touching the photograph on the table between us. The weeds on the step, the snowflakes, and I do remember him, in that room, where I am broken into pieces smaller than the grains that make up the Jerusalem limestone, and then again, I remember him looking through the window at me. His eyes, and the deep recess of the villa window in the stone wall. He blinks, and lowers his head.

'I am sorry, Prue, that I didn't protect you from harm.'

'It was not for you to do so.'

'Still.'

The rain outside has turned to hail which clatters on to the hotel window, a rippled tapping that makes us both jump. He takes the film negative from me and stands up. Looks around the room. Next to the unlit fireplace, which is guarded by ceramic dogs with the label Gog and Magog at their paws, is a bookcase. It is full of holiday romances and rows of Reader's Digest titles. He pulls a book out, and tucks the negative into its back page. Puts it back on the shelf again.

A song in my head: *grah mo chree*, here on your mamma's knee.

Harrington sits down. He runs his fingers over the other photographs, all the work of Rasul, and the last photograph at the bottom is a picture of Eleanora Rasul in a red dress, sitting at the window ledge of one of the upper rooms of Governance House. Her head is turned so she is looking out at the city, a contemplative sideways gaze, and because of the way the light is shining behind her, there's a bright white line around her, as if she's inside a flame and she herself is the red-hot burning pulse at the centre of it.

We both look at the photograph. I touch the flat, unreal face.

'I thought I had forgotten her,' I say, 'but I haven't.'

I tell Skip stories at bedtime about the secret ways we can talk to one another, using codes, or messages, or tugs. Invisible words can fly from one mind to another; it's happened to me, it has, and Skip with his wide eyes is trying to believe me but already at six he is interested in the scientific proof of everything, the bone under the surface and the root in the soil, and I wonder if this man opposite me is talking to me in his head, and I just can't hear it.

'I am going to leave,' he says, coughing. 'Wicklow will be after me. Give him these photographs, although it won't stop there; at least he will never know about that negative in this Isle of Wight hotel. There is a sort of satisfaction in that, don't you think?'

I shrug.

'These are yours,' he says, pushing letters written in my own childish handwriting towards me. He stands up again: that sense of a gate being opened, or a fence erected.

'There is something you should know,' he says, 'although it will be officially denied by the authorities.'

'Oh?'

'It was Wicklow,' he said, 'who authorised the blowing up of the Hotel Fast, and Ihsan was inside.'

When I think of Ihsan, I think of birds and dogs: a wing, a beak, a pant, the way a paw comes up and asks for more. William Harrington takes the drink glasses and puts them up on the bar and I am about to say to him: was it true, what you said, about him just using me? For information? But what is the good in knowing the answer to that? He pats the pockets of his trousers as if trying to remember where he has put something. He doesn't seem agitated, as if running away; rather he has the air of a person setting off for the market.

'Skip wanted to come with you?' I say, as he turns away. He looks back.

'Yes, but I told him we could only go if you came with us.'

I think of the Irishwoman I tried to give him away to. We try to lose each other, mother and sons, but we can't.

'I'm sorry too,' he says, 'about that business with the men near the fishing hut. The fighting.'

Billy: his face staring at me from the airfield, his usual tallness and brawn reduced by the fret and the wind from the propeller. Harrington gives me one more nod. Then he's gone. I pick up the paper in front of me. Written in shifra, but I am not sure if I can remember how to decode it. The page underneath it, however, has the key.

We are leaving Jerusalem. I am being sent back to London soon, Father will join me later, and so we are staying for a day in a German hospice on the shore of the Sea of Galilee. I am writing this on the veranda which is covered in bougainvillaea which grows here the whole year round. There are doves in the sky and it doesn't feel like the end of February but rather summer. I do not say this aloud, but I don't believe you are dead, and so I am continuing to write as before. Those other letters weren't sent, but perhaps one day this will get to you. I do hope Graylingwell is treating you well, and isn't as awful as its name sounds. I don't believe you are dead, even though they have told me that you are.

I stop reading, because the door flings open. It is the two police-men; it is Mr Wicklow.

'Did you have an enjoyable flight?' I say.

Wicklow fills the bar with bad temper and rain; he slams his briefcase on to the table, pulls out papers, sits down.

'Here you are,' I say. 'It's all here.' The two policemen hover near the door. 'You are vulnerable to charges of treason, Prudence Ashton.' At first I laugh, but then I put my hands on my knees and try to understand what he is saying. The barman has returned, and for the first time is listening in to the conversation, eyes switching from me to the policemen and back again, cheeks red. I want to get back to Skip. I rest my hands on the table, breathe.

'You provided information to pro-Arab nationalists at a time of extremely tense negotiations in Jerusalem.'

I look at his face. Long-nosed. Parrot.

'When I was eleven? I don't understand. What information?'

'Advanced notice of your father's plans for the development of Jerusalem under British rule.'

I don't speak, I chew at the inside of my cheek. 'Am I to be put on trial for being a lonely child in a city a long time ago? It seems unthinkable.' Ludicrous.

'You gave Ihsan Tameri outlines of all the proposed architec-tural plans of the city so that the Muntada group would know how to intercept, how to interrupt, how to disrupt. These plans were largely taken up by the following administration even after your father's departure from Jerusalem in 1922, and the informa-tion was used by terrorist activists.'

'Plans? I was a child, Mr Wicklow. You know that well enough, because you met me. You saw me.'

'I know that the hotel staff used to call you the Little Witness. A pertinent title, perhaps?'

'You're not serious?'

Wicklow rummages in his pocket for cigarettes and gives me one. He lights them both, and I don't know why but I am rather surprised that he smokes. He seems rather too *stiff* to have a weakness for tobacco.

'War is coming again, Mrs Miller,' he says, blowing out smoke, 'even though many of us are ready to deny it.'

Should I simply run back up to the room to be with Skip? He will only come following, banging on the door. I try to swallow saliva but my tongue, my mouth and my throat are terribly dry.

'Mr Wicklow, I am just getting a glass of water.'

'I shall get it.'

He goes to the bar, causes a commotion, finally hands me water in a dirty glass. Ihsan in a pile of rubble, a destroyed hotel on the corner of Mamila in Jerusalem. I imagine the light on the dust and wreckage and the burial mounds of the people who were blown up inside. Although, if they were blown up, their bodies exploded into small bits of skin and bone, there would be nothing to bury. So perhaps there were no mounds, in their name, in the Mount of Olives cemetery. Mr Wicklow has his hands in his pockets now, attempting to be informal. He is very minimal in his movements. I have no idea what it is he wants.

'We can come to an agreement, perhaps?' I take a breath. So he has been leading up to something. I wait.

'You might find a way to forget the image of the swastika and the Union Jack together at the hotel in Jerusalem? How shall I put it? The government's position at one time was more fluid, particularly overseas, and it of course does not chime with our current mode of thinking.'

'You mistake me for a political person, Mr Wicklow. Those sorts of things do not concern me.'

'Yes. I imagine so.' He leans against the wall and looks at me. Oddly, I remember the smell of oilskin and the profile of Mr Wicklow's face reminds me of something.

He glances down at the picture of the square; in the corner of the frame the dog, barking at something. I uncross my legs, cross them again, and sit up straighter in the chair, breathing in and rolling my shoulders back a little.

'I should forget that memory too.'

He says nothing else, and I feel, when looking at the sharp jut of his shoulder line, that the pose in which he is sitting has changed, and has become a direct threat.

'It is not that easy to ignore the past, Mr Wicklow.'

'In this case, it is important that you do,' and he gets hold of his chair and drags it so that he is sitting very close to me. He puts his briefcase on top of his knees and rummages through it again and then snaps it shut.

'It is part of my job, Mrs Miller, to conduct thorough research around people we are particularly *in communication with* and in doing so I had a little conversation recently with your benefactress Mrs Margot Eaves.'

'Oh?' He is like an octopus, pushing into every strain of my life. Like the journalists, like Piers.

'She was kind enough to talk me through your ideas for her forthcoming exhibition.'

'Mr Wicklow, please just say whatever it is you are planning to say.'

He sniffs. 'It seems that your provisional ideas, some of your sketches and thoughts, revolve around a series of ladders and spiral staircases.'

'You want to have a discussion about my art?'

Mr Wicklow produces from his magical briefcase a sketch I recognise. It is my own, given to Margot months ago, the design for the second part of my contribution, the two hanging men, which I intend to suspend from a stairwell.

'Why on earth do you have that?'

He pulls out another photograph. This one was not with the pile in the envelope, but it is still clearly the work of Rasul. It is of two men, hanging from their ankles by ropes from beams.

'It is almost exactly the same as the image in your show.'

'But I've never seen that photograph before in my life.' My hands are sweating and Wicklow, until now perfectly calm, is perspiring a little on his temples.

'You must remove these images and any like them from your show. You must speak to nobody, ever, of anything you might have witnessed in Jerusalem in the time you were there, and in doing so, I will refrain from reporting the inappropriate exchange of information by you with the pro-Arab nationalist and anti-British campaigner, Ihsan Tameri.'

I sit perfectly still. 'I did not know this image came from that time.'

'I do not believe that.'

What can I say to this man who looks like a person just returned from a long hunt? He wants to control what is inside my memory. He wants to control how my memory bleeds into what I make.

'I have all the evidence,' he continues, 'and if you don't stick to these conditions then I will be able to arrest you at any time. In

terms of treason, particularly with such long-standing conse-
quences, it does not matter that you were a child, I'm afraid.
Children are moral beings in their own right.'

'Yes, Mr Wicklow. I agree to it, then.' I push the photographs
of the Fast and of the village of Lifta towards him.

'Thank you.'

'I will keep my childish notes?'

'No, I am sorry, anything you wrote in the military encryption
codes is now the property of the British Government.'

'Fine,' I say, consigning to him my descriptions of doves and
bougainvillaea written to a mother who was dead.

He gathers his belongings and gets up to go, and as he does, as
if to applaud the relief of his absence, a valve on a pipe for the
bitter behind the bar judders and spits out froth and I stand up
too, appalled at myself for having locked my child in a hotel
room.

Malta, 1926

The Mediterranean is unusually choppy today. Several boats drift by, each with an eye painted on the bow. On Prue's knee is a soldier's Bible. She opens it randomly – Genesis 19: *and he perceived not when she lay down, nor when she arose* – and across this page she copies the eye, draws it with her black fountain pen, surrounding it with swirls and dashes.

Her drawing becomes not quite a map, but the outline of a house, a home she will one day have: a gable and a roof and an entrance and a stairwell. Saint Paul's Islands are in the distance, low purple shadows, and beyond them Sicily, the Levantine coast, Alexandria and Jerusalem. She rips the page out and rolls it so that it looks like a long cigarette, pokes it into the glass bottle she brought with her from the kitchen, though it has no stopper or cork. It once contained French vinegar. Gulls at the shoreline poke beaks into the sand. An island for magpies: the fishermen dangle blue beads on their boats, strings of glass bracelets, charms to warn off the evil eye.

She makes her way to the water's edge. The dawn happened not so long ago. A British naval officer is coming with his girl linked into his arm; she is swinging her sandals. They both smile at Prue; they have been out having fun all night, probably at a party at the Grand Harbour, and as she passes them the officer swings round and winks. The girlfriend gives him a playful shove. *Hey, look at me.* Because Prue is beautiful today: seventeen, made up of skin, and it is so very rare that she feels like this.

There the bottle goes, an arc, a small splash. Sinks, immediately resurfaces and then quickly settles into a gentle rock and lull. A shout: it's her father, standing on the veranda of their villa.

'There you are, Prue. Come now, breakfast is ready.'

Prue glances at the sun, but she does not return to the house. She leaves the Bible and pen in the sand, runs along the beach, fast as she can, splashing at the edge of the water so that the hem of her dress is wet. Her lungs are full and she runs as far as the beach stretches before it is cut off by a peninsula of craggy lime-stone rocks. She climbs over them and drops down the other side, a smaller bay; more of a cove.

There is nobody here, so she takes off her dress and lets the sun have her, walks into the water, shouts as it covers her, and goes down. Her hair is wide from her face and her skin feels free.

If she opens her eyes underwater they sting, but after one or two tries she can do it. It is just a couple of yards before it is deep enough to swim properly, though her toes still scrape against a sandy seabed. Trails of light and ticklish seaweed wrap her ankle, as if to tug her under and curl between her toes, but she doesn't remove them. She flips so that she is on her back, inflates her lungs to float. The sun wheedles out more freckles. She closes her eyes, bobs, feeling as she did long ago when Eleanora in Jerusalem photographed her: becoming nothing, reducing to nothing, delicate bone, weightless. Things in the water trace her, bump against her, nudge her, but she does not turn over. Like many seventeen-year-old girls, in her mind she sees herself in the frame of a silent movie. Or one of the photographs for sailors: a ready-made sweetheart for a long voyage. The shutter: click. The day: a dream. A photograph. Suspended in light, and what is not light.

When she arrives back at the house, dripping sea water on to the marble floor, her father is sitting with his legs crossed at the breakfast table, irritated. His mistress Andrea, who is Croatian, gives Prue a wide-eyed stare, and then, as if in profound disapproval, looks down at her Italian newspaper.

Her father puts down his copy of *The Times*, and glares. 'We had agreed on the pictures today, Prue.'

'Yes, I know.'

'I had it all set up.'

'Yes.'

Andrea looks over and frowns. Then she leans across the table, picks up a packet of cigarettes and lights one. She has brown hair, and a square, perfectly arranged face, and is only seven years older than Prue.

'Must you use your daughter as a model, Charles?'

He swings round in his chair and rubs his hand along his beard. He stretches his fingers out.

'It isn't seemly, perhaps?' Andrea says.

'Just pictures, my dear.' And Prue follows him through to the central room. He has arranged for her to be seated near the white marble fireplace which is never lit. There is a camera as well as his drawing equipment in front of him. She faces him and a breeze comes over her like a hand on her neck.

'Like this?' She sits: and as he draws her with his pencil, the water comes around her, the bobbing light sensation of being lifted up and then lowered a little down.

'Father, I would like to live in London, at the end of summer. Do you think it is possible?'

He murmurs, and is concentrating.

'Absolutely not,' he says. 'London is no place for a young woman.'

There is a faint droning sound. Prue lets the murmur of the sea around them come into her mind. She has heard a tale about a house near here, on the fishing coast on the west side of the island. Until recently people spoke of having seen pale lights above the house which was inhabited by a widow who wanted to escape. It was a part of her, floating away, they said. Each night a paler and paler light, until she was gone. Prue considers telling her father this story but does not.

She stands up.

'I haven't finished,' he says.

'Draw Andrea.'

That night, Charles Ashton has fallen asleep on the sofa and Prue is left with the young woman who is his lover. They circle one another like cats. Prue is expecting Andrea to slope off as normal, but she doesn't, as if she is making a statement.

'You are keen to leave?' Andrea says, walking towards her on the balcony. Prue is resistant to interaction, conversation. These women come and keep coming, since Frau Baum; after that Clara, now Andrea. She doesn't want to get attached to any of them. Andrea is fragile, with a long thin neck; she talks often of falling down and she has a mysterious sickness which means she drops asleep at inconvenient times. Prue cannot see that Andrea will be in her father's life for very long.

'The island, I mean. You want to leave?'

'Yes.' They are both silent.

'I saw some pictures of your mother,' Andrea says. 'She looks very much like you.'

'Hmm.' Prue won't stoop; she won't be reduced to asking: what pictures? And, do I? Do I look like her?

'Would you like to go out for dinner?' Andrea says. 'Your father is clearly not going to wake again tonight.'

A drop in Prue; a shrug. She agrees and Andrea drives them in a little farmer's truck that she uses to the other side of the island, to an inlet. They have dinner in a restaurant at the end of a stone pier with the sound of water lapping throughout the meal of fried octopi. This woman who is not much older than her, with strong black eyebrows and a steady hand, dabs her attractive lips with her napkin.

'It was such a terrible way your mother died, I was so sorry to hear about it,' she says.

This is it: this is why Prue has been brought here. Boats are dipping and rising in the mini-harbour next to them. A moth rests on Prue's thumb knuckle and then flies away to kill itself in a light somewhere else.

'Choking on bread,' Prue says. Looking at the bread basket in front of them, almost as if a joke could be made, of the coincidence of it.

Andrea's eyes open a little more. 'No,' she says, 'your father told me that she died from having a feeding tube forced into her, in hospital.'

'She died from that?'

'Well, yes, it was the feeding tube that killed her, it punctured a lung.'

Prue stops listening to this woman who has a dark look in her eye; she hears a popping in her ears. Closes her eyes and empties herself of all being, all sound, all thought, and she is simply light, as delicate and empty as a bird bone dried in the sun. Her mother used to eschew food; she would take the bread from the table and pull it into tiny pieces and say, 'Give it to the birds, Prue. They need it more than me.'

Her father asks her for a walk the next morning. It is not comfortable; he makes pleasantries, she ignores them, and they descend into gloom. They walk past the doorway of a small room. It is full of chalk and dust and hammering. It is the sculptor Karsten Azzopardi at work. He trained in Italy, as all the Maltese sculptors do, but he is one of the few to return. The artist himself comes to the door, sees them, smiles.

'An early walk?' he says, in Italian.

Her father, who is loosely proficient in many languages, master of none other than English, says, 'Ah yes. Refreshing.'

'Come in.'

'Really?'

'Of course.'

She is allowed to touch everything: the hammers and the scales and the buckets of water and the saint he is working on, a commission for a church on the smaller island of Gozo, though it is only yet lightly sketched into stone. It is possible to see the swathe of the saint's robe and the way it will fall, the line of her chin, but there is only a hint of the shape of her face, or her hands. Prue touches the stone and is surprised at how alive it feels. Al-Tanka, it is called, he tells her. It is sandy-pink, with stains on it, russet.

As they walk back to the villa along the dusty path, the heat already too much for their English blood, Prue says, 'Father, choking on bread is not quite the same thing as being put in a home and being force-fed with a tube.'

He turns, looks at her. There is his face. His long beard, and blue eyes with a red dot in the whites like a signal for a pilot, and she has this thought: when you take the details of the land you think you own – here in Malta, for instance, walking around the port of Valletta as the British Civic Advisor – measuring the stones and the distance and the bridges and the steps down to the harbour's water and counting the number of churches and considering how to rearrange this, how to rearrange that, then you control it with your bird's-eye view. You control it. A walk around Tiberias. The thick-armed muscle of a police force to do your bidding so that you can instigate your plan – cultivating the *waqf* lands, the stitching of this settlement to the unclear ownership of that land there – and she knows all of this because she has been sneaking into his study. Reading the memoirs he has begun. His working title is *Orientations, Constellations*.

'You don't know what you're talking about,' he says, as if he can read her thoughts.

Memory: her mother, sewing. Napkins or handkerchiefs or linen, or something, and she hadn't come down from the attic room of the house they were lodging in for days; it might have been a week. Prue spent the days going up and down to the char and landlady in the basement who made horrible comments about the heating and the draughtiness. Prue took breakfasts and dinners up, but her mother barely ate anything. Late one afternoon her mother had fallen asleep where she was sitting, chin dropped to her chest, her face still. Her hands laid out neatly on the handker-chiefs; her spine must have been a line of perfectly arranged bones because she was not leaning forwards, or slumped: upright, asleep. Prue picked up one of the napkins and on it was embroidered the word EVIL. The one below that EVIL too. All of them: Prue looked down into the basket; there were very many, it seemed to her hundreds, but she was little, perhaps it was simply one hundred.

Who was evil? What was evil?

Later, she had asked her mother what it meant. The needle going up and down, the long line of red cotton making holes; not a pause, not showing surprise at the question, her mother had said: 'I came to a conclusion that it was the most soothing word.'

'Oh?'

Her mother held her work up to the light. 'Live,' she said.

'Of course,' Prue said. She always saw words the wrong way round and sometimes, when writing, the words would flip back-wards, or the first and last letters would fall off. Which was what might have happened in this case. It should have been ALIVE. Or LIVED.

Jerusalem, 1920

Nothing but a white stillness over the whole of Jerusalem. After weeks of sporadic snow showers it was now a thick deep blanket, alarmingly white. It had been layering without a pause, covering every tree, every bicycle, every fence. People walked slowly, navigating the steep hills in the ice. The domes and walls of Jerusalem were hidden, changing the atmosphere of the city: less leaden and weighed down and exhausted under the struggle of being a symbolic place. Snow brought it peace, perhaps. It was so freshly landed on the streets that Willie's footsteps squeaked as they imprinted themselves in the recent powdering.

There was no warmth to be found inside the Zion Theatre. It was freezing. Willie chose a middle seat. There were several couples dotted about and a few children on the front row. He didn't want to be anywhere remotely near them. *But for the fortunate ones who seek within ... the blue bird of happiness*. This film had been running for so long that everyone in Jerusalem had seen it four or five times, so he was amazed that there was anyone in here. He lit his cigarette, paid no attention to the screen in front of him.

As a boy at Lancing he used to climb on to the wall that surrounded the school, and the view of Salt Farm fields and the roll of the downs always looked to him like a woman lying on her side. Not a particularly curvy woman, a narrow-hipped one, a boyish one with a waist for shaking. That was when he first flew. In a contraption that Piffard invented, as shambolic as could possibly be imagined; the first time he saw the land beneath him, the hip of the woman from above, the swell and scars of the earth, rather than the curve.

The door to the Zion Theatre opened and he knew from the footsteps that it was her. Clipped, light, definite, because we can tell the people we love from a crowd of thousands, from one step of their foot, from the silhouette of their arm. He glanced round. She was wearing a fur coat. Darker than previous coats of hers he had seen, which tended to be russet, foxes. This was dark, bearish.

He had resigned from the position on Ashton's team. Ashton had called him in, shortly after the Lifta affair. It is true we are looking to rethink certain aspects of the city, he had said, but what was really needed was a cadastral survey. An intensive survey of Southern Palestine using aerial photography and revision of the old maps. He was bringing in a team from Egypt who had experience in compiling maps in Sinai and Galipoli. The cosmetics, the moving of the clock tower, the polishing of the ramparts, were merely a superficial topping on a serious consideration of reforming ownership of these lands. On Ashton had gone, on and on. Willie wanted to fly with Eleanora again, to capture something: what? What if they could have rearranged the scars of the world beneath them to their own order? But Ashton was intent on scars more vivid than anything etched on to Willie's chest, and Willie had swallowed his drink, put his glass down. *I'm sorry, Charles. I might have to bow out.*

There was her smell. Tea? Grass? Freshly cut leaves? Mingled with Turkish cigarettes. She was hovering behind him and he would not look up. He pushed fingernails into palms. He remembered a walk along the promenade in Brighton, life-times ago, when he was training in Shoreham. The sea grey and the girl he'd picked up changed her mind abruptly, pulled back and swivelled on her ankles. Her name was Florence, for some reason he recalled this detail, and her little pearl-coloured hand with red nails had dropped his hand. She stared at him as if he were an absolute stranger (well, he almost was). There was even horror in her face and without explaining a thing she ran away, bird-like feet clipping on the prom, leaving him alone with the grim grey sea and the conviction that he was the most grotesque creature in the world. He recognised the moment: a beauty in bed turns, becomes bored and then repulsed. Rejection: a slipper around the face, and stamp on the toe, reasons vague, explanations untrue, coming down to: I don't want you.

All it amounted to in the end was a change of mind (change of heart, his mother used to say: *Have you had a change of heart, darling? We all do, trust me, we all do*).

Eleanora sat down next to him, protected by her fur. He looked at the screen, but he was shocked by the ferocity of his body's response. Darts pricking his skin all over; every part of him awake. A sideways glance, and finally a capitulation. He turned to her. She will always have this demeanour, he realised: serious, quizzical, entirely her own person. In other words, untouchable.

She had been recovering at home for three weeks; he dared not visit. He had dispatched a message with Ashton's daughter, who was being sent back to England in ten days' time. She was to stay there until the following year when Ashton would be posted to either Cyprus or Malta and she would join him. It was not conducive to his land-survey plans to have her here under his feet, under the tables, always having to worry about. Or so Willie understood. The child had made no reference to the day in the stone villa, to the square in the village, and he rather thought she didn't know that he'd been there. He felt culpable, sad, whenever he thought of it. Eleanora crossed her legs. Was she real, Eleanora? Or was she a hope, a first dream? Was she in fact a place, like this theatre, this shed, this walled city?

'You're here.'

'I am.'

'Are you well again?' And he meant to say it with tenderness but it did not come out that way. They both stared up at the screen where a thousand unborn children were drifting around a mother on a throne, and he flushed all over.

'This is the last thing you need to see, shall we leave?'

'It's all right,' she spoke in a low voice, 'I'm not looking at it.'

She said that, but she was watching the flickering screen.

'I told Khaled everything.'

'What?' He turned to her. 'Ellie … what did he say?'

'He disappeared for a week again.'

'He's good at doing that.'

She looked at him with a cold, still expression. She loosened her bear-fur slightly. The dress underneath had buttons along her neck and right up to her chin, as if to claim her unmovable and unreachable.

'You told him about … what you asked me to do?'

She turned, in the cinema seat. 'God no. No.' She blinked at the screen. 'He will never know that.'

Willie did not know what to say. What had she told him then?

'You know,' and she pulled from her pocket the Turkish cigarettes and, fumbling, he lit one for her. 'I had not previously understood my marriage as an architectural place, a curated castle or a city or a house. A swirl of rooms, a number of memories, an infinite number of delicate portions of time. You coming here shook the foundations of the house.'

What rot.

You're sure, old man? This is what Ashton had said to him, unconvincingly, when he had followed up with a formal letter of resignation. *Been called back home, you know, the mater and pater, stamping their feet.* And when he had returned to his hotel room, there was a flare, like the fireworks he had watched one night from the bank of the Nile, a crackle and explosion in the sky. Hope: that she might still come, but now as she spoke, this awkward, clearly prepared speech, this talk of rooms and refuge, all he felt was the hope dying, and then gone. Extinguished.

She was rejecting him for ever; that is all he heard. He stopped listening to what she was saying. The odd word filtered in. *I was lost. Confused.*

She was flesh: tainted, stained with a long thick line of blood, she was bones. Her breasts were small, her ankles thin. Why the hell hadn't he slid her on to the bed rather than that other thing? The silk dress ruffled up, the attached stockings loosened. He looked up at the rafters of the Zion. They seemed to creak.

'You came from my past and tricked me. You knew I was married.'

'I did know that, it's true.'

He was grieving already because he would never know certain elements about her. He wanted to know, for instance, how her mouth tasted after she had smoked a cigarette. Did she eat much at breakfast (he doubted it)? She was a person who craved adoration, wanted it daily, to drink it up, and yet had chosen to be married to a man who disappeared for long periods of time and, even when he returned, it was not her he came back to. Willie was mortified that Rasul would have the whole of her. Was there consolation in the fact that he knew the worst of her?

Not much.

All around them the Holy City was groaning under the weight of snow. He looked at the cinema screen.

To be perfectly truthful, what he had to say was this –

Nobody will know you better than me. Nobody will love you more than me. It is for life. You are my girl. But it wasn't true because Rasul now took the whole of her.

'Don't ever think it has cost me nothing,' she said; her hand was shaking, cold fingers touched his. 'To not be with you.'

He said nothing to that.

'My husband is a steadying force. Without him I would be dead.'

It was like a gentle but thorough drowning, that remark. He did not say anything; perhaps it helped her to be cruel. It was true that he was filled with a desire to puncture her: a masculine force, like the pin in the centre of a delicate butterfly. They were both silent for some time.

'Why do they only play this film?' he said.

'It's because it takes so long to get a new film reel from Cairo.'

In his head he was walking along the rambling corridors and landings and stairwells of Pentrohobyn. It was alarming how accurately he could see himself as a small boy, running as fast as he could through the cold empty spaces of that echoey house. He took the stairs quickly. The topmost points of tree branches rattled the glass windows, nettles everywhere outside and whatever he did, no matter how much he wanted it, he could never hold on to this place. He was not entitled to a room full of ashtrays piled with cigarettes and the cushions, still with the imprint of heads on them, and the oriental throws on old leather chairs, and heaps of books next to fireplaces and a grand oil painting of ships on the great wide sea. By refusing him, she was condemning him to walk and walk and walk and be forever displaced, and she didn't even know it.

'There's such crookedness in me, darling. I am not whole, I'm a blurred thing. I couldn't give myself to you, even if I wasn't married to Khaled. I don't want you. There is nowhere to put you, there never has been. The way you want me, *that me*, I'm afraid it doesn't exist.'

There was another creaking from the beam above them, a little further back behind them, and then there was a more serious cracking sound. He took her hand.

'Quick.' He hauled her up. The ceiling near the screen collapsed, a great rending noise of the corrugated roof giving way to the piled, heaped snow. The screen fell to the floor, but it was possible to hear the winding screech of the little projection wheel still making its revolutions. The shock of the exposed cold was like a baptism and the night sky was shimmering and intense in its blackness.

'Eleanora.' He pulled her towards the doors and they went out into the street. They stood, blinking at the strangeness of suddenly being out in the Jerusalem sky with the black night above and people standing pointing, looking at what had been inside but was now outside. As she dusted the snow from her coat she was pale and beautiful. He would be loyal to nothing, if not her. Each betrayal was a closer step to death and he understood that she was all the days of freedom before the war, all the summers, all the rooms in the great house; in other words, she was the past, and that is what he desired most.

She looked like a fragile bird in the snow, and he said, 'I don't understand why you wanted me to be there, to meet Khaled up at Lifta.'

She turned, rubbing snow from her eyelid. 'It was Khaled who requested it.'

'But why? Did he know about us?'

'He did not say. But he was very specific about you being included in those photographs. He wants to send them to prime ministers, to I don't know who.'

He looked away from her and saw a black dog, slinking along the edge of the wall, paws in the snow, ears flat. He hadn't seen many dogs in Jerusalem, he realised. It tended to be cats here. And the endless birds.

'You think I wanted to hurt you?' she said, softly. He watched the dog crouch low as two men passed it, and then continue the delicate placing of its paws in the snow.

'I don't know,' he said. From this point onwards, we live in memories and our own stories for each other; we will either die or live. Did she say this, or did he think it? He was no longer sure.

The New Movements in Art Exhibition at the London Museum (Lancaster House), 1942

Margot Eaves was fussing in her usual manner but it was clear to see from the glimmer around her eyes and the redness of her cheeks how excited she was. She was the type of woman to pile her hair on her head in great swoops and then fix within its webby matter pins and odd bits of glittering stuff so that she quite resembled a decoration. To pull off an exhibition of this nature, at these times, with so much happening, and just to get the parts into the right place, just to complete the permission, the rights, the negotiations with Lancaster House, was no small feat.

The room was a crush of people, there was a tinkling of glasses, but Skip and the little girl, Betty, did not want to stay. Skip ducked Margot's embrace and scurried past the spirals of Gabo and the work of Hepworth. *Saint Helena*, by Prudence Miller, had a central position and the twist of it was impressive, he could see. It dominated the room, and the light shone across it in exactly the way it was supposed to, but Skip had seen it so many times, he had watched it when it was a mouldy old lump of stone brought from Portsmouth and his mother had chipped and bashed away at it for so long that he did not remotely care to look at it. She had been preparing work for this exhibition for *years*.

An old woman with lipstick the colour of potted shrimp put her scaly fingers in his hair: *Are you proud of your mother?* He squirmed away, escape! Ducked under a table and there, as he guessed he might, he found Betty, sitting quietly with her feet tucked beneath her, sucking her thumb.

'Come on,' he said. Together they crawled underneath the long table towards the doors, which were very grand. When they emerged, Skip took Betty's hand, to help her. On the whole he did not agree with holding the hands of girls, but she was only six and he guessed that she was feeling strange because this was the first time she had come back to London since being billeted with them; every household in Shoreham had been forced to take an evacuee. She was from Bermondsey, which she said, being better than him on the geography of London, was one hundred miles from here, Lancaster House SW1. He tugged her, to get away from the ghastly room, but near the door a hand caught him by the neck and hauled him backwards.

'Daddy,' he said. It was Piers, laughing.

'Just a minute,' Piers said. 'What are you little horrors up to?'

'We're just going for an explore, we shall be quite safe.' His father smiled down at them both, and Betty, who did not speak to adults, put her thumb in her mouth and pretended to be invisible. The woman standing next to Piers had green powder over her eyelids so that she looked like a mermaid, if a mermaid were to be found in the middle of London on a hot summer's day, and for a moment Skip was mesmerised by her and the way her hand came around his father's waist, like a cowboy's lasso.

322

Piers called across the room to Prue, gesturing, *Can they go?* Skip looked round at his mother. She was standing surrounded by a group of people, wearing a very blue dress which she called her 'indigo number'. She looked not at all bad. She mouthed to his father, *it's fine*, smiling at them with her eyes.

Betty followed Skip. She adored him, so he needn't boss her too much. They ran out of the grand hallway of Lancaster House, away from the old, and it was only when they were outside that Skip realised he had forgotten his gas mask, but perhaps it didn't matter. Betty said, with a knowledgeable air, 'I've been here before, you know. A celebration, I think. Something like that.' And then, after all that explanation, her little face clouded. To shake her out of it, because he knew these memories caused her trouble, he gave her a shove, and they ran down the steps.

An entire corner of the street opposite was surrounded by fences. A bomb had blasted the inside of the building but left the walls so that it looked like an outdoor theatre. They continued along a narrow passage, which opened out on to a covered area, and Skip counted the signs: barbers, haberdashers, saddlers, tailors, bookshops, brewers. It was a higgledy-piggledy jumble of chaos, and Skip rather liked it. He felt at home here. He found a good rock, not quite perfectly round but a nice weight, and lobbed it, right into the heart of a crater.

Dust, everywhere, and dirt. People moved slowly, stepping over boulders and things in the wrong places: a concrete block in the middle of the road, a wall tipped down. Betty picked a wild blue flower growing from around the edges of a wall and twirled its weedy, spindly stalk. Skip paused at a metal gate and from inside they heard a wireless crackling. Betty's eyes widened. Skip pushed his shoe on to the dusty ledge at the bottom of the wall and then heaved himself up, so that he could see over the top. He jumped back down again.

'Let's go in there,' he said.

'Yes,' said Betty, his loyal follower, 'let's go in there.' She had his mother's doll, Lulu, with her. They ran through the narrow entrance together, kicking up dust, and the path opened up. There was another great pile of rubble with pipes sticking out of it and a cat tiptoeing like a ballerina across the top. The passage went under an archway and then popped out into a courtyard. Skip and Betty stood rooted. In front of them was a church, magnificent, still, with the arches where the stained-glass windows once were, but most of the front was gone, and it had no roof, just the walls forming a shell. They walked inside and as they approached there was a fluttering of bird-noise. Pigeons: hundreds of them, up in the ridges of the walls, flapping and jesting. There were pigeons bobbing their heads and hopping around the floor too. Skip shooed them. He took Betty's hand.

A church with no roof is a wonderful thing. It is the world topsy-turvy. Skip ran into the centre of the wrecked building. Fragments of Bibles lay scattered, the covers torn, thin pages fluttering. Betty was a little awed; she stood at the entrance and would not move, and when Skip looked round at her he saw how tiny she was, and went back and brought her forward, gently by the elbow. There was a bicycle, leaning against the altar, and a makeshift fireplace full of ash; signs that somebody was perhaps living here.

They sat together on the altar steps, Betty bringing her ankles together and wrapping her fingers around her feet. A man appeared then, nodded at them, but didn't say anything. He pulled a bag out of his pocket and threw seeds into the air. They scattered and landed with a patter, like rain, and in response the pigeons flew down, a cloud of wing and pecking beak, making the odd curling noise that pigeons like to do. *Ccrrrrruuu crrruuuu* and alongside the raggedy old pigeons were some tiny London finches.

Skip heard his name being called, and he stood up.

'We're here,' he shouted. Coming round the edge of the pathway was Mrs Deal, who was looking nice for her, with her hair brushed through and a smart summer jacket rather than the shapeless dresses she tended to wear at home. She had insisted on wearing a bright yellow hat, however, and looked like a sunflower turning in the sun, but Skip did not tell her that.

'Have you got Betty?'

'Yes, she's in here.' Mrs Deal was smiling, so he knew he wasn't in trouble.

'We should get back to the show,' she said, 'they are just about to start the toasts and whatnot. Your mother would like you there, I expect.' She stared around at the smashed-up church and all the broken figures on the floor.

'Goodness, look how marvellous it is,' Mrs Deal said.

'I thought you didn't like ruins and broken buildings, Mrs Deal,' Skip replied.

'I'm learning to, darling.'

His father was with the mermaid-woman waiting on the steps of Lancaster House for them.

'Come on,' he said, 'come on. Speeches.'

Skip watched his mother as she was being helped on to a stage, alongside a lot of other people in suits and bright-coloured dresses. As the talk began, he looked at the art all around him, some of which he liked, most of which he didn't. He left Betty standing next to Mrs Deal and sidled off. This was the main room of the exhibition but there was also another, smaller room, with additional 'pieces', and this is where his mother's second piece was. The titles meant nothing to him on the whole. *Abstraction. Studio. Wheels.* One called *Esplanade* was rather good because he recognised it as a broken-down image of the seafront: a pier, a bandstand, the beach. But the others? *Two Circles. Composition.* Really: the names were mostly idiotic.

This room was empty because the people had all cleared out to listen to the speeches. In the furthermost corner was the fisherman's hut that his mother had used as her studio on the beach. She had decided to turn the hut itself into the artwork. It had been disassembled, and brought in here and reassembled again. He had been allowed to help and how different it looked inside, in the city, away from the seagulls and the wind. Quite eerie, he had to admit. He ran his hand along the wooden planks. There was a peephole in the door; he used to look through it to spy on his mother working sometimes.

She had put the hut on two railway-carriage sleepers that had caused quite a lot of trouble getting here because they were so heavy. Margot, who was always squeezing him and poking his nose and hair, made a fuss about woodworm and rot, but his mother had won in the end, and here they were, holding up the hut. There was a sign on it that he himself had painted for her. YOU ARE ENCOURAGED TO ROAM AROUND THE BEACH HUT AND COME INSIDE. He had had to do it twice because on the first sign he had written RAOM. Inside the beach hut there was a secret, which only Skip knew about. Only his mother, and him. Not Betty. Or Mrs Deal. Or Margot.

'There is a secret compartment,' she'd said. 'No one else in the world knows it's there.'

The sound of applause broke through from the other room, and Skip climbed up the rickety steps to the hut and crawled inside. It was spidery, damp still, and despite the sign outside, he had the feeling that not many people had bothered to roam. There was a fake wall at the back of the hut, and he tapped the panels to find out which was loose. There it was. He pulled it off. Inside was a small cavity about the size of a Punch and Judy theatre and in this black recess, hanging from a stick, were two upside-down men, tied with rope, dangling. He tapped them so that they swung and bumped into one another. Their little heads wobbled like gooseberries hanging from a bush.

'But why have you put it there, Mummy, if you're going to hide it?'

'Because someone once told me I couldn't and I don't like to do as people tell me.' She had smiled at him mysteriously. 'It's a gift,' she said. 'A secret from me to you.'

'Why are they hanging?'

'I don't know,' she had said, 'but let's remember, we're alive.'

Shoreham-by-Sea, 1942

The train home from Victoria station is delayed by fifteen minutes so that by the time we are finally installed in the carriage Betty already looks exhausted and Mrs Deal is burrowing in her bags to see if there is a blanket that can be wrapped around her so she can have a sleep. The train is full of grey men wearing grey suits and carrying briefcases and I have drunk rather too much champagne. *Saint Helena* has sold already; a princely sum. Cause for celebration.

Skip fidgets; he will neither settle into sitting nor stand at the window but hops between the two. Running from one window to the other, looking over towards Chelsea, and then back, over towards Battersea, but after a while, though, he calms down and sits next to me, putting his head on my shoulder and patting my wrist in that oddly grown-up way he has.

'It will be a relief to be out of the city,' Mrs Deal says, 'and back into the sea air.'

'It will,' I say, watching the river disappear and the trees from Battersea Park change into the leafless roofs of endless houses.

Arriving at Shoreham has vivified us; we are no longer tired. It is late, nine o'clock, but the sun is not yet down in this heart of summer and we have unanimously decided to climb to the top of the small hill behind the station to have a look at the sea before heading home. Just off the coast a large battleship is moored, and the entire beach is decked in barbed wire.

'In a way,' I say to Mrs Deal, 'it looks rather pretty.'

She whacks me on the hand for that comment.

'Where was Cecilia, again?' Skip asks and Mrs Deal points down; *there*, she says, *there*. Skip, who is a sensitive little chap, gives her hand a squeeze because he knows she always gets sad looking down at Shoreham spit. The night that the bungalows and chalets were demolished by the army, dismantled first and then bulldozed, was a terrible one for Mrs Deal. No more Kangaroo or Puss-in-Boots. In their place is a line of ugly concrete blocks, all along the coast as far down as Brighton and beyond.

'Mrs Deal, your face is getting its melancholy look,' I say, and she laughs. There are midges coming at us, clouding our heads, and Skip and Betty, who is full of energy after sleeping the whole train journey, hop up and down, waving hands wildly to fight them off.

'You look like fools,' says Mrs Deal, being kind, pushing glasses up her nose.

There are mines on the beach so the children cannot play there, though they only feel bad about it on a hot day like this. It is me who misses the rustle and uproar of wind and shingle the most. I watch Skip move away from us towards the edge of the grassy mound where he can get a better view of the aerodrome. It is a place he returns to, and then pulls back from. Billy told him how the Home Guard have been ordered to make the airfield look like farmland, with make-believe hedges, so that when the Luftwaffe fly overhead and take photographs they won't think it's a target, and now he sits and watches the sky, all day long, looking out for the planes above and their cameras.

We walk home slowly to the house that we have taken up in the New Shoreham side of town: Mrs Deal on the ground floor, me on the top, and the children, in bunk beds, in the room at the back of the kitchen. We are still very close to the 'zone of invasion' and Billy is fond of saying that if Hitler comes to Britain we will be meeting him first. Looking out at the wide sky, I think of William Harrington. Billy, obsessive and tenacious, tracked him down through channels at the Ministry: interned by the Germans in Jersey and I wonder what the sky looks like from there; whether he regrets being trapped on that side. I suspect, somehow, that he has always been lost without Eleanora Rasul. Perhaps it didn't matter altogether, where he was?

'Should you have stayed, do you think, in London? All those people wanting to interview you and talk to you?' Mrs Deal says, putting cups of tea down for us. We have let the children drop where they are tonight rather than struggling with them into bed. Skip is flat on the rug, his face turned to the side and resting on the paper he was drawing on. Betty is curled in a nest with her doll tucked deep between her knees on the comfiest chair near the fire.

'Probably,' I say, but I have let my *Saint Helena* go: the heavy twists and turns of it inside me nearly undid me and I have no desire to talk about it any more. I hope the hut will sell too; that one is a requiem for my father – not that any of the critics with their sniffing snouts have picked up on that yet. Now, for my next work, I am thinking of something new, lighter. Taking inspiration from a large print from some fractured negatives: views from the air, but I need to find a way of making them my own. I'm planning to use chalk, and Piers of course is horrified: the most malleable, crumbling, unsuitable of substances.

I bite into an apple and swallow a pip. Funny how the old childish fear of an apple tree growing in the stomach never fully disappears. Along the window ledge of our kitchen pane is a row of skulls, collected by Skip. Most of them are bird skulls, yellowing, and I fear the odd one is a mouse or a rat. Next to them is a little cemetery of Skip's balsa aircraft that have come to bad ends. Broken tails, snapped wings, dented noses, but loved too much to throw away.

We do not have a sea view in this house, which we still call *the new house* even though we have been here now for three years. Piers visits if he is in the country and relieved of his mysterious war duties and Skip adores him and has come to accept the way things are. I meet Billy when he too is discharged from duty, and we have come to an arrangement: when and as we fancy, a drink, a talk, a fall into bed. I tell him my troubles, he doesn't tell me his. Like Mrs Deal, he found the loss of Bungalow Town particularly hard, much harder than I would have imagined. I don't know where he is stationed or what he does at war, and I haven't told him this, but I've made a little shrine for him, on my windowsill. A circle of charms. A feather, a stone, childish things. A prayer to keep him alive.

When he's home he opens up the houseboat on the Adur because for some reason the army haven't moved it. I visit some nights, and we spend an eternity covering gaps with blackout materials and when that is done listen to the honking of the geese and the ducks out on the black water. I sometimes have the disquieting sense that Billy, in other places, with other people – by which I mean boxing men, although possibly women too, I don't ask, but somehow, I doubt it – has quite another way of being when I am not with him. But there we are; we can only be the person we can be in that particular company.

I pick Skip up, he is huge now, so heavy, especially with his limbs dead-like and asleep, but I can just about do it. There is a chalk-trace from his map on the side of his cheek, the course of a river and the edges of the land, the shadowing he made of places he wants to go to and the corners of houses he plans on building. I use my finger to rub it off and put him into his bed. On his pillow is my old Eastman Kodak. I have given it to him recently, along with the manual. *Take pictures any way you like*, I say. *There are no rules. Throw the rulebook out!* But he scours the sections. Landscapes. Portraits. Snapshots. Close-ups.

When I come back into the living room Mrs Deal is asleep, too, on her chair, so I cover her with a blanket and stand by the window, and listen to the wind and for the air-raid sirens. We live in brick now, but I know, from the rubble and dust of the church that Skip found today and the hotels that are gone – the Fast, and even the Warnes was badly damaged last week – and from the sound of the Luftwaffe flying above us and discarding its final cargo, that brick is as delicate and vulnerable as rackety old wood on shingle, or limestone corroding in the sun, so I've stopped trying to hold on, and as a consequence I am no longer afraid of the wind.

Mrs Deal said today, 'I think we'll be evacuated from here, if it goes on like this.'

'But they sent us Betty,' I said. 'Why would they make us move? Where to?' Do we shunt to the city or move to another place: where is safe? An island; oh, but this is an island. A place on the other side of the map: a city with walls and minarets? Oh no: there are wars there, worse than any we have here, and I remember that they are all gone: Eleanora, with white jasmine flowers in her hair, and Ihsan. Skip makes a noise then, cries out, like he does sometimes when bad dreams come. I go to him. Put my hand on his cheek.

'What?' he says.

'Just checking.'

'Checking for what?'

'That you are all right.'

'You were checking to see if I was dead, weren't you?'

'Of course not.'

'Did I look dead?'

'No. Alive. Definitely alive.'

He smiles, points down to the floor under his bed. I look. There is a bucket, with water, and inside a sole starfish, waving one of its arms up and down, resignedly.

'Poor starfish,' I say.

'You don't think he's happy?'

'I'm not sure.'

'You don't think he's safe?'

'I don't think he thinks he's safe.'

Skip frowns. I take his hand, and put it on my own face. His hot palm, his fingers curl.

'He doesn't know that he's got you looking after him, though, does he?'

Skip smiles at this. 'Sleep,' I say. 'Sleep.' And he turns away and I cast my wish – and may you dream of flying – and when I go downstairs I pick up all the gull feathers that Betty and Skip have collected and listen to the sea for a while.

Acknowledgements

Thanks go to Arts Council England for a residency at the Shoreham Airport, particularly Kieran Phelan and Jon Prebble. Thanks to the Kenyon Institute, Jerusalem, for housing me on research trips. Thank you to Professor Roberto Mazza, Suad Amiry and Professor Salim Tamari for advice and feedback. Thank you to Kevork Kahvedjian and Varouj Ishkhanian for talking to me about the history of photography in Jerusalem and also to The American Colony Hotel, East Jerusalem for letting me stay. Thank you to Suheir Khoury for support and help and to Nadia Kara'a for the tour of the old city and for kindly allowing me into her home. In Malta thank you to Adrian Grima for inviting me to Malta and Savio Deguara who generously showed me his sculpture studio and working methods.

I researched this book at SOAS and the British Library. I edited and wrote much of it in my local libraries in Worthing and Shoreham, West Sussex; many thanks to the staff of all of those institutions, particularly Jackie Manners and her team of librarians at Worthing library and Chris Desmond and his team in East Sussex.

A huge thank you to my parents John and Lynda Joinson for love and help and for enduring years of trouble from me and thanks to Dave, Ruty, Ms Helena Rebecca Howe, Marion and David, Laila Hourani, Tamera Howard, David Parr and everyone else who has provided support, shelter, friendship, tea, babysitting and love.

Thank you to Rachel Calder for being both the loveliest and the wisest of agents and to Helen Garnons-Williams for so much help, sympathy and for continuing to believe in me. Thank you to everyone at Bloomsbury, in particular Nigel (and Joanna) Newton for the inspirational flight to Le Touquet and kind words along the way, to Nancy Miller for such wonderful support and for championing me in the US, and Alexandra Pringle for taking me under her glamorous wing. Thank you Elizabeth Woabank, Imogen Denny, Isabel Blake and the rest of the team. It has been an enormous pleasure to work with you all.

A special thank you to Florence McKinney, my grandmother, age ninety-something, who used to watch Amy Johnson land her plane near Monaghan, Neville Joinson and the rest of my family.

Thank you to all the people who have facilitated residencies, workshops, writing commissions and projects which have enabled me to live as a writer over the last few years, including Kate Griffin, Chris Gribble, colleagues Paul, Joel, Sally and Karen at the University of Chichester, Rachel Stevens and Sinead Russell at the British Council, Sarah Matthews and James Shea at CAS, Lydia Bell, editors at the *New York Times*, *Aeon*, *Independent on Sunday* and Don George at Lonely Planet. Thank you to Elizabeth White for a stay in a wonderful apartment in Baku and thank you kind hosts and colleagues from various places I was lucky enough to visit in the last couple of years, in particular Kuala Lumpur, Myanmar, Istanbul and Huangshan.

Most of all, my thanks and love go to Woody, Scout and Ben Nicholls, for everything.

A NOTE ON THE AUTHOR

Suzanne Joinson is an award-winning writer of fiction and non-fiction whose work has appeared in, among other places, the *New York Times*, *Vogue*, *Aeon*, Lonely Planet collections of travel writing and the *Independent on Sunday*. Her first novel, *A Lady Cyclist's Guide to Kashgar* (2012), was translated into sixteen languages and was a national bestseller. She lives in Sussex.

suzannejoinson.com/@suzyjoinson

A NOTE ON THE TYPE

The text of this book is set in Adobe Garamond. It is one of several versions of Garamond based on the designs of Claude Garamond. It is thought that Garamond based his font on Bembo, cut in 1495 by Francesco Griffo in collaboration with the Italian printer Aldus Manutius. Garamond types were first used in books printed in Paris around 1532. Many of the present-day versions of this type are based on the Typi Academiae of Jean Jannon cut in Sedan in 1615.